THE BATTLE LINES ARE DRAWN

"The critic who signs himself Chiron," Philippa began, "has he reviewed your book?"

Henry Ashton hesitated. "It would be quite inappropriate," he said at last. "You see, I am Chiron."

Philippa stared at him in disbelief.

"But you should take no notice of criticism, Miss Davenport. Now, if you will excuse me, I must take my leave."

Philippa watched him depart with mounting fury. He had read her books. He had found her trivial and unworthy of his attention. Philippa had been devastated by the attacks of the unknown Chiron. She was enraged by the indifference of Henry Ashton.

Francesca hurried to her side. "Didn't I tell you he was out of the ordinary?" she asked.

Philippa spoke calmly, her tone belied by the sparkle in her dark eyes. "I think Mr. Ashton is the most disagreeable man it has ever been my dubious fortune to meet. My only comfort is that it would take a very odd set of circumstances to throw him in my way again."

And in this last, Miss Davenport proved to be absolutely right.

The Courting of Philippa

ANTHEA MALCOLM

ZEBRA BOOKS
KENSINGTON PUBLISHING CORP.

ZEBRA BOOKS

are published by

Kensington Publishing Corp.
475 Park Avenue South
New York, NY 10016

First printing: August, 1989

Printed in the United States of America

For Else, Gwendolen, and Maha

People of *ton* have taken to writing novels; it is an excellent amusement for them, and also for the public.

Lady Charlotte Bury's diary, 1818

We think that a lady ought to be treated, even by reviewers, with the utmost deference, except she writes politics, which is an enormity equal to wearing breeches.

Fraser's Magazine, March 1831

What is love . . . the power of dressing up life in the colours of romance.

Almack's

Historical Note

The newspapers and pamphlets mentioned in this book were in publication in 1819 with the exception of those created for purposes of the story: the *Morning Intelligencer, London Spectator, The Phoenix, The Scourge,* and the pamphlet written by Mrs. Robinson.

Our authority for taking tea with cream and sugar comes from *Almack's,* a three-volume novel published anonymously in 1826. It was said to be the work of Marianne Spencer Stanhope, later Mrs. Robert Hudson.

Prologue

"Philippa, come with me, I know it's a dreary party, but there's a man you must meet, and I promise you he's out of the ordinary."

Lady Francesca Scott took her cousin's hand and threaded her way through the crowded drawing room. Philippa followed her with some anticipation, though she rather wished Francesca would not feel obligated to draw her into conversations. Francesca's entertainments were usually more lively—perhaps she had had obligations to discharge—but Francesca should know that Philippa, of all people, was never bored by the company in which she found herself. How else was she to obtain the material for her novels?

Francesca indicated a man standing in a far corner of the room, surrounded by four or five young women who all seemed to be talking at once. The gentleman, his manners apparently being good, was not saying a word, but there was something about him that instantly drew one's attention. He was, Philippa judged, in his mid-twenties, with a careless grace in his pose, a mop of tawny hair that fell over his forehead, and a lean intelligent face that, even in repose, showed more animation than any of the fashionable gentlemen present that evening had seen fit to display.

Francesca broke into the group with an authority that instantly stilled conversation and a dazzling smile that robbed

11

her move of any offence. "Henry, I insist that you stop monopolizing my friends, there are above a half-dozen gentlemen languishing for want of female companionship and I must see that they are not disappointed. Philippa, allow me to present Henry Ashton. Henry, my cousin, Philippa Davenport, she will keep you company. I'd say more if there were time, but I'm sure you both know all about each other."

With which, Lady Francesca shepherded the young women back into the vortex of the crowd, making them feel that the unlooked for change in their position was somehow to their advantage.

At twenty-one Philippa was no novice to the drawing room, but she felt suddenly awkward. One of her hairpins had come loose and her hair threatened to escape its moorings; her face was damp with the heat of the room; and her dress, a pink jaconet in its second Season, was not nearly as dashing as the frocks of the women who had just quitted Mr. Ashton's side. Philippa was anxious to make a good impression, for not only was Mr. Ashton attractive in a way that was unique in her experience, he was a fellow novelist whose first book, published earlier that year, Philippa had read with a great deal of pleasure.

Mr. Ashton's eyes, of a deep but changeable green, regarded her intently, as though he might have met her before but could not recall exactly where. Then they flickered with a hint of surprise or recognition. Well, why not? Philippa's novels had been generally praised, and it was not inconceivable that he could have heard her name—or perhaps even have read one of her books.

"I'm sorry," she said in some confusion, wishing she appeared to better advantage, "Francesca is not generally so abrupt. I'm afraid we have interrupted your conversation."

"On the contrary, your cousin saw that I was in need of rescue." He smiled and the intense face relaxed. She saw that he was not only intelligent, he had a great deal of charm, not to mention a sense of humour. Philippa was relieved, for this last was a quality she valued above all others.

"Let me guess," she said, feeling suddenly light-hearted.

12

"They were telling you that they were enravished, positively *in alt*, over *Robert Levering*, but they were desolated by Amelia's death, and why couldn't you have written a more comfortable sort of book?"

"Something of the sort," he admitted. "I made the mistake of claiming that Amelia was not all that important, either in the book or in Robert's life, but I think they failed to grasp what the novel was about. It was not a love story."

It was said in a matter-of-fact tone, but Philippa thought his voice held an edge of disdain for the lighter form. She was surprised. Of course, *Robert Levering*, which was set during Wat Tyler's rebellion, could hardly be called a—a *domestic* novel, not like Philippa's own first book, nor even like her second which, though more openly satirical, chronicled the limited world of the kinds of people now present in her cousin's drawing room. But while Philippa admired Mr. Ashton's work, she was proud of her own, and it had not occurred to her that he would find any disparity between them as writers.

But perhaps he did not. Though she was generally a cheerful person who thought well of herself, Philippa was inclined to be morbidly sensitive about her writing, particularly since her second novel, published only last month, had been reviewed in the *London Spectator*. Protected by fortune and family, with no beauty to arouse envy and sufficient cleverness to ward off pity or slight, Philippa had been shielded throughout her life from criticism and rebuff. She had been devastated by that review. The critic, who signed himself Chiron, had granted her a certain facility with words, but had made clear his contempt for both the style and substance of her novel. The review had seriously damaged her self-regard, and it was the more galling as Philippa had had occasion to read Chiron's work before and had found it perceptive. She could not relieve her feelings by talking to her family or friends, for they gave her facile praise, but the man before her was her equal. She could trust his judgement, and she longed to gain his approbation.

"You should not judge too harshly of your readers," she said, hoping to prolong the conversation. "They look for what is closest to their hearts, and for young women that is

13

frequently romance. When they are older they will be able to see beyond it."

"I doubt it, folly seldom improves with age. Not," he added, looking about him, "when their surroundings present little but folly to the eye."

Philippa glanced at the fashionably dressed guests thronging her cousin's drawing room and spilling over into the adjoining saloon. It was true that many of them were extremely silly, but to Philippa even the foolish—especially the foolish—were objects of endless interest. "And yet you partake of that folly," she pointed out.

He smiled. "I do not entirely shun society, Miss Davenport."

"But you are impatient with its excesses? It is a pity, for there is a fascination in one's fellow creatures, no matter how absurd they are, and they help us to know our own absurdities."

"Then you are enjoying yourself tonight?" he asked, as if the matter was of some moment.

"I always enjoy myself in company, Mr. Ashton."

"Yes, of course, it is your natural element. I did not mean to be rude about your friends," he added, referring to the women who had lately left his side.

They were not Philippa's particular friends and she thought them remarkably shatter-brained, but she chose to ignore his mistake. "You were not rude, you were protecting your work, and you had a right to do so. It is hard to be misunderstood, and even worse to be criticized, though of course a writer should take no notice of criticism. Still, you can hardly fault your book's reception. The reviewers have understood you better."

"They have been kind," he admitted.

"No more than is deserved," she said warmly. She followed this with some appreciative comments on his treatment of both characters and themes, for which he thanked her gravely. Philippa waited for some reciprocating comments on her own work, but these were not forthcoming. She had a moment of chagrin, then realized that in all probability he had never seen her books and possibly did not even know that she was a writer.

14

It was a lowering thought. There was no way to bring this gracefully to his attention, so, laughing at her own presumption, Philippa prepared to find another topic of conversation. But there was one thing he might tell her first.

"The critic who signs himself Chiron," she began, "I've seen his work in several publications. Has he reviewed your book?"

Mr. Ashton hesitated, an odd expression crossing his face. "It would be quite inappropriate," he said at last.

"Oh?" Philippa was surprised. "Are you acquainted with him?" Perhaps she could at last learn something about the gentleman who had so disturbed her peace of mind these last weeks.

"In a manner of speaking. You see," Mr. Ashton said with perfect gravity, "*I* am Chiron."

Philippa stared at him in disbelief.

"I have been both a journalist and a critic," he explained. "It takes a long time to write a novel, and I don't have the luxury of an assured income." Then, with the smile that transformed his face but that now seemed a parody of his former warmth, "But you should take no notice of criticism, Miss Davenport. If you will excuse me, I have another engagement and must take my leave." He bowed and made his way rapidly through the crowd, leaving Philippa looking after him with mounting fury. He had known who she was. He had read her books. He had found her trivial and unworthy of his attention and was unwilling to meet her on the common ground of their mutual occupation. No, unwilling even to grant that they stood on common ground. Philippa had been devastated by the attacks of the unknown Chiron. She was enraged by the indifference of Henry Ashton.

She did not notice that Francesca had reappeared at her side. "How did you find him?" Francesca asked. "Didn't I tell you he was out of the ordinary?"

Philippa turned to her cousin, her social mask well in place. "Yes, he is that. He is not a fool and he is not a bore."

She spoke calmly, but Francesca, who knew her cousin, was certain there was more. "And?" she asked.

15

"And," said Philippa, her tone belied by the sparkle in her dark eyes, "I think Mr. Ashton is the most disagreeable man it has ever been my dubious fortune to meet. My only comfort is that he does not often go into society. It would take a very odd set of circumstances to throw him in my way again."

And in this last, Miss Davenport proved to be absolutely right.

Chapter 1

1819

Felicity stared at the marquis with a mixture of astonishment and awe. The immorality of his proposal was exceeded only by the gravity of his demeanour and the dispassion of his gaze. She blushed, then blushed again for being unable to control the coursing of her blood. How was it possible that she had been so mistaken in the character of the man who now stood before her, the man for whom she had felt, if not a daughterly affection—there was that matter of the lip which somewhat impaired the symmetry of his face—at least the same dutiful sentiments that were evoked by her Uncle Augustus, the rector of Lower Basing?

In her confusion, she had turned away from him, but she now looked him full in the face, hoping to see something in his countenance that would give the lie to his words. There was nothing. He was observing her with the detached interest of a boy who has found some new species of moth to add to his collection, or a man who, though not sharp-set with hunger, fully intends to do justice to the dish set before him.

Felicity felt a little frisson of pleasure that a man as eminent and as much in the public eye as the marquis would direct his attentions to her, unwelcome as those attentions might be. She did not apprehend any immediate danger to her person, but she determined to keep her door locked that night. What an extraordinary story she would have to tell Jane and Sarah

17

when they returned from the milliner's!

Elliot Marsden, counsel for the plaintiff, paused, closed the paper board-covered book with a look of distaste, laid it carefully on the table before him, and regarded the young woman sitting in the witness-box. "Do you deny, Miss Davenport, that you penned those words?"

Philippa felt a surge of anger and carefully schooled her features. "I wonder that you ask, sir. The novel"—she laid the slightest stress on the word—"from which you have been reading is my own creation."

Mr. Marsden raised his eyebrows. "A work of fiction, Miss Davenport?"

Philippa returned his look with composure. "A work of fiction, sir."

"And the character of the Marquis of Coachfield, that also is a work of fiction?"

"The gentleman exists only in my imagination," Philippa said pleasantly, "and between the pages of my novel."

Mr. Marsden made a sound, not quite a snort, but a clear expression of disbelief. He grasped the open front of his gown and looked about the courtroom, resting his eyes finally on that portion where the jury was seated. "Coachfield," he mused, his mellifluous voice carrying clearly even to the spectators in the furthest rows, "the Marquis of Coachfield. An interesting name, that. Coach, a four-wheeled vehicle. Almost, one might say, a kind of cart."

"One would be very silly to do so, Mr. Marsden," Philippa interposed. "Carts most often have only two wheels."

A titter swept the courtroom. The barrister turned back to the witness-box. "Pray confine yourself to answering the questions put to you, Miss Davenport."

Philippa's own counsel, Julius Pettibone, had warned her most specifically about her behaviour while in court. Unbecoming levity had been his exact words. She sighed. It seemed a pity that a sense of the ludicrous should prove a detriment rather than an asset.

Judging that Miss Davenport was about to put her foot into it, Mr. Pettibone rose to object to opposing counsel's line of questioning. Mr. Marsden argued that he was trying to

18

establish the state of Miss Davenport's feelings toward his client, and the judge, Sir Williston Fortescue, wearily waved the objection aside.

Philippa meanwhile looked out into the courtroom and met the eyes of the disagreeable Henry Ashton who, by a most unfair twist of fate, was writing about the trial for the *Morning Intelligencer*. Censorious eyes, but then Mr. Ashton had made it clear at their disastrous first meeting two years ago that he considered Miss Davenport a feather-brained young woman, while his opinion of her books was even less flattering.

"I will put it to you, Miss Davenport," counsel for the plaintiff continued, "I will put it to you most strongly, that the so-called Marquis of Coachfield is a *thinly*—I would venture to say, a *transparently*—disguised depiction of the late Marquis of Carteret."

In her anger at this unfair accusation, Philippa forgot her annoyance with Mr. Ashton. She rose from the chair which had been placed in the box in deference to her sex and station and gripped the rail in front of her. "I will put it to you, Mr. Marsden, that it is no such thing!"

The dry voice of Sir Williston broke through the hush that followed Philippa's outburst like the rustling of leaves on a gust of wind. The words could not be distinguished, but their sound released the breath of the spectators and a loud murmur swept the courtroom. The judge's gavel sounded twice and the murmur receded. Philippa knew she had gone too far. "My lord," she said with pretty deference and resumed her seat.

Mr. Marsden acknowledged Sir Williston's intervention with grim satisfaction, then turned back to the woman in the witness-box. "Miss Davenport," he went on, and his voice was now almost cajoling, "you are obviously a gently-bred young woman, despite your somewhat—ah—unwomanly way of occupying your spare hours."

Philippa bit back a retort. She knew that the sympathies of the people in the courtroom were not entirely with her, and the barrister was playing on them cleverly.

"Do you read books as well as write them, Miss Davenport?"

Philippa nodded.

"Pray answer the question." Sir Williston's voice broke

into the silence again.

"I enjoy reading, my lord."

"You read widely, Miss Davenport?" Mr. Marsden said, as though her answer was of the most abiding interest. "Your reading is not confined to Mrs. Radcliffe and Miss Burney and works of that kind?" He flicked a dismissive finger at the copy of Philippa's novel lying on the table in front of him.

"Anyone familiar with the works of Miss Burney and Mrs. Radcliffe would not place them in the same category," Philippa retorted. "I read many kinds of books. I recently read Mr. Ashton's latest work, *Enfield Chase*." She glanced again at Henry Ashton, but his expression was infuriatingly unreadable. "I am very fond of history," she added. *Enfield Chase* was laid in the years preceding the Restoration.

Mr. Marsden seized on her last statement. "History, yes. An admirable study. History provides a useful guide to conduct—provided one reads it properly, of course. Its more sensational aspects may be misinterpreted when the understanding is weak. One is safer, perhaps, with those writers who address problems of moral practice." His tone was reflective, and his remarks seemed addressed to the court in general. He turned suddenly and fixed Philippa with a piercing stare. "Do you read the Bible, Miss Davenport? Do you know the difference between right and wrong?"

Before Philippa could reply, Mr. Pettibone registered a strong objection.

Mr. Marsden turned to the judge. "I am endeavouring to ascertain, my lord, whether Miss Davenport fully apprehends the seriousness of what she has done."

"I have already testified to what I have done," Philippa said, controlling her temper with difficulty, "and to what I have not done. And I certainly know the difference between right and wrong."

"You do? Admirable," Mr. Marsden returned. "And would you say you are a truthful person?"

"I am under oath," Philippa reminded him.

"Yes, you are under oath. But when you are not under oath, Miss Davenport? Are you accustomed to telling the truth? Have you never told a falsehood?"

20

The answer should have been a simple yes, but Philippa could not let it alone. "We all tell falsehoods, Mr. Marsden, they are the basis of our social intercourse. Were this not so, my books would not be so widely read."

An appreciative laugh broke out in the courtroom. The gavel sounded again.

"But I generally speak the truth, Mr. Marsden, though perhaps not as often as some people do, because when the truth is unpalatable I prefer to say nothing at all."

Three would-be Corinthians, who had been avidly following this exchange from their seats near the front of the courtroom, pounded their feet in approval, evoking his lordship's gavel once more.

"And I have never told a malicious falsehood," Philippa concluded with a resounding flourish, looking at Henry Ashton and daring him to contradict her.

Mr. Marsden picked up the offending book once more and held it high over his head, the bell sleeve of his gown making a black raven's wing as he waved the volume back and forth. "And you aver," he said in ringing tones, "you aver, Miss Davenport, that your portrait of the Marquis of Coachfield represents no more than the truth?"

"The marquis is a character in my book!" In exasperation, Philippa turned to the bench. "How often must I say so, my lord?"

Sir Williston waved a dessicated hand.

"A book," she repeated wearily. "A book which is a product of my imagination."

The barrister's manner was silky again. "Your imagination, Miss Davenport? Ah, yes, your imagination. But surely more than that? For if imagination were all, then the merest child could spin a tale, were he able to put words to paper. If imagination were all, then the ravings of any madman—or any madwoman—would be deemed worthy of publication. Surely more than imagination is needed? Surely you rely on the keenness of your observation as well?"

"Of course I do," Philippa said, agreeing with the obvious. "So do all writers, yes, and all speakers, too. If it were not for their observations on the foibles of their fellow men, what

21

would our clergymen do for sermons?"

The murmur from the courtroom now held a touch of disapproval. I have gone too far again, Philippa thought. I must watch my tongue. Her eye swept the courtroom and lit upon Mr. Ashton, but he was occupied in scribbling notes and she could not see his face. She had tried to be clever, but in tomorrow's paper he would no doubt show her to be foolish.

"Then you admit that you rely on your observations as well as on your imagination?" Mr. Marsden continued.

"I do." Philippa turned her attention back to the barrister. She now saw the danger in the direction of his questions.

"Conversely, one might say that the characters you write about in your books, Miss Davenport, the products of your imagination as you call them, are in reality based upon the observations you make of your fellow men and women— disguised, of course, by that imagination of which you are so justly proud."

"One might not say that at all," Philippa said, looking full into the shrewd face under the carefully curled wig, "not with any pretence to logic. If I am asked to give my opinion of a particular horse, I will rely, of course, on my observations of other horses, but it does not follow that my description of the legs or wind or breeding potential of the horse I am judging corresponds to that of a particular horse I have observed in the past."

There was an eruption of coarse laughter. The youngest of the Corinthians shouted "Hear, hear!" Sir Williston threatened to clear the courtroom.

Out of the corner of her eye, Philippa saw Mr. Ashton regarding her with a speculative look. "In any case," she went on before his lordship could say more, "your imputation is false. The Marquis of Coachfield was intended as a general type, not a specific person."

Mr. Marsden, who had been losing the battle, snatched at the opening. "I am very sorry, Miss Davenport, that a woman of your tender years should have been exposed to so many men of the marquis' unsavoury character."

There was a titter, instantly hushed by Sir Williston's frown.

"It is a portrait of a hypocrite, sir, and hypocrisy is not an uncommon trait."

"I beg to differ, Miss Davenport. It is a portrait of a very particular hypocrite, a man whom, if my memory serves, you described as"—Mr. Marsden threw back his shoulders, put his hands behind his back, and proceeded in a sonorous voice as though he were reading from the text itself—*"well above the average in height, with an erect carriage, a commanding presence, and a countenance that could be called handsome were it not for the small scar above his upper lip which gave to his expression a kind of permanent sneer."* He paused, then continued in his natural tones. "There are other details, of course, details which you recall quite well, details which point unmistakably to the late Marquis of Carteret. The reference was obvious to my client." He made a sweeping gesture toward the Dowager Marchioness of Carteret who was seated just behind the barrister's table.

The marchioness responded by raising a lace-edged handkerchief to her eyes. Philippa felt a pang of conscience. The reference had been obvious to half of London, but it had certainly not been intended.

"The resemblance is unfortunate," she acknowledged, "but it was not deliberate. Such things have been known to happen. After all, people are born in only so many shapes and conditions, and it is difficult to be totally original. I assure you that any similarity was purely a matter of coincidence."

Mr. Marsden again raised his expressive eyebrows. "Coincidence, Miss Davenport?"

"Coincidence, sir. I don't see how it could possibly be anything else. I never saw Lord Carteret, and I never had the privilege of meeting him."

She delivered this last with the satisfaction of a pugilist making a successful hit. At least, she thought the feeling must be similar, though she had never actually observed a prizefight. Her mama had very advanced views and would probably have allowed her to attend one, but Philippa could not imagine there to be any great enjoyment in viewing such an event. Unless, of course, she was going to use it in one of her books. Philippa considered this for a moment, struck by the idea. Handled with the right touch, it might make a splendid illustration of the idiotic pig-headedness of the majority of the male sex.

While Philippa considered her future literary efforts, Mr. Marsden consulted some notes on his table. There was a rustle among the spectators, a stirring of limbs too long confined, and a sibilance of whispers which were for the moment ignored by Sir Williston.

Philippa Davenport's third book had aroused more than usual interest. Despite her youth (at twenty-three she might be growing old for the Marriage Mart, but for a successful author she was absurdly young), her observations of her fellow men and women were remarkably keen. Far too keen for an unmarried girl, some said, but there was no denying they made enjoyable reading.

Yet though Miss Davenport's current book had proved every bit as entertaining as her first two, the delights of the book itself were nothing compared to the subsequent rumour that one of the characters was meant to be none other than the late Marquis of Carteret. There was a physical resemblance between the two, and everyone knew that Lord Carteret's behaviour had been every bit as profligate as that of the fictional Lord Coachfield. Miss Davenport's denial that the similarity was intentional had done nothing to lessen public interest, particularly as the marchioness remained convinced that the book maligned her late husband and told everyone of her acquaintance that Miss Davenport had acted with unconscionable malevolence toward the Carteret family.

Philippa had written her a pretty note of apology, but it had not helped matters. Indeed, it had only served to rouse Lady Carteret's fury to greater heights. The marchioness had sent for her solicitor and directed him to suppress the book at all costs. When that gentleman pleaded that there was no real cause to do so, Lady Carteret became quite faint and gave everyone a fright, but even in this pitiful state she was adamant that some way be found to withdraw the book from circulation.

The Carteret fortune was large and its circle of influence wide. The solicitor had bowed his head to the inevitable and approached first Philippa and then her publisher. Philippa was outraged, and her publisher, who was enjoying brisk sales and

24

contemplating a second printing, did not bend. At that point, Lady Carteret turned to some of her late husband's influential friends in Parliament and pressure was applied from higher sources.

Furious, Philippa dashed off a blistering letter to the *Lady's Monthly Museum*, a magazine which was not known for stodgy views on literary matters. As Philippa was acquainted with some of the ladies who were its editors, her letter appeared in the next issue's section on "Intelligence relative to Literature and the Arts."

Miss Davenport's letter began with the general problem of an author's freedom to write as she pleases but moved rapidly to her own case. The tone of the letter was mocking and, though not quite calling *Lady C.* a liar, served to make the marchioness appear vain, foolish, and an object of ridicule.

The letter delighted those jaded members of the *beau monde* who, not having daughters to marry off or love affairs to pursue, had expected the Season to be rather flat. The marchioness' response was decidedly different. She sued Miss Davenport for libel.

The betting at White's and Brooks' was the heaviest it had been since the Duke of Waterford had courted the divine Claudia Neville three years before, and the odds on the outcome of the trial were dead even. The courtroom was packed as tightly as any fashionable ball or rout. The trial offered all the attractions of the most sophisticated of novels, save that as yet it lacked a hero, and Miss Davenport was sadly unlike a heroine. Though she had a lovely clear voice, her brown hair was thin and straight and unenlivened by glints of red or gold, her brown eyes were much too direct, and there was no calling her a beauty. Her face was finely boned but lacking in softness. Her figure was well enough in its way, but was not, the gentlemen agreed, out of the ordinary. There was nothing precisely wrong with her appearance—many women with far less to work with achieved a notable success—but those who were well acquainted with Miss Davenport reported that, whatever her skill with words, flirtation was an art entirely unknown to her.

For some of the spectators, the plaintiff offered a more

attractive sight than the defendant. The Dowager Marchioness of Carteret was just past her fortieth year, and her fragile prettiness had endured remarkably well. Her hair was that shade of pale gold which blends naturally with grey, and her skin retained the delicate bloom of a much younger woman, a fact that led many ladies of her acquaintance to consult with her on her choice of creams and lotions. True, some found her manner cloying, but her soft femininity won her many supporters, while Miss Davenport's forthright demeanour tended to have just the opposite effect.

Philippa was aware of the image she presented. Indeed, she had been warned and warned again by Mr. Pettibone about the dangers of giving free rein to her tongue. She had also been warned about the dangers of wool-gathering (a failing that had been the despair of her governesses, though her mother had wisely told them to ignore the habit). Philippa readjusted her face, which had broken into a smile as she contemplated her preposterous pugilistic hero, and assumed an expression of gravity proper to the occasion.

Mr. Marsden seemed to be taking an inordinate amount of time to review his notes. Philippa looked at Lady Carteret. On the marchioness' left sat her adored and only child, Lord Christopher Paget, now engaged in patting his mother's hand. On her right sat her stepson Anthony, the present Marquis of Carteret, who was making his first appearance at his stepmother's side since the trial had begun. He was reputed to be a rake, and it was no secret that Lady Carteret frequently disapproved of his behaviour, but the libel suit had apparently induced him to make a show of family unity.

Philippa turned her head to the corner where her cousin Francesca, the only member of her own family present, was seated. Francesca, elegantly dressed and wearing what she described as a most amusing hat, sent Philippa a reassuring smile. Beside her sat the very pretty girl whom Francesca, in a burst of generosity, had offered to sponsor for her first Season. Philippa liked the outspoken and unaffected Claris, who was unabashedly enjoying her stay in London and flirting outrageously with any man under the age of twenty-four, so it had been quite provoking to learn that Claris' surname was

Ashton and that she had an elder brother named Henry.

Philippa had seen little of Mr. Ashton since their first unfortunate meeting, but now, thanks to the normally intelligent Francesca, he was practically one of the family. And as if that weren't bad enough, the *Morning Intelligencer* had had the gall to engage him to write about the trial. Alone of Philippa's circle—in which, due to Francesca and Claris, he must now be included—Mr. Ashton had offered her no sympathy when Lady Carteret first instigated the libel action. He rarely discussed the trial when he saw her outside of the courtroom—indeed, he rarely spoke to her at all for any length of time—but his daily articles made his opinion clear as crystal: an attempt at suppression of a book must be deplored, no matter how trivial that book might be; but Miss Davenport had destroyed all chance of a responsible discussion of this question by the intemperate tone of her letter, while her frivolous behaviour in the courtroom indicated that she had no real understanding of the issues that might be at stake.

To be fair, Mr. Ashton was equally hard on Lady Carteret, and even on the public who haunted the courtroom. It was evident that he saw the whole trial as wanton waste of the court's time and a prime example of the shallow preoccupations of the *ton*—preoccupations which no doubt also included the reading of Philippa Davenport's novels.

"Miss Davenport." Mr. Marsden was once again addressing her. "Will you tell the court if you were present at a house party at Staveley in August of 1814?"

Philippa blinked. In Mr. Marsden's barrage of sharp questions, this was the last thing she had expected, and she couldn't at all think how it might relate to the case. She remembered the house party quite well. It had been the summer after her first Season, and the group was a lively one with many other young people present. But Philippa had been writing her first novel and spent most of the visit curled up in the housekeeper's room with paper and ink.

"Yes," Philippa said, "I was at Staveley then. I went with my mother and sisters."

"And did you take part in the many entertainments offered by Lord and Lady Staveley for the amusement of their guests?"

27

"I was there," Philippa admitted cautiously, not sure where the question was leading, "but I spent much of the time by myself."

"By yourself? A young girl, just out of her first Season? You did not ride? You did not dance?"

He was bordering on impertinence. "I am not very fond of dancing," Philippa said evenly. She saw Mr. Pettibone stir in his chair and hastened to forestall him. "Mr. Marsden, if you will tell me what particular entertainment you have in mind, perhaps I can tell you whether or not I took part in it."

Mr. Marsden looked affronted. "Very well, Miss Davenport. Let me refer you to the fancy dress ball which was given at Staveley at the end of August, I believe on the 27th of that month. Do you remember the occasion?"

"I remember it, yes," Philippa said. It had been a matter of particular interest to her sister Violet who was relying on the ball to bring a certain Captain Livesey up to scratch, a hope in which she was bitterly disappointed.

"And were you also present at the dinner Lord and Lady Staveley gave before the ball?"

"Yes, of course. All the Staveley guests were there."

"Quite so. You have said that you never met the late Lord Carteret, Miss Davenport. And yet on the night in question, the night of the 27th of August, Lord Staveley's neighbour, Sir Thomas Griswold, drove over to Staveley and brought along some friends who were staying with him at the time. Not only did Sir Thomas and his friends attend the ball, they were asked to dinner beforehand. And among those friends whom Sir Thomas brought to Staveley—who sat down to dinner at the table at which you yourself, Miss Davenport, by your own admission, were also seated—among those friends was the late Marquis of Carteret whom you so earnestly assured the court you never had the privilege of meeting."

There was a shocked murmur from the courtroom. That clever Mr. Marsden had caught Miss Davenport in a lie.

Stunned, Philippa looked involuntarily at Henry Ashton and knew that it was what he had expected all along.

Chapter 2

Philippa stared bleakly out the carriage window at the crowd pouring into Middle Temple Lane, calling for their carriages and no doubt gossiping excitedly about the turn the trial had taken that afternoon. How was it possible that she had sat down to dinner with a man whose name and face she could not recall? For the first time since the trial had begun, Philippa had lost some of her self-possession.

Fortunately, Mr. Marsden's revelation about the late Lord Carteret's presence at Staveley had come late in the day, and to Philippa's relief Sir Williston had seen fit to adjourn immediately thereafter. She would have the rest of the day to compose her thoughts, control her anger at Mr. Marsden's imputation of duplicity, and plan how she was to defend herself against the slurs that were bound to appear in tomorrow's *Morning Intelligencer*. She could begin by not dwelling morosely on what was in the past and could not be helped.

Philippa turned from the window and forced herself to smile at Francesca who was sitting beside her in the carriage. "I'm sorry, people who sit and brood about their problems are dreadfully tedious. I'd never allow one of my heroines to be so poor-spirited."

"Nonsense," Francesca returned warmly. "Recollect that I am standing *in loco parentis*, Philippa. It is my positive duty to take an interest in your problems."

Philippa smiled again, partly in gratitude, partly at the absurdity of the twenty-seven-year-old Francesca serving as

29

a parental substitute. Though she was normally a most independent young woman, Philippa suddenly found herself wishing that her mother or one of her sisters was beside her. But Mama was currently on the Continent, travelling with her new husband, Violet and Ianthe were in the country, preparing to add to their nurseries, and Juliana was in Ireland, raising horses. If Francesca's soldier husband had not been transferred back to England, and if he and Francesca had not agreed to take up residence in the Davenport house in Green Street, Philippa would now be in the country herself, for a young lady—even a young lady who had written three books and who, at twenty-three, was decidedly on the shelf—could not reside alone in London without being thought, at best, positively eccentric.

Francesca had been marvellously supportive throughout the business with Lady Carteret, and Philippa had always been fond of her cousin. Of course, with her pale blonde hair and finely drawn features, Francesca was impossibly lovely, but Philippa was used to that. Her own mother was still renowned for her beauty as well as for her wit and vivacity, and her three sisters had all been rated Incomparables during their very successful Seasons. Long before any of them had come out, when she was still quite young, Philippa had learned that she was different, thanks to the comments of well-meaning visitors who murmured that "it's a pity poor little Philippa takes after her father's side of the family." Philippa had convinced herself that her appearance was of little moment. And if occasionally a longing for a fuller figure or more luxuriant hair crept into her thoughts, she harboured no ill-will toward beauties like her mother and sisters.

Nor her cousin. Francesca had a tongue very nearly as sharp as Philippa's own and that gave them a common ground.

"Are you quite certain you were present at the dinner table?" Francesca said, turning to the immediate problem. "There's no chance you could have stayed in your room with a headache? or been delayed by an accident to your frock?"

"No, I remember the dinner," Philippa said ruefully, "though it was a confused sort of affair. There must have been near thirty people sitting down to table." She closed her eyes, trying to visualize that long-gone evening. "I remember the dining room. It was large and dark, not at all what one likes to see in the country, and the walls were hung with a series of depressing portraits of the Staveley ancestors. The curtains had been drawn, though it was still light outside, and there were candles and a great quantity of silver. I remember a great epergne and, oh yes, the soup tureens. Mama told me later they were by Storr and very valuable, but we laughed about it at the time for we thought them extremely ugly—they had tortoises for feet and were covered with writhing fish and acanthus leaves and all manner of vegetables." Philippa opened her eyes and looked at her cousin. "I know what you're thinking, Francesca. How could I possibly recall the tureens and not the faces of the people who were seated at the table? But I was eighteen and not used to such oppressive splendour, and I'm sure I was paying more attention to the young officers there—remember, the war in the Peninsula had just ended—than to men as drearily old as the marquis. I suppose we had been presented to him and the other guests before dinner—you know the sort of thing, the Davenport girls all in a cluster, with little Philippa standing rather toward the rear—but I have no specific recollection of it. I doubt he would have noticed me any more than I noticed him, and of course we were seated nowhere near at table, for he would have occupied a much more exalted place."

Francesca laughed appreciatively. "I know the feeling exactly. The young live in a different world, and it's no wonder Lord Carteret made no impression. But let's think of all the possibilities. Lord Carteret was, after all, a marquis. He must have attracted some attention, or some comment, particularly with that scar. If you didn't notice his face, could something have been said at the ball, something you could have overheard?"

Philippa shook her head. "Nothing that I recall. Of course, many more people came for the dancing—it was a dreadful crush, and I was persuaded at the time that a number of the younger guests had not been properly invited—and I doubt that Lord Carteret would have spent the evening in the ballroom when he could have been comfortably playing cards.

Perhaps someone mentioned him the next day when they were talking the ball over, but by then I had gotten Belinda into the most dreadful scrape and had no idea how to extricate her in time to keep her appointment with Edward. You can understand my preoccupation, since the plot hinged entirely on the meeting being witnessed by Mr. Tilworthy, who of course misunderstood what was happening and thus caused a breach between Belinda and Charles, which had to take place so they could become reconciled in the end. So I'm afraid I didn't pay very much attention. Besides, I'd been up half the night with Violet. She was inconsolable because of Captain Livesey's defection, and Mama was not at all sympathetic, and Ianthe was being spiteful because Violet had been allowed to wear Mama's pearls, and Juliana never cares about anything but horses, so it rather fell to me." Philippa looked her cousin in the face. "And that, Francesca, is all I can remember of that wretched evening, I swear it is."

Francesca covered Philippa's hand with her own. "I believe you, Philippa."

"Mr. Ashton does not." Philippa was unable to keep the bitterness from her voice. "I could tell by his face that it was only what he had expected. He knew all along that I had been telling an untruth. And it will all appear in the *Morning Intelligencer* tomorrow."

Francesca looked at her in some distress. She had never understood why, in that brief quarter-hour two years ago, her cousin had taken Henry Ashton in such dislike. It was the more unfortunate as Henry's sister was now living in their house—Philippa's house—and Henry as a matter of course was a frequent visitor. His role as a respected commentator on Philippa's trial only added to Philippa's sense of injury.

"Surely you exaggerate," she said, but Philippa had turned away and Francesca held her tongue. Francesca had to admit that Henry could be difficult to know. That had not always been the case. He had been such an engaging companion when she first met him, with an ardent imagination and a ready smile. But by the time she introduced him to Philippa, he had grown harassed and driven, unable to enjoy the success of his first novel and his growing literary reputation. Francesca thought the change was due to his father's death which had not only been a personal blow, but left the family in straitened circumstances. As the only son, Henry was responsible for the welfare of his mother and five sisters. The income from his writing was not large. Francesca suspected that he had beggared his own portion to see his sisters properly dowered, and it was partly for this reason that she offered to sponsor Claris, the youngest and the only one still unmarried. Francesca had never regretted the offer, for Claris was an enchanting girl who kept her constantly amused.

Yet when Henry opened the door and handed his sister into the carriage, Francesca saw that Claris was looking mutinous and Henry was white-lipped with anger, though, when he addressed Francesca, his voice was quiet and controlled. "I'm sorry if Claris has kept you waiting," he said without further explanation. "I understand you do not go out tonight. I'll call this evening if I may. Miss Davenport." He bowed briefly to Philippa, closed the door, and gave the coachman the signal to start.

After a quiet dinner, the ladies retired to the drawing room. Francesca's husband Gerry (whose business at the War Office had kept him from attending the trial) declined to sit over a lonely bottle and retreated to the library with his dispatch box. Francesca kept up desultory chatter with a subdued Claris while Philippa thought about her recent interview with Mr. Pettibone. He had called late that afternoon, together with Mr. Herrington, her solicitor, to inquire dryly why Miss Davenport had not seen fit to acquaint them with her introduction to the late Lord Carteret. Wearily, and at somewhat greater length, Philippa had repeated what she had said to Francesca in the carriage. Mr. Herrington, an old friend of the family, patted her hand and told her not to worry. Mr. Pettibone, who was not a stupid man, agreed that the mistake was understandable, though it might not sit well with either Sir Williston or the jury, and Mr. Marsden was sure to make much of it. Still, they must do the best with what they had, and he would recall her to the stand the next morning. He was certain, yes, he could say he was quite certain, that they would be able to prevail. With which cold comfort the two men had taken their leave.

Philippa roused herself to attend to the others, but at this moment Francesca was called upstairs to attend to her baby daughter who was cutting a tooth and calling for her mother.

Philippa was left alone with Claris, a situation she would normally have enjoyed. Claris was just eighteen, a pretty girl with large sky-blue eyes, honey-coloured hair, and a rounded little figure that was judged by her dancing partners to be perfectly designed for the intimacies of the waltz. Claris had spent her life in the relative seclusion of the Dorset village where her father had held a living and her widowed mother still made her home. She had not yet been spoiled by London. She had a ready laugh, a disposition to be pleased by whatever befell her, and a frank interest in the doings of the other sex.

But Claris had been blue-devilled ever since she had entered the carriage that afternoon, and Philippa was wondering what she could say to cheer her when Claris ran suddenly to her side and took her hands. "Philippa, I am in the most dreadful coil! Please, please, may I talk to you? Francesca has been very kind, but I don't think she would take me seriously and I do not know where else to turn."

Astonished, Philippa gave a ready assent, and Claris plunged into an account of her plight.

"He is the most unexceptionable young man and quite the handsomest in London," Claris began, "and Henry had no cause to be so Gothic about seeing us together, we would have told him in the end, but Crispin said we should wait until the end of the trial—he has such a sense of delicacy, though I think it is quite unnecessary myself, for I'm sure you would think nothing of it, but of course I agreed to do whatever he thought best, and don't you think it is extremely hard that we should have to wait?"

Philippa did not fully understand this outburst, but she could at least agree that Henry Ashton could with justice be accused of barbarous behaviour. There was no reason on earth why Claris should have to suffer for her association with the notorious Miss Davenport. "I take it," she said, feeling her way, "that you have developed a *tendre* for a young man and

34

that your brother does not approve?" Who, she wondered, thinking of all the young men who regularly clustered around Claris. There was no one she knew by the name of Crispin.

"Oh, Philippa"—tears filled Claris' lovely eyes—"Henry will forbid our meeting, and if he does, I know that I shall absolutely die!"

"Nonsense! Your brother can hardly forbid you to meet, and if you have a mutual liking you should certainly have the opportunity to get to know each other better."

"There's no need for that, we are desperately in love, and we already know each other as well as two people ever can."

Philippa looked at the young girl sharply. This had gone further than she had realized, but surely Claris would not have—no, Francesca had been raised with a good deal of freedom, but she was a careful chaperone. "Claris, he is not absolutely ineligible?"

Claris shook her head.

Philippa had a sudden suspicion. "Does he have money?" It was, after all, the chief reason Claris had come to town, though her brother, of all people, should not object to a man who worked for his living.

"I don't know much about such things, but I think he will come into a comfortable fortune." Claris was not without a practical side.

Then why should Mr. Ashton throw Claris into such a fright? It was true she had not been long in town, but she had come to be married. If she had attached herself to a handsome young man with a comfortable fortune, her brother had every reason to felicitate her, not to ring a peal over her head.

"Who is he, Claris? Do I know him?"

"Yes. No. Well, I am not absolutely sure whether or not you have met. It is Crispin, Lord Christopher, Lady Carteret's son."

Philippa stared at the girl at her side who was dabbing at her eyes with a damp handkerchief embroidered with gooseberries. Where in heaven could they have met? No, that was nonsense, the families did not move in quite the same circles, for the Davenports had long been Whigs and the Carterets were equally staunch Tories, but the young couple could have met at any of a dozen places. And it was hardly surprising that Claris should have been attracted to Lord Christopher. He was an excessively handsome young man, neatly formed, with well-drawn features, an engaging manner, and a head of splendid gold hair that clustered around his forehead in curls that nature might have given him. Still, it was deucedly awkward, for not only was Claris living in the house of the woman Lord Christopher's mother had taken into court, but Lady Carteret, as Philippa knew to her sorrow, had a great deal of family pride and was not likely to welcome an alliance between her only son and a nobody of a girl whose only male relative earned his living by his pen.

Philippa put Lady Carteret aside. There were no insuperable objections. If they were sincerely attached and the attachment weathered the Season, there was no reason why their friends should not applaud their union. True, he seemed very young and there was much to be learned about him, for Claris was obviously blind to all but his external charms, but Philippa determined to support the young couple, against their families if need be. She knew this resolution had a little to do with her present animus toward Lady Carteret and a great deal to do with her animus toward Claris' brother, but no matter. Though she did not consider herself a romantic, Philippa thought that love, a rare commodity, should be nurtured whenever it dared to show its fragile bloom.

Claris' tears had abated and her breathing had quieted when the door opened and Tuttle, the Davenport's butler, announced the arrival of Mr. Ashton. Claris seized Philippa's hand again. "Do not leave me," she whispered, "I beg you!"

Philippa nodded. The two women rose and went forward together to meet Claris' brother.

Mr. Ashton had his feelings under control. He bowed to Philippa, bade her good evening quite civilly, and kissed Claris on the cheek. His sister suffered this in silence, then retreated to the sofa on which she had been sitting. Mr. Ashton stood irresolute a moment. "I do not wish to discommode you, Miss Davenport, but I have something particular to say to my sister. Is there some place where we can be private?"

Philippa could not in justice deny him, but she saw Claris'

pleading face and determined that she would not accede to Mr. Ashton's wishes. "I believe your sister would be more comfortable with another woman present."

Mr. Ashton raised his brows. "I am not a monster, Miss Davenport. Believe me when I say that I have my sister's best interests at heart."

"Then I honour you for your sentiments. Nonetheless," Philippa went on as she seated herself beside Claris, "I have been asked to remain, and I intend to do so. Pray be seated, Mr. Ashton. Lady Francesca is occupied with her daughter, but if you care to wait, you may make application to her and I will be guided by her decision."

Philippa watched the play of emotions across Mr. Ashton's face and almost felt sorry for him. She did not doubt his sincerity, and Claris had no doubt tried his patience. He chose a chair opposite her, declined refreshment, and stared fixedly at his sister who in turn stared at the twisted handkerchief in her hands.

After some moments, Philippa broke the silence. "Claris has told me that she has formed an attachment for Lord Christopher Paget and that you do not approve. I hope that her position in this house has nothing to do with your feelings in the matter, for I would not want to be the cause of any disappointment on her part. It is difficult at present, of course, but the trial will not last long and will soon be forgotten."

"The trial, Miss Davenport, is of no importance whatsoever."

"Then surely—"

"Then surely my confiding little sister—look at me, Claris!—should have told her obliging friend that she has formed more than an attachment." He leaned forward in his chair. "When court was adjourned this afternoon, my sister begged leave of Lady Francesca to remain behind a moment to speak to her brother. She did not want to speak to her brother, she wanted to escape his notice. And when he left the courtroom some minutes later and glanced about him in the corridor outside, whom should he see but his own sister hiding in a corner clasped in an indecent embrace?"

Claris could not let this pass. "It was not indecent!"

"For a young girl it was ruinous! You were fortunate no one but your brother was witness to it." He turned back to Philippa. "And when I had occasion to object to this treatment of my sister, the young whelp informed me that he and my sister were betrothed."

Philippa could not conceal her dismay. So this accounted for Mr. Ashton's thunderous look when he brought Claris to the carriage. The girl had been disingenuous. "I don't wonder at your concern," she said, "the betrothal is unconventional—"

"The betrothal is impossible, he's underage." He turned again to Claris who had made a sound of protest. "And don't think you will run off to Gretna Green to be married, his family would have it annulled."

Claris drew herself up. "He will be twenty-one in August. We will wait."

"By all means," her brother said with heavy sarcasm. "Wait if you can. If he can. What will you live on? He has no money of his own until he's twenty-five."

Claris' face fell. She and Crispin had not envisaged the need to live anywhere at all. She lifted her chin. "Then we'll live with his family."

Mr. Ashton threw up his hands at this piece of folly. He rose and gripped the back of the chair. "His family will never receive you. And why should you want to be received by them? His mother has the brains of a mouse, his half-brother is an affected fop who does nothing at all to justify his existence, and the object of your affections is a puling infant who hides in corners for fear of being found out by either of them."

"Henry!" Claris jumped up and faced him.

"Unjust, unjust!" Philippa said, hastening to Claris' defence.

"I grant his pretty face," Claris' brother said grimly, ignoring Miss Davenport's outburst, "but it will not do."

"You don't want me to marry well," Claris wailed.

"I want you to marry a man of sense."

"I don't want a man of sense," Claris cried, "I want Crispin!" She burst into tears.

Philippa rose and took the girl in her arms, rocking her gently while her sobs abated. Mr. Ashton could not have it both ways. If he wanted his sister comfortably settled—and that, after all, was why he had agreed to let her come to Francesca—he would have to accept a husband who moved in the circles of which he disapproved. "Can't you see she's overwrought?"

"I can see she wants her own way," he said. "But the match is impossible, and even were it not, he's not the man I'd want to have the care of my sister."

"You judge harshly, sir." Henry Ashton, she remembered, had a low opinion of love stories.

"You would approve this folly?"

"I would give this folly time to grow and learn if it is folly indeed."

"Then, madam, I must protect my sister from you as well as from herself."

They stood glaring at each other while Claris continued to sob out her heart, drenching the shoulder of Philippa's gown.

The door opened and Tuttle appeared once more. Carefully ignoring the tearful Miss Ashton, he informed Miss Philippa that Mr. Herrington had called again to see her, and he had taken the liberty of showing him into the jade saloon. Philippa said she would be there directly and, after seeing that Mr. Ashton had no intention of further harshness toward his sister, gave Claris into his care and left the room.

When Philippa saw Mr. Herrington out of the house some half-hour later she was puzzled, for he had brought her news that was both encouraging and disturbing. She returned to the drawing room to find Claris sitting quietly on the sofa and Mr. Ashton playing backgammon with Gerry. Francesca had come back downstairs and ordered tea.

Philippa accepted a cup gratefully. "The oddest thing has happened," she told her cousin. "Lord Carteret, the new Lord Carteret, Lady Carteret's stepson"—he was also Lord Christopher's half-brother, but there seemed no point in calling it to anyone's attention at the moment—"has sent Mr. Herrington a letter saying that he would like to call on him later this evening. I thought he might be going to propose a settlement of the case, but Mr. Herrington says the tone of the letter leads him to think Lord Carteret has something else in mind."

"How curious," Francesca said. "It's not usual to approach the opposition this way. I'm not sure it's even proper."

"All the Pagets are mad," Mr. Ashton was heard to mutter.

"Perhaps he's going to change sides." Gerry left the game table and sat down beside his wife, dropping an arm around her shoulders. He was a large, handsome man with a generous fund of careless good-humour. "From all reports, Carteret's not the type to be concerned with the family honour."

"I wouldn't count on it," Francesca returned. "Rakes are often tiresomely conventional underneath. And he seems to be standing by his stepmother. I can't imagine what could cause him to change his mind."

Claris looked up, her face cleared of all traces of past tears. "I can," she announced. "It was obvious in court this afternoon," she added in response to the curious looks of her companions. "He couldn't take his eyes off Philippa. I'm sure he's conceived a *tendre* for her."

It was a preposterous statement, even for Claris—Lord Carteret's taste ran to women both beautiful and safely married—and it was met by silence. Her brother threw up his hands once more and rose from the game table.

The accumulated tensions of the day were too much for Philippa—Mr. Marsden's attack, Claris' disclosures, Mr. Ashton's threats, and now this unlikely message from the present Marquis of Carteret. She went off into a peal of laughter. "But I don't even know him!"

Henry Ashton looked at her with narrowed eyes. "Are you quite sure, Miss Davenport?" he asked with withering sarcasm. "Perhaps he dined at Staveley, too."

Chapter 3

Anthony Bertram Cedric Paget, seventh Marquis of Carteret, walked boldly across the courtroom and took his place in the witness-box. To the astonishment of the court, the plaintiff, and the plaintiff's attorney, he had been summoned as a witness for the defence. Even Philippa's counsel, the eminent Julius Pettibone, appeared a trifle put out by the irregularity of the proceedings. Only Carteret himself seemed perfectly at ease. He mounted the steps to the box, turned to face the courtroom, and prepared to take his oath. The young men among the crowd of spectators observed with envy the coat of dark blue superfine that fit his broad shoulders without a wrinkle, the buff-coloured pantaloons that covered his long, well-muscled thighs, and the Hessians polished to so high a gloss they might have served as mirrors. The young women admired the lustrous hair, the fine nose that had been generations in the making, and the hint of sensuality in the delicately carved lips.

Philippa, normally not one to be caught by a handsome face, observed Lord Carteret with distinct interest. She had been astonished when, on her arrival in court not half an hour since, Mr. Pettibone had informed her that Lord Carteret had some testimony which might be of benefit to her case. There had been no time for Pettibone to elaborate, and Philippa hadn't the least idea what Lord Carteret could be about. Claris' contention that he had conceived a *tendre* for Philippa was clearly preposterous, but Philippa was sure there was more

41

behind his action than a freakish whim.

Whatever odious remarks Henry Ashton might make, Philippa was unacquainted with the present Lord Carteret, though she knew him by reputation. He had been considered a matrimonial prize almost from the day he came down from Cambridge, but he was notorious for his aversion to Almack's and the other haunts of respectable young women. Those ladies of the *beau monde* whom he did distinguish with his attentions were invariably already supplied with husbands.

In addition to his country estate which dated to the fourteenth century (and, more remarkably, was in excellent repair) and his income (rumoured to be in the vicinity of 30,000 a year), Lord Carteret's personal characteristics were enough to turn the head of the most clear-sighted young woman. His hair was dark enough to be called black, his eyes a cool grey, and elder brothers who frequented Gentleman Jackson's boxing academy were able to assure their sisters that he stripped to distinct advantage. Like so many men who could afford to lose, he had uncanny luck at the gaming table, he drove recklessly, but with consummate skill, and he was a capital shot, though sadly he had not actually fought any duels. And his skill at tying a cravat was almost legendary.

Philippa looked at Carteret critically, wondering what it was that sent half the young women in London into such a pucker. She was not impervious to his good looks, but good looks, while all very well in their way, were scarcely sufficient justification for a sustained interest. She glanced involuntarily at the corner where Henry Ashton sat, pencil and paper in hand. Mr. Ashton had spoken harshly of the entire Paget family on the previous evening. How had he described Lord Carteret? *An affected fop who does nothing at all to justify his existence.* Philippa turned her eyes back to the marquis. If Mr. Ashton thought him worth disliking, perhaps there might be more to Lord Carteret than met the eye.

Henry looked up from his notes in time to see Miss Davenport fix her gaze upon Lord Carteret and was conscious of surprise and disappointment. Carteret had clearly turned the heads of most of the young ladies in the courtroom—Henry's sister was looking defiantly at Carteret's younger brother—but Henry had thought better of Miss Davenport. Though she frittered her talent away upon trivial subject matter, she was a woman of considerable intelligence, and Henry would have expected her to see past Carteret's elegance and sang-froid to the shallowness which no doubt lay just beneath the surface.

Lord Carteret himself appeared oblivious to the attention he was attracting. He had been accustomed to it since his thirteenth year and, to his credit, no one had ever accused him of the sin of vanity. He took his oath in a resonant voice and prepared to answer Mr. Pettibone's questions. Philippa leaned forward with interest. Henry jotted down a comment of more than usual acidity.

Mr. Pettibone cast a brief glance in the direction of the Dowager Lady Carteret, who was regarding her stepson with a mixture of outrage and disbelief. Lady Carteret might be suing Pettibone's client, but she was the witness' stepmother, and Pettibone did not like to see family obligations disrupted. He began to wish he had never agreed to argue this case, but since he had his first duty was to his client. He cleared his throat and commenced his examination.

"Lord Carteret, you are familiar with the nature of this trial?"

"I was in court yesterday," Lord Carteret returned affably. "Had to get up monstrous early. It's quite extraordinary the hours you fellows keep."

A titter went up from somewhere in the courtroom, followed by the sound of Sir Williston's gavel.

Mr. Pettibone looked pained. It was not the place of a witness to make clever remarks, but he could hardly admonish a man who had volunteered to come forward on behalf of his own client. He cleared his throat a second time and tried again. "You are aware, my lord, that a charge of libel has been laid against my client, Miss Davenport?"

Lord Carteret acknowledged that he was so aware.

"Miss Davenport wrote and caused to be published a letter which, it is alleged, contained words of contempt and ridicule referring to the person of the plaintiff, Lady Carteret, and the plaintiff is seeking damages for the consequent loss of her

43

comfort and enjoyment of society." Mr. Pettibone adjusted his gown. He was clearly not at ease with this unexpected witness. "My learned friend, Mr. Marsden, has argued that Miss Davenport bears some animus, not only toward Lady Carteret, but toward your entire family. In support of this ridiculous contention—"

Here Mr. Marsden predictably objected and Sir Williston predictably sustained it.

"Mr. Marsden has introduced in evidence," Mr. Pettibone continued blandly, "a novel called *Worldly Wisdom* which was written by Miss Davenport, and specifically the character of the Marquis of Coachfield which, he claims, was based upon that of your own father." Mr. Pettibone held up an admonitory hand. "Let me be more precise. What has been alleged, or at least what my esteemed colleague has endeavoured to demonstrate"—here he turned and bowed slightly to Mr. Marsden who was staring at the witness with a perfectly impassive face—"is that the appearance of Lord Coachfield, as described in Miss Davenport's book, bears some slight resemblance to the appearance of the late Lord Carteret."

Mr. Marsden was on his feet, but the witness answered before the barrister could voice his objection. "I wouldn't have needed to come to court to be aware of that," Lord Carteret pointed out. "It's been all over London for weeks."

A somewhat louder laugh arose from the courtroom, but Mr. Pettibone's voice soared above the laughter and the sound of Sir Williston's gavel. "Mr. Marsden claims that there is a strong similarity in appearance between the two men and that it leads the uncritical reader to assume that the *character* of the fictional man is intended to portray the character of the real one.

"Mr. Marsden further claims that my client drew the physical similarity knowing full well that her readers would reach this conclusion, that she did so with deliberate and malicious intent, and with the knowledge that such a conclusion is a false one. This, Mr. Marsden claims, led his client to conclude that Miss Davenport was acting with unparalleled malice toward her late husband—whom Miss Davenport cannot even recall having met—and toward your entire family. Lady Carteret has made these accusations publicly on a number of occasions, despite Miss Davenport's representation that they are entirely false and without foundation."

Mr. Pettibone was now getting into the swing of his argument. "Miss Davenport," he went on, including the jury as well as Lord Carteret in his gaze, "generously overlooked these attacks on her veracity. But when Lady Carteret took steps—the exact nature of those steps is in dispute, but that some steps were taken has not been denied—when lady Carteret took steps to have Miss Davenport's book withdrawn, my client not unnaturally made an effort to protect herself and the work of her creation by writing a letter to a respectable magazine in which she protested the suppression of literature.

"Lady Carteret, maintaining the fiction that my client was animated by ill will toward your family"—Mr. Pettibone's voice soared over Mr. Marsden's protests—"took the letter as an attack on her own reputation and brought an action against Miss Davenport for libel." Mr. Pettibone paused impressively. "Do you understand, Lord Carteret?"

"I have a tolerable understanding, Mr. Pettibone." Lord Carteret's voice pronounced his boredom with the tediousness of the proceedings, but his closest friends would have noted that he was following the argument with care. "Miss Davenport wrote a book describing someone with a vicious character who looked something like my late father. Miss Davenport says the resemblance was accidental—she does not recall meeting my father or paying him the slightest attention if she did. My stepmother, however, believes the similarity in appearance was intentional and was intended to denote a similarity in character. And even if Miss Davenport did not intend it, the reader of her book would assume that such was the case. It seems a chancy business. If the reader assumes that my father was like Lord Coachfield in his character as well as his features, then it should be the reader's malice that is inferred, not the writer's. And in that case, my stepmother should have taken on half of London."

There was an uproar. Sir Williston called twice for order. Lord Carteret examined his nails. Philippa tried to school her

45

features, but her eyes were dancing. The impossibly handsome marquis was proving far more interesting than she had expected.

Henry found he was grinning in spite of himself. Carteret had a sense of humour, one must give him that. But the man was clearly playing with them all and might just as readily have amused himself by testifying for the prosecution. Miss Davenport, with her keen powers of observation, should realize that this was the case.

"But," said Lord Carteret when the courtroom was quiet once more, "I have no real understanding of the law."

Mr. Pettibone, who had stood stolidly throughout the last few moments, drew his brows together and was heard to murmur, "Just so, just so," before he continued in his courtroom voice. "Have you read the book in question, my lord?"

"I don't read books in the ordinary course of things," said Carteret, as the courtroom became suddenly hushed, "but I thought in this case to make an exception. Had the devil of a time finding it yesterday and had to borrow one, there's not a copy left for sale in all of London."

"But you read it, my lord?"

"I read it. I read it," Lord Carteret continued, a note of wonder in his voice, "all the way through. I believe it was the first time I'd done so since I was eleven. After two years at Harrow, one learns to avoid unnecessary tasks."

Pettibone ignored this aspersion on the public school system with masterful restraint. He was an Etonian. "And, having read Miss Davenport's book, do you believe that the fictional Lord Coachfield was unmistakably meant to be your late father?"

Carteret paused carefully before he spoke. "Certainly not. There is some physical resemblance, but it is of the most superficial nature. As for his character, my late father, as my esteemed stepmother is perfectly well aware"—Carteret inclined his head politely in the direction of Lady Carteret who was staring at him with wounded eyes—"was a man of principle and would never have accosted a well-bred young girl under his own wife's roof."

46

This filial tribute was greeted by a confused murmur. Mr. Pettibone hastened on. "Yet according to popular reports, reports which I myself have not heard though they have been testified to in this courtroom, it is widely believed that Lord Coachfield was modelled on your late father."

Lord Carteret smiled. "No sensible man believes half of what he hears. Nor half of what he himself swears to be the truth."

"Let us move then to another question, my lord," Mr. Pettibone said when the laughter had died down. "You have read Miss Davenport's book. Do you share Lady Carteret's opinion that the book was written with malicious intent?"

"Lord, no." Carteret smiled affably. "I enjoyed it immensely. I may even read another book before the year is out."

Mr. Pettibone paused to allow the laughter and the gavel to run their course. Lord Carteret was a difficult witness, but he was proving more helpful than Pettibone had hoped, and he intended to get full value from him. "Let me understand you, Lord Carteret. Are you, as the head of your family, telling the court that you are not disturbed by Miss Davenport's book?"

"I don't think I could make myself any plainer," Lord Carteret said firmly.

"You would not, in deference to your stepmother's feelings, undertake to suppress this work even though you do not personally find it objectionable?"

"I have always had the very greatest consideration for my stepmother's feelings," Lord Carteret said, "but I can't see that any good is served by attacking a piece of paper."

"Am I to conclude, then, that you find Lady Carteret's response to Miss Davenport's book somewhat"—Mr. Pettibone paused, searching for just the right shade of meaning—"excessive?"

Mr. Marsden was on his feet. He opened his mouth, then made a gesture of resignation and sat down again.

"My stepmother is a woman of great sensibility," Lord Carteret said carefully.

"Just so." Mr. Pettibone put his hands on the desk in front of him and leaned forward. "Lord Carteret, have you read the letter from Miss Davenport that appeared in this issue of the *Lady's Monthly Museum?*" He held a copy of the magazine aloft.

"It's not a publication I'm put much in the way of," the marquis admitted, "but yes, I have seen the letter."

"And what is your opinion of the letter, Lord Carteret?"

A hush swallowed the court. Lord Carteret waited a fraction of a moment, and when he spoke his voice betrayed his amusement. "I found it somewhat excessive. But then, I expect Miss Davenport is a woman of great sensibility, too."

Philippa ran a brush through her fine hair and savoured the sensation of having an immense burden suddenly lifted from her shoulders. Though it had taken the remainder of the morning to conclude the legal proceedings, Lord Carteret's testimony had marked the end of his stepmother's case. A murderous Mr. Marsden had declined to cross-examine Carteret and asked for a recess. Lord Carteret had been observed bending over his stepmother, talking to her earnestly. What he said was unknown, but Mr. Marsden was eventually called to their side. Mr. Marsden then spent some time closeted with Sir Williston and Mr. Pettibone, after which the charges against Miss Davenport were withdrawn.

The spectators had been divided on the outcome of the trial. It was a pity to have it cut short so abruptly, but Lord Carteret's testimony had provided a delicious new piece of gossip. Miss Davenport's supporters felt she had been quite thoroughly vindicated, but those who sided with Lady Carteret considered that Miss Davenport's escape was owed solely to Lord Carteret's perfidy.

Until the case was actually dismissed, Philippa had not realized how much it had disturbed her, nor how worried she had been. Now she felt positively giddy with relief—so giddy that she had actually agreed to accompany Francesca and Claris to Almack's this evening. Philippa smiled and set down her brush. The trial must indeed have made her light-headed, for she generally avoided that matrimonial bazaar. It reminded her too much of her own first Season, which she had disliked almost as much as Claris was enjoying hers. But it was different now that Philippa was old enough to be one of the observers

48

rather than one of the young women on display. And if she had to face society after her pillory in the courtroom, better in the staid confines of Almack's than in a drawing room where tongues were less constrained.

Besides, tonight she felt like celebrating and Francesca had clearly desired her company. Philippa's cousin preferred wittier entertainments—her attendance at Almack's this Season was owed almost entirely to her obligations to Claris—and Philippa knew that Francesca would welcome her conversation as an antidote to the tedium. Gerry, normally the most uxorious of husbands, had flatly refused to set foot inside the assembly rooms, saying that the liquid refreshment was undrinkable and that he had, after all, already found a rich wife. Francesca threatened amiably to box his ears and prevailed upon Henry Ashton to serve as their escort.

Philippa reached for her hairpins—she had dispatched her maid Nancy to see to Claris—and found that she was grinning. No doubt Almack's was even less to Mr. Ashton's taste than it was to Gerry's but, as Francesca was attending the assembly for his sister's sake, he could scarcely have denied her request. Philippa was sure that Mr. Ashton would take her own attendance as another example of her frivolous preoccupations. In all honesty, it was that thought which had really convinced her to make one of the party. Never let it be said that a desire for Mr. Ashton's approval motivated her actions.

In any event, it was rather fun to be going into company and Philippa found she actually enjoyed preparing for the outing. She had taken longer than usual to choose her dress, settling finally on a deep rose sarcenet of a conservative cut but of a shade that was flattering to her skin. Her hair, of course, was hopeless. Even were she to crop it short all over, like poor Caro Lamb, it would remain completely straight. Any attempt to coax it into ringlets invariably led to disaster, so Philippa simply wore it pulled off her face and anchored with as many hairpins as possible. It was a style which Francesca sometimes affected, but while it looked regally lovely on Philippa's cousin, on herself, Philippa thought, it looked merely plain. She tugged at her front hair, trying to soften the severity of the style. A lock of straight brown hair slithered free of its pins and hung limply in front of her right eye. Sighing good-naturedly, she picked up another pin and jabbed the offending lock firmly into place.

She looked critically in the glass. As they left the courtroom, Claris had repeated her assertion that Lord Carteret had conceived a *tendre* for Philippa, but Philippa continued to find the idea laughable. Whatever had persuaded the marquis to come forward in her defence, it had nothing to do with her person, for he more than most men could be discriminating in his choice of companions. She would not meet him tonight—according to Francesca he made it a matter of personal pride to avoid the Almack's assemblies—but it was not impossible that they would meet one day. Philippa rather hoped they would, for he was certainly an intriguing man and she would like to engage him in conversation.

Her thoughts were interrupted by a bark from the floor near her feet. Hermia, a dog of small size and dubious pedigree—her mother was a King Charles spaniel and her father had been very determined—stood up, stretched, settled herself in a fresh position, and closed her eyes again. Philippa patted her pet's head and abandoned all thoughts of the marquis.

Feeling suddenly silly for having spent so much time on her toilet, she clasped a necklace of garnets around her throat, arranged the Lyons shawl which her mother had given her just before departing for the Continent, picked up her gloves and reticule, and went downstairs to find that she was still ready well in advance of Francesca and Claris.

As the little party disembarked from their carriage before the assembly rooms in King Street, Claris prophesied cheerfully that their arrival was sure to receive a great deal of attention, "for everyone will be wanting to see Philippa."

Philippa knew this was an exaggeration—most of the young women and even more of their mothers would have serious business in mind—but the trial was sure to be much talked of, and there were bound to be many curious stares, and not all of those friendly. No doubt many of Lady Carteret's friends regularly brought their daughters to the assemblies.

When she entered the grand ballroom, Philippa saw that it was even worse than she had expected and wondered if she should have remained at home with a book. Lady Carteret herself did not seem to be present, but a formidable woman in puce satin and diamonds was standing just beyond the entrance. Though the woman had almost nothing in common with Lady Carteret's soft prettiness, and though she had not attended the trial, Philippa knew her by sight as the Countess Buckleigh, Lady Carteret's sister. Lady Buckleigh's daughter, Lady Edwina Thane, a fashionable beauty who had had London at her feet for the past two Seasons, was just leaving the dance floor, and the engaging young man at her side was none other than Lord Christopher Paget.

Philippa glanced at Mr. Ashton and saw that he was observing Claris' would-be fiancé with every appearance of calm. She was relieved, for it would make the evening much pleasanter, though she suspected Mr. Ashton's manner betokened a change of tactics rather than any lessening of his opposition to Claris' betrothal.

In this last, Philippa was perfectly correct. On the previous evening, once his sister and Miss Davenport had retired and his own temper had cooled, Henry had discussed Claris' situation with Francesca and Gerry. Gerry observed that in his experience it was futile to attempt to control one's sisters. Francesca managed to persuade Henry—she was not a diplomat's daughter for nothing—that opposition would only strengthen his sister's resolve. Both Claris and Lord Christopher were, after all, extremely young, and very likely to grow out of their infatuation if left to themselves. As for Henry's fear of an elopement, Francesca gave him her word that there would be no possibility of that while Claris remained under her roof.

Henry had seen the sense of Francesca's words, and now he did not even attempt to catch his sister's eye. Not that it would have served any purpose if he had done so, he thought wryly. Oblivious of her brother, Claris gave a brilliant smile which embraced the entire ballroom, but her eyes were directed at Lord Christopher. The young man, who was passing just beyond the rope which separated the dancers from the

51

onlookers, glanced in their direction and hesitated, his eyes fixed on Claris with a look which instantly convinced Philippa that he was as much in earnest as her young friend. He seemed about to approach them, then suddenly turned away and followed Lady Edwina off the floor.

Claris raised her chin a fraction and looked elaborately unconcerned. "It's his cousin," she said, "and she's years too old for him."

"He would find it awkward, you know, speaking to you in front of Philippa." Francesca's tone was gentle. First love could be a painful experience and she had no desire to see her young charge hurt.

"Most people would," Claris said, "but Crispin's not like that at all. I'm sure he doesn't care a fig for whatever people might say. It's all Lady Edwina's doing."

"I'm sure she finds it awkward as well," Philippa observed.

"I wish Lord Carteret was here." Claris could not let the matter alone. "He wouldn't let Lady Edwina cut you like that."

Philippa laughed. "She didn't cut me. She doesn't know me. In any case, why should Lord Carteret have any control over Lady Edwina? She's only his stepcousin."

"She's much more than that. She's his fiancée."

Startled, Philippa turned inquiring eyes to Francesca.

"There's generally thought to be an understanding between the families," Francesca said, "but the matter isn't fixed. Carteret scarcely seems eager to settle down, and his cousin has more than her share of admirers."

Philippa studied the lovely Lady Edwina with a writer's detachment. She and Carteret would make a handsome pair, and they both had a certain arrogant self-assurance.

Philippa turned back to Claris, hoping Lord Christopher's behaviour wouldn't ruin the girl's evening, but Claris was not one to be so easily cast down. Her hand was soon claimed by Harry Warwick, a connection of Francesca's. Harry had a cheerful disposition and some wit and seemed to enjoy Claris' company, though he could hardly be considered a serious suitor for her hand. Young Warwick preferred women in the dark exotic mould, and he was presently enamoured of Lady Edwina Thane whom he worshipped from afar. This suited

Claris very well. She had long since—at least a fortnight ago—given up the thought of taking any man but Crispin seriously, and she took Harry's arm quite happily.

Philippa was relieved, both because Claris' spirits seemed restored and because Claris was now well away from her own contaminating presence. From the thinly veiled looks and whispered conversations around her, it was clear that no one was quite certain as to the proper line to take with the young woman who had bested Lady Carteret that morning.

"Philippa." Emily Cowper, the least formidable of Almack's patronesses, materialized out of the crowd to greet the new arrivals. "How very pretty you look. And how splendid to see you here. I was telling Francesca just the other day that she must persuade you to come to our assemblies more often."

Philippa could not but be grateful for Emily's intervention, though she put the compliment on her appearance down to kindness. She had known Emily for years, and at the age of nine had been a guest in the drawing room at Melbourne House when Emily had married the regrettably stolid Earl Cowper. Francesca had been there too—she and Emily had been friends since they were both in the schoolroom—and Philippa recalled thinking her cousin and the bride looked like two princesses in a fairy tale.

It was a description which would not be inappropriate fourteen years later, Philippa decided as Emily greeted Henry and slipped an arm around Francesca's waist. With a full figure, masses of curling dark hair, and large, heavily fringed brown eyes, Emily radiated warmth and soft femininity. She deserved better than Peter Cowper—and, Philippa knew, had gone to some trouble to find it. Philippa suspected that Emily's mother, the ambitious Lady Melbourne, had had a great deal to do with the match and not for the first time rendered silent thanks for her own mother's refusal to meddle in her children's affairs. She cast an anxious glance in Mr. Ashton's direction. Despite his frequently high-handed treatment of his sister, surely in the end he would respect Claris' feelings and allow her to make her own choice. Wouldn't he?

Emily made no mention of the trial, but instead asked Philippa about the latest news from Violet and Ianthe and whether Juliana was really happy in Ireland. Philippa in turn inquired after Fordwich, the Cowper heir, William and Spencer, the younger boys, and Minny, the only girl and Emily's special pet. The interchange had the desired effect. Lady Carteret's close friends might continue aloof, but Philippa's acceptance at Almack's was assured.

Once pleasantries had been exchanged, it seemed only polite for Henry and Philippa to move a little way off, leaving Francesca and Emily to enjoy a more private conversation. Politeness also decreed that, having done so, they did not immediately desert one another. Despite Henry's frequent visits to the Davenport house in recent weeks, this was one of the first times they had been alone together—or, if not precisely alone, at least without others to lean on for conversational support. Both felt extremely awkward, and both told themselves they were fools to feel so.

Philippa smoothed one of her gloves and tried to hit on a suitable topic of conversation. She was not about to discuss writing and face Mr. Ashton's condescension. Yet despite her earlier assertion that Mr. Ashton's opinion meant little to her, she could not quite stoop to discussing the weather. She began at last to speak of the Summer Exhibition. Mr. Ashton followed her lead, but his responses were rather stilted. Philippa, who felt her customary facility with words had quite deserted her, was pleased to note that Mr. Ashton was in a similar predicament.

Henry, in fact, was feeling not only awkward, but more than a touch guilty. It was not the first time he had experienced that emotion in Miss Davenport's presence, the most notable occasion being their first meeting in Francesca's drawing room two years before. With the hindsight of experience, he had more than once told himself that he should never have accepted the invitation to Francesca's soirée, knowing that Miss Davenport was Francesca's cousin and knowing the things he had so recently written about Miss Davenport's book. Of course, as Miss Davenport herself had said, a writer must learn to deal with criticism, even to converse politely with critics. So Henry had reminded himself when he arrived at Francesca's, realizing he might very well come across

Francesca's cousin. He had thought he was prepared for the meeting. What he had not bargained on was finding Miss Davenport so eager, so direct, so *young*. And so unlike the fashionable woman he had expected. Nor had he bargained on her bringing up the damn' review and asking him directly about Chiron's identity.

At the time, his main concern had been to end the conversation as quickly as possible, with a minimum of embarrassment on both sides. Looking back, he realized that he had only made matters worse. He had thought of writing her a note of apology, but had decided that that would only seem condescending.

Some of his guilt had been assuaged when he met Miss Davenport again two years later. She was clearly a most self-possessed young woman whom it would take more than a review to devastate. She was also clearly not eager for further acquaintance with him. Henry obliged her by staying out of her way as much as possible.

And then, shortly after Henry brought Claris to London, Lady Carteret brought suit against Miss Davenport. It was only natural for the *Morning Intelligencer*, for which Henry had written in the past, to call upon him, as a novelist, to cover a trial involving a literary matter. He could have refused, of course. He had considered doing so. But the paper had made an unusually handsome offer, and there was no denying that the money would be of use. He and his mother had managed to provide Claris with an allowance for her London sojourn, but Henry suspected that it would prove woefully inadequate for a young lady making her way in the fashionable world, and he did not want to see Claris living off Francesca's charity.

Having accepted the assignment, he was determined that it not be said that he softened his commentary because of his connection to Miss Davenport's family. In any event, Miss Davenport was scarcely in need of assistance. No longer as young and ingenuous as she had appeared at their first meeting, Philippa Davenport was clearly well able to take care of herself, and the situation, after all, was of her own making.

At least, Henry reflected, replying to a question from Miss Davenport on the differences between English and French approaches to portrait painting, he had thought the situation was of her own making. Certainly she should not have written such an intemperate letter, especially if Lady Carteret's accusations were grounded in truth. Having read Miss Davenport's latest novel—as clever, and, he judged, as superficial as her earlier work—and having heard a description of the late Marquis of Carteret, Henry had been convinced that Miss Davenport had drawn the similarity between Carteret and Coachfield deliberately. Now, as he thought back over the events of the past few days, he had to admit that her demeanour in court argued against this interpretation.

There were, it seemed, several reasons he owed Miss Davenport an apology. Whatever their differences—he thought back, with a flash of temper, to their scene with Claris on the previous evening—they would be thrown much in each other's way for the remainder of the Season. Surely they could contrive a more amicable relationship. The least he could do was make some sort of peace offering.

"Would you like to dance?" Henry asked.

Philippa stared at him in surprise and confusion. There had been a slight lull in the conversation, but this was the last thing she had expected to hear on Mr. Ashton's lips. Not that he did not dance, of course. She had seen him partner Claris and Francesca as well as several other ladies of his acquaintance and he had done so with unusual grace. He had never before solicited Philippa's hand, but then, Philippa reflected fair-mindedly, when they were in company together she always stayed well out of Mr. Ashton's way. Still, he could have no real wish to dance with her. His unexpected offer, made as the conversation was beginning to dwindle, could betoken nothing more than a sense of obligation.

These thoughts chasing each other chaotically through her mind, Philippa blurted out, "No." Then, realizing that her response was even more curt than Mr. Ashton's invitation, she hastened to add, "Thank you. It's just that dancing isn't my favourite occupation."

Balked in his first attempt at a *rapprochement*, Henry tried another tack and offered to escort her to the tearoom and procure her some refreshment. Philippa accepted, though she wished, for Mr. Ashton's sake as much as her own, that some of her acquaintances would arrive and allow Mr. Ashton to leave her side, as she was convinced he must be longing to do.

They drew a good deal of attention as they made their way to the tearoom, but some of it, Philippa realized, particularly that of the young ladies, was as much on Mr. Ashton's account as on her own. Whatever Mr. Ashton's opinion of the fashionable world, his novels had won him his share of fame within its ranks. His radical views and his avoidance of polite society before his sister's arrival in London would have been enough in themselves to interest the more daring. And, while Mr. Ashton might lack the romantic air which had made Lord Byron all the rage, there was something undeniably attractive about his person. Philippa herself had been very much aware of it at their first meeting, though that, of course, was before she realized how disagreeable he could be.

Thanks to Mr. Ashton's surprising skill at negotiating a crowded room, Philippa soon found herself seated and supplied with a glass of lemonade and a plate of bread and butter. She realized it was once again incumbent on her to supply some polite conversation and was searching for a suitable remark when an unexpected smile crossed Mr. Ashton's face.

"I was wondering," he explained, setting down his glass, "whether the lemonade is even sweeter than on my last visit or whether it's simply that my memory didn't fully allow for its cloying quality."

Philippa bit back a giggle, realized there was no need to do so, and grinned appreciatively. "Memory *couldn't* fully allow for its cloying quality," she assured him.

"You think so too? Good, it seems that we have at last found a subject on which we can agree."

Philippa felt a sudden and unexpected exhilaration. It was impossible, of course, that she and Mr. Ashton could ever see eye to eye, but perhaps she had judged him too harshly in the past. It seemed that, when he put his mind to it, he could be a diverting companion.

As they sipped their lemonade in a more comfortable silence, Philippa became aware of the buzz of conversation about them. More than one group of people were debating the interesting question of why Lord Carteret had publicly affronted his own stepmother. Some thought he had done so out of idle amusement, but others maintained that Carteret, despite his languid manner, always knew precisely what he was doing.

Philippa met Mr. Ashton's eyes and realized that she was listening shamelessly and that he was perfectly well aware that she was doing so. "I know," she said, "I'm an inveterate eavesdropper."

"I have yet to meet a writer who isn't," Mr. Ashton returned.

This was more and more promising. He had actually acknowledged that she was a writer, too. "I must confess to my own share of curiosity about Lord Carteret's behaviour," she said. "I expect I'll never know and it's a pity, for he seems a most interesting man."

"All shallows," Mr. Ashton returned, "you'd be disappointed."

"Oh, dear," said Philippa, "I'd quite forgotten your opinion of the Paget family. And here we were getting along so nicely. Do let's change the subject. Tell me what you think of the bread and butter."

But before Mr. Ashton could reply, he was distracted by a disturbance near the door. Claris was making her way swiftly through the tearoom, followed by a young man whose face showed embarrassment mingled with the consciousness that he was escorting a very pretty girl.

"I told you I was right," Claris announced breathlessly, releasing the young man and clutching Philippa's arm. "Oh, Philippa, do come. I'm sure he's here expressly to see you."

Philippa looked up at Claris in bewilderment. Henry was more adept at interpreting his sister's dramatic pronouncements. "I think," he said, "that my sister is endeavouring to inform you that the Marquis of Carteret has deigned to honour Almack's with his presence."

Chapter 4

Popular opinion was divided as to the exact date of Lord Carteret's last appearance at Almack's. Some claimed he had never attended an assembly. Others argued that he had most certainly put in an appearance five years ago, during his brief and desperate flirtation with Corinna Grantham. (In fact, there had been rather an unpleasant incident with Mrs. Grantham's husband later in the evening, though fortunately it had taken place elsewhere, owing less to any particular sense of delicacy on the part of the gentlemen than to the fact that Mr. Grantham had not been at the assembly, but visiting his mistress' apartments.) Still others claimed that Lord Carteret had come to Almack's at least once during his cousin Edwina's first Season two years ago, though the majority were loath to believe that he had done anything so conventional.

As in the courtroom that morning, Lord Carteret seemed unaware that he was the focus of all eyes. He surveyed the crowd, nodded to Lady Buckleigh, Lady Edwina, and his half-brother but did not approach them, and began to make his way around the room.

Philippa had flatly refused Claris' entreaties to "come back to the ballroom, do, he's obviously looking for you," and sent Miss Ashton off to dance with her embarrassed escort. Philippa and Henry remained in the tearoom to finish their lemonade and nibble the bread and butter, but somehow they could not return to the rapport they had established before Claris' arrival. No doubt Mr. Ashton was growing bored. Feeling oddly depressed, Philippa asked him to escort her back to Francesca.

But only moments after they entered the ballroom, long before either of them had been able to locate Philippa's cousin, Sally Jersey, resplendent in turquoise satin, cut a swath through the crowd and materialized at their side.

Like her fellow patroness Emily Cowper, the Countess of Jersey was an attractive woman in her thirties, but she lacked Emily's lush beauty. Her regular features and rather thin mouth would have appeared merely commonplace, were it not for the constant animation which lent vivacity to her countenance. Though some feared her sharp tongue, Philippa did not find the countess intimidating. But as Lady Jersey approached, she was conscious that a number of eyes were suddenly turned in their direction, which was not surprising, considering that Lady Jersey had the Marquis of Carteret in tow.

To be at the centre of attention was not a novel experience for Sally Jersey, but even she considered it quite a coup when Carteret asked her to present him to Miss Davenport. It made up in some measure for the fact that she had not been in the courtroom to hear his testimony. Despite his neglect of the assemblies, Lady Jersey, like so many other women, nourished a soft spot for the marquis, and in the matter of the trial her sympathies had been firmly with Philippa. True, she herself had seen to it that Caroline Lamb was blackballed from Almack's after the publication of the wretched *Glenarvon* three years before. (Caro had eventually been readmitted—against Lady Jersey's wishes—thanks to the efforts of her sister-in-law, Emily Cowper.) But *Glenarvon* had contained wicked portraits of half of London, very much including Lady Jersey herself. One could really not feel similar outrage toward someone who had caricatured the late Marquis of Carteret, whether or not the portrait had been intentional.

"Philippa," said Lady Jersey, her eyes betraying her enjoyment of the situation, "I think this gentleman cannot be unknown to you, but it has come to my attention that you have never been properly introduced. May I present the Marquis of Carteret? Carteret, Miss Davenport." She paused only long enough for Carteret to bow and Philippa to incline her head before continuing, "Carteret, I don't know if you are acquainted with Mr. Ashton, but he is the brother of that uncommonly pretty young woman with whom your brother is presently dancing."

Henry and Philippa looked involuntarily toward the dance floor, Carteret temporarily forgotten. A quadrille was in progress, and through the crowd they caught a glimpse of Claris' white dress and Lord Christopher's golden curls. If Lord Carteret followed their gaze, he gave no sign of similar concern for his half-brother.

"Servant, Ashton," he drawled, in response to Lady Jersey's introduction. "Er—you're a writer too, ain't you?"

Philippa choked. Mr. Ashton, rather to her regret, retained his calm manner. "Yes," he said simply. "Though I don't believe I can boast of Miss Davenport's readership."

Philippa bit back a protest and suppressed an accusatory glance. Mr. Ashton's statement was not only disagreeable— and most annoyingly couched in the guise of a compliment—it was patently untrue. He might complain that the *ton* did not understand his novels, but a number of its members most certainly read his books. If they did not, people like Sally Jersey would not accord him such notice.

Subtlety might not be a quality for which Lady Jersey was noted, but she was not unaware of the undercurrents in the conversation. She would have dearly loved to stay and discover more, but Carteret would dislike that excessively, and now that he had at last been enticed to Almack's she must make some concessions. She turned to Henry Ashton. An interesting young man, he would warrant further attention.

"Mr. Ashton, pray give me your arm, Millicent Brandon's been begging to be presented to you for the past fortnight. Penhow's youngest, you know. A charming girl, though I've never been able to get a word out of her. I'm sure Lord Carteret will be happy to look after Miss Davenport."

It was said pleasantly, but Henry knew that such a request from Lady Jersey was in the nature of a command. When he had agreed to bring Claris to London, he had committed himself to doing as the Romans did—within reason. Besides, Miss Davenport wanted to talk with Carteret. She thought he would be an interesting man. As he gave Lady Jersey his arm, Henry found himself hoping that Miss Davenport would be disappointed.

Left alone with the marquis, Philippa was conscious of some confusion, not, she told herself, owing to the quality of Lord Carteret's smile, but to the difficulty of knowing how to address him. She was grateful for his testimony in court that morning, but any expression of thanks on her part would suggest that Lord Carteret had testified for her benefit, and that of course was not the case. If she thanked him for something he had done merely to please himself, she would appear presumptuous, and if she thanked him for an action that was intended to disoblige his stepmother, she would look rather worse.

Still, she could scarcely ignore the fact of the trial, and this meeting at least gave her an opportunity to relieve some of the guilt she had been feeling since the trouble with Lady Carteret began.

"Lord Carteret," Philippa said, "I should like to tell you that I am very sorry for any unhappiness I may have inadvertently caused your family."

Carteret's eyes were amused. "There's no need to apologize to me, Miss Davenport. I found your book nothing but a delight."

"I am relieved to hear it. But I'm afraid I caused your stepmother genuine grief. I was angry when she tried to suppress my book, but please believe that I had no intention of injuring her or anyone else."

"Don't waste your assurances on me, Miss Davenport. My late father and I were not on the best of terms."

"I'm sorry," Philippa said.

"Do not refine too much upon it. I certainly do not. I leave all of that," he added with a charming smile, "to my dear stepmother."

So he wasn't overly fond of his stepmother, either. That and his feelings about his father no doubt accounted for his behaviour on the witness stand. But what had brought him to Almack's, and why had he gone to the trouble of getting himself presented to her? Perhaps he had been aware of the stir his entrance would create, tonight of all nights, particularly if he was seen talking with the young writer who had just triumphed over his stepmother in court. Philippa suspected that creating a stir was something the Marquis of Carteret very much enjoyed. She waited with some interest to see what he would say next. Lord Carteret asked if he could procure her a glass of lemonade.

Philippa was disappointed. "I've already had one," she told him. "And it was quite enough."

"Allow me to compliment you on being a woman of taste. May I at least escort you to a less crowded spot? I feel rather like a prize pig on display at a village fair."

Amused, Philippa gave him her arm and permitted him to escort her through the crowded ballroom. Lord Carteret did not negotiate the crowd quite as well as Mr. Ashton had done, probably, she suspected, because unlike Mr. Ashton he quite enjoyed the attention they were receiving. As with her earlier progress, Philippa judged that not all of that attention was on her account. If the young women in the ballroom had shown an interest in Mr. Ashton, they—and their mothers—positively fawned over Lord Carteret. Which, considering his fortune, was not surprising.

The marquis at last managed to steer a path to a bench set against the wall and partially obscured by a gilt column. "I did read your book, you know," he said, settling himself on the bench beside her. "All the way through."

"I am flattered."

"In all fairness I should confess that I may have read one or two other books since I was eleven."

"Take care, Lord Carteret. That could be grounds for perjury."

"Good God!" Carteret exclaimed with a look of horror. "I hadn't thought of that. And I suppose in this day and age there's little safety in being a peer. Shall I prepare to fly to France?"

"The French record is hardly reassuring," Philippa pointed out, "though they seem to have been making up for it in recent years. But I hardly think anything so drastic will be necessary. Your secret is safe with me."

"I can't tell you how much you relieve my mind. Do you know," said Carteret frankly, "you are quite as refreshing as your book. I scarcely dared hope that would prove to be true. If all books were as entertaining as yours, I daresay libraries wouldn't grow so devilish dusty. Your friend Mr. Ashton should take a lesson from you."

"He's not—you've read Mr. Ashton's books?" Philippa asked quickly.

"Looked at one of them once," Carteret admitted. "My—er—a friend of mine had been reading it. But I didn't get beyond a chapter or so," he hastened to assure her. "Rather slow going."

"Oh, no," Philippa said involuntarily. "That is, Mr. Ashton may not aim to be amusing, but he writes with tremendous power and he has a wonderful sense of irony. And a sense of humour, too, though it may not be apparent at first glance."

"A most vehement defence." Carteret eyed her speculatively. "Am I to infer, Miss Davenport, that you consider Mr. Ashton something more than a friend?"

Philippa stared at him in amazement. "Mr. Ashton? Good heavens, no, whatever gave you that idea?"

"He was present in the courtroom this morning and the whole of yesterday. I'm not sure I would do the same for a lady to whom I was betrothed, but I am quite certain I would not do so for a lady who was not my betrothed or—er—something rather closer."

Philippa's lips twitched. "I assure you Mr. Ashton and I are not betrothed. Or anything closer."

"My dear Miss Davenport," Carteret exclaimed, genuinely apologetic, "I did not mean to imply—"

"No," said Philippa, "I didn't think you did. Mr. Ashton was in court because the *Morning Intelligencer* engaged him to write about the trial."

"I see. Then as I needn't fear being called out, and as I already seem to be making confessions, let me admit that I came here tonight in the sole hope of meeting you."

Philippa looked into the marquis' dark grey eyes, which contained an expression calculated to wreak havoc on the heart of any female over the age of twelve, and burst into

64

giggles. "Doing it much too brown, Lord Carteret. You could not possibly have known I would be here."

"On the contrary. I had it on the best authority—my younger brother, he's a bit of a scamp, but quite reliable—that Lady Francesca and young Miss Ashton meant to attend the assembly this evening. I assumed you would accompany them."

"Then you were very nearly disappointed. I only decided to do so at the last minute."

Carteret looked at her in surprise and growing respect. "You don't care for Almack's, Miss Davenport?"

"No," said Philippa frankly. "Do you, Lord Carteret?"

"Certainly not," he said cheerfully. "I haven't set foot inside the place for years. But I thought all young women liked dancing."

"I've always been old for my age," Philippa told him. "And I much prefer observing to dancing."

"Observing?"

"I am a writer."

"I rather think you terrify me. Shall I expect to find myself between the pages of your next book?"

Philippa was genuinely contrite. "That," she said, "was a very poor choice of words. My observations are general, not specific. Lord Carteret, you must believe that I had no intention of satirizing your father. I suppose we must have met at Staveley, but I have no memory of it."

"As I told you, there is no need to waste your assurances on me. You are infinitely more delightful when you are not being serious."

"I shall remember that," said Philippa tartly, "if I ever aim to be delightful."

Carteret flung back his head and laughed. "*Touché*. I think you may be even *more* refreshing than your novel. May I hope you will give up observing long enough to dance with me?"

The musicians were striking up a waltz. His invitation surprised Philippa, but then so had the whole last quarter-hour, her own behaviour as well as his. This was the way she conversed with her family and close friends, but here she was talking so with a man she scarcely knew, a man who was one of

London's most sought-after bachelors, with a rakish reputation into the bargain, a man with whom she could have almost nothing in common. And she was enjoying herself.

Moreover, Philippa found, for the first time in several years, she very much wanted to dance. She gave him her hand. "I'd be delighted, Lord Carteret."

After a few minutes conversation with Miss Brandon—who, once Lady Jersey had left, proved quite talkative—and with Miss Brandon's particular friend, Letty Greystoke, Henry excused himself and began to make his way around the room. It was a slow progress, for he was frequently stopped by acquaintances, many of whom had other friends who wished for an introduction. When he had begun squiring his sister about, Henry had been surprised at the number of people—outside the small circle of reform-minded Whigs who had hitherto constituted his only real acquaintance among the *ton*—who knew his name and claimed to have read his books. He suspected that the majority of those at the assembly viewed him as something of a curiosity, but he had achieved a certain distinction. It really had been inaccurate, not to mention unfair, to say he couldn't boast of Miss Davenport's readership.

Henry smiled ruefully. There was something about that woman that drove him to say the most damnable things. True, he thought her novels trivial in subject matter, but it was not as if he did not like many members of the frivolous world that she chronicled.

Henry Ashton had the heart of a revolutionary tempered by a strong streak of pragmatism. He might deplore the very idea of inherited wealth, but he did not condemn individual men of means because they did not turn their fortunes over to charity and seek honest employment. His articles might savagely attack Parliament's failure to deal with rising poverty and unemployment, but he had a good deal of respect for those politicians, like Francesca's brother-in-law Nicholas Warwick, who were struggling to bring about change. He was on good terms with Francesca's husband Gerry—who had married into the polite world, if he had not been born one of its members—and he was very fond of Francesca herself, though she was clearly a woman of fashion.

Moreover, having faced the fact that, the world being as it was, his sisters must marry if they were to have a secure future, he had recognized that a Season in London would be to Claris' advantage. Why then did he find Miss Davenport so provoking when he was perfectly tolerant of his own sister and Miss Davenport's cousin?

Henry stopped to exchange pleasantries with the clever Lady Granville, then moved on again, the thoughtful look on his face prompting more than one observer to infer that he was planning a new novel. Was it, Henry wondered, that, unlike Claris and Francesca, Miss Davenport had a chance to move beyond the confines of her world? Her talent was undeniable.

Henry believed strongly in the power of the written word. Miss Davenport was squandering this power disgracefully. So far. For all her self-possession, she was still quite young. Perhaps she would change. Perhaps he could help her to change. They had been getting along rather well this evening, amazingly well considering their past history. Perhaps—

But at this point, Henry, who had been idly surveying the crowd, turned his eyes to the dance floor just in time to see Miss Davenport whirl by in the Marquis of Carteret's arms.

No. Thank you. It's just that dancing isn't my favourite occupation. Henry prided himself on being a shrewd judge of human nature and no longer in the least naive, and he had taken Miss Davenport's words quite at face value. Yet here she was not only dancing—the waltz, too—but smiling warmly at her partner and giving every evidence that she was thoroughly enjoying herself.

Henry resolutely turned his back on the swirling couples. Not only was Miss Davenport proficient with words, through one simple action she had made her opinion of him very clear indeed.

Claris gave a delighted squeal. "I knew he had conceived a *tendre* for her! Only look, Crispin, it is the most romantic thing imaginable!"

Claris had spent the past quarter-hour attempting to convince her beloved that his half-brother was undoubtedly in a fair way to being head over heels in love with Philippa Davenport. Twenty some years acquaintance with Anthony Paget and the worldly wisdom of a young man who has been down from Cambridge for a full year made Lord Christopher highly sceptical of this assertion, but as he followed the direction of Claris' gaze he let out a low whistle.

"Edwina's going to be livid."

Claris nobly refrained from saying that it served Lady Edwina right and instead pressed her own point. "And you thought he just came to Almack's out of curiosity," she reminded Crispin, putting the "I told you so" into her inflection.

Crispin turned his eyes from the dance floor to look down at the enchanting young woman he meant to make his wife. Claris was a darling, but very young and inclined to queer starts. He was three years her senior, and it was incumbent on him to act as a restraining influence. "He might just be dancing with her out of curiosity," he cautioned.

"Nonsense," said Claris firmly. Crispin was a paragon in every way, but men, as her mother said, took longer to mature than women, and Crispin was still distressingly blind to nuances in affairs of the heart. "Only perceive the way he's smiling at her. And the way she's smiling back. I think she looks quite pretty."

Miss Davenport did indeed appear more animated than usual and, in contrast to the sober ensembles she had worn in the courtroom, her rose gown lent her skin an appealing vibrance. All the same . . . "She's not at all Tony's usual type," Crispin pointed out.

"And would you say that your brother conceives *tendres* for his 'usual type?'" Claris shot back.

For the first time Crispin was silenced. He cast another, more thoughtful look at his brother and Miss Davenport.

"Well?" Claris persisted. "What do you think?"

Lord Christopher gave a disarming grin which, in a decade or so, might rival his elder brother's smile. "I think," he said, giving Claris his arm, "that Tony would skin me alive if he caught me speculating about his conduct, and he has an unholy knack of overhearing what's said about him. Let's go talk to Thornton and Metcalfe before you land us both in a pickle."

Like Henry, Claris, and Lord Christopher, most of those present in the assembly rooms took note of Lord Carteret and his dance partner. People like Sally Jersey found it an interesting development in the ongoing drama that had begun with the publication of *Worldly Wisdom* and were most grateful that the end of the trial had not rung down the curtain on the performance. The mothers who had tried in vain to secure Carteret for their daughters and the daughters who had secretly cherished dreams of the elusive marquis felt varying degrees of bitterness and envy.

The Countess Buckleigh refused to betray the least sign of interest and her expression dared the group of matrons with whom she was conversing to so much as allude to Carteret's behaviour. Her daughter, Lady Edwina, waltzing with the Honourable Lionel Thurston, was not seen to even glance in Carteret and Miss Davenport's direction, but close observers detected storm warnings in her deep blue eyes. Georgina Nelliston, a full-figured, auburn-haired beauty commonly held to be the current recipient of Carteret's favours, made a more elaborate show of ignoring the marquis and began to flirt rather desperately with Captain Trent. Carteret's former mistresses, more than one of whom were in the assembly rooms, could have told her it was wasted effort.

Francesca observed her cousin and the marquis with far warmer feelings. She had long felt Philippa was far too retiring and was delighted to see her on the dance floor. There were not many young women who could look so unaffected while waltzing with the Marquis of Carteret. That Philippa could do so was owing, no doubt, to the fact that she considered Carteret's interest in her completely unromantic. In this, Francesca thought, studying the couple, her cousin might be mistaken. There was a look in the marquis' eyes which was far from impersonal. It might do Philippa a world of good to receive the attentions of an attractive gentleman. Provided, of course—Francesca remembered that, for all her assurance, her cousin was a novice in affairs of the heart—that she did not let herself be hurt.

When the couple left the dance floor, Carteret escorted Philippa back to her chaperone. He had met Francesca once or twice and he remained with them for a few minutes, conversing on topics of no particular moment. The marquis then spoke briefly with Lady Buckleigh and Lady Edwina, smiled at Sally Jersey, and left the assembly rooms.

Not long after, Lady Buckleigh called Lord Christopher to her side. Claris returned to Francesca and said that she didn't feel like dancing anymore, and Francesca decided it was time to gather up her own small party. Neither Philippa nor Henry made any objection to leaving early. Henry, Francesca thought, was looking rather grim. Philippa, in contrast, positively glowed. She had not danced again after her waltz with Carteret, but she had talked with a number of people and for once she had seemed quite comfortable as the centre of attention. As Francesca made her way out of the assembly rooms on Henry's arm, she heard Philippa giggling with Claris, for all the world as if she, too, were eighteen.

Henry handed the ladies into the carriage and informed them rather curtly that he would walk home. Philippa, who was in a mood to be charitable even to Mr. Ashton, was surprised and rather annoyed at his behaviour. What on earth was he being disagreeable about now?

Resolutely shoving the matter aside, Philippa set herself to answer Claris' questions about the wicked marquis, determined that Mr. Ashton should not be allowed to spoil the most enjoyable evening she had spent in weeks.

She was very nearly successful.

Chapter 5

Aurelia Paget, Dowager Marchioness of Carteret, lifted her head in response to the butler's inquiry and said in a faintly affronted voice that of course she was not at home. She was lying on a delicately carved mahogany sofa upholstered in pale blue-and-cream satin, propped up by a half-dozen pillows, her still lovely arm draped carelessly along its back. In deference to the indifferent state of her health, the curtains had not been drawn, and though the room was normally a sunny spot in the late mornings, it was now filled with shadows. The filtered light was kind to the marchioness' face, which was just a trifle puffy under the chin, and a casual observer, seeing the pose and the arm and the golden ringlets which escaped her lacy cap, might have concluded they belonged to a very young woman. The butler, whose name was Nesselbank and who had known her ladyship since the time she came to Carteret House as a bride of eighteen, had no such fancies. His face impassive, he nodded, bowed, and turned toward the door.

"Of course you are home, Aurelia." A forceful woman whose majestic presence lent her height swept into the room and crossed to the figure on the sofa. "Nesselbank, open the curtains. One cannot think clearly in the dark, that accounts for the appalling state of one's dreams. Aurelia, sit up properly, if you are ill, you should be in bed, and if you are not, you have no call to behave as though you are going into a decline." Lady Buckleigh leaned over the recumbent figure with an expression of anxiety belied by her manner and felt her sister's

71

forehead. "No, there's no trace of a fever. Nesselbank, you may bring tea, but no cakes please, some plain buttered bread. Edwina, come pay your compliments to your aunt, then go find your cousin or a pianoforte or something and amuse yourself, I want to talk to Aurelia."

This last was directed to a slim young woman with a mass of dark hair and large, almond-shaped eyes who had followed Lady Buckleigh into the room. Edwina Thane bent gracefully over her aunt, brushed her cheek, then retreated to a nearby chair. "If you don't mind, Mama, I will have some tea first. I'm sure that Crispin is out, and I don't intend to drink it alone." She propped her parasol against a nearby table and carefully removed a pair of fine doeskin gloves in a shade of lavender that exactly matched the spenceret she wore over a silk frock striped in violet.

Lady Buckleigh ignored this display of filial disobedience. She never engaged in contests of will on trivial matters, the secret of her success in greater ones, and she knew that her daughter required careful handling. She seated herself on the sofa beside Aurelia, who was now sitting more or less erect, and waited for tea to appear.

Aurelia scarce felt the faint wave of resentment that always followed her elder sister's high-handed behaviour. If truth be told, she rather welcomed this visit, for she had begun to be bored with her self-imposed isolation in the blue parlour, even though it was her favourite room. She was a woman of strong but fleeting emotions, inclined to fret when left alone, and her son had been absent from the house more than usual in the past few days. As for her stepson, he was seldom at home, and in any event she was not speaking to Anthony, but still he might have had the grace to inquire now and then how she did. The marchioness felt she had a right to a certain sympathy, even from her sister. "I have been poorly, Catherine."

"Nonsense. You're in a temper because Anthony insisted you give up that ridiculous lawsuit and you think you were made to look foolish. Well, so you were, but what did you expect from trying to do away with a novel? Everyone adores them and no one takes them seriously. If you would only bestir yourself and go out a little in company, you would find that you would get a great deal of sympathy. If you'd won the suit, you'd have had no sympathy at all."

Lady Carteret lifted a perfectly dry handkerchief to her eyes. "Anthony was unbelievably brutal."

"Fustian. Anthony was being clever, which is something men like to do, and like most men he cannot see further than the end of his nose. Still, you should thank him, for he put an end to that farce. If you are wise, you will ignore his behaviour. I am certain he intended no disrespect, and you may find you have gained more credit with him than otherwise as a result of his display in the witness-box."

Lady Carteret, who did not seem to have followed this last remark, turned to her niece who clearly did.

"It is quite simple, Aunt Aurelia," Edwina explained patiently. "My cousin will know that his behaviour was painful to you and will thus feel obliged to be kind."

"He has a strange way of showing it," Lady Carteret said with a show of spirit. "I've heard no word of apology from him and he has not been near me these several days. I'm sorry for you, Edwina, his behaviour does not bode well for your future happiness."

Lady Buckleigh told her sister that she was a fool. "One should never expect men to apologize, Aurelia, it makes them feel abject and wounds their self-esteem, and they are liable to engage in the most inconsidered acts in an effort to retrieve it. Ah, tea at last. Can you manage, Aurelia, or would you like Edwina to pour?"

Lady Carteret straightened her back and informed her sister that she was quite capable of this domestic office. Even Lady Buckleigh, who gave credit where it was due, admitted that she performed the ceremony with felicity.

The two sisters were not much alike, for where Lady Carteret was fair, Lady Buckleigh was dark, and where she was small and delicate, her elder sister was tall and inclined to be angular. Still, they were both accounted handsome women and in their youth had been reputed beauties. Both had made good marriages, though here Lady Carteret could be said to have the edge over her sister, for her husband, though dead, had left her a marchioness while Lady Buckleigh could only claim the title of countess.

Lady Edwina united the best of both sisters in her person. She had her mother's colouring and the fine bones of her aunt, while her figure, which was admirable, was all her own. She drank two cups of tea, declined the bread and butter and the cakes which, contrary to Lady Buckleigh's request, had appeared on the tea-tray, and entertained her aunt with light gossip and a description of the dresses she was having made by Madam Dessart. Then, knowing she had pushed her mother as far as was wise, she rose and said she could be found in either the music room or the library.

Lady Carteret's spirits had been much improved by the refreshments and by her niece's chatter. She quite admired Edwina, and though she suspected the girl would one day turn out to be very like Catherine, Edwina had never shown her anything but the most flattering consideration.

The room had grown warm from the sunlight streaming through the windows. Lady Carteret removed the shawl she had been wearing and turned to her sister. "Very well, Catherine, what is it you have to say? It can't be anything more about that unfortunate trial, for you have been talking about it since you arrived, and pray don't scold me about anything else for I am not sure my nerves can stand it."

"I want to talk about Anthony, Aurelia, and I have no intention of scolding you about anything. Indeed, I never scold you at all. I've been giving you advice for almost forty years, and you've been ignoring it for nearly as long, which makes me wonder why I bother, but old habits die hard. And this time you really must pay attention, for Anthony is behaving in the most foolish manner imaginable and is likely to embroil us in something quite distasteful."

Aurelia looked at her sister in astonishment. Her stepson's behaviour was no different than that of many other young men of large fortune and healthy appetites, and though its excesses caused her some distress—particularly since it stirred painful memories of Anthony's father—she was not aware that Anthony had done anything of late, beyond his appalling performance in court, that could call forth her sister's strictures. "I don't know what you're talking about."

"Almack's, at the beginning."

"Almack's?" A puzzled frown creased Lady Carteret's smooth forehead.

"He was there, the night the trial ended."

"Yes, you told me so. I'll admit it was odd, but scarcely reprehensible."

"I'm persuaded he went solely for the purpose of being presented to her. It was quite obvious," Lady Buckleigh went on, "though at the time I put it down to vulgar curiosity. I would not have expected her to show her face at the assembly, but Francesca Scott brought her along. You know, Lyndale's daughter, the one who threw over a coronet and married a nobody of a soldier, they're cousins or something. I would hardly have thought Anthony would be interested, for she's not at all in his usual style and with no pretence to any kind of looks, though I admit her books are rather clever."

Lady Carteret's bewildered face showed sudden comprehension. "You mean Miss Davenport."

"Yes, I mean Miss Davenport," Lady Buckleigh said with some impatience. "He got Sally Jersey to present him and talked to her for some minutes and asked her to dance. It caused no end of comment and was rather hard on Edwina, though I must say she carried it off creditably, and Anthony, to do him justice, did pay his respects before he left. I thought it all one with his behaviour in court that morning and hardly anything that would last."

At this, Lady Carteret sat up very straight. "Do you mean to say that he's seen her again?"

"I do."

"But in heaven's name, where? They don't frequent the same houses, and Anthony has never been one for conventional amusements."

"He's pursuing her, Aurelia. There's no doubt of it. He's been seen leaving the Davenport house in Green Street, he's taken her driving more than once, he put in an appearance at Lady Pembroke's rout three nights ago, though I know for a fact that he hasn't responded to one of her invitations before, and he took her down to supper at the Windhams' ball. He's amusing himself, of course, but she's nothing like his usual flirts, she's unmarried and hardly safe. What if she begins to take him seriously?"

"Anthony wouldn't . . ."

"That's hardly the point. The question is what Philippa Davenport would do. I told you the woman is clever. Look at her mother. Married off her youngest daughter to some Irishman, then eloped with Braithwood who was a splendid catch and a full ten years her junior."

Lady Carteret looked at her sister in disbelief. "Edwina?" she said faintly.

"Edwina is being sensible. But Anthony's making it very public and she's in a difficult position. We have to put a period to it, Aurelia, before he commits himself to anything rash. He's at a dangerous age and is quite capable of a quixotic gesture. The woman has to be stopped."

Of course she had to be stopped. Not that Lady Carteret, in her innermost heart, would not prefer that her stepson spend his entire life unmarried, for then her darling Crispin would inherit the title, but that was too much to hope. Anthony was fond of women and would undoubtedly be caught sooner or later. Far better Edwina than an unknown woman who would have neither consideration nor respect for the family.

Catherine and Aurelia had decided long since that the Paget heir would marry a Thane and unite the two families. When the children were young, they had planned to wed Anthony to Lady Buckleigh's eldest daughter, but the headstrong Demetra had put a stop to that by falling in love with a young man with no prospects and dangerous political views. Lady Carteret barely repressed a shudder as she recalled the six-year-old scandal. Demetra's disastrous flight to Gretna Green had been the talk of London for weeks. They could not afford to have another scandal in the family.

Nor another unsuitable marriage. For bad as the elopement had been, the talk had eventually died down. But Demetra's husband had not the grace to succumb to a chill or a hunting accident and remained a constant thorn in the family's side, though he at least had the sense to remain in the country. It would be a thousand times worse if Anthony married the impossible Miss Davenport and brought her to live under Lady

Carteret's own roof. It did not bear thinking of, but it must be thought of if it was to be avoided.

Alive with a sense of purpose, Lady Carteret said good-bye to her sister and her niece, sat down at her desk, and wrote a brief note on heavy cream-coloured paper, then rang for Nesselbank and told him to see that it was delivered immediately to Mr. Marsden in Middle Temple Inn. She would show Catherine that she could manage her stepson better than Catherine had managed her eldest daughter.

Lady Buckleigh's visit persuaded her sister that it was to her advantage to appear once again in society. Lady Carteret was welcomed back into her accustomed circles and found, true to Catherine's prediction, that she was received with a good deal of sympathy, though the sympathy was short-lived. After two or three days, the trial was no longer spoken of and, as far as she could discern, was not even remembered.

She would have found this a matter for some chagrin had not her energies been devoted to learning as much as she could about the doings of her stepson Anthony. The matter took all of her attention until a casual comment from an acquaintance met at one of Mrs. Humberstone's musical evenings gave her fresh cause for alarm. The next morning she made an unexpected appearance in the breakfast parlour for the express purpose of having some conversation with her son Crispin.

As a result of this conversation, Lady Carteret made further inquiries, then dispatched another cream-coloured missive, this one to Mr. Henry Ashton in Little Russell Street requesting that he wait upon her at four o'clock that afternoon.

On receiving this peremptory request, Henry was tempted to tell the messenger that he was much too occupied to pay a social call, but he thought better of it. It was unlikely that Lady Carteret proposed to take him to task for journalistic excess in his reporting of the trial, and even more unlikely that she was using him as an approach to Miss Davenport. It had to be about Claris.

Fortunately, Henry had a meeting with his publisher and

was kept too busy to give much thought to his forthcoming interview with Lady Carteret. But as he hurriedly ascended the steps of the massive pile of the Carteret house in Cavendish Square—for he was somewhat later than the appointed hour—he remembered the marchioness' histrionic behaviour during the trial and warned himself that the encounter might be difficult.

He was ushered into a small parlour on the ground floor and left to wait. Nicely calculated, he thought. No drawing room for that journalist Ashton, not even for Ashton the nearly respectable writer of novels. This would be the room where Lady Carteret saw her man of business. No, hardly that, she would not have the head for it. It would fall to that idler Carteret or, more likely, the family solicitor.

After a quarter of an hour, the butler returned and conducted him up the broad staircase which rose leisurely from the majestic entrance hall to the gallery above, past double doors that must lead to the drawing room, and along a corridor to a room at the back of the house. The butler pronounced his name, then closed the door discreetly behind him, leaving Henry to adjust his sight to a room dimmed by drapes of azure blue silk over sub-curtains of gold-embroidered muslin.

Lady Carteret was seated in an armchair with her back to the window. She thanked Henry for the favour of coming and waved him to a nearby seat. He had to admit she was a lovely woman, and he could see that she had decided to be gracious. The faint air of condescension was, he guessed, her customary manner with people she could not place precisely upon the social scale. Henry crossed his long legs, leaned back in his chair, and prepared to follow whatever direction she chose to take.

She adjusted the flowered silk shawl which covered her upper arms and trailed over the soft blue material of her dress—a sign of ill-ease, though it might have been deliberate. "Mr. Ashton," she said, looking somewhat away from him, "the matter is awkward, and I scarcely know how to begin. I believe we may have some interests in common." At this last she looked him full in the face, opening her blue eyes in an expression of earnest entreaty. The effect was devastating. The chin held high to combat the growing softness of her face, the mouth slightly parted, the fair curls escaping her cap and falling over her forehead, all combined to form a picture of vulnerable womanhood. Surely, she seemed to be saying, you cannot wish other than to help me.

Perhaps she was not speaking about Claris. Was it possible that she saw him as some kind of ally in her vendetta against Miss Davenport? His articles might have given the impression that he would welcome such an alliance, but he had been scarcely kinder to the marchioness and she had no call to think well of him. Henry inclined his head briefly in acknowledgement, but said nothing. He thought she was disappointed.

"Let me be frank, then," she said after a moment. Her voice held more decision than she had hitherto shown. "As perhaps you know, I have a son, Lord Christopher Paget. He has formed an acquaintance with a Miss Ashton who I believe is your sister."

"My sister is acquainted with a great many young men," Henry said dryly. "It was for this purpose that she came to London."

It was a crude statement, but it had its effect. Lady Carteret sat just a little straighter in her chair. "One of them, I repeat, is my son."

Henry shrugged. "Very likely. I assume your son is acquainted with any number of young women."

Lady Carteret was clearly displeased with this imputation of frivolity. "Crispin is a Paget, but he is also a Montagu, and the Montagus have always been known for their deep feelings." She raised a wisp of handkerchief in the direction of her face. "It gives us great sensitivity, but it is also our curse."

"Ah," Henry said, "I think I begin to understand." Damn the posing woman. "Your son has deep feelings, and you would rather he had no feelings at all."

"Yes. No! Crispin could never be an unfeeling person."

"But you would prefer that he were so, at least when he is in the company of young women. As a matter of curiosity, Lady Carteret, is this something you wish to bring about with respect to my sister or to all the young women of his acquaintance? Do you plan a number of interviews of this sort?"

She looked at him in astonishment. He had been insolent and she should have told him so, but instead she took refuge in the wounded expression she had used to such advantage in the courtroom.

Henry felt a moment of contrition. "I beg your pardon," he said in a more temperate tone, "that is not my affair. My sister, of course, is. Am I to believe that you are uneasy because you think your son has more than common feeling for Claris?"

She nodded. "He is scarcely twenty," she said with a note of genuine concern.

"True. And Claris is also very young. But surely we should not fret ourselves over these youthful attachments, ma'am"— here he was echoing Francesca's advice—"it is common at this age, and will soon pass."

"My son is an uncommon man, Mr. Ashton."

"And Romeo fell out of love with Rosaline at the sight of Juliet." It was an unfortunate reference. "Opposition only strengthens caprice."

She looked at him doubtfully, wondering if he quite understood. "Crispin is a most exceptional young man. It would be no wonder if your sister looked upon him with—with unusual interest."

"Claris is a girl of great enthusiasms."

His tone distressed her. "Mr. Ashton, you do not take my meaning. The thing is impossible!"

Henry looked at her in cold inquiry. "What thing is impossible, Lady Carteret?"

She was now clearly flustered. She made vague gestures with her hands. "That they should . . . that she should . . . that there is any question of . . . young people are so impulsive. Marriage is not to be thought of!"

Henry drew his legs up and sat forward in his chair. "Of course it is not to be thought of," he said, his voice dangerously quiet. "In that we are agreed."

"Ah, I knew you would be sensible of the fact!" She leaned toward him, relief evident in her pose. "Crispin is much too young to marry, but even were he not, the match would not be suitable. He is a Paget. The family is very old, and one must take care in making alliances. I am sure your sister is a charming girl, but she should not expect to—she should not aspire to—"

Henry's face grew warm, but his voice was glacial. "Claris should aspire as high as she pleases. Provided, of course, that she is sensible of her future happiness." He rose and picked up his hat. "I hope to see my sister settled well, Lady Carteret, but her happiness would certainly not be assured by an alliance with a shallow-witted twig of the house of Paget, no matter how old the tree. I would never consent to such a match. In that, at least, my resolve is as firm as your own. Good day."

Henry left the room and found his way to the front door, surprising the butler who had expected Lady Carteret to ring when she was through with her visitor. Nesselbank was just opening the door to another caller and Henry, in a temper and not watching where he was going, nearly collided with the gentleman entering the house. Henry was halfway down the street before he realized that there had been something familiar about the man. He stopped and tried to recall where he had seen his face before but could not place it. He had turned into Green Street before the answer came to him. The dark, well-built man with the long nose and the clever face had been Lady Carteret's barrister, Mr. Marsden.

Henry arrived at the Davenport house with no clear idea of why he had come. He frequently dropped by at this hour to see Claris, but he was not sure that it would be wise to communicate the results of his interview with Lady Carteret to his sister. The marchioness had, it was true, insulted both Claris and his whole family, but it was no more than he would have expected from a woman who thought of little but her bloodlines. Francesca had warned him against overt opposition, and if Lady Carteret took the line with her son that he had taken first with Claris, she might drive the young cub into a rash act. He ought to talk to Francesca again, if only to warn her to be doubly on her guard.

But as he entered the hall, Tuttle informed him that Lady Francesca and Miss Ashton were from home. Henry, who was ready to talk, was conscious of disappointment and he stood indecisive, hat in hand, debating whether to wait in the hope of an interview or return to his rooms and get back to work. Then he heard footsteps and saw Miss Davenport coming down the hall, Hermia at her heels.

Miss Davenport was wearing a simply cut dress of a dark green, her colour was high, and she was looking, he thought, rather pretty. He had not seen her for some days, and, though the scene at Almack's still rankled, her low-pitched voice and lack of artifice were a welcome contrast to the posing woman he had left a short time before. When she asked him to keep her company until Francesca and Claris returned, Henry gratefully accepted.

Philippa was as grateful for his presence. Somehow, without ever exactly planning to do so, she had spent an extraordinary amount of time from home since the end of the trial. She hadn't gone out so much since her first Season. But then she had trailed behind her mother and sisters, dutiful and feeling out of place. She had never been bored in company, but she had always been as happy alone in her study. Now she was thoroughly enjoying herself, and she positively looked forward to a new ball or rout. She had Lord Carteret to thank for that. Though his attentions could hardly be taken seriously, they had earned her much popular regard and she never lacked for dance partners. She would probably even have enjoyed herself had she accompanied Francesca and Claris to the milliner's this afternoon. Only yesterday she had been thinking that she would quite like a new straw— What on earth had come over her? She was neglecting her novel shamefully.

So today she had ruthlessly denied all callers, including Lord Carteret himself, and stayed by her desk, though to little effect. Carteret's pursuit had given her a heady and unaccustomed sense of being a desirable creature, and her thoughts kept straying to the time she spent in his company.

At length she had thrown down her pen in disgust and left her study. She was pleased to find a caller and rather glad that it was Claris' brother rather than Lord Carteret. For despite her feelings about the marquis, he did take some effort. With Mr. Ashton, whatever his faults, she could be quite herself.

She led Mr. Ashton to the library, a long pleasant room at the back of the house, less gloomy than such rooms usually are, for the shelves of books had been broken on two sides by tall windows which admitted the late afternoon sun. Hermia padded after them and curled up in a patch of sunlight.

"Shall I ring for tea?" Philippa asked. "Or would you prefer something stronger?" She gestured to a side table where, a tribute to the rectitude of the Davenport servants, the decanters stood at the ready.

Tea, he assured her, would be welcome. He walked to one of the long windows and stared out into the garden where the wallflowers, in velvety shades of rose, pink, and burgundy, were just coming into bloom. "I've been calling on Lady Carteret," he said. He had not intended to discuss the interview, but he found he wanted to talk about it. Miss Davenport was sure to appreciate its ironies.

Philippa gave the order for tea, then joined him at the window. "Surely an odd choice for a companion, Mr. Ashton. But perhaps you did not initiate the meeting."

He turned to her and grinned. "It was something in the nature of a command performance. A note on very heavy and very expensive paper, with a great many flourishes to the s's. Delivered by hand by a very tall footman in a coat cut considerably better than my own, favour of a reply requested immediately."

Philippa laughed. "And she wished to consult you as a journalist?"

"As a guardian and brother. Claris, it seems, has had the temerity to dance with her heart's darling, the sole offspring of the Pagets and the Montagus. Claris, of course, has had the temerity to do a good deal more than that, but I doubt that her ladyship is aware of it. In any event, that must surely be laid at her son's door."

"I thought Lady Carteret no more than foolish. This borders on the impertinent."

"Would you really expect otherwise from the family? I was informed—at first with much indirection and veiled glances, then quite openly—that my sister is undoubtedly a charming girl, but she must not aspire to the exalted heights on which the

Pagets reign. Claris quite simply is not good enough for the golden-haired Lord Christopher."

"Which is nonsense, of course, And you, I assume, told Lady Carteret that Lord Christopher was not good enough for your sister."

He looked at her sharply. "Do you think he is, Miss Davenport?"

She ran her hand idly down the drape. "I know nothing against the young man save his youth, and that fault will surely be cured with time. Claris herself is young."

"Exactly. Which is why she needs a husband with a modicum of sense."

"Poor Claris. Because she is young, she cannot seek a young husband. Yet men seek young wives. Don't they too value sense in their life companion?"

"Not nearly often enough."

"There!" she said triumphantly. "Then what right have you to foist Claris—whom I have heard you call to her face a remarkably silly girl—on a man of sense? Surely if Lord Christopher is too young to marry, then Claris is as well."

He threw up his hands and laughed. "It is different with women." She bridled, and he went on quickly. "Not that it should be, but what other choice does a woman have? Do most women have? Claris has no fortune, and no particular talents that will let her honourably support herself."

"So you would auction her off to any man who can keep her?"

"Spare me your indignation, Miss Davenport." His eyes were angry and his voice turned cold. "This is the world you live in and write about so charmingly. Accept it as it is, or do what you can to change it. I am not happy with the games Claris must play, but I am a realist. And I would not force her into a marriage without affection."

"Then—Lady Carteret aside—why not Lord Christopher? For affection is surely there, and the promise of being respectably kept."

"No doubt you think it a good connection, but the boy has nothing to recommend him save his golden hair. He's been overindulged by a remarkably silly woman, he runs with St.

George's pack who are all arrogant poseurs, and he models himself on an elder brother who plays at being clever and lives for nothing but his own pleasures. You may choose to ally yourself with the Paget family, Miss Davenport, but the Paget cub is no match for my sister."

The mention of Lord Carteret made Philippa angry, and even more the imputation that she was throwing herself at the marquis. How had they gotten into this quarrel? Lady Carteret had been arrogant and insufferable, but that had nothing to do with Lord Christopher who, Philippa had observed, was quite free from any sense of his own consequence. And why should Claris' brother take it on himself to judge the circumstances that would make a woman happy?

She tried to keep her temper in check. "So you condemn the young man not for himself but because you dislike his mother, his friends, and his brother. His mother is perhaps too indulgent, but he is her only child. Lord St. George is his cousin and he can hardly help the acquaintance. And his brother you do not know at all!"

"I have not had your opportunities," he said smoothly. "No doubt the marquis is a charming companion. But his person, his name, and his fortune are his merely by accident of birth, and he is spending his life squandering them away. Besides, they're Tories, Miss Davenport, and of the worst kind. The Ashtons do not look at the world in that way."

This brought Philippa up short. "Neither do the Davenports," she said, "but Lord Carteret doesn't show his father's interest in politics."

"Exactly. He doesn't show much interest in anything."

Philippa raised stormy eyes. "How can you say so? He has a position and he maintains it, but no one has accused him of running through his fortune. He has estates to look after, and they're known to be well kept."

"He's fortunate in his bailiffs."

"Give him credit for choosing wisely."

"Oh, I do. And for his choice of the cattle which he races successfully at Newmarket. I wish he took as great care of his own family."

Philippa looked at him in exasperation. What did the man

85

expect? Lord Carteret lived as did other men of consequence. He had the arrogance of wealth and was prone to affectation, but there was no denying that he was amusing and he had a great deal of charm. As for taking care of his brother, she could only applaud a relationship that allowed Lord Christopher to live as he pleased.

She sought futilely for some way to put this into words. When the tea tray arrived, she took refuge in being a hostess until Francesca and Claris returned. Then, judging that this was no time for Claris to endure a prolonged encounter with her brother, she took the girl upstairs by affecting an interest in the purchases she had made that afternoon.

Claris came quite readily, but once inside her room she threw her parcels down without ceremony. "Oh, Philippa, I am so glad you took me away," she said breathlessly. "He has sent me a note, you see, and says we must speak privately at once and can I meet him by the Serpentine tomorrow morning at nine? I thought I could slip away, but someone is sure to see me and then Henry is bound to hear and be very disagreeable. So may I go with you, please? I know you take Hermia for an early run, and if I join you no one will remark it."

Philippa hesitated. Claris would meet her lover one way or another, and it would be far more prudent if she were kept under observation. Philippa reached down and picked up her dog who had followed her upstairs. Pushing aside the thought that she ought to consult Francesca, she gave her agreement. At nine in the morning, nothing untoward could possibly occur.

Chapter 6

Hermia was trotting by Philippa's side when she caught sight of a pair of ducks in the grass and bounded after them. The birds rose awkwardly and waddled to the safety of the water where they circled in agitation, loudly protesting the intruder. Hermia was quite capable of following them in, but she looked back at her mistress, then lay down at the edge of the Serpentine and put her head between her paws, contenting herself with an occasional bark. The ducks, having made their point, swam lazily away and Hermia ran off in search of new diversion.

The morning was fresh, with a slight mist, and few people were abroad. It was Philippa's favourite time of day and she relished the hour to herself, with only her dog for company. This morning, however, she had another companion, and that companion was much on her mind. She almost regretted consenting to Claris' meeting with Lord Christopher, for she had acted, she knew, as much out of pique at the brother as desire to serve the sister. Still, a promise was a promise, and when Claris had appeared in the downstairs hall that morning, Philippa had not been able to deny her.

She glanced involuntarily toward the clump of willows near the bank where the young couple, screened from view, were engaged in conversation. She trusted it was no more than conversation. Lord Christopher had looked serious enough, and Philippa suspected that he had been spoken to by his mother. If so, Lady Carteret had been as foolish as Claris' brother, for opposition would only throw the would-be lovers together. Philippa turned away. It was a pity, for they showed an uncommon attachment. Still, it would not do for them to take any rash step. She thought Claris was sensible, but she would have to keep an eye on the girl.

Philippa moved slowly down the path. Ordinarily she used this hour for a brisk walk, but though she wanted to give Claris and young Paget some privacy, she was not wholly lost to propriety and was determined to keep the clump of trees in sight. Impatient with her dawdling, Hermia was now some way ahead, making friends with a nursemaid and a perambulator. A handful of other pedestrians were in view, and an occasional horseman, but the park seemed blissfully empty compared to its state in the fashionable hours of the late afternoon.

Not far ahead, one of the horsemen had reined in his mount. The horse caught Philippa's eye—it was a superb glossy black that her sister Juliana would have given half her dowery to possess. Philippa raised her eyes to the horseman and realized that she was looking at the Marquis of Carteret.

He dismounted and came toward her and she was conscious of the wave of pleasure she always felt when she saw him. He was fully as handsome as his mount, with the same glossy black hair and the same animal grace. This of course should not weigh with her, but she would be less than human if she did not respond to his attraction. Besides, his manners were easy and his smile disarming. So she smiled in return and gave him her hand and said that she would not have expected to see him abroad so early. Hadn't she heard him complain about the hours kept in court?

"You shame me, Miss Davenport. I frequently ride in the morning. At least, I do so in the country, and this was much too splendid a morning to lie abed. Are you accustomed to walk out so early yourself?"

"You know that I am, for I told you as much the other day. I bring Hermia for a run every morning."

"Ah, I had forgotten." He smiled, and she knew perfectly well that he had come out in search of her and that he was aware of her knowledge. "May I join you for a while?"

Philippa acquiesced, then remembered that Lord Carteret's

younger brother was standing hidden not two dozen paces away with a young girl who should not be without a chaperone. "If you don't mind my going after Hermia. She's run off and I want to be sure she hasn't gotten into mischief." Philippa turned her back on the clump of trees. "Your horse?"

"Do you mind his company as well?" Lord Carteret looped the reins about his hand and prepared to lead the animal along with him. "He's quite well behaved."

"I'm sorry I can't say the same of Hermia. I'm told she scratched your boots when you called yesterday."

"I would have minded less had you been willing to ride with me."

"I was working, Lord Carteret."

He raised a brow but said nothing.

She stopped and looked at him. "Do you find that a paltry excuse? Or do you think it mere pretext? I assure you, I do work, and I am quite serious about it."

She had never spoken sharply to him before, and he seemed taken aback. "I'm sorry, I had no desire to make light of your writing. I only regretted that it kept you from me."

Philippa felt subtly in the wrong, but could not tell why. Carteret continued at her side, oddly subdued. "Was it a productive day?" he asked, swinging at the grass with his crop.

It was Philippa's turn to feel abashed. "Tolerably so," she lied. "A dozen pages." Then, in a burst of honesy, "In fact, they wouldn't quite do and will have to be thrown away. There are days like that." She was silent for a while. "And yours?"

He looked puzzled. "Mine?"

"Your day? Was it productive?"

He smiled. "Perhaps like yours, there are pages I will have to throw away. I rode, Miss Davenport, alone. I looked in at Tattersall's but saw nothing fit to mount. I spent an hour or two at White's and glanced at the papers." He did not add that he had kept a rendezvous that afternoon with Lady Nelliston and managed to quarrel with her, then found to his surprise that he had no desire to make it up and take her to bed.

"I dined with my friend Worthman," he continued—Lord Worthman was an avid hunter and reputed to have one of the finest stables in England—"and later we went on to the

Haymarket where we saw no one we had not seen a thousand times before."

"And the play?"

"Hardly worth noting." His smile was disarming. "I confess I paid it little attention. It was a day much like any other." His horse had stopped to graze and he tugged gently on the reins. "And yours, Miss Davenport? After the dozen pages that wouldn't quite do?"

"I had tea with Lady Francesca and Miss Ashton and was asked to give my opinion on three bonnets and the exact shade of blue ribbon that would best suit Miss Ashton's sprigged muslin." She grinned. "Then we dined with the Warwicks— Mrs. Warwick is Colonel Scott's sister—and spent the evening there. They had a few people in. It was," she echoed, her eyes dancing, "a day much like any other." She did not add that she had quarelled with Henry Ashton and spent the entire evening avoiding his company.

Lord Carteret looked at the woman walking by his side. "You lead a quiet life, do you not?"

Philippa acknowledged that she did.

"Are you never bored?"

"Bored?" she laughed. "Sometimes cross and out of sorts, but I am never bored."

"How very strange. For my life is not at all quiet, Miss Davenport. In fact it is quite full of moving about from one place to another, and do you know, I am frequently a prey to ennui."

She stared at him in surprise. "You want occupation."

"But I told you, I am much occupied."

"Serious occupation, Lord Carteret."

"I have serious occupation, Miss Davenport."

He was setting a trap, but she did not care. "I have heard of none," she countered.

"I can name you at least three things."

"Well?"

"My horses."

"And?"

"My cravats."

"And?"

"My dear Miss Davenport, need you ask? Yourself, of course."

Philippa turned her head away. As a rule, she felt quite easy in Lord Carteret's company, but there were times when a most disturbing look crept into his eyes. She forced her eyes to his and found the disturbing look very much present. She was annoyed and, perversely, pleased, but it was not in her to respond in the same key. "You are not taking my words as they are meant, Lord Carteret."

"Then instruct me," he said simply.

"I wouldn't dream of doing anything so impertinent."

"You don't approve of me, do you?" Carteret feigned a sigh. "A great many people don't. My stepmother for one. She thinks I lead a shameless life and set a bad example for her son."

Philippa turned to look at him, wondering exactly how this odd conversaton had come about. "There is no cause for approval or disapproval. I have no objection to the amusements of your life, nor to their morality. Or lack of it. But it does seem strange to me that, with all the friends and leisure and fortune you command, you cannot find some antidote to boredom."

"Ah, yes," he said ruefully. "My estates."

"Well, why not? Many men find it absorbing."

He shuddered. "Parliament."

She was a shade annoyed. "Do not mock, it is perhaps an imperfect system, but it is necessary. And surely there is much to be done if you will only look around you."

"I might," he said lightly, "try my hand at a novel."

Now she was seriously vexed. She forced her tone to match his. "You might, but I am not sure you have the gift for it. Writing is serious business."

"Ah, you think me a hopeless case."

"Not at all. It is you who condemns yourself to boredom."

He offered no reply. He had been amused, then piqued, and was now genuinely puzzled. It was one thing to be disapproved of. He had been accustomed to—had indeed courted—disapproval for the past ten years or more. But to have a young lady—and, moreover, the first young lady whom he had

91

distinguished with his attentions since he came down from Cambridge—not take him, well, *seriously*, was both surprising and annoying. She had attracted his interest by her demeanour in court. He had sought an introduction out of curiosity and the pleasure of hearing her thanks for his help. He had pursued the acquaintance because she was pleasant to converse with. She seemed free of artifice and vanity, she had some wit, and he was comfortable in her presence. This last was no small thing, for he had long been wary of the petty deceits of women. But now, as he walked beside her, he knew that he wanted something more. He wanted her approval, or at least her interest in his reformation.

Philippa too was silent. She had gone much too far, and she regretted speaking so to the man whose eyes held such disturbing messages. She longed to be able to play his own game, but she suspected that her attraction for Carteret was that she did not. She had had no intention of telling him how he should live his life, and then he had tricked her into saying things that were—well, very suspiciously like the things Henry Ashton had said to her the previous afternoon. They were certainly not Philippa's ideas and she did not know how they had gotten into her head.

The thought of Mr. Ashton reminded Philippa of Claris and the wisdom of getting the marquis to mount his horse immediately and ride far out of sight of that troublesome clump of trees behind them.

But Hermia drove these concerns from her mind. She had been running happily back and forth by the side of the path while Philippa and Carteret conversed, until the sight of another dog sent her dashing off in expectation of fresh amusement. The second dog had broken away from his master and was trailing a lead. He was large and black, much like Carteret's horse, and seemed quite friendly, but the amusement he—for it was clearly a he—had in mind caused Philippa to scream Hermia's name and run frantically to the rescue of her pet.

Seeing her distress, the owner of the black dog ran toward her, calling his own dog to order. This animal, which seemed to go by the name of Coverley, did not pay him the slightest heed and continued circling Hermia, trying to position himself behind her. Hermia was in a playful mood but seemed uncertain about his advances, and she circled in turn, barking ecstatically into his face.

Breathless and laughing, her hair escaping from its pins and her face shiny from her dash across the grass, Philippa scooped Hermia into her arms at the same instant that Coverley's master retrieved the dog's lead and drew him out of danger. "I'm sorry," he said, "I had no idea . . ."

"Nor did I," Philippa said, breathing hard. "I would never have brought her here had I realized it was her time. Or almost her time, she does not seem quite ready."

The man grinned, perhaps in appreciation of her outspoken response. He looked about Carteret's age, and though he could not be called handsome, he had an arresting face. It was the eyes, perhaps, a dark clear grey shaded by heavy brows, and the firm squared jaw, and the long nose that was not quite straight. Philippa had seen that face before, and the knowledge was written in her countenance.

He seemed to be amused. "You're quite right, we have met before, Miss Davenport, but we have not been introduced. May I suggest that Coverley has done it for me? I am Elliot Marsden."

He would have attempted a bow, but Coverley was straining at the lead. Philippa took an involuntary step away, cradling Hermia in her arms. "Mr. Marsden," she said faintly. It seemed impossible that this pleasant stranger—who had seemed a full twenty years older in his wig and gown, with a voice a full octave deeper—should be the man with whom she had sparred in court, the man of whom she had almost been afraid.

Hermia began to struggle and Marsden, seeing Philippa's distress, took Coverley firmly by the collar. "This is clearly no time to talk. I apologize, Miss Davenport, for Coverley's behaviour. I trust there are no hard feelings." He put his hand to his hat, but the dog turned round and tried to nip his wrist and he was forced to retreat, pulling the unwilling Coverley after him.

"None at all," Philippa called, wondering whether he

referred to the dog or to their earlier encounter. Hermia ceased her struggles and began to lick Philippa's face. Philippa turned her head away and shifted the dog in her arms, then looked round for Lord Carteret whom she had momentarily forgotten.

Carteret was standing a short distance away, and he now began to walk toward her. At Miss Davenport's scream, he had stayed only to calm his horse, which had started at the sound, then run after her to find that she had retrieved her dog and was in conversation with a man who appeared to be an acquaintance. He could not see the man's face, but he was well dressed and carried himself like a gentleman. Carteret did not like to intrude, but neither did he intend to leave the field. Ordinarily he would have strolled up to the couple, making his claim to the lady clear, but there was something about Miss Davenport that did not call for ordinary behaviour. So he waited until the man walked away and she turned in his direction.

"It was the strangest thing," she said as they met. "That was Mr. Marsden."

His brows contracted. "Marsden?"

"The barrister. I could hardly credit it." Her eyes danced. "He seemed quite human, and much younger than I thought him in court. Anyone who likes dogs must have some redeeming qualities."

He laughed. "Ah, now I know your secret. Let me assure you, Miss Davenport, that I am exceedingly fond of dogs. I have a full dozen at Carteret Park. Is Hermia all right?"

Hermia wriggled at the sound of her name and Philippa tightened her hold. "Yes, but I must take her home. I'll leave you to get on with your ride."

But he would not hear of it. She should not walk unattended, and certainly not with the animal struggling in her arms. He would be only too glad to carry her pet to her door. She protested, pleading her better knowledge of the dog, but he held firm.

Philippa was in a dilemma. She had already left Claris alone far too long. She could not go off and leave her, nor could she risk having Lord Carteret see Claris with his brother. She made rapid calculation. "But I am not alone," she said, hoping her

94

smile would forestall any question as to why she had not yet acknowledged Claris' presence. "I left my friend over there by the water, near the willow trees. She did not care to walk so far, but it is time I fetched her." She knew he was quite capable of following her, so she thrust Hermia into his arms. "Pray hold her, I'll be back in a moment and then we would be glad of your escort."

She turned and walked off rapidly toward the willows, not waiting for his response. Carteret stared after her, a bemused expression on his face, while Hermia struggled to escape his hold. He did not see the children passing with their nurse, nor hear the quarrelling of sparrows, nor the splash of a duck as she waddled into the Serpentine. Nor was he aware that Elliot Marsden had stopped in his retreat to watch them, while his dog wound his lead around his legs, nor that Henry Ashton had come into view and was striding purposefully toward Miss Davenport.

Whether it was the sight of Henry, or the shaggy brown dogs accompanying the children, or the memory of her former freedom, Hermia was roused to fevered effort and she slipped from Carteret's hands and ran headlong over the grass, voicing her joy in a series of staccato barks. Cursing, Carteret ran after her. Hermia turned. Good, it was a game. She waited for him a moment, then changed direction and set off again before he could reach her. The breeze was fresh and blew her scent and the shaggy dogs, sensing uncommon sport, broke free, leaving a pair of squalling boys in their wake. This was too much for Coverley. He leaped forward, taking Marsden with him, but the barrister was unprepared and fell prone. The lead snapped and Coverley too was free.

Four people now gave chase, for Marsden was back on his feet, Henry had joined in the effort to retrieve Hermia, and Philippa, alerted by the barking, had turned back to see her pet once more the object of unexpected attentions.

"Hermia!" she screamed again, then knew it was a waste of breath. In a display of canine coquetry, Hermia—oblivious to human blandishments—was leading her three admirers in a game of advance and retreat, circling now in one direction, now in another, frustrating the efforts of the three dogs and of the four poeple who would bring her game to a close.

It was Henry who brought some order to the uncoordinated attack. Like a commander encircling an enemy, he deployed his small troops so that the dogs were driven toward a large grassy area that jutted into the ornamental waters of the Serpentine. Philippa was conscious of his presence, but not of surprise. Indeed she was past all surprise on this most surprising morning. It was no stranger to find Henry Ashton in the park at this early hour than to find Lord Carteret or Mr. Marsden. Or to find that they as well as she responded naturally to Mr. Ashton's directions.

They had slowed down, keeping the dogs in sight, moving to head off any dash into the vastness of the park, gradually narrowing the animals' area of freedom. The three male dogs, concentrating on Hermia, seemed oblivious of the encroaching humans, but Hermia, seeing clearly what was in store, made straight for the water.

The other dogs followed. Their human pursuers had not expected this, and they were galvanized into action. It was Marsden who reached the bank first, in time to put a firm hand through Coverley's collar and drag him back from the edge. The shaggy dogs were already in the water, pursuing Hermia who was swimming down stream. Philippa glanced at Marsden. He was out of breath. He had lost his hat, his cravat was askew, his trousers and the sleeves of his coat were stained with grass, and he was cursing fluently as Coverley dug his haunches into the damp ground and refused to be taken.

Overcome by the absurdity of the situation, Philippa burst into laughter. Marsden looked affronted; then he grinned and together they hoisted Coverley into his arms.

Philippa did not stay to see Marsden move back toward the path with the struggling dog, searching for the lead which had disappeared during Coverley's flight. She ran along the bank to keep pace with Hermia, but the dog circled and began swimming back. Carteret had stripped off his coat and plunged into the water toward the milling dogs. Hermia saw him coming and turned down stream again, but the shaggy dogs were confused and Carteret collared them before they could follow.

Philippa ran toward Carteret and, kneeling in the damp grass at the edge of the bank, reached out to take one of the dogs he was forcing into shore. The two boys who claimed acquaintance with the shaggy dogs appeared at her side, while in the distance she could see the distraught nurse who was coming after them as fast as her years would allow.

The dogs were exuberant after their swim, but their desire seemed to have cooled and Hermia was forgotten. They shook themselves dry, drenching boys, nurse, and Philippa. Carteret's boots and breeches were already soaked, but Philippa, who had been concerned for him, saw the light in his eyes and knew that he was a man who relished adventure.

Philippa turned round and looked for Hermia. She had no real concern, for this was not Hermia's first swim, but was relieved to see her pet still paddling downstream. She would have to go after her, and without the distraction of the other dogs perhaps Hermia would be willing to come to shore by herself. But as Philippa made to leave, she saw that they were not yet through with the shaggy pair, who showed some disposition to return to the water and take the boys with them. The nurse raised ineffectual hands and cries, but neither dogs nor boys attended. Carteret was moving to head them off and Philippa joined him, wondering what on earth had become of Mr. Ashton. They could use his help.

Then she saw him. He had run down stream to head off Hermia and the two were converging near a clump of willows that trailed their fragile leaves over the water. The willows. Dear God! Philippa picked up her drenched skirt and ran, leaving Lord Carteret alone to sort out boys, nurse, and shaggy dogs.

The problem, Henry saw, was to recapture Hermia and take her out of the park, leaving the other dogs to their own devices, and to that end he followed the path of the Serpentine in the direction Hermia had taken. The animal, of course, must be recovered, but Henry had a greater concern. He had returned to his lodgings the night before to find a letter from his mother and had called at Green Street that morning to leave it for Claris to read. But Tuttle told him that his sister was not in bed as he had expected. She had left early with Miss Davenport who was accustomed to take her dog for a run at that hour.

Henry felt like a walk and decided to follow them to the park. He had found Miss Davenport and the obstreperous animal readily enough, but what had the woman done with his sister? When he had arrived, Claris was nowhere in sight and Miss Davenport appeared to be enjoying a rendezvous with her marquis. Claris would hardly come to harm at this hour, but she should never have been left alone.

Henry was tempted to abandon Hermia and have it out with Miss Davenport. He glanced over his shoulder and saw her with Carteret, struggling with the shaggy dogs and some children. He could see Hermia ahead, slowing her pace as though she was tired. Henry ran to the water's edge and called her name sharply.

The dog turned and paddled toward shore, happy to hear a familiar voice. Henry knelt at the edge, heedless of his trousers, and lifted the dripping animal out of the water. She seemed content to be helped up and tried to lick his face.

Henry intended to carry the dog back to her mistress and demand that she produce his sister, but first he stepped prudently back, and while Hermia relieved herself of the worst of the water, looked again at the others. Carteret appeared to have the shaggy dogs under control—he was resourceful enough, Henry admitted—and Miss Davenport had restraining arms around the two boys.

Henry turned to pick up the errant Hermia but in that instant the dog made off for the willows and Henry was forced to the chase once more. He doubled over as he entered the shelter of the trees, and their soft leaves whispered as they closed after him. Sounds were muffled here, but the quiet was broken by Hermia's sharp barks. Henry followed the sound. The dog was sitting on her haunches, her tail thumping on the hard earth, her eyes raised to a young couple who had taken refuge under the trees.

Giggling, the girl reached down to pat the dog's head. Her other hand was still firmly clasped by her would-be lover who held it ardently against his chest. Perhaps it was an unintended tightening of that grasp that caused Claris to look up and see

98

her brother regarding them with thunder in his eyes.

An assignation. And Miss Davenport must have known. In a wave of disappointment and fury, Henry swept up the still wet dog and thrust her into his sister's arms. Then he turned to Lord Christopher who had broken apart from Claris and stood bewildered, ready for some action in defence of his beloved. As the young man debated, Henry's fist smashed into his face and he fell abruptly and lay quite still.

Claris screamed. Ignored, Hermia jumped down and ran to investigate the strange behaviour of the man on the ground. Henry intercepted the dog, tucked her firmly under one arm, seized Claris with the other and dragged her protesting out of the shelter of the trees.

"Henry, no! You've killed him! Stop! I must go back!"

Claris was a small girl, but she was compact and well made and showed surprising strength. Henry was quite capable of carrying her off bodily, but he was impeded by Hermia who objected to her undignified portage and snapped at his arm. He was about to let go of the dog when Philippa arrived, breathing hard from her sprint toward the trees.

"Philippa!" Tears were streaming down Claris' cheeks and her voice rose to a wail.

Henry gave Philippa a scathing look and redoubled his hold on his sister. "Take your dog, Madam! And when you walk again, pray leave the rutting females safely at home."

Colour flooded Philippa's face. She clasped an ecstatic Hermia in her arms, but the retort on her lips was silenced by Claris' renewed outburst. "You can't leave him, Henry! He's hurt, he's dead, I have to see him! Philippa, tell him! Henry, please!"

"He'll soon recover," Henry said, "and be fit to seduce other girls. Now walk or I shall put you over my shoulder and carry you like a sack of meal."

Claris was mutinous and would not move. In exasperation, he turned to Philippa. "Tell her, Miss Davenport. I hold you responsible."

But Philippa was staring past him at the trees. Lord Christopher had emerged, leaves and twigs adorning his golden hair, blood staining his face and snowy cravat.

Claris screamed again and struggled in her brother's arms. Henry saw that not much was amiss with the young man, then turned back to Miss Davenport. Lord Carteret had come up and was standing by her side. Disapproval was written on the marquis' face, but whether of Henry's actions or of Lord Christopher's was not clear. In truth, Henry did not much care. "Carteret," he said abruptly, "see to your brother. Miss Davenport, I am taking my sister back to Green Street. You may come with us if you like, or you may find your own way home." He made off for the path leading out of the park, pulling the now unresisting Claris with him.

Philippa stared at the retreating pair in mingled anger and dismay. She glanced at Lord Carteret, shrugged helplessly, then clasped Hermia more firmly in her arms and set off after them.

Chapter 7

At ten-thirty, Tuttle opened the door to admit Miss Ashton whose pretty face betrayed signs of recent tears, Mr. Ashton who looked murderous, and Miss Philippa who was struggling to hold onto a damp and squirming Hermia. They were clearly on the verge, if not in the midst, of a crisis. More than twenty years experience of the Davenport girls had given Tuttle considerable acquaintance with crises and his only response was to close the door behind the arrivals as quickly as possible.

Once the door was safely shut, Philippa relinquished Hermia with a sigh of relief. Freed from the indignity of being carried, Hermia barked excitedly, scampered across the checkered marble floor, sniffed at the foot of the staircase, and ran half-way up to the landing. Philippa called her usually well behaved pet to order, just as Francesca came in from the garden carrying her year-old daughter, Linnet. Before anyone could speak, Claris' tears began afresh, suddenly and dramatically, heedless of the presence of Tuttle, hovering discreetly in the background, or of one of the maids, who got up from her dusting and peered over the stair rail, then hastily withdrew at a look from the butler.

Though Claris said nothing coherent, her tears and her brother's tight-lipped expression were enough to give Francesca a fairly shrewd notion of what had happened. Like Tuttle, she was no novice at handling a crisis. Clearly the first priority was to get Claris out of the hall and into a quiet place where they could begin to sort out the problem. Philippa and Henry could take care of themselves.

"Philippa," Francesca said, turning to her cousin, "could you be a love and take Linnet up to Adèle? There you are, darling, go with Aunt Philippa—"

But Linnet, already disturbed by Claris' tears, experienced glimmerings of jealousy as Mummy handed her over to Aunt Philippa and turned her attention to Claris. The child began to cry, rather more loudly than Claris had done. Hermia did not improve matters by running back to Philippa and barking sharply to indicate that she forgave her mistress.

At this point Henry, who had four younger sisters and numerous nieces and nephews, roused himself from frowning contemplation of a bowl of early roses on the hall table and fished in his pocket for his watch.

It did the trick. Her tears ceasing, Linnet seized the watch with one hand and Philippa's shoulder with the other. Philippa beat a hasty retreat upstairs. Francesca cast a grateful glance at Henry, put an arm around Claris, and led her up to her dressing room.

After giving Linnet over into the care of Adèle, her young nurse, Philippa went to her own chamber. She stripped off her pelisse—which, thanks to Hermia, the damp grass, and Linnet, was both stained and rumpled—and cast it on a chair together with her hat. A cursory inspection revealed that the hem of her walking dress was also soiled and damp. Philippa exchanged this garment for the old green muslin she usually reserved for days spent in her study—this was clearly not a morning on which to waste one of her newer frocks—repinned her hair, and decided she could no longer put off the inevitable interview with Mr. Ashton. His expression on the walk back to Green Street left her in little doubt of what he meant to say to her, and the fact that the accusations she was about to face were more than a trifle deserved did nothing to improve her temper. Besides, she reminded herself as she descended the stairs, she might have been wrong to help Claris meet Lord Christopher, but if it were not for Mr. Ashton's unreasonable attitude there would have been no need for the meeting in the first place.

As she had suspected, Mr. Ashton was in the library, alone except for Hermia who was lying on his feet. Hermia raised her head at Philippa's entrance, but seemed to feel no need to abandon her present position. Traitor, Philippa thought, closing the library door. Mr. Ashton's head was turned away, but the cup in his hand and the coffee service on the table beside him testified that he had at least recovered his temper sufficiently to ring for refreshment.

At her entrance, he set down his cup and rose, disturbing Hermia who got up and waited patiently for him to resume his seat. Philippa cleared her throat and prepared to launch into the quite reasonably conciliatory speech she had prepared, but he forestalled her.

"Out of curiosity, Miss Davenport, would you mind telling me if you actively connived at my sister's assignation with young Paget or if you were simply too preoccupied with Carteret to pay Claris any heed?"

All thoughts of conciliation forgotten, Philippa advanced into the room and stationed herself before the fireplace. "I know your opinion of me is low, Mr. Ashton, but you should know that I would never allow my—my personal concerns to supersede my obligations to others."

"Then you did connive at the meeting. Judging by the clever way you manage such scenes in your books, I would have expected you to do rather better, but I suppose you hadn't bargained on my interference. Or Hermia's."

"If you had permitted Claris to speak with Lord Christopher in the ordinary course of things, there would have been no need for the meeting to take place at all."

"But I have permitted Claris to speak with Lord Christopher in the ordinary course of things. I have no objection to her standing up with him, or going into supper with him, or even spending half the evening in his pocket, provided she is suitably chaperoned."

"You know as well as I do there's precious little chance for private conversation at a ball or in someone else's drawing room," Philippa retorted.

"It is evidently enough to allow most couples to become acquainted."

"Which is certainly insufficient, considering the marriages one sees," Philippa shot back.

"If word of this morning's little adventure ever leaks out," Mr. Ashton said evenly, "it is unlikely that Claris will marry at all."

"Nonsense," said Philippa crisply. "People would not be so idiotish."

"No?" His tone was dry. "You are, of course, better acquainted than I with the ways of the *ton*. I leave it to you to imagine the results if someone else had stumbled into the willows at that particular moment."

It was not a line of thought Philippa cared to pursue, so she took refuge in attack. "And do you imagine that you improved matters by planting Lord Christopher a facer?"

"What would you have had me do? Walk off peacefully and leave them in each other's arms?"

"Judging by the high-minded ideals of your heroes, I would have expected you to arrive at a neater solution."

Mr. Ashton started to speak, drew a breath, and said in a dangerously controlled voice, "Will you do me the favour, Miss Davenport, of remembering that Claris has neither your birth nor your fortune to ensure her place in the world and refrain from interfering in her life any further?"

"I am very fond of Claris. I can't help but be concerned for her happiness."

"Do you seriously mean to tell me that your actions this morning did anything to advance Claris' happiness?"

Despairing of Mr. Ashton's feet, Hermia had crossed the room to stand by her mistress. Philippa checked the retort which sprang instantly to her lips and bent down to stroke her pet's head. When she straightened up, Mr. Ashton was still regarding her, his gaze challenging.

"No," she said, "I don't mean to tell you anything of the kind. What I did this morning was inexcusable. Please believe that I had no intention of leaving Claris alone for so long a time. I did not expect Lord Carteret to arrive, and I most certainly did not expect Hermia to create such a disturbance. Nevertheless you are right, I should not have agreed to the meeting in the first place. I have been feeling abominably guilty, and I have taken it out on you, for both of which reasons I owe you an apology."

It was clearly the last thing Mr. Ashton had expected her to say, a circumstance which afforded Philippa no small amount of satisfaction. His posture relaxed and she almost fancied the ghost of a smile begin to play about his lips. "You never fail to surprise me, Miss Davenport. Thank you. The apology is appreciated on both counts. I must confess to my own share of guilt. Theoretically I abhor violence."

"Theoretically," said Philippa, retreating to a carved rosewood chair, "I am a rational person and never lose my temper without just cause." She glanced down at Hermia and had a sudden image of four able, intelligent people quite unable to control four equally intelligent dogs. She giggled and looked up to find Mr. Ashton grinning in response.

"It's an open question which is more difficult to control, my sister or your dog."

"There can be no comparison," Philippa returned. "Hermia is much the faster runner, but then she isn't obliged to wear skirts. Would you mind giving me a cup of coffee?"

"We seem to do better over refreshments, don't we?" Henry handed her the coffee and seated himself opposite her.

"Over refreshments?" Philippa looked puzzled, then remembered. The tearoom at Almack's. Just before her introduction to Lord Carteret, an introduction which had had a marked effect upon her life and given her and Mr. Ashton a fresh source of disagreement. She thought of Mr. Ashton's caustic comments on Lord Carteret's way of life, made in this same room less than twenty-four hours before, and of the way she herself had echoed those comments in her talk with Carteret this morning. Well, she had to admit that there was more than a grain of truth in Mr. Ashton's criticism of the marquis. The thought that there might also be more than a grain of truth in Mr. Ashton's criticism of herself had only just intruded on Philippa's consciousness when she ruthlessly suppressed it and hastened to change the subject.

"Do you know who the man with the black dog was?"

"Ah yes, your opponent of the courtroom. He looks much more human without the gown and wig, doesn't he?"

"You recognized him?" Philippa felt a twinge of jealousy at the thought that Mr. Ashton's powers of observation had proved greater than her own.

"Yes, but in all fairness I've seen him in mufti before. Yesterday in fact."

"Have you?" Philippa was intrigued. "Were you near the courts?"

"No, I was in Cavendish Square, and I saw him—actually, I almost collided with him—outside the door of Carteret House."

"That's hardly remarkable. I daresay he was calling on Lady Carteret."

"But the case has been closed for some days now."

"Perhaps it was a purely social call."

"Perhaps. I doubt I'd have given the matter a second thought if it weren't for Marsden's appearance in the park this morning."

Philippa set down her coffee cup. Really, Mr. Ashton was making entirely too much of the incident. And that was odd, for over-dramatizing was one fault of which she'd never accused him. "What is there to wonder at in a man's taking his dog for an early run in the park?"

"That's just it. I don't think it *is* his dog."

"What on earth makes you say that?"

"He seemed to have spent very little time in its company."

Determined to be equitable, Philippa thought back to the scene in the park, searching for a piece of evidence that would give Mr. Ashton the lie, and instead found much to support his assertion. Mr. Marsden had not seemed comfortable with his dog, and the dog had paid little or no heed to Mr. Marsden's attempts to control him. Still, there was no doubt a perfectly simple explanation. "I daresay he was walking him for a friend," Philippa said.

"I daresay." Mr. Ashton's voice was polite, but his expression remained infuriatingly noncommittal.

Philippa swallowed the last of her coffee, smiled with determination, and changed the subject.

"Henry is a beast! He had no right to lay hands on Crispin. He might have done him serious injury, and if he had I should never have forgiven him. Indeed, I *shall* never forgive him in any event!" To emphasize her point, Claris blew her nose defiantly into the clean handkerchief Francesca had provided.

Francesca prudently made no attempt to contradict these assertions. "In my experience," she said, "gentlemen tend to lose all pretence to rationality when it comes to matters of their sisters' honour."

"But Crispin would *never* do anything dishonourable," Claris protested.

"No," Francesca agreed, reasonably satisfied on this score herself, "but you must admit that if someone other than your brother had come across you the consequences might have been decidedly unpleasant."

"The consequences were unpleasant enough when Henry came across us," Claris retorted. Francesca suppressed a smile.

"Henry," Claris continued, twisting the soiled handkerchief between her fingers as if she wished it were her brother, "doesn't have the least idea of what love is. It's true," she insisted, fixing Francesca with stormy eyes. "Why, he killed Amelia off more than fifty pages before the end of *Robert Levering*. Even before Papa died and he got so serious—Henry I mean—his stories weren't in the least romantic. We used to complain about it dreadfully—that is, Susy didn't so much, because she was older and married and had the children, and I didn't at first, because I was too young, but Beth and Penny and Meg were always teasing him to write a real romance and as soon as I was old enough to be sensible I quite agreed with them." Claris rubbed vigorously at her eyes. "If Henry had the smallest particle of romance in him he'd understand that Crispin and I are simply meant to be together for the rest of our lives. You understand that, don't you, Francesca?"

This last was spoken with just the smallest note of uncertainty. Claris had grown very fond of her chaperone, but she sometimes wondered if anyone with Francesca's sophistication could truly remember what it was like to be young. The pause before Francesca answered merely served to increase Claris' doubts. Well, at least she still had Philippa on whom to rely. Surely Philippa, who was clearly far from indifferent to Lord Carteret, could be counted on to sympathize.

Francesca chose her words carefully. "I don't doubt the reality of what you and Lord Christopher feel for each other." Her tone was uncharacteristically gentle.

"But you don't believe it will last," Claris said flatly, drawing back slightly into her corner of the sofa.

"I can't possibly know how long it will last. But I can say from experience that people have a way of outgrowing their first loves." And their second and third, she added to herself, but there was no point in turning Claris into a cynic. She had a sudden image of herself, in seventeen years' time, having a similar conversation with her daughter.

"Are you telling me to forget Crispin?" Claris demanded.

"On the contrary," Francesca returned, feeling her age. "I think you are quite right to enjoy yourself. I am merely advising you not to do anything that may jeopardize your future."

Claris carefully folded the handkerchief into quarters. "Tell me one thing, Francesca. Did you outgrow it?"

"Outgrow what?"

"Your first love."

Francesca paused. Her first love had been a young ensign named Germanicus Scott. She had been even younger than Claris and he had been much Lord Christopher's age. Gerry had had scruples about marrying a well born heiress, and Francesca had been a widow of twenty-four before she'd finally been able to convince him that those scruples were groundless. But she could not, with any degree of truth, claim that she had outgrown it. She met Claris' gaze, which suddenly did not look so naive, and felt absurdly young.

Claris had a fairly shrewd notion of her chaperone's thoughts—had she not done so, she would not have asked the question. She wondered if Henry had outgrown his first love, and then she wondered if Henry had had a first love at all. Certainly there had not been anyone of whom she had heard. Then she thought of Philippa. Lord Carteret, Claris strongly suspected, was Philippa's first love. Well, if she had anything to say about it, neither she nor Philippa would have any need to give their hearts again.

"Never mind," Claris said, with one of her most brilliant

smiles. "It was rude of me to ask. Thank you for the handkerchief. And for talking to me. I think I'd best go change my dress. And don't worry," she added, pausing by the door, "I shan't do anything silly. I know I mustn't do anything that will embarrass my future husband's family."

Twenty minutes later Claris came downstairs, wearing a sunny yellow muslin and a matching smile, and went into the library. Francesca had joined Henry and Philippa and returned Henry's watch. No mention of the morning's incident was made, but it was clear from Claris' manner that she had condescended to forgive her brother and from Henry's that he did not intend to rake his sister over the coals any further.

Henry left soon after, saying he had already avoided his work much too long. Claris' parting smile was as sweet as ever, though she did not kiss his cheek as was her wont. After luncheon, Philippa declined to accompany Francesca and Claris to Ridgeway's bookshop and shut herself up in her study, determined to make progress on her novel. She wondered briefly if Mr. Ashton's remarks about *his* work had influenced her decision, but assured herself that that was nonsense. Mr. Ashton might have seemed almost human during the latter part of their conversation in the library, but she would never tailor her actions to suit his measure.

She surveyed the untidy papers on her desk—it had been her father's and made up in size for what it lacked in grace and elegance—and tried to imagine Mr. Ashton at work. She had long been convinced that he was one of those infuriating people who kept their papers in neat stacks and never forgot to number their pages. She had forgotten to number hers for the last chapter or so, and it took her some minutes to find where she had left off. Then she had to discard most of yesterday's work, but before long she was happily absorbed in the tangle into which her characters had worked themselves. She very nearly did not hear Tuttle when he came to the door an hour or so later to say that a Mr. Marsden had called and was she at home?

She should have said no, but she had been making good

progress, and she needed a stretch, and—oh, why not be honest—she was curious. She wiped her hands free of ink, tucked her hair into place—as if it wasn't slippery enough on its own, she had a distressing tendency to pull at it when she was working—and left her study.

She found Mr. Marsden standing by the window in the jade saloon. Though he had set himself to rights since the morning's adventure and was dressed, if not with Lord Carteret's style, certainly more fashionably than—for instance —Mr. Ashton, he seemed curiously out of place in the room. The flowered wallpaper and delicately carved furniture only served to emphasize the energy and force that Philippa had been aware of in the park that morning.

He turned as she closed the door and came forward to greet her. His words were perfectly correct, but Philippa thought she sensed something else in his manner, something which she could not define except that it seemed related to the disturbing look she sometimes glimpsed in Lord Carteret's eyes.

Fanciful nonsense, Philippa told herself firmly. She had been working on a scene between Anne and Nigel when Tuttle interrupted her. No doubt that accounted for the absurd turn of her thoughts. She seated herself on a scroll-backed chair, gestured to the seat opposite her, and hastened to apologize for the disturbance her dog had caused.

"I rather think the apologies should be made on my side," Marsden returned. "Coverley clearly lacks an understanding of what is owing to a lady."

Unbidden, Mr. Ashton's comments about Marsden and the dog echoed in Philippa's head. Well, she would ask Mr. Marsden. It would give her great satisfaction to pass on his no doubt perfectly satisfactory explanation to Henry Ashton. "Have you had him a long time?" she asked.

Marsden started to speak, checked himself, gave Philippa a look she was at a loss to decipher, then grinned. "You are quite as quick out of the witness-box as you are in it, Miss Davenport. I have not had Coverley for any length of time whatsoever. He belongs to the youngest son of a fellow barrister in my chambers who, I have no doubt, could have controlled him a deal better than I did this morning."

"I see. Then you aren't generally in the habit of walking him for your young friend?"

"I never encountered the animal before in my life. In fact, I have been at some pains to locate a dog at all these past few days."

"Locate a dog?" Philippa was torn between interest and regret. Her perfectly satisfactory explanation was fast slipping away.

"Yes. I only needed it for an hour or so, you see. The hour from nine to ten, to be precise. I had ascertained that that is generally when you take—Hermia, is it?—for a run. In short, Miss Davenport, our meeting this morning was entirely my own contrivance, though I take no credit for the subsequent events."

At this pregnant moment Tuttle re-entered the room with tea and biscuits. Philippa dismissed the butler with a smile, determined that Mr. Marsden required neither cream nor sugar, and carefully poured two cups before saying, "Surely that was a bit excessive."

"Not in the least. I had to manage an introduction somehow. I was—I am—most eager to make your acquaintance."

"I see." This was not at all the scene Philippa had envisaged when she abandoned chapter ten. Indeed, it was proving far more interesting than Anne and Nigel's conversation. "I trust you had your reasons."

"I never act without reason, Miss Davenport. Quite frankly, you intrigue me. It isn't often that I'm bested by a woman."

This blunt and surprising statement might have shocked Philippa into silence had his last comment not been so beautifully open to retort. "Am I to infer that you frequently find yourself bested by men, Mr. Marsden?"

He hadn't seen it coming, but he accepted it with good will. "No, Miss Davenport, you are not. I don't frequently find myself bested by anyone."

It was an arrogant remark, but Philippa suspected it was close to the truth. "You must admit it was a rather foolish case," she pointed out, offering him the plate of biscuits.

"It was," he agreed, declining the biscuits.

"Why did you accept it?"

Marsden gave an ironic smile, very different from Lord Carteret's charming expression, but in its own way no less attractive. "An ambitious young barrister does not refuse briefs from the Paget family. However ridiculous. My father may have gone to the same schools as yours, Miss Davenport. He did not leave the same fortune."

Philippa stirred her tea slowly while she formulated a reply. Her family's acquaintance included a number of persons who were considered unconventional, but Mr. Marsden's style of plain-speaking was something entirely new. He was the antithesis of Lord Carteret, who seemed to make it a matter of personal pride never to speak his mind directly. In fact, Mr. Marsden's last statement had sounded very like something Henry Ashton might say. Except that Mr. Ashton, Philippa felt sure, would sooner starve than seek patronage from the Pagets. Or from anyone else.

"Shall I apologize for my fortune?" she asked at length.

"On the contrary," Marsden said easily. "I fully intend to have one equally large in the course of things."

Philippa set down her cup. "Tell me, Mr. Marsden, are you always so direct?"

"Oh, I can prevaricate as well as the next man. But I see no need to hide my ambitions from the world." He returned his cup, now empty, to the Pembroke table between them. "Should I continue to call on you, as I have every intention of doing, you will no doubt be informed that I am pursuing your fortune."

"And are you?" Philippa was pleased to note that her voice remained composed.

"That I leave you to judge for yourself. I shall give you ample opportunity to do so." He rose to take his leave. "I am late for a meeting, I must go. If I call again, may I take it that I won't be shown the door?"

"I am not in the habit of denying callers, Mr. Marsden." She smiled and gave him her hand. "Unless I am working."

Philippa returned to her study but Anne and Nigel were far from her mind. The extraordinary interview with Mr. Marsden had left her bemused and more than a trifle shaken. Beside Mr. Marsden's manner, Lord Carteret's attentions seemed light-hearted and almost restrained. Philippa was certain that Mr. Marsden had spoken the truth when he said that he never acted without reason. He had gone to some pains to make clear his interest in her and, unlike the marquis, he had not done so simply out of boredom. Why then? True, she was something of an heiress, but she had fended off fortune hunters in the past, and they were not in the habit of drawing attention to their lack of wealth or of looking at her in quite that way. . . .

Oh, this was absurd. She scarcely knew the man. He scarcely knew her. Her flirtation—if it could be called that—with Lord Carteret had turned her head. She was reading too much into Mr. Marsden's behaviour and acting like a green girl in her first Season, the result, no doubt, of having been so defiantly practical when she *was* in her first Season. Her sisters had warned her this would happen.

By the time Francesca and Claris returned, Philippa had convinced herself that her impression of the scene with Mr. Marsden was due to a bad case of over-active imagination. But the next evening, when he presented himself at the Scotts' opera box, she was forced to reconsider.

In the succeeding days he asked her to dance at Lady Swinnerton's ball, crossed her path in St. James's Park, found his way to her side at Mrs. Walgrave's rout, and called again in Green Street. By the end of the week Philippa could not deny that he was actively pursuing her and had given up speculating about his motivation. He claimed to be intrigued by her. Well, she was intrigued by him. He might be—he admitted to being—arrogant and ambitious, but one could not by any stretch of the imagination accuse him of frittering his life away. He was a welcome change from Lord Carteret's clever superficiality. Mr. Ashton should approve.

She was thinking of this, and also thinking that Mr. Ashton had not seemed to notice there were now two gentlemen frequently in her company, when she walked into the breakfast parlour on Monday morning to find Claris' brother seated at the table with the *Morning Chronicle* and a cup of coffee. He greeted her with a friendly smile—since the adventure in the park they had been on comparatively good terms—and explained that he had shared an early breakfast with Gerry and intended to wait for his sister, provided she rose before noon.

"I shouldn't bargain on it," Philippa told him, pouring a cup of coffee and sipping it thankfully. "We didn't return from the Ossulstons' until nearly four. You've no notion how exhausting frivolity can be."

"Perhaps not, though in Claris' case it can scarcely be called frivolity. Husband-hunting is serious business."

Philippa conceded that this was so, but added that she did not have any such excuse. She was helping herself from the dishes on the sideboard and so missed the speculative look which crossed Mr. Ashton's face. He was silent while she filled her plate, but when she had seated herself at the table he said abruptly, "If by any chance you don't have an engagement Wednesday afternoon, I can offer you some entertainment which couldn't possibly be called frivolous."

Philippa looked at him in surprise and inquiry. "Entertainment?"

"In a manner of speaking. It's a meeting at Miss Neville's."

Sophronia Neville was a distant connection of Gerry's. She was also a well known reformer. Philippa set down her fork and considered. "Am I to take this as a challenge, Mr. Ashton?"

"You may take it as whatever you like, Miss Davenport. If you care to come I can call for you at half past one."

He was watching her closely, but his expression was unreadable. Well, she had never been one to refuse a challenge. "Half past one, Mr. Ashton. I shall be waiting."

114

Chapter 8

When Henry called for Philippa on Wednesday afternoon, he told her he had a hackney waiting at the door. Caught by surprise, Philippa was obliged to retire and tell Tuttle her carriage would not be required and then pretend to Mr. Ashton that she did not know that he was perfectly aware she had expected to be driven in one of her own carriages.

It occurred to her for the first time that Mr. Ashton was a proud man, and then it occurred to her that she had actually spent very little time with people whose situation was less comfortable than her own. Philippa did not often think about money and did not spend it lavishly, but it was always comfortingly there, and its presence insulated her from any charge of eccentricity. How different it must be for Claris. She thought once more of her culpable carelessness and of Mr. Ashton's anxious concern for his sister's welfare and resolved to be very pleasant to him this afternoon.

"I don't know Miss Neville," she said when they were seated in the hackney, "though Gerry's talked about her, of course. And my father was acquainted with her. He said she had a head of fire and a tongue to match."

Henry was amused. "The description's apt, but I'm afraid her hair has turned to ash." He leaned back against the dark leather squabs. "She's a gadfly."

"But people listen to her?"

"Yes, they do listen. It helps if your name is Neville."

She decided to ignore the hint of sarcasm. "I'm looking

forward to meeting her. No doubt," she added, her expression quite innocent, "it will contribute to the improvement of my mind."

Henry looked at her sharply. "Improve your mind, Miss Davenport? I would never so interfere. Though," he continued with a slight smile, "it might do no harm to broaden your acquaintance."

Henry wondered what Miss Davenport would make of the coming afternoon. For all her family's advanced views, she had led a sheltered life. Would she be surprised by what she heard? Would she be offended? Or would she refuse to take the proceedings seriously? He could not believe that she would be indifferent, but mockery often served to mask distress.

"You will be pleased to know that I've already begun." Philippa reached for the strap as the carriage made a sharp turn. It was abominably sprung. "Mr. Marsden has been to call, and you can hardly take exception to him as a fit companion. His father may have been a baron, but he's a younger son and has had to make his own way in the world. Though I confess that he is not very successful with dogs, he has risen fast in his profession. Or so I've been told," she added, remembering her inquiries of Francesca. "Of course he does go out of an evening, but that should hardly tell against him, should it, Mr. Ashton? I have seen you do the same."

Henry made her a mock bow. "I have no quarrel with Mr. Marsden." Privately he was not so sure. Claris had told him of that first afternoon call and of several others. He had seen a man who looked like Marsden talking with Miss Davenport in St. James's Park, and he had certainly seen him dancing with her at Lady Swinnerton's on Friday last. Marsden might, like Carteret, have simply become intrigued with the outspoken young author after their encounter in court, but he might also be using their scant acquaintance to further his own fortunes. And there was the matter of his puzzling call on Lady Carteret. For reasons he did not fully understand, Henry had been moved to make inquiries about Elliot Marsden.

"Then I think I understand," Philippa said. "It is idleness you abhor. At least for men. Tell me, Mr. Ashton, what is your stand on the idleness of women?"

She was baiting him, so he replied in kind. "You find your sex idle? Between conferring with the housekeeper and paying and receiving calls—"

"And shopping, Mr. Ashton. You must not forget shopping. Or is that an idle occupation?"

"Frequently. But it does keep our shopkeepers in business. We've arrived, Miss Davenport. Let me introduce you to some women who are far from idle."

The cab had pulled up in Berkley Street just off Manchester Square. Henry led Philippa up the steps to Miss Neville's door. There were several people before them, and they waited in the hall while their hostess greeted the guests, having a few words for each. Philippa observed Miss Neville with interest. The famous red hair was now almost entirely grey, but she carried her thin body with authority, and though she rarely smiled, her finely lined face was animated and her blue eyes alive with understanding.

As Henry introduced her, Philippa found herself observed in turn, but there was no malice in Miss Neville's scrutiny. "I'm pleased to have you, Miss Davenport. I knew your father. He was a sensible man, for a politician. You write, that's good. Writers are good observers and that makes them good reporters, and we need reports, yes, we do, honest ones. Haven't read your books, don't intend to, I never read works of fiction—as you know very well, Ashton, haven't read yours either—the real world is sensational enough, there's nothing you have to tell me. Still, bless the writers, we need them. Go in, go in, while there are seats to be had." The raspy voice stopped for a moment, and she turned toward the door to welcome some new arrivals.

Philippa and Henry moved into a large room which seemed to occupy half the ground floor. It was arranged much like a public hall, with rows of chairs facing a large table on which stood a speaker's lectern, a pitcher of water, and several glasses. Along the side wall a number of other tables displayed books and tracts and a collection of newspapers. The *Manchester Observer* Philippa had seen before, and the *Political Register*, but there were others that were new to her and with names far stranger—*The Phoenix* and *The Medusa* and *The*

117

Black Dwarf. Philippa browsed among these, for she was an inveterate reader, and was deep in a copy of *The Rights of Infants* when she heard a booming voice behind her.

"Henry! Henry, m'boy. Didn't expect you. Are you working? Of course you are, this is no house of waste, more's the pity. Sorry, m'dear." This last was directed to Philippa whose presence Henry made known by a gesture.

Henry hastened through an introduction. "My friend, Gordon Murray. Gordon, this is Miss Davenport."

Murray was a short, heavy man, clearly given to the pleasures of table and tankard. His face fell in loose folds under his chin, his nose was broad and splayed over the wide mouth beneath, his eyes were bright with mischief. Philippa liked him on sight.

He professed himself delighted to meet Miss Davenport. "Enjoy your books, m'dear, I've read them all. They make me laugh, and laughter's a rare commodity these days."

Philippa stole a glance at Mr. Ashton. If he was discomfited by this praise of her work from a man he called his friend, he did not show it.

"Like Henry's scribblings, too," Murray went on, "though like as not they make me cry. Still, it's all the same, you know, have to escape from the real world one way or another."

And with this dubious compliment he slipped away into the growing crowd.

"Chastening praise," Philippa murmured.

"Quite." Henry was amused. He took her arm and guided her to a chair against the far wall. The room was filling rapidly and the voices rose in pitch and volume as in the moments of expectation before the beginning of a play.

"Is he a critic?" Philippa asked when they were seated. "Does he write?"

"Are those contrary questions, Miss Davenport?"

"Not at all," she returned sweetly. "I have found critics often write very well indeed."

He ignored her barb. "You might call Murray a critic of the world—certainly he sees it as his stage. He edits, writes, publishes a newspaper, *The Phoenix*. I doubt that you would have seen it, but it boasts a modest circulation. It was formerly

118

called *The Scourge*, but that was while he was in Newgate."

"A pity." Philippa was little acquainted with the radical press, but she knew that its editors were as likely to publish from inside prison as out.

"A slight disagreement with the Stamp Office. Murray tried publishing without stamped paper, an effort to increase his readership by lowering the price of knowledge. It was bound to fail, of course. Murray's a gadfly, like Miss Neville, but unlike her he is not quite respectable."

Philippa looked up at the speakers' table where Miss Neville now stood. "Then her respectability is an asset in her work?"

"She does a great deal of good."

"And what particular good is she intending to do today?"

"Don't mock her, Miss Davenport."

"I had no intention of doing so," she said quietly, controlling her annoyance at the rebuke. "I really want to know." She could never resist the urge to be clever. It was a failing that made even her sincere utterances liable to misinterpretation.

He would have answered her, but a sudden hush in the room, accompanied by the shuffling of feet and settling of skirts, indicated that the meeting was about to begin. Philippa looked curiously about, studying the expectant expressions of her fellow guests, and found herself staring into the grey eyes of the Marquis of Carteret.

When Claris had managed a few clandestine words with her beloved at Lady Jersey's the evening before, she had informed him that her brother was taking Philippa to a meeting at Miss Neville's near Manchester Square and Lady Francesca was going to a china warehouse with her sister-in-law and she, Claris, was going to have a severe cramp and have to stay at home, so would he please take advantage of the situation and call at about three on the following afternoon.

Knowing his brother's interest in Miss Davenport, Crispin had seen fit to convey the first part of this message to Anthony when they met at breakfast the next morning. Anthony had nodded and gone on to talk of something else. But on the way to a party at Richmond, Lord Carteret had taken a sudden freak and, in the middle of the King's Road, turned his curricle and made his way to Manchester Square, leaving his friends to agree that Carteret had been acting deuced queer in the past few days.

Anthony himself could not have told them why he chose to return to London. He had been unsettled ever since that morning in Hyde Park when Elliot Marsden put in so unexpected an appearance. At the time, he thought the meeting a mere coincidence, but when Anthony saw Marsden dancing with Miss Davenport at the Swinnerton ball, observed him conversing with her at Mrs. Walgrave's rout, and then encountered him the following afternoon in the Green Street drawing room, he knew that Marsden was pursuing Miss Davenport.

The knowledge caused the most peculiar feeling in Anthony's breast. Another man would have recognized it as jealousy, but that was an emotion entirely foreign to Lord Carteret who had never had anything to be jealous about.

Then there was the matter of that conversation by the Serpentine. Anthony knew that Miss Davenport enjoyed his company, as he intended she should, for he set himself to be pleasing, but he had come away with the distinct impression that she did not take him seriously.

And in the end, it was this perhaps that caused him to turn back toward London. Marsden had only passable looks, no particular address, and no fortune to speak of. But he clearly filled his days with serious activity. Perhaps that was why Miss Davenport found him so interesting. Anthony could certainly find serious activity as well.

He arrived late, thus missing a greeting from Miss Neville in the hall. He was waved into the parlour by a whispery female in a serviceable dark brown worsted who informed him that the meeting had commenced and he should be quiet as he entered.

Anthony stood in the doorway, scanning the room. Ah, Crispin was right, Miss Davenport was there, against the wall, seated by that writer fellow, the brother of that engaging bit to whom Crispin was so attracted. He caught her eye and bowed

120

slightly, letting her see the seriousness of his mien. She coloured prettily and the ghost of a smile hovered about her lips. Then she turned toward the speakers and Anthony found a convenient wall to lean against, all the chairs now being taken. He had a clear view of Miss Davenport and she, if she cared to look, could mark his attention to what was at hand.

Miss Neville opened the meeting with some announcements and very little ceremony. They were to have the pleasure of hearing from Mrs. Cornelius Tucker with whose work they were all familiar. There was a scattering of applause and Mrs. Tucker rose and came to the lectern. She was a large woman of indeterminate years with an untidy mass of brown hair and a sheaf of foolscap which she arranged neatly before her. Anthony shifted his position, folded his arms, and prepared to wait her out.

She proved an earnest speaker, but her voice was flat and she had a habit of bobbing her head to emphasize her points. The subject of her discourse gradually made itself apparent: the young women from villages who made their way to the capital to escape from rural drudgery and isolation, only to become domestic drudges find themselves at the mercy of their masters, and like as not be gotten with child. It was a familiar story, robbed of any poignancy by the speaker's monotonous delivery.

Anthony recalled that his own father had had a penchant for the rosy young virgins found below stairs. Anthony thought it a dubious pleasure at best, and his own code—which he had never clearly articulated—led him to prefer women of experience. As a boy, he had wondered what became of all those girls—interchangeable they seemed to be, with names like Lucy and Sarah and Bess—who came and went with regularity. Mrs. Tucker was speaking of it now, and he looked across the room at Miss Davenport, who was sitting forward in her chair, mouth slightly parted, absorbing the dry accounts of dozens and scores and hundreds. Philippa Davenport, he knew, was not missish, but it was a distasteful subject, and he would have liked to take her away.

Mrs. Tucker gathered her sheaf of papers at last and left the lectern. There was applause and a general stirring in the audience who had been sitting quiet too long. Anthony looked once more at Miss Davenport, but she was in conversation with Ashton. As soon as Miss Neville closed the meeting, he would join them.

But the meeting was far from over. There was some kind of colloquy at the table, and it was evident that there were to be more speakers. Anthony refolded his arms and suppressed a sigh. Aside from Miss Davenport, to whom he dared not pay too obvious attention, there was no one worth watching. They were a drab lot on the whole, and, aside from a curious glance or two, they seemed quite oblivious of his presence. It was a novel sensation and not a very pleasant one.

The speeches were beginning again. A woman who was the twin of Mrs. Tucker told the story of a girl who had delivered her infant in Hyde Park, drowned it in one of the fountains, and been found half-frozen and gibbering the next morning, her face smeared with her own blood. A thrill of horror went through the audience.

She was followed by the rector of a parish in Spitalfields who deplored, at some length, the incontinence of the employing classes. For his father's sake, Anthony winced.

Finally, a thin, pale young woman, clearly ill and looking far older than her seventeen years, described how she was hounded from her parish so she and her child would not fall upon the parish's charge. From the general to the particular. It was nicely calculated, Anthony thought with a touch of admiration for Miss Neville. The audience was clearly roused to action. Miss Neville was coming forward now, no doubt to make some closing remarks and call for help of a more material kind.

Anthony was not wholly without feeling for what he had heard that afternoon, though he was inclined to believe that little could actually be done. The problem alluded to was a natural part of life, men being what they were. Still, the afternoon had not been uninstructive. He had had the pleasure of watching Miss Davenport unobserved, and the seventeen-year-old had really touched him. Anthony promised himself the satisfaction of a large donation.

*   *   *

Henry's attention had also been divided between the speakers and Miss Davenport. She followed the speeches with intent interest, showing neither disgust nor surprise, and it occurred to Henry that she had been less sheltered than he had supposed.

"Was it what you expected?" he asked when the speakers had finished.

"I don't know that I had any clear expectation," Philippa admitted. "I found it instructive. Not so much in what was said, for one knows, of course, that such things go on, but in hearing it firsthand."

"And now that you have?"

"I have a great deal to think about." She smiled. "And so, I hope, does Lord Carteret. He, too, is willing to broaden his mind."

"Did you ask him to come?"

"No. But he must have taken my words to heart."

"Your words?"

"Never mind, Mr. Ashton." Philippa might have come to see the truth in his criticisms of Lord Carteret, but she was not about to tell Mr. Ashton so.

"He is willing to please you," Henry observed.

"I did not invite him," Philippa insisted. "There is no way he could have known I would be here."

"He must know that he gains credit in your eyes by his attendance."

"And so he should! Whether for my sake or for his own, he is here. I came out of curiosity, but that does not mean I will learn nothing from the afternoon. And the same is true for Lord Carteret. What drove him here is of no importance."

They had been whispering, but were now hushed by their neighbours. Miss Neville was returning to the lectern. But she was not bringing the meeting to a close nor was she using the occasion to solicit donations. She summarized the points made in a few pithy sentences, then invited the audience to comment on what they had heard.

There was a general stirring in the crowd. A clergyman near the back recommended a return to piety for the poor unfortunates they had heard described.

"Fiddle-de-dee!" Philippa and Henry heard Gordon Murray's deep murmur somewhere behind them.

Philippa smiled. "Bravo," she said softly.

A stout woman dressed in black said that scripture was all very well, but it would feed neither babe nor mother. It was what they deserved said another, and a mild shouting match ensued.

A frail old woman called for attention. "I've been in service all my life," she said, "and I go to church every Sunday, but it happened to me anyway when I was young."

"You should have resisted temptation," said the clergyman.

"It was no temptation, sir, that it weren't. He were stronger than me, and he threatened to have me turned out, and he could've done so for he were nephew to my mistress. And if she weren't a kind lady and sent me off to the country to have the babe and found it a home, I'd be on the streets today. Or dead, more like. So to my way of thinking, the gentleman"—here she nodded toward the clergyman—"should seek to bring his own kind back to the ways of the righteous, for women can look for little protection when men play the devil."

This was followed by a spattering of applause. Henry was pleased to see that Miss Davenport joined in. He got to his feet.

"I must apologize for my sex, ma'am, and in your own case there is much to censure. But surely the blame does not always lie solely with us. Women have been known to play the devil as well as men." He paused and looked round, as if to gather the group's attention. "It is futile to apportion blame. The question is, what can we do once the mischief has been done?"

"What indeed, sir?" He was interrupted by a tall woman who rose and instantly commanded everyone's attention. She was built on ample lines, of uncertain years but with the remnants of considerable beauty. Her hair was loosely dressed and a brilliant gold in hue, her eyes were a deep blue shaded by dark lashes, and her complexion had a rosy underlay that seemed wholly natural.

"Rubens," Philippa murmured. Henry turned and nodded, then resumed his seat.

The woman made her way through the rows of chairs and walked toward the front of the room, moving with quiet purpose and with no trace of self-consciousness. Despite her somewhat florid appearance, she was dressed with great propriety in a three-caped, dark blue pelisse and a high-crowned straw hat. Both manner and clothes announced that she was someone of importance in the world.

She nodded to Miss Neville and turned to face the room, and neither Miss Neville nor anyone else questioned her right to stand there. "What indeed?" She echoed the words with which she had first taken the floor. "The gentleman is right, let us not blame one another for our frailties." She looked out calmly over the room, ignoring the murmurs that followed this opening. Not all members of the audience cared for that all-embracing pronoun.

"Let us by all means be charitable," she went on. Despite her proportions, her voice was light and clear, almost girlish. "Let us open our hearts to these girls. Let us support those who provide shelter when girls are in trouble. And when that trouble is over, let us open our homes as well. These young women must not be deprived of a livelihood, lest they be forced onto the streets and pass disease to our sons."

These were stronger words, and the stirrings in the audience became more noticeable. "And let us also bring what pressures we can on their seducers. Let them be shamed into paying for their pleasures. Let them acknowledge their bastards.

"Let us do all this," she continued, "because it should be done, because it must be done." She turned to the young girl who had spoken earlier. "I offer a position to Miss Rivers here, if she will have it, and she may bring her child with her."

A murmur of approbation swept the room. The statuesque blonde woman turned back to the audience. Henry watched her appreciatively. She was playing them well, but he sensed that she had not yet made her point.

"You applaud my action. Good. But if you think I am doing any lasting good, you are wrong. Nothing will change." Her voice rose. "Nothing will change until such children are not conceived."

There was some murmured assent, but Henry was disappointed. "A pious hope," he muttered. "What else are the poor to do for entertainment?" Then he remembered Miss

Davenport's presence. He looked at her, uncertain how she would take it.

She grinned. "Just so, Mr. Ashton."

But the blonde woman had not finished. "Now I am a practical woman," she continued. "I have been acquainted with a great many men, and I hold out no hope for their reformation. Nor do I trust to the strength of women to resist men's blandishments or force, or to resist their own desires. But women have it within their power to prevent the worst effects of these encounters, to prevent the loss of their employment, to prevent the ruin of their health." She placed her reticule on the speakers' table behind her, opened it and withdrew a small wash-leather bag.

"Men sometimes go in armour, though they do it for the sake of their own health rather than that of their partners, and I would not in any case rely on a man. But here"—she held the bag up for all to see—"here is a means that a woman can rely upon without trusting to the good offices of a man. They have known of it in France for years. It is shameful, it is shameful that it is not better known here!"

The drift of her remarks was now clear to most of the audience. There was complete silence in the room. Then the clergyman stood up and cried "Abomination!" And in that same instant the Marquis of Carteret unfolded his arms and in a voice that rang through the room cried, "Madam! There are ladies present."

There was a scrambling among the chairs and several women surged toward the door. Others sat quietly in rapt attention, and a few took advantage of the confusion to move to seats closer to the front of the room. Miss Neville made no move to interfere. Henry looked at Miss Davenport, but she showed no sign of distress and continued to regard the speaker with interest.

Philippa in fact was eager for details. She knew perfectly well how babies were made, and she knew that men and women had reasons other than the making of children for engaging in this practice. She was more vaguely aware that there were steps which could be taken to prevent conception, but no one had ever volunteered the details. Her mother, she felt certain, knew all about it. After all, there had been eleven years between Juliana's birth and Papa's death.

This must be what Mama had, in private colloquy, told each of her sisters shortly before their marriages. Juliana, Philippa recalled, had emerged from Mama's dressing room with a bemused expression on her normally lively face, looking as though she had passed some rite of initiation. When Philippa had asked her younger sister what was the matter, Juliana had said, "Nothing, nothing at all. In fact, it's quite wonderful," and gone humming down the stairs.

"Sponges," the blonde woman was saying, opening the bag and holding up a small soft object in her hand. A loop of ribbon depended from it, making it look rather like a miniature bonnet. "Cloth will do, but I have found that sponges are more comfortable. Dipped in a little brandy and water and inserted before congress. Or vinegar may be used. As you see, a thread or ribbon is attached to help in removal. I will be glad to speak later with anyone who cares for more precise instructions."

She raised her voice over the growing tumult of the crowd. "I speak to the married as well, for nothing is more injurious to a woman's health than being forced to bear children without end. And nothing is harder for a poor man than to father children for whom he cannot provide."

By the time the handsome blonde woman had reached this point, the room was in an uproar. Lord Carteret moved rapidly through the crowd, determined to remove Miss Davenport from a scene that was offensive and promised to become unruly.

Henry looked again at Miss Davenport. "How very sensible," she murmured. "Why should anyone be offended?"

Someone was heard to demand that the speaker be called before a magistrate. At this point Miss Neville came forward to intervene, but before she could do so, Henry was on his feet. "Let her speak!" he cried. "Are you afraid of words?"

"They are impious and unclean. No decent woman should know about such things." The speaker was a tall, thin man of sober mien who had been sitting at the back of the room and who stood now, rigidly erect, his hands opening and closing in his agitation.

"Then no decent woman should titillate her mind with stories of young girls fallen into error. How in thunder do

127

decent women suppose the girls got that way?" Gordon Murray rose slowly to his feet and turned around. "I was sure I knew that voice. Eleazer Nobb, Society for the Suppression of Vice. Good God, man, what are you doing in this nest of reformers?"

Mr. Nobb, who considered himself the only true reformer present, raised his right arm on high and opened his mouth but no words came. His spare frame shook with the intensity of his emotions.

The woman in black had no such difficulty. "Does this not encourage young women in vice, ma'am?" she addressed the speaker. "I can see how it would be a help to married women, for I've borne thirteen myself, and buried seven of them before they'd been on God's earth three years, and still it's hard on us to provide for so many. But to tell such things to innocent girls is only to reward a life of depravity."

Philippa in turn was on her feet. "But haven't we been hearing, ma'am," she said to the black-gowned woman, "that a life of depravity is often a consequence of that very innocence? Surely what could do good to so many should not be forbidden because it might harm a few."

Henry watched her appreciatively. He had been about to say something of the sort himself.

Carteret had now reached Philippa's side. "Miss Davenport, Miss Davenport, I beg you to let me take you away."

"Not on any account," she told him. She was surprised and disappointed that he had asked. Rakes, she remembered Francesca saying, are often tiresomely conventional underneath. Carteret's tall figure obscured her view of the woman to whom she had been speaking, and she pushed past him to continue the conversation.

A number of people had quitted the room in the last few minutes, including Mr. Nobb who had been shepherded out by two female companions. A small knot of men clustered at the back of the room, heads bent intently toward one another. Several of the more venturesome women had taken advantage of the blonde woman's offer and were grouped around her at the front of the room.

There was no longer even a pretence of a meeting. Miss Neville had moved to the parlour doors some time since where

128

she was talking earnestly with her departing guests, soothing or exhorting as the case might be.

In his frustration, Carteret turned to the woman who had caused the trouble. "You, madam," he called in a voice that commanded attention, "you who choose to remain nameless, do you see what you have done here?"

The blonde woman broke through the circle around her and walked toward him. "My name is Mrs. Robinson," she said with dignity, "and I have done nothing but open the windows of ignorance. Shall women be denied what many men already know? What you must know yourself, Lord Carteret, for how do you suppose a man's mistresses keep their liaisons within decent bounds? You cannot have it both ways, sir. If you enjoy the company of women, you must be prepared to allow them to protect themselves against the consequences of your attentions."

And with this shot she returned to the group of women who were seeking her specific instruction.

Anthony stood as though he had been struck, as indeed he had. How dared this unknown woman refer publicly to his mistresses? By what right did she speak to him in that familiar tone? He had put her down as a rich cit's wife or widow and certainly did not know her. Nor would he have expected her to know his name. There had been some curious looks as she pronounced it, but the discourse that afternoon outweighed any curiosity about the presence of a peer of the realm.

He turned to a man standing near him, a short, squat man with bushy eyebrows that grew low over the bridge of his nose and shot up in a straight line to his temples. "Who is that woman?" he asked in a strangled voice.

"Upset you, did she, m'lord?" Gordon Murray's tone was cheerful. "She's got a fair tongue. Used to run one of the finest houses in Tothill Fields, just south of Westminister. Handy. Retired now, does what she can for girls caught in the game."

The man with the bushy eyebrows nodded and wandered off. Anthony stared after him in stupefaction. Then memory returned in a flood. He did not, as a rule, frequent brothels, but he remembered this particular one. It had been a memorable night, for he had surprised his father there. He remembered the woman too, though her name had not been Robinson.

Then the enormity of her appearance in this house struck him. Was her former calling known? Should he tell Miss Neville? No, from what he had observed, Miss Neville would probably not mind. Nor, he suspected, would Miss Davenport who was still engaged with the woman in black.

"See here, Ashton," he said, turning to Henry with sudden decision, "You've got to get Miss Davenport out of here."

Henry returned the marquis' look calmly. "Miss Davenport does not seem eager to leave."

"That's hardly the question. It was bad enough bringing her here in the first place, but once that woman started talking—"

"You have some objection to Mrs. Robinson?"

"Damnation, Ashton," Anthony hissed, "the woman's a trollop!"

"I don't think so," Henry said blandly. "I understand she retired several years ago."

"No need to fret, m'lord," Gordon Murray said quietly. "This is a respectable house. Miss Davenport will come to no harm here."

Anthony looked round helplessly. There was clearly no danger to Miss Davenport's person, and it was already too late to shelter her from the unseemly ideas that had been expressed. He was out of place in this house where none of the rules seemed to apply. Boundaries were crumbling. It was a sign of his distress that he sought help from a man who did not look quite a gentleman and to whom he had not even been introduced. "She doesn't belong here. Persuade her that she must leave."

Murray's voice was soothing. "Ashton will see her safely home. Don't worry, m'lord. She's got a tough mind and she won't be corrupted." Murray put an arm on his shoulder and Anthony did not even think to resent the liberty taken with his person.

Anthony nodded briefly at Miss Neville as he left the room, then strode out of the house and down the street, quite forgetting that his groom was waiting patiently with his curricle in the opposite direction.

What had he got himself into? He had spent an afternoon with a group of people of whose existence he had barely been aware. He had been touched by a story told by a waif who was doubtless making the whole thing up. He had been subjected to an attack on his way of life and that of his whole sex by a common whore. And all for the sake of a woman who was critical of his behaviour and indifferent to his wishes.

He stopped and remembered the curricle. Retracing his steps, Anthony took himself in hand. It was time to beat a prudent retreat before his interest in Miss Davenport led him into uncharted seas. He would drive down to Carteret Park and spend a few days with his horses and dogs.

Miss Davenport had exceeded Henry's expectations. After her conversation with Carteret, she had joined the circle around Mrs. Robinson, and it was with some difficulty that he at last persuaded her to come away. She seemed exhilarated by the experience of the afternoon. Her eyes were bright, her face animated, and she insisted on walking all the way to Green Street. She had made a conquest of the woman in black, convincing her at last to speak with Mrs. Robinson, but she was most pleased by her conquest of Lord Carteret. "And if he was upset by what occurred, that is quite understandable," she said as they turned into Green Street, "but that he came at all is quite a triumph. You see, he is not what you thought him. His wealth has kept him in ignorance, but he is willing to learn, and willingness is all."

Henry doubted that was the motive for Carteret's appearance. He wondered what it was Miss Davenport had said which had caused the marquis to brave the neighbourhood of Manchester Square. And why she had said it. "What about you, Miss Davenport?"

"Oh, I am willing, too." And with that ambiguous comment he had to be content.

Henry stayed in Green Street long enough to take tea with his sister and Francesca, then returned to his lodgings where he found a message from Will Brixton, a Lincoln's Inn clerk with whom he was casually acquainted. Will would be at the Pig and Bottle and, if Henry would stand the blunt, he would tell him what he had learned of Elliot Marsden.

131

Chapter 9

Lady Edwina Thane walked through the front door of Buckleigh House in Bruton Street, nodded absently at the footman, crossed the hall—not as palatial as that in Carteret House, but quite grand enough for all usual purposes—and started up the stairs, pulling off her riding gloves.

"Good, you're finally back. Come into the breakfast parlour. I want to talk to you."

"Oh, it's you." Lady Edwina turned her ungloved left hand resting on the stair-rail. "Can't it wait? I want to go up and change my dress. I won't be a minute."

"You'll be close to an hour, and by then Mother will be up and there'll be precious little chance for private conversation. This is important." Quentin Thane, Viscount St. George, turned and started back for the breakfast parlour, not looking to see if his sister would follow. Edwina hesitated, annoyance warring with curiosity. Curiosity won. Besides, much as she might hate to admit it, when Quentin said something was important it usually was.

Lord St. George was four years his sister's senior and like her was possessed of dark hair, excellent bone structure, and supreme self-confidence. He might lack the angelic charm of his cousin, Lord Christopher Paget, and his cravats might not be tied with quite the cachet achieved by his stepcousin, the Marquis of Carteret, but his name, his assurance, and his not inconsiderable wit had made him the acknowledged leader of his set.

"I must say this is a fine welcome," he remarked, holding open the breakfast parlour door. "I return to the bosom of my family after two months' absence—"

"Six weeks."

"—and no one makes an effort to see me."

"It's hardly my fault you chose not to dine at home on your first night back in London," Edwina retorted, moving past him into the room and laying down her gloves and crop, "nor that you came in even later than Mama and I did."

"I was hearing all the latest *on dits*. It seems rather a lot has happened since I left London." Lord St. George sampled his coffee, found it cold, and poured himself a fresh cup.

"I wish you would come to the point," Edwina said impatiently.

The viscount surveyed his sister critically. She was wearing a habit of deep blue, lavishly trimmed with black braid. The highstanding collar admirably became her long neck and the blue ostrich feather which ornamented her beaver hat curled fetchingly against her creamy skin.

"That's a remarkably fine rig-out," St. George observed. "Pity there were so few on hand to see it at this hour. You weren't keeping a rendezvous by any chance, were you?"

"Don't be a beast, Quentin. And if you won't tell me what you are about—"

"I simply thought that since Tony seems to have developed other interests, you might have done so as well," St. George said mildly.

Lady Edwina gave a short laugh. "Oh," she said, "is that all. Tony and I have never lived in each other's pockets."

St. George regarded his sister in some surprise. "Doesn't it bother you?"

"No, why should it—" Lady Edwina began, and then, in a rare burst of candour, "I own it did at first, a bit. But it's not as if it's the first time he's embarked on a flirtation. Mama advised me to do nothing. She said if I acted concerned I would only appear spiteful."

"Mama is a very wise woman. But in this case I rather think she may be too wise."

"That's quite clever, Quentin. What does it mean?"

"It means that when a confirmed rake suddenly begins lavishing attention on an unmarried young woman of no particular beauty, he is engaged in something very different from his usual flirtations."

Lady Edwina smiled. "Well, of course. I don't think even Tony would go as far with Philippa Davenport as he does with his married flirts."

"Not without a ring on her finger," St. George agreed dulcetly.

Edwina looked at him sharply. The most provoking thing—one of the most provoking things—about Quentin, she decided, regarding her brother across the breakfast table, was that one could never tell whether he was in earnest or merely being clever. He could break through her cool veneer as no one else could, but she always put up a good fight and in this case she was not yet ready to admit defeat. "You're quite out for once, Quentin. The flame is already beginning to dim. Tony left for Carteret last week and he still hasn't returned to town."

"Do you mean to say that the plain Miss Davenport has managed to drive Tony to the country at the height of the Season?" St. George demanded, setting down his fork. "This has gone farther than I realized. Take care, sister mine. Now that Waterford's been caught, there's a distinct dearth of dukes, and eligible marquises don't grow on trees. Unless you want to settle for an earl—or less—you'd best use your wits."

This was the last straw. At twenty, Edwina was not bothered by her single state. There were advantages to being married, of course, but there were also encumbrances and she was in no hurry to begin increasing. At least, that was how she had felt, secure in the knowledge that Tony would one day make her his marchioness. And yet they had never been formally betrothed. There might be some raised brows if he took another woman to wife, but Tony was the last person to cavil at a raised brow. And if Edwina could no longer count on marrying him—

She thought, with mounting panic and indignation, of the number of eligible offers she had refused in the past two years, and of the fact that there had perhaps been rather fewer of them this Season than in previous years.

"I knew you'd see sense," St. George said with approval,

134

reading her expression in the odious way he always could. "I daresay you'll manage quite handily, though mind you don't lose your temper. It's your besetting sin, you know, and it won't get you anywhere with Tony, no matter what that fool Easthampton said about the martial light in your eyes. Are you going? We were just beginning to see things eye to eye."

Lady Edwina had pushed back her chair and risen. The martial light was very much in her eyes and, were her thoughts not full of the errant Anthony, her brother might have been treated to one of her more spectacular bursts of temper. "Poor Quentin, you'll have to finish your breakfast alone. I have a battle strategy to plan." She picked up her gloves and crop. "Thank you for the warning."

"Don't mention it. Our sister's already made a shocking mésalliance, can't afford to have another in the family. By the way," he added casually, "speaking of mésalliances, I understand Tony isn't the only one who's fallen prey to infatuation."

"I told you I wasn't—oh, you mean Crispin and that chit from the country. She lives in Miss Davenport's house, you know."

"Does she? This is becoming more and more interesting." St. George leaned back in his chair. "Do you know who her brother is?"

"Mr. Ashton? Yes, I've seen him several times, he's been taking his sister about. I haven't been introduced, but Milly Brandon was and she's talked of nothing else ever since. He is rather attractive."

"I was thinking of his opinions, not his appearance."

"Well, the sister hardly looks a fire-breathing reformer," Edwina said, moving to the door, "and she's the one Crispin's been spending time with."

"A great deal of time. According to Trevelyn, Crispin's been shunning all his old haunts for the most insipid of entertainments. I suppose I shall have to do the same if I want to make the girl's acquaintance. Where are you and Mother engaged tonight?"

"We're going to the theatre with Aunt Aurelia. As Crispin was at some pains to attach himself to the party, I daresay Miss

Ashton will be there. I'm sure he'd be happy to introduce you, if you think it's worth an evening in Mama and Aunt Aurelia's company."

"It is, I own, not a pleasant prospect, but I think it must be endured. After all, Miss Ashton may become one of the family."

Edwina paused at the door, her brows raised.

"Metcalfe says Crispin considers himself betrothed to the girl," St. George explained.

Edwina was surprised, but she was in no mood to waste thought on Tony's younger brother. "I'll say this for Crispin, his taste is better than Tony's. She's pretty enough, if you care for the type."

"Not in general, though they can be amusing. And clever, more's the pity. It may be difficult to rescue Cris."

"Must he be rescued?" In Edwina's eyes the defection of her own putative fiancé was a crisis of uncommon order, but if Crispin chose to make a cake of himself that was quite his own affair.

"Good God, Edwina"—St. George sounded affronted—"I'm not going to stand by and let my cousin marry the sister of a dashed radical."

He returned to his breakfast, but something in his tone alerted his sister to danger. "Quentin, what are you—"

"Never mind." St. George reached for the *Morning Post* which he had pushed aside when he heard his sister return to the house. "You see to Tony, my dear. Leave Crispin to me."

Philippa stood in the doorway of Francesca's dressing room, a dissatisfied expression on her face. "What do you think?" she asked bluntly.

Francesca turned from her dressing table mirror, masking her surprise. The hour was advanced—she herself had already dismissed her maid and was just finishing her toilet—and she would have expected Philippa to have gone downstairs to the drawing room some twenty minutes since. She most certainly would not have expected Philippa to be soliciting advice on her appearance. At least, she would not have expected it before

136

Philippa met the Marquis of Carteret and Elliot Marsden.

"Very nice," Francesca said. "I've always liked that dress."

Philippa turned to the cheval glass and studied her gown, a fawn-coloured crêpe with short sleeves, a demure square neck, and a single flounce. Francesca's sea-green gown was also crêpe and also simpler than the prevailing mode, but the sleeves were puffs of embroidered net and the neckline, which left bare Francesca's elegant shoulders, was hardly demure.

"I feel a hopeless dowd," Philippa announced.

"No," said Francesca honestly, "though you could do with a bit more colour." She turned back to her dressing table, considered resorting to cosmetics, decided against it, and began to rummage through her jewel case. "Ah, yes, the very thing. Come here and take off those pearls. They're pretty enough, but you're quite right, something more dashing is called for." She stood up to give Philippa her seat at the dressing table and held out a pair of ruby pendant earrings set in gold filigree.

Philippa stared at the offering in surprise, started to protest, then laughed and followed her cousin's instructions. "There's a necklace as well," Francesca said, as Philippa removed her tiny pearl earrings, "but one doesn't want to be overpowering. There, a vast improvement, don't you think?"

Philippa looked into the glass and found to her surprise that she agreed with Francesca. The rubies caught the light and cast a warm glow over her skin, and her simple dress and plain hairstyle became an elegant background for the dramatic earrings. It was a subtle effect, but it did wonders for Philippa's morale. She turned to thank Francesca and was interrupted by an exclamation from the doorway.

"Oh, Philippa, they're perfect!" Claris flew across the room, her precipitate entrance having no effect on her blue-spotted jaconet nor the charming arrangement of her curls. She seized Philippa's hands and surveyed her with approval. Having grown up in a household in which every penny counted, Claris knew how much could be achieved with the simplest accessories. "What a pity Lord Carteret won't be at Drury Lane tonight," she sighed.

"Yes," Francesca agreed, with a slight smile, "but I daresay

137

Mr. Marsden will be there."

Philippa looked sharply at her cousin, then returned the smile. She was new enough to flirtation to find this sort of teasing rather embarrassing, but she had to admit she enjoyed it.

Claris was less well pleased. Lord Carteret's absence from town in the last few days, coupled with Mr. Marsden's continued attendance on Philippa, created a most unsatisfactory situation from Miss Ashton's point of view. Claris had made up her mind weeks ago—when she first saw Lord Carteret observing Philippa in the courtroom—that Philippa was to marry the marquis. It would be a splendid match, which Philippa certainly deserved, and if Philippa would then be able to smooth the way for Claris' own marriage to Crispin, well, that was so much the better. Mr. Marsden had no business interfering.

Still, careful observation of her sisters' romances had taught Claris that there was nothing like jealousy to pique a man's interest, so perhaps Mr. Marsden's pursuit of Philippa would bring Lord Carteret up to scratch.

Claris moved to the cheval glass to check her flounced skirt, while Francesca added some extra pins to Philippa's hair which had not come through all the excitement unscathed. Gerry, who had three sisters, came into the dressing room in the midst of all this and said it seemed quite like old times, and they all went down to dinner in very good spirits. Even Henry, who was dining with the family, partook of the mood, though to Philippa's disappointment he gave no indication that he noticed any change in her appearance. Lord Carteret and Mr. Marsden could have been counted on to pay her the most flattering of compliments, which no doubt was why recognition from Mr. Ashton would have meant rather more to her.

Conversation was general at the dinner table and in the carriage, but when they arrived at the theatre Gerry and Francesca were stopped by Corisande and Charles Ossulston, and Claris' attention was claimed by a trio of young gallants. Philippa made a remark calculated to take Mr. Ashton completely by surprise.

"I read your account of the meeting at Miss Neville's." She let her gaze stray over the crowd of elegantly dressed theatre-goers, but watched him carefully out of the corner of her eye.

"Did you?" If Mr. Ashton was surprised he hid it disgustingly well. "I didn't know you were in the habit of reading the *Register*."

"I'm not," Philippa said frankly. She turned to him, her chin slightly raised. "I wanted to see what you had to say."

"And?" Philippa could not be certain if there was a hint of laughter in Mr. Ashton's eyes or if she merely imagined it.

"I thought it interesting," she said, choosing her words with care. "But I wish you'd treated the subject a bit more—directly."

"Yes," said Mr. Ashton gravely, "so do I. But you must remember that not everyone shares your advanced views on the subject, Miss Davenport. A great many people would be more inclined to the opinion of your friend, the Marquis of Carteret. I believe Mr. Marsden is trying to get your attention."

It was a far more direct sally than Philippa's own, and, like most of Mr. Ashton's barbs, quite and maddeningly unanswerable. Not even a particularly flattering compliment from Mr. Marsden could restore Philippa to good humour before the play began. She spent most of the first act trying to think of an impressive counterattack.

She applauded mechanically at the end of the act, and it was some moments before she emerged from her thoughts and glanced around the box. Emily Cowper had come by with her most enduring lover, Lord Palmerston, the Secretary at War. They were talking to Gerry and Francesca about the Slave Registry bill which was being introduced in the House that evening. Mr. Ashton had disappeared. Claris was sitting quietly beside Philippa, but her eyes sparkled with anticipation. The reason for this was apparent when Lord Christopher entered their box a few moments later. But for once he did not seem bent on a tête-à-tête with Claris, for he was accompanied by Lady Edwina Thane and a gentleman who must be Lady Edwina's brother, the Viscount St. George.

From a box on the opposite side of the theatre, Lady

Carteret watched with astonishment and dismay as her beautiful niece, the woman who was to marry Anthony and become the next Marchioness of Carteret, shook hands with Philippa Davenport.

"I would not have thought it of Edwina," she said in a low voice.

"Nonsense, Aurelia." Lady Buckleigh responded to her sister in her usual bracing manner. "Edwina is curious, and you must admit that she has a right to be. Besides, whatever you think of Miss Davenport, you can hardly fault the family lineage. Of course Buckleigh didn't care for her father's politics, and her mother made herself the talk of the town with her second marriage, but there's never been any real scandal."

Lady Carteret sniffed and said that scandal or not she knew perfectly well what sort of things went on in Whig houses.

Lady Buckleigh looked from her daughter and Miss Davenport to Emily Cowper who was conversing with Miss Davenport's cousin. She had no moral objection to women like Lady Cowper or her late and equally promiscuous mother, Lady Melbourne, but she did consider that they showed a shocking lack of concern for the family line. To feel one had done one's duty by presenting one's husband with a single legitimate heir was flying in the face of providence, as had been demonstrated by the death of the Melbournes' eldest son several years before. No one with a particle of sense believed that William Lamb, the current heir, had been fathered by Lord Melbourne. Still, despite so many noted examples among the Whigs, one must be fair and admit that such behaviour was not confined to the Opposition. Lady Buckleigh said so.

Lady Carteret, quite unable to deny this, took refuge in another sniff and said that at least they could be glad that Anthony's interest was on the wane, for he had been absent from London for some days now.

"I shouldn't be so sanguine, Aurelia. If his interest was really on the wane he would have had no need to retire to the country in the first place." She glanced sharply at her sister. "I wonder you do not bestir yourself more in the matter."

"I told you, Catherine," the marchioness returned with dignity. "I have taken certain steps."

"What steps?" Lady Buckleigh demanded, not at all impressed.

"That I cannot disclose at the moment. You must trust that I have the matter in hand."

Lady Carteret was rarely in a position to take this tone with Catherine, and her enjoyment of the moment was only marred by the sight of Edwina still in conversation with the Davenport woman. "You should have prevented Edwina from speaking to Miss Davenport," she informed her sister.

Lady Buckleigh lifted her opera-glass and began to scan the other boxes. "You should have prevented Crispin from presenting Miss Davenport to Edwina."

Lord Christopher had been surprised when Edwina asked to meet Philippa Davenport, but he himself was eager to present Claris to Quentin, so it fit in nicely with his plans. It was most imperative, as Crispin had impressed upon his beloved, that Quentin support their betrothal, for his father, Earl Buckleigh, was Crispin's guardian. Not that there was any doubt Quentin would be on their side, he was the best of good fellows and was sure to adore Claris as much as Crispin did. Well, perhaps not quite that much, but they would no doubt get on famously.

Accordingly, Crispin had made his excuses to his mother and aunt and shepherded his two cousins to the Scotts' box. Having performed the necessary introductions, he drew Quentin and Claris off to one side, leaving Edwina to become acquainted with Miss Davenport.

There was a momentary silence while the two ladies took stock of each other. Lady Edwina's first impression left her both disappointed and alarmed. On close inspection Miss Davenport was not at all the drab little thing Edwina had thought her. She would never be able to rival Edwina in beauty, but she dressed with style—the combination of her simple dress and dramatic earrings almost made Edwina regret her ruched skirt and frilled bodice—and she carried herself with real distinction.

Philippa was more sanguine. She could guess at the reasons for Lady Edwina's visit and she retained enough detachment to derive considerable amusement from the scene. She waited with a good deal of interest to see what Lady Edwina could possibly find for them to talk about.

"What do you think of the play, Miss Davenport?"

"I must confess I find it hard to understand what a sensible woman like Helena sees in Bertram," Philippa admitted.

"Ah, but that is easy. Position. And fortune, of course."

"You think that is all it is? It would take more, surely, to inspire such passionate poetry."

"She is certainly single-minded in her determination to wed him." Edwina unfurled a small fan of painted silk which matched her lemon-yellow gown. "Tell me, Miss Davenport— I'm sure we both know how the play ends—what chances do you give a marriage such as theirs, a marriage which is founded on a trick?"

"I rather think its success depends on how much and how quickly Betram grows up."

"Then you lay all the difficulties at his door?"

"His behaviour is far from exemplary," Philippa replied with spirit. Any member of her family might have warned Lady Edwina that Philippa could argue more passionately about fictional personages than most people could about real ones.

Lady Edwina, however, had a different objective in mind. "Yes," she agreed. "But I can't help but think that if Helena really loved him she would leave him to a woman of his own sort. He would be much happier—and for that matter so would she."

Philippa started to retort that one could not possibly know this was the case, but she saw the measuring look in Lady Edwina's eyes and realized with a jolt that they were not talking about Shakespeare's characters at all.

It was not surprising that Lord Carteret's attentions to her in the preceding weeks had aroused some jealousy on Lady Edwina's part, and Philippa had assumed that this was the reason for Lady Edwina's visit. But it had never occurred to Philippa that Carteret's cousin might take her seriously as a rival. Dear God, could Lady Edwina actually consider her a competitor for the position of Lord Carteret's marchioness? True, the marquis' interest was enduring longer than Philippa had expected—at least, it had endured until his departure for the country—but he could have no more intention of offering for her than—than she would have of accepting him if he did so.

But here Philippa was brought up short. It was true that she assumed she would never marry, but that had not always been the case. When she made her début she had expected quite the opposite. But by the end of her first Season she had faced the fact that no men—no interesting men—paid her much heed. And so she had ceased to think much about marriage, but more from lack of options than lack of interest.

And now? Philippa had suspected that Lord Carteret's departure for the country meant he was tired of the chase, but Lady Edwina's conversation indicated that she thought otherwise. Could she be right? She had known Carteret much longer than Philippa had done. And if Lady Edwina was right . . . ? What, Philippa wondered, would she do if Lord Carteret—it was absurd, of course, to think that he would—but what would she do if Lord Carteret, against all expectation, offered her his coronet?

And what about Mr. Marsden, who had not taken himself off to the country and who seemed motivated by more than desire for novelty? Philippa had determined to enjoy his attentions, as she did Lord Carteret's, but she had never thought that those attentions might have consequences for the future. What would she do if Mr. Marsden made her an offer? And what, oh what, would she do if both men did?

For the first time, Philippa considered her two suitors side by side and faced the disturbing realization that she could not possibly say which she preferred.

Philippa returned Lady Edwina's gaze, her own equally appraising. "As to that," she said, "I rather think I should have to know more about the people in question before I could form a competent judgement."

Soon after Lord Christopher brought his cousins to the Scotts' box, Elliot Marsden entered the anteroom to find Henry Ashton leaning against the wall, seemingly lost in thought.

"Evening, Ashton."

"Servant, Marsden. Go in by all means, but I think you'll

143

find it rather crowded."

A peal of laughter and the threads of several conversations, drifting through the partially closed curtains confirmed his words. Marsden hesitated, wondering if Miss Davenport was engaged, and if so with whom, and whether or not she would welcome his appearance.

"She's talking with Lady Edwina Thane," Henry volunteered.

Marsden turned to him, failing to conceal his surprise.

"Yes," Henry agreed, "I thought it odd as well. But then there's no accounting for behaviour, is there?"

"No," Marsden conceded, his thoughts still on Miss Davenport. "No, I suppose there isn't."

"That is," Henry continued meditatively, "there's no accounting for it based on what one can observe. I imagine the explanation would be clear enough if one was privy to all the facts. Take your own case, for instance."

"My own case?" What on earth could Miss Davenport be finding to say to Lady Edwina? Marsden wondered. If he joined them would she—

"Yes, you seem a straightforward enough fellow, and yet you quite baffle me. What's your game precisely?"

Marsden stared at Henry, all questions about Philippa Davenport forgotten. Having ascertained that Ashton could not be reckoned a suitor of Miss Davenport's, Marsden had spared him little thought. It appeared that he had made a grave mistake. He couldn't imagine what the devil the fellow could be driving at—or why—but clearly it behoved him to discover more. And to tread warily in the process. Ashton was on good terms with Miss Davenport's cousin. "I'm not sure I take your meaning, Ashton," Marsden said, keeping his tone easy.

"You represented Lady Carteret in the libel trial," Henry returned, his manner equally friendly.

"Her solicitor engaged me."

"Quite. And after the trial I nearly collided with you on the steps of Carteret House. I don't know if you recall the occasion. You looked rather preoccupied."

"I daresay it was a social call. I am somewhat acquainted with the marchioness."

"So I understand." Henry studied the moulding on the opposite wall. "But I think you understate the matter. I've heard her described as your patroness."

"She has been kind to me," Marsden said evenly. "Our families were acquainted."

"I didn't know that. But I can readily see that Lady Carteret's assistance could be invaluable to you. Particularly if you stand for Parliament. Miss Davenport says you have political ambitions."

Marsden smiled dryly. "Every man has ambitions, Ashton. Men like me—or you—who have to make their own way in the world are forced to be rather more aggressive in pursuing them."

"Certainly," Henry agreed affably, turning to face Marsden directly. "Which makes me wonder why a sensible man like you would risk offending his patroness by so publicly courting a young woman whom the patroness has—equally publicly— made it apparent she regards as her bitterest enemy."

Marsden returned Henry's regard. "What's your game, Ashton?" he asked bluntly.

"Purely professional. Inconsistent behaviour fascinates me. The stuff of good novels, you know."

"In that case, it would be most injudicious of me to respond. The issue of libel has been thrashed out quite enough for one Season. Pray tell Miss Davenport that I did not wish to interrupt her conversation and will pay my compliments later in the evening."

Marsden returned to the corridor, but Henry remained in the anteroom and was still standing there a moment or so later when Philippa came through the curtains from the box. "I'm afraid you've just missed Mr. Marsden," Henry informed her. "He asked me to tell you he'll come round later."

"You've been missing Lady Edwina and Lord St. George," Philippa returned, sitting on the low couch which had been placed in the anteroom for spectators who grew fatigued with the play. "Are you sure you don't want to go in? I'm certain Claris would be happy to present you."

"Thank you, Miss Davenport, but *it is an honour that I dream not of.*"

Philippa grinned, and felt her spirits begin to improve. Her conversation with Lady Edwina had left her disturbed. Francesca, understanding the symptoms if not the cause, had appropriated Lady Edwina and allowed Philippa to escape into the anteroom. Philippa had not thought to find Mr. Ashton there, but strangely his presence did not disturb her. In fact, it was rather a relief to talk to him. She was, she discovered, glad that Mr. Marsden had not remained to speak with her and very glad that Lord Carteret had taken himself off to the country. She would as soon not face either of her suitors—what an odd term that was—until she had a chance to sort out the exact nature of her feelings for them. But Mr. Ashton was another matter. Her feelings for him were blissfully uncomplicated.

"Did you mean what you said about being interested in my article on Miss Neville's meeting?" Mr. Ashton asked, sitting beside her.

"Of course. Why shouldn't I have meant it?"

"I once heard you say that falsehoods are the basis of our social intercourse."

"Certainly, but with you I know I need not bother with social niceties. Didn't I seem interested?"

"Very." Mr. Ashton was smiling and his tone, if not quite admiring, was certainly friendly. "So I expect you'd be even more interested in some pamphlets my friend Murray is having printed as a result of the meeting. They were written by Mrs. Robinson, and I think you will find that they address the subject very directly indeed."

Philippa's eyes began to dance. "That I should most certainly like to see. Will you bring one next time you call in Green Street?"

"I'd be happy to. Or I could take you by Murray's office. I think he'd be flattered, though of course he won't admit it."

Philippa seized on this offer. She was curious and she liked what she had seen of Mr. Murray—he had won her heart by telling Mr. Ashton that he enjoyed her books—but most of all this was the perfect opportunity to give her thoughts a new direction. No member of the fashionable world was likely to be anywhere in the vicinity of Gordon Murray's office, and for a few hours she could escape from Claris' teasing about Lord

Carteret and any calls Elliot Marsden might make in Green Street.

"I'd like that," she said. "Would tommorow suit?"

Henry concealed his surprise with an effort. Pleased as he had been at her response to the meeting at Miss Neville's, he had not expected her to accept his new invitation quite so eagerly. Miss Davenport had altered her appearance this evening—to considerable effect, he admitted. Perhaps other things were changing as well.

"Tomorrow would suit admirably, Miss Davenport."

Chapter 10

Anthony returned to town in an unsettled frame of mind, having reached no clear decision about Miss Davenport. He was not ready to give her up, of that at least he was sure. Philippa Davenport had none of the ripe charms of Georgina Nelliston, but he could not stop thinking about her. There was a simplicity and directness in her manner that quite enchanted him, and though she was distressingly independent he longed to protect her.

Above all, he wanted her to notice him. Anthony would not have phrased it in quite this way, for he had never been other than the pivotal point of any group in which he found himself, but he was aware that the pleasure she found in his company was no more than the pleasure she appeared to take in that of Elliot Marsden or that writer fellow Ashton. There were even moments when he thought she would as lief be companioned by her dog as by any of them.

Marriage. The thought had come to him at Carteret Park as he rode dutifully around the estate with his bailiff who was overjoyed that the young marquis had taken the time to make the journey to Worcestershire at the height of the Season. Anthony knew that he would get married someday. The state had nothing to recommend it, but a gentleman had to leave an heir. Edwina was, of course, available. She was undeniably a handsome woman and she would make a discreet and tolerant wife. Had he not known her since the cradle he might have found her worth the chase, but he had never taken particular pleasure in his cousin's company. The mystery was not there, and the element of surprise.

So it was not with the image of Edwina Thane by his side that Anthony rode and looked at calves and foals and piglets and observed the progress of the north fencing. Philippa Davenport would be constantly surprising. But did he really want to take this unlikely and uncomfortable woman to wife?

After four days of indecision he set out again for London, spending one night on the road near High Wycombe where he drank two bottles of claret to no useful effect. He arrived in the capital before noon and drove directly to Miss Neville's house where some discreet inquiries produced the name and address of Gordon Murray. By half past one, he brought the curricle to a halt at the entrance to Portpool Lane.

Anthony had not been in this particular street before. It was a depressing bywater off the livelier stream of Gray's Inn Lane. Handing the reins to his groom with an injunction to wait—an unnecessary addition, for the marquis' groom was used to waiting on his lordship's pleasure—Anthony strode down the narrow street in search of number 15.

The house was a mean one, with a print shop below attended only by a thin boy with ink-stained hands and the look of a ferret. Anthony tossed him a coin and was rewarded with the information that the writing gentleman could be found on the first floor front.

The stairs were narrow and worn and Anthony took them two at a time. Three paces brought him to a door which was slightly ajar. Without preamble, he flung it wide and entered Gordon Murray's domain.

It was only at this point that Anthony had some misgivings about the wisdom of his visit. Murray seemed larger than Anthony remembered him. He overflowed his chair as his table overflowed with papers and newsprint and books and crusts of bread. There was a dark stain on the carpet near his chair and a smell of stale wine mingled with the scent of freshly printed paper. Murray's hair was rumpled and rose in a feathery grey halo around his head. He was hunched over the table, pen in hand, scratching rapidly on a sheet of paper.

"Come in, come in," Murray said without looking up, "just

149

a line or two to put a period to the argument." He wrote a few words, then paused, pen in mid-air, and stared at the paper in front of him. A drop of ink fell unheeded on the manuscript. Anthony waited, feeling obscurely out of place.

"Aha!" Murray dipped his pen in the inkpot and scratched rapidly over the paper, read the lines with satisfaction, then threw down his pen and turned round. If he was surprised at the identity of his visitor, he did not show it.

"Ah, m'lord, good of you to come by." Murray struggled to his feet, waved a hand at a nearby chair, then subsided into his own. He picked up a neglected cigar which was threatening to burn the edge of the table and drew on it gratefully. A long ash fell on his trousers and he brushed it off absently, meanwhile staring at Anthony with a bland face and shrewd eyes. He made an ineffectual effort to wave the smoke away from his guest. "Do you mind?"

Anthony said that he was not averse to the smell of tobacco.

"Can't work without them, myself." Murray patted his coat, then rummaged among the detritus of his work table. "Have another one here someplace, can't seem to lay m'hands on it."

Anthony assured him that he had no present desire to smoke. He had not yet made known the reason for his visit and was not sure that he could properly explain it. He had come to Murray because he was a friend of Ashton's, and Ashton had brought Miss Davenport to the meeting at Miss Neville's house, and Miss Davenport had taken an unseemly interest in the events of that meeting, but he could not quite say so.

Murray continued to rummage through the papers on his table, the cigar clenched in his teeth. "Aha, I thought so," he exclaimed with satisfaction as he unearthed a large sheaf of pamphlets which seemed freshly printed. "You might be interested in this, m'lord, it's by our friend Mrs. Robinson."

Anthony took one unwillingly into his hands where it promptly soiled his York tan gloves. Mrs. Robinson was hardly a friend, at least of his, and he resented the imputation.

Murray leaned back in his chair and stretched his short legs out before him. His feet were encased in felt slippers and his waistcoat, one or two buttons left undone for comfort, gaped over his sizeable paunch. "Well written, if I say so myself.

Helped her with it, but the tone is all her own. Dedicated to married ladies, so no one can take objection."

Anthony doubted this last was true. He had considerable objections himself. He put the offending pamphlet back on the table. "I can't say I agree with you, Murray. A public speech is bad enough, but once in print there's no telling whose hands will find it."

"But that's the beauty of it, ol' chap." Anthony winced. He had not been spoken to in that avuncular tone since he was fifteen, but it was difficult to take offence at the genial Murray. He could not quite place Murray. He had the accent of a gentleman and the manners of a boor, but there was no doubt that he considered himself every inch the equal of the Marquis of Carteret.

Murray placed his cigar on the edge of the table. "Thing is, we need to get the widest possible circulation. Married, unmarried, it's all the same. And it's the unmarried girls who need it most, can't go peopling the world with unwanted brats just for gentlemen's pleasure. Not fair to the brats. Not fair to the girls. Deuced awkward for the gentlemen."

Anthony smiled in spite of himself. "It's not that I don't recognize the problem," he began, "but—"

"Ah, thought you would. There's more in your upper storey than you let on. Had some dealings with your father once. Clever man. Can't say I liked him, though."

Anthony had not much liked his father either, but this was not a remark he would ordinarily have let pass. He was silent and wondered why. Murray took liberties he would not have tolerated in even his close friends. But if Murray saw himself as Anthony's equal, he saw Anthony as his own. There was no censure in his manner, and no condescension. And Murray wanted nothing from him. It was a shade unsettling, not unlike the feelings evoked by Philippa Davenport.

Anthony turned this idea around in his head, conscious that he was on the verge of a discovery. He had lost the thread of Murray's discourse, and it was with difficulty that he brought his attention back to what was being said.

"So you see what I mean. Girls have to defend themselves, can't expect fair treatment from their seducers, so what have

151

you?" He raised his shoulders in an expressive gesture. "Mrs. Robinson."

Anthony picked up the pamphlet once more and weighed it in his hand. He was a man of some experience and the information was hardly new to him. Nor, he suspected, to many women of fashion who had probably brought back the knowledge from Paris. He was not a prude and had no objection to the spread of such knowledge among married women, provided the information was spread discreetly. Word of mouth was how such things should be done. As for the lower orders, he could see the justice of Murray's argument, perhaps even for unmarried girls, though he suspected it would only enhance their lewd behaviour. But to talk of such things openly, in public meetings and in public print, to subject gently bred young women who were as yet unmarried to sordid explanations of things they should neither know nor desire to know . . . He put the pamphlet down once more. "Mrs. Robinson is a dangerous woman."

"Oh, my stars, yes." Surprisingly, Murray agreed with him. "Exactly, m'lord. She stirs things up, don't she? Good, suspect you need stirring up. We all need stirring up a bit now and then."

"Some things, Murray, should not be stirred."

"Ah," said Murray, as though the idea had just occurred to him, "you're thinking of the little Davenport girl. Don't worry about her, she's not been corrupted. Girls know more than they let on. Remember her face? She wasn't surprised, just eager for the details."

That had been all too true, but it did not make it right. Anthony struggled to find the words to express his concern. "It's—it's indelicate."

"Bosh! Think of your mistresses. What of their delicacy of mind?"

Anthony had to admit that they showed scant acquaintance with that commodity. In fact, he was frequently amazed at the readiness with which women, when won, threw off all trappings of gentility. Georgina, now, was a woman whose appetites matched his own. But it was hard to think of Philippa Davenport in the same class with Georgina Nelliston. Or—and

152

this was a new idea—were all women so underneath? It was a disturbing thought. On the other hand, it might mean there would be compensations in the married state. "So you see nothing wrong with Miss Davenport's"—he chose the word with care—"enthusiasm for the subject?"

"Lord, no. Thank God she has the mind and energy to be enthusiastic about something. Better that than a passion for horses."

Horses, Anthony thought privately, would be a far more suitable subject. Or children. Her own, of course—they always settled a woman. Anthony found it somehow reassuring that the clever Miss Davenport might only be playing at new ideas and in the end would settle down to the production of heirs. Not that Anthony wanted a large family. Two or three boys would ensure the line, and beyond that he didn't care. And after all, if a woman weren't constantly breeding, she might make a more interesting companion. He eyed the pamphlets once more.

"Take them, take them," Murray said. "I have plenty more. I daresay you have some friends who might put them to good use. We need to reach the men as well as the women."

Anthony's mouth twitched. He had a sudden vision of entering the serene precincts of White's with a sheaf of pamphlets in his hand. He smiled and shook his head.

While Anthony sat in contemplation and the ash burned longer on Murray's cigar, the door was pushed open and a slender boy with a mop of curly black hair entered the room. He took a few steps forward, then stopped and stared with unfriendly eyes at the room's occupants. Behind him came a fair-haired woman followed by a little girl of perhaps four years with a long pale face and straight fair hair. The woman held a still younger child in her arms and carried another in her protruding belly.

Startled, Anthony stood up and swept off his hat, a courtesy he had not hitherto extended during his visit.

The woman looked uncertainly from one man to the other. "Mr. Murray? I come from Mrs. Robinson."

By this time Murray too was on his feet. He shuffled across the worn carpet and led her to the chair just vacated by the marquis, seating her as though she were a duchess.

Which she clearly was not. Her voice was genteel enough, and the stuff of her gown was of good quality. But the gown itself was soiled and neither its colour, a brilliant red, nor its cut, which gave promise of the soft and ample breasts beneath, seemed suited to her condition. Her hair, her best feature, cascaded luxuriantly beneath the plumes of her bonnet. Her eyes—slightly protuberant and of a curious pale blue—looked appraisingly from Anthony to Murray, then settled on the latter as the proper object of her visit.

Anthony took up a stance in front of a bookcase and studied her. The woman must be an object of Mrs. Robinson's charity, like the pale girl that lady had befriended at Miss Neville's house, perhaps a castoff mistress. Or she might be—yes, that was more likely—a follower of Mrs. Robinson's profession. Strange, he had never thought of those women having children, or at least having children close at hand. He had supposed that such accidents were left conveniently in the country.

Having reached these conclusions, Anthony thought it prudent to withdraw. He had no wish for another encounter with a woman of Mrs. Robinson's ilk.

His way was barred, however, by the young boy who had come over to inspect the fine gentleman and stood now not two paces away. He looked perhaps six or seven years of age, and his serious, fine-boned face stared up into Anthony's own with a mixture of curiosity and insolence.

"Bertie, come here," the woman said wearily, and Bertie retreated a step, not taking his eyes off Anthony's face. The elder of the two girls came to stand beside him, and the youngest also came to investigate. Being unsteady on her feet, she fell down in front of Anthony with a suddenness that made her sob. Then her face cleared and she reached a grubby hand for the tassels on Anthony's boots.

Anthony resisted an urge to step over the child and flee the room. "Pick up your sister, boy," he said in a commanding voice, "and return her to your mother."

Surprised, the boy hastened to obey.

The way now clear, Anthony prepared to take his leave.

154

"Madam." He made the fair-haired woman the slightest bow. "Murray, your servant." And with that he put his hat on his head and made for the door.

His hand was on the latch when the woman uttered two words that stopped him dead in his tracks. "Tony Paget."

No, Anthony thought in despair, not another!

He would have ignored the summons, but generations of training in politeness, even to whores, had left their mark.

The woman rose and came forward.

"Madam?" he inquired coldly.

"I thought it was you," she said, all traces of weariness vanished. "You must be Lord Carteret now."

In her youth, he thought, she would have been quite pretty. "You have the advantage of me, madam. I don't believe we have met."

"Mrs. Mecham," Murray supplied helpfully.

"The name is unknown to me. Madam. Murray, once again, good day." Anthony turned to the door to find Bertie standing defiantly in front of it. "Step aside, sir," he commanded, but the boy held firm.

"You do know me, Lord Carteret, and I will have you acknowledge it." Mrs. Mecham's voice had grown hard. "And I will have you acknowledge the boy in front of you who is your own image."

Anthony swung round in astonishment and even Murray was moved to protest.

Mrs. Mecham quickly followed her initial assault. "Look at him," she cried, "and you will see the justice of what I say!"

His son? Anthony stared at the boy and wavered. No, the thing was impossible. "I do not bear responsibility for every black-haired brat in London. I repeat, madam, I have never known you."

Bertie had come to stand by his mother and Anthony's eyes strayed to him involuntarily. He had something suspiciously like the Paget nose. If not himself, could it have been his father? Good God, was the child before him his own brother?

"Jenny," the woman said unexpectedly, her tone more friendly. "Swinforth's Jenny. You remember now, love, don't you? We had a bit of a ran-tan at his box in Suffolk."

Anthony remembered. It had been seven or eight years ago. Swinforth was a casual acquaintance whom Anthony had known at school and whom he had never particularly liked. He had ignored his invitations until the time when, frustrated at the failure of an expected liaison, he had agreed to make one of a large party that Swinforth had down for the races. They had stayed drunk for the better part of a week, and there had been several complaisant girls who were passed around. But Anthony could not recall this particular one, and had she been there he would not have bedded her. Even in those days, he was fastidious.

The woman was trying to blackmail him. If she genuinely believed he had fathered her child, she had had many years to press her claim. The fact that she had not done so, that she had never made a move to approach him, argued against its justice. And for a woman of her kind to accuse any one man in particular was outrageous. Anthony felt a swell of righteous anger. He made a move toward the door. Then he looked at Bertie and wavered. Caught between indignation and doubt, Anthony was transfixed.

Mrs. Mecham watched him closely, shrewdly gauging the play of emotions across his face—the recognition, the anger, the final uncertainty. Then her eyes closed. She took a tentative step, swayed, and—whether in calculation or in consequence of her condition—fell to the floor in a faint. In response, her eldest child—who had been watching the duel with scant comprehension but who knew that the well-dressed gentleman harboured some ill-feeling toward his mother—leaped at Anthony and dug his teeth into the marquis' wrist.

Resolutely pushing aside thoughts of her two suitors, Philippa prepared to enjoy her visit to Gordon Murray. Whatever her differences with Henry Ashton, it was her head he had challenged, not her heart. And Philippa was not afraid of new ideas.

They had come in a hackney along High Holborn, then at Philippa's suggestion had descended at Gray's Inn Lane and walked along that thoroughfare toward their destination. It

156

was not the first time Philippa had been in this part of London, but she was seeing it with new eyes. Though it was no more crowded than the fashionable streets to which she was accustomed, the feel of the place was different. The pace was quicker, there was a greater sense of purpose in the air, and colour and sound and smell seemed harsher and more alive.

They walked past the bulk of Gray's Inn and then the gardens beyond. Philippa looked with interest at the black-gowned men moving by on the street and wondered if Elliot Marsden was among them. But no, they were too far north, his chambers were in Middle Temple. She was relieved, for though she was curious about the life he led, a life which seemed filled with urgency and resolution, she did not want to see him today.

"Down here," Henry said, leading her into a narrower street where the buildings were smaller and meaner and the cobbles rough under the thin leather of her shoes. He guided her expertly around a cart and past a knot of men quarreling in a doorway. "There it is, the fourth house on the left. Murray has his office above. His lodgings too at the moment, I'm afraid. His last fine was heavy and near ruined him."

Philippa looked up at the windows of Murray's office. "It seems an innocuous place to give rise to something as fierce and splendid as *The Phoenix*."

Henry laughed. "Gordon's ferocity is in his head." They were standing at the edge of the street, waiting for an ancient berline to pass so they could cross. "The place is convenient," Henry went on, "there's a print shop below and the man's a friend, though he doesn't do all of Gordon's work. Printers stand in as much danger as publishers, and they tend to move frequently."

The carriage moved on, its driver cursing at the carts and pedestrians that had blocked its movement. Henry took Philippa's arm and led her across the street. Neither noticed the man walking toward them until he halted abruptly in the middle of the road, raised his hat and called Philippa's name.

She turned round. Her heart gave a leap and then sank. It was Elliot Marsden, and it was most unfair. She did not wish to see him, not now when her head was full of printers and disreputable newspapers and his presence could be nothing but an unwelcome distraction.

But she greeted him pleasantly, noting the faint air of calcuation in his eyes as he looked from her to Mr. Ashton. She could not see Ashton's face, but she was surprised by the coolness of his voice as he greeted Marsden.

The moment passed quickly. Marsden bowed slightly and might have passed on had not their attention been diverted by a thin boy with ink-stained hands who erupted out of the print shop door. "Mr. Ashton!" he called. "Mr. Ashton, come quickly. They be screaming up above, and I daren't leave the press."

"Wait below," Henry said and dashed toward the shop.

Philippa of course did not wait. As she reached the doorway she saw that the boy had retreated behind the press and Mr. Ashton was nowhere in sight. The boy pointed and Philippa ran up the stairs. There were heavier footsteps behind her, and she knew with certainty that it was not the boy who followed, but Elliot Marsden.

They paused at the top of the stairs to get their bearings, then moved toward an open door at the front of the house. Philippa had a confused impression of movements and shouts and the smell of stale cigars and stale wine. Then the figures took familiar form. Mr. Ashton was holding a struggling boy beneath the arms while the lad shouted and kicked wildly at his shins. Another man was engaged with a small girl with straight fair hair who appeared to have wrapped herself around his leg. Philippa looked beyond the men and saw a figure on the floor clad in an improbable shade of red. It was a woman and Mr. Murray was on his knees beside her, exhorting her to "sit up, madam, pray sit up." And beyond them, under a table at the far end of the room, a very small girl was carefully shredding a cigar butt and putting the pieces in her mouth.

Philippa was across the room in a moment. Talking all the while in a soothing voice, she removed the remains of the butt and carefully cleaned out the small girl's mouth. The child suffered this ministration without response, then stood up and reached for the edge of the table, her hand outstretched for whatever object might be at hand. Philippa moved the inkpot out of reach, then picked the child up and turned back to the others. The little girl spoke for the first time. "Mama's sick."

That much was clear. The woman was still on the floor, Murray and Marsden kneeling beside her, but she was recovering from her faint. Her bonnet had come askew and, as Philippa watched, Mr. Marsden undid the ribbons, then picked her up and carried her to the largest chair in the room which, by its position in front of the work table, must be Mr. Murray's own. Mr. Marsden bent over her and inquired gently about her condition while Mr. Murray hovered around her chair, his face creased with worry.

Shifting the child in her arms, Philippa turned to see how the other men were faring with the older children and once more found herself staring into the eyes of the Marquis of Carteret.

She might have known. Scarce wondering at the oddity of his being in the room at all, Philippa moved forward to aid him with the fair-haired child. The girl was now disentangled from his boots but was trying to bite his arm. Mr. Ashton had barely subdued the black-haired boy who was threatening further violence if he ever got his hands free.

It took a few moments to bring order to the room. The woman, Philippa learned, was Mrs. Mecham, and these were indeed her children. The little girl that Philippa was still holding in her arms was known as Dee, the fair-haired girl was Alice, and the boy was Bertie. Bertie had been defending his mother's honour, for reasons Philippa could not ascertain, and had bitten Lord Carteret on the wrist. When Mr. Ashton removed him, Alice had rushed forward to take her brother's place. It was not clear whether their mother had fainted as a consequence of this attack or whether the attack was a reaction to her fall.

Murray, who had been genuinely concerned about Mrs. Mecham, sat down heavily and wiped his head with a large handkerchief. Marsden had disappeared which Philippa considered tactful. But he reappeared a few minutes later bearing a glass of wine for Mrs. Mecham which, Philippa concluded, showed some presence of mind.

Bertie was brought reluctantly to stop kicking Mr. Ashton. He returned to his mother and stationed himself behind her chair, from which position he glared at the assembled company. Alice went to stand beside him, her face solemn and without any trace of curiosity. Philippa put Dee in their care and went to inspect Lord Carteret's wrist. He protested that it was nothing, but she demanded soap and water to cleanse the wound lest it fester and bound his wrist with her own handkerchief.

"I could almost be grateful for the brat," Anthony said, "to have you attend me so."

"A pretty speech, Lord Carteret. But I might not be so conveniently near next time, so I strongly advise you to stay out of the way of small boys' teeth."

"It was only a misunderstanding."

"It was no misunderstanding, sir," Mrs. Mecham, who had been following this scene with narrowed eyes, now found her voice. Ignoring Murray's protests, she pushed herself out of the chair and came forward. Her eyes swept the room, then came to rest on Philippa. "Your friend—I trust he's no more than a friend, dearie, for he's shown himself no gentleman—would deny that he knows me, that he ever knew me, when I have proof right in this room that he once knew me very well indeed. Come here, Bertie!"

Obedient, the boy came to her side and Mrs. Mecham thrust him forward. "Look at them and deny it!"

Startled, Philippa looked involuntarily from Bertie to Lord Carteret. It was true, they were something like, with the same colouring and the same lean grace. She was not surprised nor particularly offended. Philippa knew that such things happened, and even if she had not, her afternoon at Miss Neville's would have fully enlightened her. If there was a chance that the boy was his son, Lord Carteret should certainly acknowledge him and do something toward his education.

But Carteret was not about to acknowledge the child. "I do deny it!"

"You deny that you have known me?"

"I may once have made your acquaintance, madam, but I have never known you. Not in any sense. Nor would I ever be likely to," he added under his breath. His voice was bitter, but his eyes kept straying to the boy as though he would convince

160

himself that the accusation was not true. Philippa watched him with concern. She would have to bring him to a sense of his obligations.

Marsden spoke up unexpectedly. "Can you prove that he is the boy's father, Mrs. Mecham?"

"Can Lord Carteret prove that he is not?" Mrs. Mecham returned.

"Well, we seem to be at something of an impasse, don't we?" Murray's voice was genial. He was the only member of the group seated, and he regarded them all with the interest of a playgoer watching a drama unfold, caring only that he be amused. Dee sat by his feet, trying to remove his slippers.

Mrs. Mecham, despite her bravado, was not well and Philippa urged her back to her chair. Here she turned tearful and begged Philippa to intercede with Lord Carteret on her behalf. Philippa stayed by her side, uttering soothing words. Carteret must not be allowed to walk away from the consequences of his acts. She looked round to tell him so, but he had moved to the other end of the room and was conversing, improbably, with Henry Ashton.

Henry wanted the matter resolved. He had no love for Carteret, but there was an issue of justice involved. So he took the marquis aside and spoke to him hastily. "You can walk away from this, Carteret, but I don't advise you to do so. I think," he added deliberately, "that Miss Davenport would be disappointed."

This last argument appeared to have some force. "What would she have me do?"

"Acknowledge the child, if it's yours."

"It can't be."

"But you know the woman?"

"She says so. It's possible, I won't deny it, though I don't recall her face. There were a lot of us there, we'd gone for the races and people were in and out of the house all week. I know what you're thinking, Ashton, but I didn't, not with this one." Anthony's face was grim. "And I won't be taken in."

Henry had some sympathy for his predicament. It would be hard to prove. "When?"

Anthony was sure now, for he had been thinking of little else

161

the past quarter-hour. "Eight years ago. I was twenty-two."

Henry nodded. "Wait here." He left Carteret and moved to the centre of the room. "Bertie, come here. I need to talk to you."

The boy glanced at his mother, but she was occupied with the lady and the gentleman who had carried her to the chair. He hesitated, then came forward slowly and stared with suspicious eyes at the man who had restrained him just a few minutes ago.

Henry dropped down to the boy's level. "Bertie, how did you get here? Did you walk?"

The man's voice was gentle. The boy nodded.

"Your mother isn't well. When you leave, I want you to see that she takes a carriage." He pressed some coins into the boy's hand. "I can see that you take good care of your mother and sisters. That's not easy at your age."

"I'm nearly six," the boy said with a touch of pride.

Henry smiled, but his heart sank. He sent the boy back to his mother, then got to his feet and motioned Carteret to join him. They crossed the room and stood before Mrs. Mecham. "I am afraid, ma'am," Henry said, "that you are attempting to extort money under false pretences."

Philippa gasped and reached for Mrs. Mecham's hand.

"I protest, sir," that lady said.

"Lord Carteret admits that he once stayed in a house where you may have been present, but he denies that any intimacy occurred. On this point I make no judgement between you. But the occasion that brought you and Lord Carteret together was eight years ago, and your son admits to no more than six. He's a clever lad and looks old for his age, but you know quite well that he was not fathered by Lord Carteret." Henry turned on his heel and walked away.

Mrs. Mecham stared after him with hard eyes, then took refuge in tears.

Confused and angry, Philippa went after Henry. "I did not expect that of you," she said, her voice shaking.

He looked at her in surprise. "I thought you believed in the truth, Miss Davenport. The child is clearly not Carteret's. You would have her bleed him?"

162

"No, of course not. But—" She stopped, not knowing how to put her feelings into words. She would hardly have expected Ashton to take Carteret's side, nor would she have expected him to treat Mrs. Mecham so harshly, no matter what she was. Perhaps especially because of what she was.

She was about to say as much, but Lord Carteret had come to thank Ashton for his intervention. Then he turned to her to take his leave, apologizing for the unseemly episode she had witnessed. Philippa gave him her hand without comment, obscurely disappointed. Carteret did not spare a glance for the woman who had accused him, now deep in conversation with Gordon Murray, nor for the boy who might have been his son.

As the marquis reached the door, Murray called on him to wait. Pushing himself out of his chair, he took a sheaf of papers from the table and followed Lord Carteret out of the room.

Mrs. Mecham was gathering her children and preparing to leave. Henry picked up Dee, now asleep under the table, and proposed to escort them downstairs. Strangely, Mrs. Mecham did not seem to bear him any animosity. Philippa would have gone to help, but she was forestalled by Elliot Marsden who wanted to say good-bye. "Your friend Ashton is a clever man," he said. Philippa nodded, not trusting herself to speak. Then Mr. Marsden too was gone and she was left alone in the room.

She moved to the window and looked out on the street below. She could see Marsden's confident figure striding down the street, but Mrs. Mecham was out of sight.

"Kicked up quite a dust, didn't we?" Gordon Murray had come back in the room, wheezing slightly from the effort of climbing the stairs.

"The poor woman," Philippa said.

Murray looked at her curiously. "She was trying to bleed him, you know."

"I know. Still—"

"Yes." He waved her to a chair and sat down heavily in his own.

"Who is she?"

"Friend of Mrs. Robinson's."

"She ought to take instruction of her friend," Philippa observed.

"Won't. Says she's a good Christian."

Philippa laughed. "There must be something else she can do."

"Precious little. And she likes the game. Ah, Henry!"

Mr. Ashton had come back in the room and was perched on the windowsill. "We came to see your pamphlets, Gordon. Miss Davenport takes exception to my indirection."

"Good girl. I've got them here someplace." He rummaged through the papers once more. "By the way, what did you give her, Henry?"

"What I had."

Philippa stared at him. She had been furious with Henry Ashton. He had taken Carteret's side, he had cozened the child into betraying his mother, he had caught the woman in an apparent lie and, without a word of sympathy for her condition, had accused her of extortion. Then he had turned round and given her everything in his pocket.

He had accused Philippa of having no respect for the truth. In her mind she had accused him of having no humanity, but it appeared she had been wrong. Mr. Murray had known immediately what Mr. Ashton would do. Shaken in her judgement, Philippa took the pamphlet Murray was handing her and turned her attention to Mrs. Robinson.

Chapter 11

The journey back to Green Street was silent but companionable. Philippa's thoughts were full of her new insight into Mr. Ashton, and only when he was handing her down from the carriage did she remind herself that her opinion of Mr. Ashton was of very little moment and her feelings for her two suitors were, if possible, more confused than ever. Her attempt to escape the problem had proved ridiculously futile. She would have to confront it head on. She very much wanted to talk about it—she would have given a great deal for some of her mother's worldly wise advice—but it was not of course a matter she could discuss with Henry Ashton, however charitable she felt toward him.

To Philippa's relief, Gerry came sauntering around from the stables as they mounted the front steps. The three entered the house together and were informed by Tuttle that Miss Ashton had gone driving with young Mr. Warwick and his friend Mr. Newfield but that Lady Francesca was in her dressing room with Miss Linnet. Philippa made her excuses to the gentlemen and took herself and her problems upstairs to her cousin.

"It's so dreadful," she announced without preamble. "I was sure I never would and I'd quite resigned myself to it, only now it looks as if perhaps I might after all, only I haven't the least idea which I prefer and this isn't at all the way it's supposed to be."

Francesca was sitting on the Wilton carpet, while Linnet pulled at the violet ribbons on her mauve linen dress.

"Must you prefer one of them?" she asked.

"Of course I must. I haven't heard that bigamy's been made legal and even if it has I'm sure it would a shockingly uncomfortable way to go on, no matter how well they managed at Devonshire House." Philippa dropped down on the carpet opposite her cousin. "Not that I think they'll both offer for me, or even that one of them will, but what would I do if they did?"

"Why not wait and see how you feel when the time comes?"

"When the times comes—if it comes—I'm sure I shall be too flustered to think clearly." Hermia, who had been sleeping by the window, woke at the sound of her mistress' voice and padded over to her. Philippa rubbed her pet's back. "Besides, they wouldn't both propose at once. I ought to know whom I prefer so that I can give him helpful hints and nudge him along. That's what Violet and Ianthe did. Not that it always worked," Philippa added, remembering the disaster with Captain Livesey.

Seeing a new object of interest, Linnet had abandoned her mother and begun to investigate the buttons on Philippa's pelisse. Francesca leaned back on her hands and surveyed her cousin. "Are you sure you want to get married at all?"

Philippa looked at Francesca in surprise. "Don't you recommend it?"

"Highly, if one can find the right person. But that's me, not you."

Philippa considered a moment. "I don't know that I'd care for living alone." She removed a button from Linnet's mouth. "And I think I might quite like one of these. Or maybe two." Linnet transferred her attention to Hermia. "But I was resigned to spinsterhood. I would never get married unless I was truly in love."

"Very sensible of you," Francesca said with a smile. Then she turned thoughtful and after a moment added, "I know how it is. You like them both, you find them both amusing, and until now you hadn't given a thought to anything as dreary as marriage."

Philippa grinned. "What a perceptive woman you are, Francesca. That's it exactly."

"Put it down to memory more than perception. That was my own state of mind, back in my distant youth when I was in Lisbon with Father."

Throughout her childhood Philippa had listened with fascination to Francesca's stories of her travels with her diplomat father, but this was something new. Philippa waited expectantly for her cousin to continue.

"The city was full of officers," Francesca explained, "so I got considerably more than my share of attention, but there were two in particular. One was Justin and the other was Gerry."

This was even more intriguing. Philippa knew that Francesca had known Gerry long before their marriage and that Gerry and Francesca's first husband, Justin Warwick, had been friends, but Francesca had never volunteered the details.

"We laughed and got into scrapes," Francesca went on, "and I was delighted to have the two most attractive young officers in the city at my feet and didn't give a thought to the future. But they did. Gerry didn't think a penniless officer could offer for an earl's daughter, so he got himself transferred back to the front. Not long after that Justin asked me to marry him and I accepted. I think I must have been in love with Gerry even then. I didn't understand why he had left. I thought he was indifferent, and I was hurt, and so I married Justin.

"Oh, I wouldn't have put it that way at the time," she amended, responding to Philippa's surprised gaze. "That's just it. I didn't even realize it was Gerry whom I preferred. I think perhaps I refused to realize it, because I thought he didn't care for me. And then after Justin was killed, I very nearly made the same mistake all over again and married the wrong man a second time, only most fortunately I came to my senses and proposed to Gerry myself."

"Any everything turned out splendidly," Philippa finished for her.

"Yes. But what I'm trying to say is that it's fiendishly difficult to know one's mind—or one's heart—and it's not the sort of thing one can afford to make mistakes about."

"So I should be very certain of where my feelings lie before I do anything?"

"Very certain indeed."

"But that just makes it worse," Philippa protested, half laughing, half serious. "I haven't the least idea if I'm in love with either of them, and I'm not sure I'd know it if I was. It's not at all like my books. Of course, my heroines usually don't know until the last chapter—in fact they frequently dislike the hero excessively—but it's all perfectly plain to me. I don't think I'd ever fully appreciated how horrid it is not to know one's own mind. I like Lord Carteret and I like Mr. Marsden. No, it's more than that. They're both—"

"Very attractive men," Francesca supplied.

"Exactly. In a way they couldn't be more different, but there's something quite exciting about both of them. And they make me feel like a—well, like a woman. A desirable woman. No one's ever made me feel like that before." She drew up her knees and wrapped her arms around them.

"But?" Francesca prompted.

"But—well, Lord Carteret is distractingly handsome, and he's clever, and amusing, but sometimes I wonder how I can take seriously a man who seems to have no interests beyond gambling and horses and other's men's wives." Philippa had the sudden suspicion that she was blushing, for that was not quite the list Lord Carteret had recited. He had included Philippa herself in place of the other men's wives and instead of gambling—oh, yes.

"And his cravats, of course," she said quickly. "It must take him half the morning to arrange them." Philippa was intrigued by this last image. She giggled. "It really is very funny. It wouldn't do for a hero, but one might make something of a secondary character." She thought for a moment, relieved to be able to retreat into the safer world of her imagination, then said, "*The Honourable Peregrine Fenton*— No, something longer than that. Ferguson? Fitzsimmons?"

"Feggington," Francesca supplied.

"The very thing. *The Honourable Peregrine Feggington was overtaken by the most inexpressible disaster on Thursday last. Rising at his usual hour of three-quarters past eleven of the clock, he found an unaccustomed stiffness in his right thumb and was consequently unable to tie his neckcloth with his usual cachet.*

Having gone through all his clean neckcloths without success, he— What would he do?"

"Send a servant out for new ones, I presume. Unless he fancied spending the day in bed." Francesca stifled her laughter and took up the story. *"Having gone through all his clean neckcloths without success, he sent his valet out to purchase some new ones, while he remained trapped in his bedchamber for hours and hours—"*

"Hours and hours?" Philippa interjected.

"The valet ran into difficulties. Or perhaps he was disposed to loiter. Don't interrupt me. I'll lose the thread and I'm not as good at this as you are.... *he remained trapped in his bedchamber for hours and hours without a scrap to cover the enlarged Adam's apple which disfigured his otherwise unblemished appearance,"* Francesca finished triumphantly. Her lips were quivering.

Philippa dissolved into giggles. Francesca stopped holding her own mirth in check. Linnet, understanding their mood if not the words of the story, joined in, her bubbly laughter only fuelling the two women's sense of hilarity.

"We can't just leave him in the bedroom," Philippa protested, when the first wave of laughter had died. "There he is, waiting for his valet, pacing the room, and—I know. *While in this sad predicament, he was surprised by Mrs. Leamington, a recently discarded mistress who—"*

"—who, in revenge," said Francesca, *"spread the story about London—"*

"—causing Peregrine such embarrassment that he was forced to rusticate for the remainder of the Season—"

Philippa could have gone on indefinitely, but at this point Linnet pulled on Hermia's tail and Hermia, who had hitherto submitted patiently to Linnet's ministrations, gave a warning bark. Philippa and Francesca reached for dog and child respectively and it was some moments before both were calmed.

"I thought," said Francesca, settling a temporarily compliant Linnet on her lap, "that Lord Carteret had been at some pains to demonstrate to you that he has broader interests?"

Philippa thought of the meeting at Miss Neville's and how

169

pleased she had been by Lord Carteret's presence, and then of the scene in Mr. Murray's office and the easy way Carteret had dismissed Mrs. Mecham and her brood once it was clear he bore no relationship to them. "Yes," she agreed hesitantly. "But I can't help thinking it's still all rather a game to him."

"And that bothers you?"

"Yes," said Philippa again, rather surprised. When, in her more romantic moments, she had considered the qualities she might look for in a husband, idleness was not a fault which had troubled her. Not until her conversation with Henry Ashton. How odd that he, of all people, should have influenced her so strongly on this point.

"And Mr. Marsden?" Francesca asked. "One could hardly accuse him of frittering his life away."

"Hardly," Philippa agreed, scratching Hermia's head. "I don't believe I've ever met a man who is so open about his ambitions. There's something rather fascinating about it. But I sometimes wonder if he could ever care for anything quite so much as he cares for his own future."

"I suppose you've considered the fact that he has very little money?"

Philippa stared at her cousin in astonishment. Francesca, of all people, should not object to a match where fortune was unequal. "I should never let a consideration like that weigh with me," Philippa said fiercely. "And in any event I have plenty of money of my own—oh, I see. You mean he might be after it. Is that what people have been saying?"

"Someone did mention it," Francesca admitted.

"Mr. Marsden warned me it would be so," Philippa said. "I'm not so naive that I don't realize my money would be a tremendous help to him. In fact, I daresay he's a great deal more likely to offer for me than Lord Carteret is, for he needs a wife a great deal more. But I don't think he's only interested in my fortune. Is that dreadfully conceited?"

"No, I've watched him when he's with you." Francesca studied Philippa in silence, as if weighing the consequences of a decision. "Philippa, has he ever said anything to you about Lady Carteret?"

"About Lady Carteret? Good heavens, no, why on earth

should he? Even Lord Carteret doesn't talk about her very much and she's his stepmother."

"She's Mr. Marsden's patroness," Francesca said quietly.

"His patroness?" Philippa's brows drew together. "You mean because he acted for her in the libel case—"

"It's rather more than that. She's introduced him to some influential people—friends of her late husband—who have been helpful in his career. And the Paget solicitor has steered briefs Marsden's way, the sort of briefs that help a man rise quickly in his profession."

Philippa continued to frown. "There's no particular reason he should have told me any of that," she said.

"No," Francesca agreed.

"But," Philippa continued, "you're wondering why he would risk offending Lady Carteret by paying such particular attentions to me. Lady Carteret would hardly continue to help the man who married the odious Miss Davenport, would she?"

"Philippa—" Francesca's eyes were full of concern. "I'm sorry, perhaps I shouldn't have said anything."

"No, I'm glad you did. It's something I shall have to consider. The truth is, I know very little about him—" She broke off, remember that what little she did know had been gleaned from Francesca. "I only wish you'd told me this a fortnight ago."

"I didn't know it myself a fortnight ago."

Philippa's frown deepened. "Do you mean you've been making inquiries about Mr. Marsden?"

"I did nothing so high-handed. I had it from a friend. No, darling, that hurts."

This last was addressed to Linnet, who had discovered her mother's amethyst beads and was tugging on them. Francesca unclasped the necklace and relinquished it to her daughter.

Philippa was not to be deterred. "Which friend?" she demanded.

"His identity is immaterial—"

"*His?*"

"Philippa—"

"Francesca, someone has come very close to accusing Mr. Marsden of practising a deception. I think in fairness to Mr.

Marsden—and to me—you must tell me who it is."

Francesca hesitated. She should have handled it more adroitly. Now nothing short of the truth would satisfy Philippa. In fairness, perhaps she did have a right to know, but the result was likely to be decidedly unpleasant. "It was Henry," Francesca said at last, "and he—wait a minute, Philippa, listen—"

But Philippa had no intention of doing anything of the sort. "Mr. Ashton!" she exclaimed, springing to her feet and disrupting Hermia, who protested volubly. "How dare he? Isn't it enough for him to tyrannize over his sister without interfering in my affairs as well?"

Decidedly unpleasant had been an understatement. Francesca watched the fragile foundation of amity which Philippa and Henry had established in the past few days crumble before her eyes. She began to protest, but decided to let Philippa vent her wrath first.

But Philippa was not about to waste her anger on the wrong object. "I'm sorry, Francesca," she said. "I'm sorry you were caught in the middle of this. I should deal with Mr. Ashton directly, and I shall do so at the earliest possible opportunity."

Gerry settled back in his chair and gave an appreciative laugh as Henry finished recounting the events in Murray's office. "Poor Carteret," Gerry murmured. "One can almost feel sorry for him."

"It will do him a deal of good to realize his actions may have consequences."

Gerry sipped his brandy and eyed his friend speculatively. "You don't much care for him, do you?"

"Carteret? Good God, no. Do you?"

"I scarcely know the man. Can't say I think much of the type, but I don't bear him any animosity."

Henry had the grace to look a touch embarrassed. "Animosity's too strong a word."

"Contempt then."

Henry laughed. "You weren't privileged to see him this afternoon. Or at Miss Neville's last week." Henry reached for his glass and stared meditatively into it. "And the devil of it is, Miss Davenport admires him for it. She thinks it shows a willingness to learn."

"And it doesn't?"

Henry snorted. "It shows a willingness to pursue Philippa Davenport even to the lengths of Manchester Square and Portpool Lane."

"He's in earnest then?"

Henry thought of the scene in Murray's office and of the expression in Carteret's eyes when they rested on Miss Davenport. "I'm afraid so."

"Afraid?" Gerry raised his brows.

Henry was not looking at his friend and did not seem to realize how odd his words had sounded. "I'd hate to see a woman of her understanding throw herself away on Carteret. Besides, the marriage would be sure to be a disaster."

"You think he'd grow tired of her?"

"I think she'd grow tired of him."

"I see." Gerry's eyes still held a speculative gleam. "But Francie says you don't think any better of Carteret's competition."

"The estimable Elliot Marsden? I don't think that's putting it strongly enough."

"You think he's after Philippa's money?" Gerry was very fond of his cousin-in-law, but he would never have dreamed of interfering in her affairs. Still, he supposed he and Francesca had an obligation to fend off fortune hunters, or at least to be sure Philippa's eyes were well and clearly open.

"Perhaps," said Henry. "But I think there's more to it than that. Did Francesca tell you he's Lady Carteret's protégé?"

"She said Lady Carteret had been influential in helping Marsden's career."

"Exactly. And Marsden, who, by all accounts, has been single-mindedly bent on his own advancement since he came down from Oxford, risks destroying it all at one fell swoop."

"Lady Carteret could do that?"

"Her late husband was an exceedingly powerful man. Liverpool was one of his cronies. So was Sidmouth. So was Buckleigh, who also happens to be married to Lady Carteret's

173

sister. And it's the Paget solicitor who sends a good many briefs Marsden's way. Lady Carteret would only have to say a few words in the right places."

"And would she?"

"Oh, yes. She prides herself on the strength of her feelings, and family feeling's probably the strongest of these. I can't see her aiding the husband of the woman who made a mockery of the Paget name. And if Marsden is to realize his political ambitions, he will most certainly need aid."

Gerry rose, went to the side table, and picked up the decanter. "Marsden might think he would gain equally valuable patronage by marrying Philippa."

"Perhaps. But it would mean becoming a Whig."

"Is he a man of such strong beliefs then?" Gerry asked, refilling Henry's glass.

"I doubt he's a man of any beliefs at all. Which is why he would think twice before transferring his allegiance to a party which offers him no opportunity for office in the foreseeable future."

"You make a convincing case. Why then is Marsden flying in the face of his own best interests and courting my wife's cousin?"

"I don't know, but I'd venture to guess it's because Lady Carteret asked him to do so."

"I see." Gerry returned to his chair. "I take it she too would have had her reasons?"

"Oh, yes. She's a meddler. She made that abundantly clear in the matter of Claris and Lord Christopher, though that's neither here nor there."

"You're a clever fellow, Henry," Gerry said approvingly. "We regimental types are a bit more slow. Why would she meddle by asking Marsden to court Philippa?"

"I don't think she actually asked him to court Miss Davenport. I imagine it was something more on the order of, 'rescue my stepson from the wiles of that horrid woman, I don't care how you do it.' And Marsden who, whatever else he may be, is certainly not a fool, realized that the best way to detach a lady from one gentleman is to cause her to fall in love with another."

174

"He thought he could compete with Carteret?"

"Why not? I don't think he's one to undervalue himself. And he's a shrewd man. Perhaps he realized that considerations of wealth and fortune wouldn't weigh with Miss Davenport."

Gerry swirled the contents of his glass. "It's quite an accusation."

"It's the only logical way I can account for Marsden's actions. And from my one interview with Lady Carteret, I'd wager she'd go to considerable lengths to save her stepson from Miss Davenport."

"Have you told Philippa any of this?"

Henry laughed. "I don't know that I'm a clever fellow, Gerry, but I'm not a complete idiot. A warning from me would be more likely to send her off to Gretna Green than anything else."

Gerry smiled. "That at all events we must avoid. Her mother wouldn't thank us for interrupting her honeymoon with the news of her daughter's elopement. But I think Francesca should have a word with Philippa. She knows how to put things tactfully."

Henry had already suggested as much to Francesca, but before he could say so Philippa herself entered the library.

She was still wearing her pelisse, but she seemed to have undergone a complete transformation since the two gentlemen had left her in the hall less than an hour before. Her eyes sparkled, her back was alarmingly straight, and when she spoke her voice fairly crackled with control. "Mr. Ashton, I must have a word with you directly. Could you oblige me by stepping into my study? I'm sorry, Gerry," she added, turning to her cousin's husband with a belated apology.

"That's quite all right." Gerry moved toward the door. "And there's no need to leave. I should go up and see Francie and Linnet. You'll stay and dine with us, Henry?"

"Er—yes. Thank you." Henry was looking at Philippa.

"Capital," said Gerry and took himself off as if he wasn't perfectly aware of the undercurrent of tension he left behind.

Philippa stood in icy silence while Gerry quitted the room.

175

Unfortunately, Hermia, who had followed her mistress downstairs, rather spoiled the effect by scampering across the floor to greet Mr. Ashton, her tail wagging vigourously. Mr. Ashton bent down to return the greeting. "You wish to say something to me, Miss Davenport?"

His tone was polite. Philippa's was not. "I should like to know what the devil you mean by interfering in my affairs for all the world as if I were eighteen years old and so unfortunate as to be related to you!"

Mr. Ashton abandoned Hermia and straighted up to face Philippa. He knew what she was talking about, of course. The man was infernally perceptive.

"I don't like to see people taken advantage of," he said coolly.

"And what made you certain I was being taken advantage of?"

"I was not certain. But there were things about Marsden's behaviour which disturbed me."

"You could not understand why Mr. Marsden would devote himself to me without an ulterior purpose. Thank you for the compliment."

Her voice was more bitter than she had intended. Perhaps she had not become quite as reconciled to her appearance as she had thought.

"Miss Davenport—" Mr. Ashton stepped toward her, then checked himself. "You know that is not how it was."

"No? I know that on the slenderest of pretexts you jumped to the conclusion that Mr. Marsden has some nefarious purpose and that you then asked questions about him behind my back. I would be angry if Francesca had done as much without speaking to me first."

"And if I had come to you first, Miss Davenport? What would you have done?"

"Told you to go to the devil," said Philippa with feeling.

"Precisely. You must perceive my dilemma."

"There was no dilemma at all. The matter was no concern of yours. Is no concern of yours. What possible interest can you have in my affairs?"

"That of a friend, I hope," he said quietly.

There was a time when Philippa would have given a great deal to hear Mr. Ashton call her a friend, but now she let the statement slip by unnoticed. "One does not treat a friend like a child," she retorted. "Good God, how would you feel if I formed the opinion that a lady who had shown an interest in you was a shameless fortune huntress and I made inquiries about her behind your back?"

Henry smiled. "My dear Miss Davenport, a shameless fortune huntress would have to have a very weak understanding to pay the slightest attention to me."

"That is immaterial! I am aware that you think me a feather-brained creature, but I am not wholly incapable of looking after myself, and even if I were that would still not give you the right—"

"I know you can look after yourself. And I don't think you anything of the kind."

"No? You think my books are frivolous, it's much the same thing. Couldn't you be content with attacking them without criticizing the way I choose to live my life and the friends I choose to make? Mr. Marsden may not be a gentleman you would have for a friend—"

"Mr. Marsden," said Henry, goaded into counter-attack, "is a schemer who would very likely climb on his own mother's back in order to make his way in the world."

"That is pure supposition," Philippa shot back, very pleased that he had lost his temper as well.

"Perhaps. But you will permit me to point out, Miss Davenport, that I am in a far better position to form an unbiased judgement."

"On the contrary. You have been determined to disapprove of everything about me from the outset. In fact, I'm surprised you tolerate Hermia so well."

"Hermia at least is worthy of your regard."

At this point Hermia, hearing her name, indicated that they had been neglecting her shamefully. Henry acknowledged her once more, causing Philippa to say bitterly that she might have known he would take her dog's complaints more seriously than her own, at which inopportune moment Tuttle knocked at the library door. Perfectly aware that he had interrupted a scene of

177

high drama, Tuttle informed Miss Davenport in his most wooden accents that Lord Christopher Paget had called and desired to speak to her immediately.

Philippa was annoyed to have her quarrel with Mr. Ashton broken off just when it was becoming really satisfying, but it seemed Lord Christopher had something of moment to communicate, so she told Tuttle to show the young man into the library directly.

"Would you like me to leave?" Henry asked.

"You may do as you please, Mr. Ashton. You have made it abundantly clear that you consider yourself part of the family."

Henry hesitated, but as it was likely that Lord Christopher's visit concerned Claris he determined to hold his ground. When Tuttle ushered young Paget into the library a few moments later, the boy's air of barely suppressed excitement instantly assured Henry of the wisdom of his decision.

"Miss Davenport—" Lord Christopher began. "Oh, Ashton, I didn't realize you were here."

"Your servant, Paget. You needn't be alarmed. I am only violent when taken unawares."

"Pray sit down, Lord Christopher." Philippa indicated a chair near a window and seated herself in one opposite it, so that Mr. Ashton was left standing alone.

"Thank you, though the truth is—well, actually—it's really you I was looking for, Ashton."

"Is it?" Henry strode across the room. "If it's about my sister, I think I have made it perfectly plain—"

"No, it's nothing to do with Clar—with Miss Ashton. Tony sent me."

Philippa turned accusing eyes on Mr. Ashton. Had he had dealings with both her suitors behind her back?

"Tony said to tell you there's been a kick-up about the pamphlets he had from a man called Murray," Lord Christopher continued. "He wants you to warn him."

"Gordon gave pamphlets to Carteret?" Henry asked. "How very enterprising of him. Do you mean Carteret actually did something with them?"

"Oh, yes," Lord Christopher assured him. "He left them on

178

a bench at White's."

Philippa bit back a giggle. She looked involuntarily at Mr. Ashton and saw his lips twitch. "I think," he said, "that perhaps I owe you an apology, Miss Davenport. I seem to have underestimated the marquis. One must give him credit for being inventive." He turned back to Lord Christopher. "How many did he—"

"Never mind about that," Philippa interrupted. "You said there had been some sort of row?"

"Yes, Nelliston actually threatened to have Tony expelled from the club."

"Did he?" said Henry, much interested. "Clearly a threat of dire proportions. What did your brother do then?"

"He challenged Nelliston to a duel," said Lord Christopher.

Chapter 12

The Marquis of Carteret came out of Portpool Lane and looked around for his curricle. Thanks to Ashton, he had avoided a nasty scrape. He should have been elated, but he felt curiously uncertain. His visit to Murray's office had hardly forwarded his cause with Miss Davenport. Or had it? Would she at least give him credit for appearing in such an improbable place?

His groom, who had been on the watch for him, brought the curricle round. Still musing about the events of the afternoon, Anthony gave the office to his greys, drove at a smart pace down Chancery Lane, through the crowded thoroughfare of The Strand, round Charing Cross, into the quieter precincts of Pall Mall, and pulled up at last in St. James's Street. He had had nothing to eat all day and nothing but a tankard of ale, procured at an inn near Denham, to quench his thirst. It was time to go to his club.

He pulled in at the top of the street and handed the reins to his groom. It did not occur to him that that long-suffering man had had no sustenance either, but he had some concern for his cattle so he directed Mugford to return to the stables and see that the horses were properly rubbed down, fed, and bedded.

As he turned to ascend the steps of White's he paused and glanced back at the seat of the curricle. There were the pamphlets Murray had thrust upon him as he was leaving his office. At the time it had seemed simpler to take them than to protest, and he had fully intended to toss them away. But perhaps he would take one in to share with his friends. Worthman was sure to appreciate it. He walked back to the curricle and reached for a copy, then paused again. Why not the lot? It was what Miss Davenport would want. A fugitive smile crossed his face. As Mugford and the horses waited patiently for his lordship to make up his mind, Anthony picked up the entire pile of pamphlets and walked into the sacred precincts of White's.

. The day was warm and the awnings had been lowered over the windows so that the morning room was in a restful dim light. Anthony paused at the entrance, nodded to a couple of acquaintances, debated calling for a drink, then withdrew. He was really very hungry, and there was no one with whom he could share the events of the afternoon. But as he mounted the curving stairs, he ran into Worthman and Finnbury.

"Carteret, haven't seen you in an age, where've you been keeping?" Lord Worthman inquired.

"Business, Freddy, business."

"Unlike you, Tony." Lord Worthman was sensible enough not to inquire further. "Come along with us, we're going to Manton's, he's made me a detonating gun, seventy pounds and worth every farthing. I'll challenge you."

Anthony declined and would have passed upstairs, had not Worthman's hanger-on, Thomas Finnbury, a portly young man with an extravagant waistcoat, inquired about the papers in Anthony's hand. They must be important, he observed, for Carteret had quite ruined his gloves by carrying them.

Anthony obliged by passing one to each of them. Worthman thumbed through the pamphlet, which was inscribed *To Married Ladies, for the Relief of the Female Burden*, and gave a shout of laughter. "Damnation, Tony, where'd you come across this?" This caused two elderly gentlemen who were descending the stairs to frown in disapproval. The younger men ignored them.

"Oh, around, Freddy, around. Thought it would amuse you." The men parted and Anthony continued up to the landing where, not knowing what else to do with them, he deposited the remaining pamphlets on a high-backed bench before proceeding into the coffee room. Here he dined in a quiet corner on a large and very rare beefsteak and a bottle of claret and promptly forgot all about the work of Mrs. Robinson.

But not about Philippa Davenport. His uncertainty had vanished. He recalled her headlong dash across the room to rescue the Mecham infant, her solicitude for the detestable Mrs. Mecham, and her more welcome solicitude for his own well-being. She was kind and resourceful, and she would make a splendid mistress of Carteret Park. With Philippa at his side, he might have less occasion to avoid the place. She would make no excessive demands on his time. She would have her writing to occupy her, and then of course she would have her children. His children.

The face of young Bertie rose unbidden to Anthony's mind. When for a fleeting moment he had thought that the boy could be his, he had dimly sensed that a son might be something worth having. Philippa would be a good mother. And though she was not too discriminating in her choice of companions, he was sure that she would be a chaste wife. This last was important. He could not bear to have a Georgina Nelliston as his marchioness and live to wear horns.

Anthony lingered over his wine, dwelling on the image of Philippa Davenport as his marchioness. He rose finally and leisurely made his way downstairs. A knot of men were talking in the hall below, but they grew oddly silent as he descended. Ignoring the covert looks, Anthony turned into the morning room from whence issued the sounds of heated argument, punctuated by oaths and laughter.

Anthony was not a stupid man. Worthman must have passed the bloody things around.

Anthony's mouth twisted. It would be good for the old buffers to be shaken up a bit. He could see them in a far corner of the room, bent with rheumatics, their heads close together as they leaned forward in their chairs. Worthman was speaking to them earnestly, but that ass Finnbury had gathered the younger members about him and was holding forth on the topic of the pamphlet amidst shouts of ribald laughter.

The joke had gone on long enough. Anthony strolled over to the younger men. Several of them had copies in their hands, and Anthony belatedly remembered the pile he had deposited on the bench upstairs. In a cool voice he remarked that it hardly seemed a matter of jest. This comment evoked renewed hilarity. "I say, Carteret," said a pink-cheeked cub, "are you promoting these among the fair sex?"

"Best do it among your own," Anthony retorted, which caused the cub to blush a brighter pink. The youth had recently been rescued from some unpleasantness involving a tradesman's daughter. The group erupted in laughter once more, and in the silence that followed this outburst a voice came from across the room. "Carteret, did you bring this filth in here?"

Anthony turned slowly and stared at the man who had spoken. He was standing by a round pedestal table on which several of the offending pamphlets were displayed. He was a man of middle years, heavily built, with a florid complexion, sagging face, and dark narrow eyes under dark level brows. He seemed to view the world with perpetual suspicion, as might befit a man with four daughters and a young and ardent wife. If there was a shade of extra bitterness in his voice when he addressed Anthony, no one wondered at it. Lord Carteret was the latest in the series of his wife's lovers.

There was no trace of guilt in Anthony's feelings toward Lord Nelliston, but he did not like Georgina's husband. "Can't say I did, Nelliston."

Lord Nelliston was momentarily confused. "I understood . . . What do you know about them?" he demanded, belligerant once more.

Anthony walked to the table and picked up one of the offending pamphlets. "You aren't obliged to read it, you know," he said as he flipped through its pages. "If I were you, Nelliston, I'd stick with *The Times*."

Nelliston bridled at his tone. "You did bring them," he insisted.

"I came across them," Anthony admitted, "and thought they might amuse one or two of my friends. I did not expect them to be seized on eagerly by the entire membership." He turned around. "By the way, does anyone know how they got in this room? I distinctly remember carrying them upstairs."

"They're vile, Carteret. They're worst than vile. They're seditious. How could you soil your hands with them?"

"Only my gloves, Nelliston. The subject's a tender one, I confess, and it's curious to see it in print, but the information is hardly a matter of surprise. Why should you be offended?"

At this last, there were murmurs from some of the older members and snickers from some of the younger ones. Someone was heard to mutter that he would like to be allowed to read his paper in peace. "Ah, I agree," Anthony said. "Let us drop the subject which Lord Nelliston finds so distasteful and restore the room to its customary quiet. No one, after all, is obliged to read anything unless he chooses to do so."

He turned away and found his younger brother by his side. "I didn't know you were back in town, Tony. I say, you kicked up quite a dust."

Anthony shrugged. "Are you going home? I need to change."

"No, I'm with St. George and some other fellows."

Anthony looked up and saw Crispin's cousin regarding them with sardonic eyes. He clapped his brother on the shoulder. "Take care, Cris. They play high." He prepared to leave the room but found his way blocked by Lord Nelliston.

"Where did you get them, Carteret? I'll have the man up on charges. He ought to be hanged!"

Anthony looked down at the shorter man. "Strong words, Nelliston," he drawled. "Strong words."

"I repeat, Carteret, where did you get them?"

"I really can't remember. If you'll move aside, Nelliston, I'm on my way out."

"Not till you remove those pamphlets. Not till you apologize to the members."

Anthony stared at him in astonishment. "If the pamphlets offend your sight, Nelliston, ring for someone to take them away. I owe no apology, but I rather expect one for the tone you have taken with me this afternoon."

Anthony had grown angry, but his face was expressionless. Lord Nelliston read insolence in it, and the wrongs he had suffered at the hands of his wife and of her lovers and of this particular lover welled up in his throat and threatened to choke

184

him. "You're a blackguard, sir. I'll see that you're black-balled."

The room was absolutely quiet. Anthony's voice was silky. 'I am not sure, sir, that I have heard you aright."

"I repeat, sir. You're a blackguard, a vile blackguard!"

"Ah, I thought that was the word. Then, sir, you will be good enough to give me satisfaction. At a time and place to be appointed by our seconds." He looked round and found Crispin still beside him.

"Tony, let me."

Anthony shook his head. He was protective of his brother and would not involve him in what promised to be an unsavoury affair.

Worthman moved forward, but St. George reached Anthony first. "At your service, Carteret."

Anthony nodded and turned back to Lord Nelliston whose skin was drained of much of its colour. His temper too had cooled, and he said in a tight voice, "Mr. Ingoldsby will act for me." Then he turned on his heel and left the room.

He was followed by several other men who recollected that they had urgent business elsewhere. Some others drifted up the stairs, talking in muted tones, and the remainder settled down in the customary peace of the morning room.

Anthony turned to Crispin. "Come with me," and Crispin followed him out of the club without question. They were in Piccadilly before Anthony spoke again. "Find Ashton, the brother of your pretty little friend. Tell him what happened, and tell him to warn Murray."

"Murray?"

"The man who gave me the pamphlets. Hurry. And for God's sake, don't tell your mother."

Crispin looked at his brother with hurt eyes. "Tony, what do you take me for?"

Crispin hadn't intended to mention the duel, and as soon as it was out he wished that he had not, for Miss Davenport took it excessively hard. "But they can't!" she said. "It's got to be stopped!"

185

"Oh, St. George and Ingoldsby will see to that," Crispin assured her, trying to put the best face on it. "They're acting for them, you see, and that's their business, though I doubt they'll get anywhere. Tony doesn't get angry as a rule, but I've never seen him so furious."

"Wait, Paget," Henry said. The duel was a matter of small moment. "What exactly was said about the pamphlets?"

Crispin turned in relief to Claris' brother. "A lot of things were said. But," he added, with a nod toward Miss Davenport, "most of them won't bear repeating. Some of the fellows thought they were a great lark. Well, I rather thought Tony did, too, he'd given one to Worthman, you see, and another to Finnbury, and they were the ones that started talking, and then someone brought a pile of them into the morning room and the fat was in the fire. The older men didn't much like them, of course"—this group included, in Crispin's eyes, anyone over the age of thirty—"because they tend to take things seriously. Nelliston was the worst, but he don't much like Tony." Crispin hesitated, then rushed over this point. "He wanted to know where Tony got the pamphlets and threatened to turn whoever it was over to the authorities, but Tony of course wouldn't say, and Nelliston—I say, Ashton, is Murray a friend of yours? He's likely to be in a bit of trouble over this."

Henry nodded. "Go on."

"Well, then it got personal. Nelliston called Tony all kinds of names and that's when he threatened to have him expelled from the club—can you imagine it, a Paget expelled from White's?—and he wouldn't back down, so of course Tony challenged him. There was really nothing else he could do."

Philippa could think of a score of things he might have done. She had little patience with the niceties of the male code of honour and a healthy respect for firearms. A duel was the ultimate stupidity. "There's no of course about it. Surely no one would take Lord Nelliston seriously."

"Well, Tony did, and if you'll forgive me, Miss Davenport, I don't think you quite appreciate how men feel about this sort of thing."

Philippa made a rude noise which caused both men to stare at her in surprise.

"What are the chances of their coming to some accommodation?" Now that he understood the role of the pamphlets, Henry could attend to the problem of the private quarrel.

"Precious little, I'd say. St. George will go through the forms, but he tends to be high in the instep, and he won't take an insult to the family lightly. On Edwina's account." He looked at Miss Davenport and was somewhat confused.

"Then it will take place quite soon?"

"Tomorrow morning, at a guess. Best to do these things before tempers have cooled."

"Best not to do them at all." Philippa was appalled by this turn of events.

"I say," Crispin said as though it was a new idea, "you don't suppose Tony will get hurt, do you?"

"Someone is bound to get hurt. Mr. Ashton, we have to do something."

"We?" The faint smile told Philippa that Henry Ashton had no intention of doing anything at all.

"Mr. Murray is your friend," she pointed out, "and if it weren't for Mr. Murray, the challenge would not have have been given and Lord Carteret wouldn't be facing the possibility of death—"

"Oh, don't say that. Tony's a capital shot, and I'd lay whatever odds you like on him."

"—or exile," she concluded, ignoring Lord Christopher's outburst.

They were all standing and had drawn close together, their varying concerns linking them in a common thread of anxiety. Henry turned to Philippa, an ironic light in his eye. "If Lord Carteret hadn't followed you to Manchester Square, he would never have set eyes on Murray. The responsibility is at your door, Miss Davenport."

"And if you hadn't taken me to Miss Neville's, there would have been no need for Lord Carteret to follow me there. Not that he did follow me," she added.

'Oh, but he did." Crispin was eager to set the record straight. "Claris told me you were going and I told Tony at breakfast."

Phillipa was more disappointed by this disclosure than she would admit. Then, struck by the absurdity of the argument, she turned back to Henry. "Oh, very well, don't help. I'll stop it myself."

Henry gave her a long look. "How?"

She returned the look, full in his face, "I'll take Hermia."

Henry laughed and threw up his hands.

Out of charity with Henry Ashton, Philippa turned the force of her persuasion on Lord Christopher. "You must find out what is happening and come and tell me immediately. At what hour it is to be, and what place."

Crispin was horrified. "Oh, I couldn't do that! One doesn't interfere in these things. Tony would never forgive me." He turned to Henry as the only other sensible person in the room. "Ashton, you understand, explain it to her."

Henry observed that Miss Davenport was in no mood to have anything explained to her this afternoon. Philippa did not take this lightly and, while the two were contending, Crispin reflected that it had been a mistake to tell Miss Davenport anything at all. Now that he had delivered Tony's message, all he wanted was to leave the house and find out what was happening to his brother.

But as he waited for a break in the argument between Miss Davenport and Mr. Ashton so that he could take his leave, the library door opened and he saw the face and form that would have rooted him for eternity to any place on earth. Claris had returned from her drive, her face flushed with a delicate wash of pink, her honey-coloured curls escaping from the confines of a charming bonnet ornamented with cherry-coloured ribbons which were tied under her deliciously rounded little chin. A fatuous look came over Crispin's face, and he put his hat back on the table and walked forward to take her hands.

Claris was delighted to see her betrothed—or, if not her betrothed, the man to whom she felt bound by ties of the heart stronger than any socially sanctioned bond. For a few moments their eyes said everything.

This behaviour at last reached Henry's notice, and he greeted his sister in tones that recalled her to a sense of what was seemly. She moved quickly away from Lord Christopher and crossed the room to kiss her brother prettily on the cheek. "How nice," she said, "I didn't expect to find you here. Nor did I expect to find Lord Christopher," she added with a look of inquiry at Crispin. He had distinctly told her he was engaged with St. George this afternoon.

"Well, I wasn't actually paying a call," Crispin said, anxious to make it clear that he was not slighting the divine Claris, "that is, I called to see Ashton, that is, I called to see Miss Davenport because I had a message for Ashton. From my brother," he explained, "but it's done now and I was just leaving, but of course . . ." His voice trailed off while his eyes held onto Claris who was removing her gloves and untying her bonnet.

Philippa was anxious to keep Lord Christopher in the room. "I'm going to ring for tea," she said. "Please stay, Lord Christopher. And you too, Mr. Ashton, though if you feel you must warn Mr. Murray at once, we will understand."

To her annoyance, Mr. Ashton said that Murray would not be home for at least another hour and a cup of tea would be most welcome.

Philippa lost no time in acquainting Claris with what had transpired. She needed an ally to convince Lord Christopher to provide her with the requisite information—for she was quite determined to act, though she did not quite know how—and though Lord Christopher was being positively pig-headed in the matter, Philippa knew that he would melt once Claris' entreaties were joined to her own.

Claris was a girl of quick parts and she understood the problem immediately. But Crispin had a mutinous look. It really didn't do to talk about these things, he pointed out, they were private affairs between gentlemen and should not be noised about.

"Oh, but I wouldn't dream of telling Lady Francesca," Philippa assured him, "and certainly not Colonel Scott for I wouldn't want to embroil him in any scandal. But Claris is different, she is so nearly concerned in the matter, and of course I trust her discretion absolutely."

Henry snorted. Claris made a face at him.

Crispin, whose eyes were on Philippa, had to agree that Claris was different, though if asked he could not have said how the matter concerned her at all. He would not for the world cause Miss Ashton any distress, but it was after all Tony's affair and not their own, and Tony quite knew how to take care of himself. "And I promise I'll be there myself," he added, "and if St. George hasn't been able to bring a reconciliation about, I'll see what I can do." He looked beseechingly at his beloved who, to Philippa's surprise, thanked him warmly and acquiesced in his decision.

But when Tuttle returned with the tea tray, Claris managed to get Crispin aside and renewed her attack. "I know I don't understand these things," she said in a low voice, "and I have to be guided by you, but you must understand that Philippa is quite devastated by your news. Surely she has a right to be there. If he's mortally wounded, she'll want to be with him at his last moments. And if he has to flee the country, she'll want to bid him good-bye. Please, Crispin, you would not be so cruel as to deny her that." She had no opportunity to say more, but she could see that Crispin was wavering.

Philippa guessed what was happening and turned her attention back to Mr. Ashton. "Pray tell Mr. Murray I am sorry for any distress this episode at White's may cause him. If there is anything I can do—if there is anyone I can talk to—if money would be a help—please tell him he may call on me."

Henry looked at her in surprise. So she was not totally preoccupied with Carteret's safety. It occurred to him that she would seek as urgently to stop any such event for which she felt responsible. It was a revelation that caused Henry to have second thoughts about letting the duel run its foolish course.

When Philippa called the others to the table, he said as much. "I'm sure your brother can handle himself, Paget, but we should give some thought to his safety. If Nelliston is as foolish as he sounds, he's likely to get himself killed and then Carteret won't dare show his face."

"It's not your quarrel," Crispin said, but it was clear the arguments of brother and sister were having an effect.

"Ah, but I have a stake in it," Henry explained. "I abhor violence and—like our late colonies—I stand for freedom of the press. Besides, Murray's a friend of mine."

"The challenge was Lord Carteret's," Claris said. "Suppose we go to him and beg him to withdraw it?"

"He'd never listen." Crispin spoke with the certainty of a younger brother.

"He'd listen to Philippa."

"He'd only say what Lord Christopher has already said for him," Philippa returned. "It's not a question for women."

"Then we shall have to prevent him from meeting Lord Nelliston," Claris insisted. "Crispin, you must stop him from leaving the house tomorrow. Henry will help you."

"Henry will do nothing so bird-witted," Claris' brother assured her.

"That would be dishonourable," Crispin said at the same time. "He has to go."

"Then we'll have to be there to meet them." Philippa pushed her cup away. She had poured tea, but the cups lay untasted on the table. "If they have to deal with us on the field in the chill of the morning it won't be so easy to fob us off."

"Especially if Philippa and I go alone." Claris grew enthusiastic. "We'll fling ourselves between them."

"No!" shouted both men.

"But we have to do something!"

"They're right, Claris," Philippa said. "We have no real right to interfere, and playing hysterical females won't help. Their pride won't allow them to abandon their quarrel, so we must give them a reason to do so."

This met with a depressed silence. Then Henry spoke up. "I think I have an idea."

It was not yet six and a fine mist lay over the ground when Lord Nelliston's carriage approached Putney Heath.

Nelliston was in a state of considerable agitation. He was not a brave man, and he had long nursed a large and ill-defined grievance against the world which he considered had treated him most unfairly. His first wife had been a dull and dutiful woman who presented him with four daughters and two still-born sons, following which she expired without complaint. The girls were pretty, wheedling little things who spent his money freely and seldom remembered to thank him for it. His estates prospered, but he took no pleasure in their management and found himself in continuous litigation with his neighbours over questions of boundaries and the killing of foxes.

Then his prosperity brought him another wife, the young and beautiful and quite penniless Georgina, and for a few short weeks Lord Nelliston thought his luck had changed. But Georgina spent his money as freely as his daughters and treated him with amiable contempt. She had not even provided him with an heir. It was true that she never denied him her bed, but to come on her hot and damp from an afternoon with one of her lovers, took away some of the pleasure he could still find in her body. He would have minded less had she been more discreet, but her liaisons were becoming more and more flagrant, and that with Lord Carteret was by far the worst. This time Georgina was quite smitten. With the falling away of the marquis' attentions in the last few weeks, her jealousy had known no bounds and she had become almost unbearable.

Lord Carteret had not only made him a cuckold, he had destroyed his domestic tranquillity. It seemed quite unfair that he should parade his conquests and his contempt for the opinion of others by bringing that filthy sheet into the club and making sport of it. The pamphlet, of course, would have to be stopped, but it was the sight of Carteret that had sent him into a rage, and though he knew at the time that he was being irrational, he could not help himself.

The marquis was everything Lord Nelliston was not, yet secretly wished to be—tall, elegant, admired by men and women alike, at ease with both himself and the world. Moreover, he was reputed to be a capital shot. This last had almost determined Lord Nelliston to offer an apology for his words, but despite his cowardice he was a stubborn man, and in the end he had found himself unable to do so. Mr. Ingoldsby did not press the matter, for a few words with the Viscount St. George had led him to understand that no apology would be accepted.

So here he was, shivering in the cold of the morning and with the knowledge that a man he detested might shortly put a bullet through his heart. What then of Georgina? Hah! If she were available, Carteret would be off like a shot. Lord Nelliston took a small grain of comfort from the thought.

He huddled in a corner of the carriage, eyes bent unseeing on the ground outside, ignoring Ingoldsby's efforts at conversation. When the carriage pulled up at the edge of the heath, he sighed and descended heavily from the vehicle. His legs were stiff with cold and he felt a faint stirring of the rheumatism that afflicted him in damp weather.

"Wait here," Nelliston said curtly to his coachman, a dour man with a leathery, taciturn face. Without looking at Ingoldsby, he made his way round the carriage and peered into the mist, willing the other carriage to appear so that the matter might be over quickly.

It was then that he noticed the horseman, a solitary rider who was just in the act of dismounting. Puzzled, he watched the man tether his horse. He did not have the careless arrogance of Carteret or St. George, but he was behaving as though he intended to stay for some time. Damnation! Lord Nelliston was not looking forward to his encounter with the marquis, but he did not want any delay to prolong the period of waiting.

Then he heard horses and an approaching carriage. His mouth went dry. Carteret must be arriving.

But it was only the surgeon, a small birdlike man with a brusque manner who brought his carriage to a halt near Nelliston's, jumped down, and said he hoped they would not be too long about it as his day promised to be full. Ingoldsby assured him that the hour was set for six and it lacked but seven minutes of that time.

Engrossed in this exchange, the three men did not notice the arrival of a curricle which had approached the heath from a different direction and pulled up near the man who had tethered his horse. The driver descended and approached the horseman. At this point Lord Nelliston looked up and saw them. "What the devil—" he said, for the men appeared to be arguing. Then one returned to the curricle, reached under the seat, and brought out some sort of box which he tucked under his arm. The men had some more words and began walking toward the centre of the heath.

"It appears," said the surgeon dryly, "that there is more than one affair of honour on the field today."

"Nonsense," Nelliston said, "where are the seconds?"

"Perhaps one of them is the second," Ingoldsby said, scanning the pair critically. "There may be more to arrive."

"Or perhaps they're here to murder birds," said the surgeon, who had little use for bloodletting though he made his living by it. "Let us hope your other pair is not behind time so you, at least, may conclude your business." He walked off, seeing little profit in continued intercourse with his companions.

Nelliston grunted and began to pace the ground, keeping his eye on the other pair who had stopped some distance away and seemed again engaged in argument. He wished that Carteret would arrive, yet he nourished a faint hope that his assailant—his opponent—might not appear. But the hope was doomed, for even as he looked down the road, the marquis' curricle came into view. What little courage Lord Nelliston had mustered was oozing rapidly away.

Lord Carteret descended from his carriage in a leisurely fashion and strolled toward his opponent. Carteret's assurance, his coolness, and the fit of his coat were alike a further affront to the agitated man with whom he was soon to measure distance.

He was followed by the Viscount St. George who was if anything more deliberately casual in his manner. It had been agreed that Carteret would supply the guns, neither Nelliston nor Ingoldsby possessing suitable weapons, and St. George now reached into the carriage and brought them forth. Ingoldsby came forward and St. George opened the case.

The surgeon made a show of drawing out his watch. Ingoldsby inspected the weapons and exchanged a few words with St. George. Carteret nodded briefly at Nelliston and looked about him, his glance passing over the other two occupants of the heath as though they were not there. Then his head swung suddenly back and he uttered a wordless exclamation.

And at the same time one of the strange pair began walking toward them. He was a slender man, with hair that fell carelessly over his forehead, and a long lean face that was now suffused with anger.

"If you please, gentlemen," he said, "we were here before you."

Lord Carteret stared at him in disbelief. "Ashton, what the devil are you doing here?"

"It's none of your business, Tony." The other man came forward. His golden curls were awry, there were circles under his eyes as though he had not slept, and he stared at his brother with a defiance Anthony had seldom seen. "It's a private quarrel."

"A—" Anthony was nonplussed. Then he realized the implications of their presence on the heath. "Ashton, if you've challenged my brother, you'll have to answer to me."

"No, thank you," Henry said coolly, "I don't choose to risk my neck with more than one Paget. The quarrel was not of my making. And," he continued, his voice suddenly bitter, "I intend to teach the young whelp a lesson."

Crispin's acquaintance with firearms was meagre. Ashton's skill was unknown. Anthony had a sudden vision of his younger brother lying bloody on the hard scrub of the heath. "Cris," he said, "you can't."

"Why not, Tony? You are."

"That's different," Anthony insisted, uncomfortably aware that this was an answer his father had often given to his questions.

"I fail to see any difference at all." Crispin's teeth were clenched. "In fact, I would say I have the stronger case. The man grossly insulted me, and he's already bloodied my nose."

Anthony might have repeated this operation had not St. George intervened. "I fancy what Tony is trying to tell you, Cris, is that you can't go about matters in this harum-scarum way. Where are your seconds? Where is your surgeon?"

The surgeon present was heard to mutter that if they didn't get on with it neither pair of antagonists was likely to have one.

"I could, of course, offer my services—" St. George began.

Anthony was outraged. "Quentin, don't you dare!"

"This is a quarrel, gentlemen, not a *fête champêtre*." Henry's voice was scathing. "Nothing is needed to settle it but some space and a brace of pistols. So would you have the goodness to withdraw and leave us to it." He took off his coat and began to roll up his sleeves. Crispin followed suit.

Lord Nelliston was growing agitated again. He could not bear the delay. "Go away, sir, go away!" He made flapping movements with his hands. "We have chosen this ground."

"As have many others," Henry said, "Lord Castlereagh and Mr. Canning among them. But we arrived first."

"But our quarrel dates from yesterday afternoon, sir! Can you say as much for your own?"

"No," said Henry firmly, "but we are here. Bear with us. It will not take me long to put a bullet through those golden curls."

This assertion was followed by a scream and a sharp bark. A small dog of indeterminate pedigree flung herself at his breeches. "Oh, my God!" said Henry Ashton. He hadn't expected Miss Davenport to bring her dog.

The others had been too preoccupied to hear the phaeton. They turned as one and saw a girl in a white dress and blue cloak racing toward them, her skirts held up to reveal shapely legs encased in pink stockings. "Henry!" she shrieked.

Behind her came a young woman whose pace nearly matched the girl's, but her concern appeared to be directed to her dog who was launching an assault on Lord Carteret's immaculate biscuit-coloured pantaloons. "I'm so sorry," Philippa said to the marquis as she swept her pet into her arms, "but we have to stop it, you see."

Of all the damnable interference! At any other time Anthony would have been overjoyed to see Philippa Davenport, but the field of honour was no place for a woman. He was about to tell her so, but she had turned back to Miss Ashton who was hanging on her brother's sleeve and begging him to reconsider.

"Worried about your pretty boy, little sister?"

Lord Christopher made a lunge at Henry but Claris placed herself in front of her brother. "No, no, you must not," she pleaded, "I never wanted you to quarrel, not about me, and Lord Christopher has been utterly in the wrong." She turned anxious blue eyes toward Henry. "But you, Henry, the Pagets are deadly shots, everyone says so, and what will become of Mama and me if you are killed?" On this last her voice rose to a wail.

"I thank you for your confidence, Claris, but I have no intention of getting killed."

"If you persist in pointing those ugly things at one another, someone is bound to get killed." Philippa's matter-of-fact voice broke through the miasma of hysteria that was rapidly building on the field. "I never heard of such an idiotish way of settling an argument. If you can't be rational about it, at least use your fists."

"Miss Davenport clearly has no head for abstractions," St. George observed in an undertone that carried clearly to the others.

"Would someone get those women out of here!" said Mr. Ingoldsby, ordinarily a mild-tempered man, and Lord Nelliston echoed his words.

"Gentlemen, gentlemen," said the surgeon wearily.

"Oh, St. George," Claris said, turning beseeching eyes on the viscount. "I know you're right and we don't understand these things, but you must consider my distress, it is gentlemen who choose to fight, but it is women who must bear the pain. I say nothing about Lord Carteret's quarrel, but surely this one does not warrant so drastic a remedy. Pray do not let them!"

The viscount gave her an appraising look. He did not like Ashton, but he had no stake in the outcome of this particular quarrel. Cris had done himself no good with the pretty Miss Ashton by provoking it. If he succeeded in putting a hole in the girl's brother, it would put a stop to any romantic attachment on her part. (St. George, a well-educated man, here conveniently forgot the example of Shakespeare's young lovers.) On the other hand, he didn't want to see Ashton put a hole through Cris. And then there was the possibility of gaining some credit with the girl.

"Cris," he said. "I find I must withdraw my offer to second you. You win no honour by pursuing the quarrel. You cannot even do it properly, and you'll only hold yourself up to ridicule by trying to carry it out in this fashion. Withdraw the challenge."

The young man shook his head.

"You're making Tony look ridiculous."

Crispin allowed his face to show some uncertainty.

The viscount followed up his advantage. "I'm sure Ashton will withdraw whatever words led up to it."

"Never!" said Mr. Ashton.

"Of course he will!" said Philippa and Claris simultaneously. "And if you don't, Henry," Claris added, "I will do something that will make you very sorry indeed."

This argument appeared to have some effect on Claris' brother.

"I was obliged to you yesterday, Ashton," Anthony said. "Dare I ask you to oblige me once again? I suspect that Cris deserved your words, and I'll see that he makes you a proper apology."

"Tony!" Crispin was outraged. "See to your own quarrel!"

"That's not—"

"By God it is!"

The brothers glared at each other.

St. George was clearly amused. "You'll have to let me try again, Tony." The marquis stared at him, then nodded curtly and turned away.

"Ingoldsby," St. George said, "I think we should talk."

"My time, gentlemen," the surgeon said.

"Will be recompensed," St. George assured him. The two seconds walked apart.

There was quiet and uncertainty on the field. Hermia barked. Henry turned to Philippa. "Is it too much to ask, madam, why you had to add that dog's presence to your own?"

Philippa looked up at Claris' brother and continued to play her part. "I always take her for a run in the morning," she told him. "It's quite all right, it's past her time. And as for my own presence," she added tartly, "which I quite see is unwelcome, I came for Claris' sake. In principle, I abhor violence, but it's all one to me whether you choose to kill yourself or not."

And with that she turned her back and walked toward Lord Carteret who was standing by himself, his brother declining to have anything to do with him. "I must apologize for our interference," Philippa said in a gentler voice than she had used with Henry. "I know it was quite unpardonable. But I plead Miss Ashton's concern for her brother."

Anthony's face softened.

Philippa lowered her voice. "And I must take the opportunity to tell you that I thought it simply splendid, what you did at White's." She was talking about the pamphlets. The subsequent challenge was the height of arrogant folly.

Anthony's spirits, dampened by the unaccustomed events of the morning, rose under her apparent approbation. They continued talking quietly while St. George and Ingoldsby conferred. St. George then asked for some conference with Anthony, and Ingoldsby spoke apart with Lord Nelliston.

It was, surprisingly, Lord Nelliston who resisted. Now that all actual danger was past, he found his courage perversely returning, and he balked at the idea of humbling himself to Carteret. Ingoldsby pointed out that the insult had been on his own side, and he could hardly expect Carteret to apologize for bringing to Nelliston's attention a pamphlet that had never been intended to fall into his hands. Then he made some reference to the weapons the viscount had brought onto the field. It was this last that did the trick, and Lord Nelliston reluctantly agreed to have some words with the marquis.

He did so with ill grace, but the thing was done. Lord Carteret put out his hand and the other man was forced to take it. Then Anthony turned away, and neither he nor St. George saw Nelliston wipe his hand on his breeches.

The surgeon pocketed the fee St. George pressed upon him, picked up his bag, and returned to his carriage, muttering about his wasted morning.

Crispin had been watching the others, his face a scowling mask. When the surgeon had left and Nelliston and Ingoldsby were preparing to follow, he shrugged and said, "Oh, very well," and went and made his peace with Henry. None of the others could hear what passed between them, but they were observed to shake hands at last and neither was disposed to negate the clasp.

Anthony appeared quite satisfied with the way the morning had turned out. "Well done," he said. "Breakfast, I think. Cris, Ashton, will you join us? We'll be at the Cup and Rose in Walham Green."

Henry disentangled Claris' arms from his neck where she had flung them after the healing handshake. "With pleasure," he said. "If you will allow me to see my sister to her carriage first."

Claris made no objection, though she stopped to thank St. George in tremulous tones for the immense service he had done her.

Crispin had put on his coat and was making his way to his curricle. Lord Carteret paused before Philippa. "You will not be offended if I do not extend the invitation?"

"But of course not," Philippa said demurely, "I quite understand that there are times when gentlemen prefer to be left alone."

Anthony smiled and raised her hand to his lips. Then he walked off, followed by the viscount who held the pistol case under his arm. St. George said something to Anthony and their laughter floated back onto the field where only Henry and the two women remained.

"Thank you, Henry," Philippa said. It was the first time she had called him by his given name, but she seemed unaware that she had done so. "Thank you for coming. Thank you for everything."

"Wasn't he absolutely splendid!" Claris' face was glowing. "And wasn't Crispin! I swear I was actually afraid they might go through with it."

"Don't impose too much on my good nature, Claris," Henry took her arm and offered his other to Philippa.

"Oh, no," she said, "we must find Hermia first."

Henry stopped and took a deep breath. "No," he said. "On no account." And he stalked toward their phaeton, pulling Claris with him.

Laughing, Philippa ran after them. When they neared the carriage, Henry called the dog's name sharply and Hermia bounded toward him, doing further damage to his breeches before he could restore her to her owner's arms.

"Tell me, Mr. Ashton," Philippa said as he helped them into the carriage, "just what did you say to Lord Christopher that he took in such very great dislike? The insult must have been fearful indeed, for I'm sure he's ordinarily a mild-tempered young man."

Henry stared at her, the rueful smile she had come to know so well just breaking over his lips. "I don't think I can remember the exact words. You know how it is in the heat of anger. Now if you'll forgive me, I have an appointment for breakfast." He raised his hand in farewell and strode back to his horse.

Chapter 13

As Lord Carteret had challenged Lord Nelliston in front of half the members of White's, the duel was hardly a secret. The details of the meeting were rather more difficult to ascertain, none of those involved seeing anything to be gained from discussing the affair. The curious had to content themselves with observing that neither Carteret nor Nelliston showed any sign of injury and that in the succeeding days Carteret did not so much as dance with Georgina Nelliston and was more attentive to Philippa Davenport than ever.

So was Elliot Marsden. Marsden, though unacquainted with the particulars of the duel, was aware that the episode had—at least temporarily—given Carteret the primary place in Miss Davenport's thoughts. He made haste to mount a counter-attack by escorting Miss Davenport and Miss Ashton to the Tower of London. Miss Davenport had of course visited the Tower many times before, but she had expressed a wish to return as she was thinking of using the setting in her new book. The Royal Menagerie seemed an appropriately absurd location for the scene in which Anne overhears Lord Chilton and Alexander conspiring to ruin Nigel. Unfortunately, Miss Davenport was somewhat abstracted during the expedition. It was Miss Ashton who really seemed to enjoy herself, particularly after they encountered Lord Christopher Paget near Tower Green.

Philippa had no doubt that this meeting was pre-arranged, but Claris and her suitor behaved most properly, strolling only slightly behind the others. They had, Philippa admitted, been remarkably circumspect since the horrendous morning in Hyde Park. Still feeling guilty for her own role in that débâcle, Philippa was grateful for the young couple's prudence.

She had Lord Christopher to thank for this. He had been alarmed by his mother's reaction to his involvement with Claris and particularly by her threat to pack him off to her brother who was attached to the British delegation in Washington. Crispin determined to wait until his mother's temper had cooled and then present his beloved to her. Surely Mama could not be other than enchanted by his adorable Claris.

In the event that he proved to be mistaken in this regard, he would be forced to turn to his uncle, Lord Buckleigh, who was his legal guardian. Uncle Horace was inclined to be severe, and Crispin was reluctant to approach him. Still, he knew he could count on his cousin for help. St. George might claim, with a disarming smile, that he had very little influence over his father, but Crispin placed great faith in his cousin's abilities. And St. George certainly seemed quite taken with Claris and was now in her company more than any other young man save Crispin.

Lord St. George's attentions had not been lost on Claris' brother who remarked caustically that his sister's taste in men seemed to be going from bad to worse. Claris retorted that her brother could not accuse her of living in Crispin's pocket and then turn around and citicize any other gentleman who paid her notice. Philippa, who was in the room at the time, took up Claris' cause and had a most enjoyable argument with Mr. Ashton. It ended in a stalemate, but then none of their squabbles produced a clear victor. That would rather take the fun out of things.

Philippa and Henry's quarrels seemed, if anything, more frequent than ever. The difference now, as Gerry remarked to Francesca, was that they both seemed to quite enjoy these bouts. Francesca nodded, an odd look in her eyes, but did not pursue the subject. She also did not pursue the matter of Mr. Marsden. Philippa now had the necessary information, and it was up to her to act as she saw fit. True, Philippa was not privy to Henry's notion that Marsden was acting at Lady Carteret's behest, but in Philippa's present mood it seemed impossible that she would give any credence to what was, as yet, mere speculation.

Philippa would indeed have been angered by further accusations against Mr. Marsden, but she did not dismiss Henry's information, however wrong it had been of him to obtain it. Between her uncertainty about Mr. Marsden, her conflicting feelings about Lord Carteret, and the necessity of confronting both her suitors nearly every day, frequently at the same time, she was more perplexed than ever. As the week drew to a close she looked forward with relief to diversion in the form of the Warwick House ball.

Though it could not compete with Holland House, Warwick House occupied a unique position in Whig society. At thirty-five, Nicholas Warwick had risen to a position of prominence within the Opposition. If some members of the party thought his vews veered dangerously close to Radicalism, his intelligence and the impeccable credentials of the Warwick family ensured that he was treated with respect. It was that same combination of unorthodox views (which brought Nicholas into contact with equally unorthodox people) and the Warwick pedigree (which made the most stiff-necked think twice before turning down an invitation from the Warwicks) that made the Warwick House entertainments such a delight.

Philippa considered the Warwicks practically family. Francesca's first husband, Justin, had been Nicholas Warwick's younger brother. Her second marriage had not severed the link between the families, for the same year that Francesca married Gerry, Nicholas Warwick had married Gerry's sister, Livia.

This particular ball promised to be one of the Season's successes. Francesca had had several consultations with her sister-in-law as the entertainment was planned, and both Philippa and Claris were privy to all the details, from the supper menu to the guest list. The latter included several persons who did not normally frequent Warwick House.

Philippa assumed that Elliot Marsden had been invited as a compliment to her, and the Paget family as a compliment to her and Claris. She was somewhat surprised that the marchioness had accepted the invitation, but what really startled her was that a card had also been sent to the Buckleighs.

The invitation was really to the Hansfords, Francesca explained. They had recently returned from abroad and were staying with Lord and Lady Buckleigh. Mr. and Mrs. Hansford had scarcely a thought in common with the Warwicks, but they were connections of Nicholas' mother and could not be overlooked. Claris observed that no doubt Harry, Nicholas' younger brother, had added his entreaties, for he was quite besotted with Lady Edwina.

These explanations, while perfectly satisfactory, did nothing to allay Philippa's glimmerings of alarm. The combination of Lord Carteret, his stepmother and half-brother, Claris, the Buckleighs, Lady Edwina, Lord St. George, Mr. Marsden, and Mr. Ashton did not, she felt, augur well for the success of the evening. But then, she reminded herself as she prepared for the ball, with some four hundred persons present, there would be scant opportunity for private conversation, let alone for quarrels. She tossed aside her concerns and prepared to enjoy the evening.

She had ordered a new dress for the occasion, a soft cream-coloured gauze embroidered with sprays of burgundy which exactly matched the stones in Francesca's earrings—once again loaned to Philippa—and worn over a slip of pale pink satin. The neckline, though not as revealing as the styles Francesca affected, was considerably lower than what Philippa was accustomed to. It made her feel delightfully dashing.

Thanks to Francesca, Claris also had a new dress, a celestial blue foulard, the skirt festooned with swags of a darker hue caught up with bows of ribbon which matched the ribbons threaded through Claris' hair. Francesca herself was in green lustring shot with gold, her blond hair encircled by a gold chain from which a single emerald was suspended over her forehead (a new fashion known as the *ferronière* after the da Vinci painting). Both were in their best looks, but for once Philippa did not feel they cast her into the shade.

When the ladies came downstairs, Gerry paid them all the nicest compliments, which was fortunate as Mr. Ashton could never be relied upon to compliment anyone. Still, it had been rather more than twenty-four hours since he and Philippa had last quarrelled, and the party left Green Street in convivial spirits.

By prior arrangement they arrived before the other dinner guests. Nicholas greeted them at the drawing room door with a ready smile. Philippa could recall a time when he had seemed almost forbidding. Marriage was good for him. Or marriage to Livia was good for him, Philippa decided, returning Livia Warwick's embrace. Livia herself, in a gown of rose gossamer satin, her hair attractively cropped, looked radiant. She was just Philippa's age, but this was her second marriage and there was a maturity and assurance in her manner which Philippa was certain she herself completely lacked. Would she acquire it if she too was married, the mistress of a large household with an established position in society? Philippa tried to visualize herself as Mrs. Elliot Marsden, and then as the Marchioness of Carteret, but found the images curiously blurred.

As they settled themselves in the drawing room, Philippa found herself addressed by Gwendolen, Nicholas' thirteen-year-old daughter from his first marriage, who had been permitted to come downstairs and greet the family before the other guests arrived. Gwendolen, who was going through an awkward adolescence, said that Philippa looked absolutely splendid and rather like the portrait of Aunt Rowena which hung in the Davenports' country house. No one had ever before suggested that Philippa remotely resembled her mother. She gave Gwendolen a hug, her spirits soaring.

As the dinner guests were confined to family and close friends and therefore did not include the Carterets, the Buckleighs, or Elliot Marsden, Philippa's good humour continued throughout the meal. Claris, seated between young Harry Warwick and his friend Jack Newfield, giggled a good deal and seemed to be having a capital time. Philippa did not, of course, spare much attention for Claris' brother, but she did note that he too seemed to be enjoying himself.

By eleven, the ballroom was beginning to fill. Emily Cowper, who had been among the dinner guests, began to flirt with Poodle Byng. Lord Cowper did not seem to notice and took himself off to the card room. Lord Palmerston looked explosive. Francesca went and said soothing things to him. Emily's sister-in-law, Caroline Lamb, on the other hand, seemed unusually and blessedly restrained.

Scrope Davies, John Hobhouse, and Douglad Kinnaird, who shared radical views with their exiled friend Lord Byron and were frequently at odds with the Whigs, arrived together. They had opposed the Whigs in the last two elections in the borough of Westminister and had been notably absent from Holland House since, but Lord Holland was seen talking quite amiably with Hobhouse. Everything seemed in train for a pleasant and peaceful evening.

Philippa stood up with Gerry for the first dance. In the weeks since her meeting with Lord Carteret at Almack's—how long ago that seemed—she had grown much more at ease on the dance floor and no longer had any aversion to the exercise.

When they left the floor, they were stopped by Lord John Russell who wanted to talk to Gerry about the current temper in the War Office. Glancing across the room, Philippa saw that Mr. Ashton had been cornered by Louisa Myerson who scarcely had two thoughts to rub together and was just the sort of young woman he despised. Deciding that in Christian charity she could not do other than rescue him, Philippa excused herself and went to his aid.

"My compliments, Miss Davenport," Mr. Ashton said, when Miss Myerson had been dispatched. "That was very adroitly managed."

"Yes," Philippa agreed, "I rather thought so myself. Are you enjoying the evening?"

"Very much. Aren't you?"

"Certainly. But then, as I think I told you once before, I always enjoy myself in company. After all, it is the stuff of my novels."

To her disappointment, Mr. Ashton did not respond to this sally. "Very true," he agreed politely. "But didn't you also once tell me that dancing is not your favourite occupation?"

"Did I?" Oh yes, of course she had, at Almack's, the evening she met Lord Carteret. That was the only time Mr. Ashton had ever asked her to dance. She rather regretted having turned down the offer. "I've changed," she told him truthfully.

"Indeed, ma'am." There was, Philippa thought, an odd look in Mr. Ashton's eyes, but he made no further comment.

"In any event," said Philippa, returning to her earlier point, "it is you who is not fond of society."

"On the contrary, Miss Davenport. I have no quarrel with the society in which I find myself this evening."

Philippa let her eyes roam about the ballroom. "I don't think the Carterets are here yet," she said judiciously, "or the Buckleighs or Mr. Marsden, so I suppose I can let that statement pass without quarrel. You do not, I collect, object to seeing your sister in the company of Harry Warwick or Jack Newfield? They are, after all, little older than Lord Christopher."

"And scarcely more sensible. True enough. However Claris seems to regard them in a purely sisterly way and is not in the least blind to their faults. She has no illusions when it comes to brothers."

"I've noticed. And Harry and Jack, of course, view her as a sort of little sister. Harry, I understand, has conceived a *tendre* for Lady Edwina Thane."

"I don't doubt it."

"You don't?" Philippa was surprised.

"I have long since ceased to puzzle over the strange attractions of that family."

Philippa decided to ignore this. "You must admit," she said, "that Lord Christopher has been showing himself far from irresponsible."

Mr. Ashton's eyes were free of mockery. "I don't deny it. I will even admit that my opinion of him has improved somewhat. But not my opinion of the wisdom of his marrying my sister." His gaze returned to the scene at large. "I am desolated to prove you wrong, Miss Davenport, but it seems the Carteret party has already arrived and Claris is therefore not in the company of Harry Warwick or Jack Newfield—oh, good God, the young fool."

This last remark, delivered in a markedly changed tone of

voice, caused Philippa to glance quickly around the ballroom. There was Claris, walking decorously on Lord Christopher's arm. And there was Lord Christopher, his golden hair shining in the light from the chandelier, leading Claris toward—

"Oh, dear," said Philippa.

"A masterpiece of understatement, Miss Davenport."

As Philippa and Henry watched in horrified fascination, Lord Christopher led Claris to the sofa on which Lady Carteret, Lady Buckleigh, and Mrs. Hansford were ensconced. So much for thinking the disparate guests at the ball would not be likely to meet, Philippa thought bitterly. Still, Lord Christopher certainly had a perfect right to present Claris to his mother and perhaps Claris' natural charm—

"Lady Carteret is smiling," Philippa pointed out.

"She hasn't seen them yet," Henry retorted, his face intent. He could not bear, Philippa realized, to see his sister slighted.

Two young women, laughing and walking with their arms around one another's waists, temporarily obscured Henry and Philippa's view. When the prospect was clear once more Lady Carteret's smiling face had dissolved into a set social mask. Lady Buckleigh looked positively glacial. Mrs. Hansford appeared confused and embarrassed. Lord Christopher appeared confused and mortified. Only Claris continued to smile as if the encounter were a perfectly pleasant one.

"They might at least have made more of an effort to be civil," Philippa muttered.

"You said that young Paget was far from irresponsible?" Henry inquired dryly.

"You can scarcely blame Lord Christopher because his mother and aunt choose to behave shabbily," Philippa returned, transferring her gaze to Mr. Ashton.

"But I already knew Lady Carteret's attitude toward Claris was impertinent. If Lord Christopher had any sense he'd have realized it as well and spared my sister a painful scene. And if Claris had any sense she would have avoided an encounter that could only prove embarrassing."

"That," said Philippa roundly, "is monstrously unfair. How on earth is Lady Carteret to see Claris' good qualities if Lord Christopher does not bring them together?"

"My dear Miss Davenport, in Lady Carteret's view 'good qualities' are no doubt limited to birth and fortune. Claris does not and never will possess them."

This was unanswerable. Then Philippa remembered something Mr. Ashton had once said. "Didn't you tell me that if one doesn't like the world as it is one should seek to change it?"

"Very likely," he said with equanimity. "I was speaking of the general, not the particular. The world being as it is, Lady Carteret's attitude is, I fear, nothing out of the ordinary."

Philippa's brows drew together in frowning concentration as she searched for a reply.

"Frowning Miss Davenport? Good God, Ashton, what have you been saying to her?"

It was Elliot Marsden. Philippa gave him her hand, wishing he could have put off his arrival just a few minutes longer, until she had concluded her exchange with Mr. Ashton. Not that her exchanges with Mr. Ashton were ever concluded, but—

"You'll excuse us if we desert you, Ashton," Marsden was saying, retaining Philippa's hand. "Miss Davenport is promised to me for the next waltz."

Elliot Marsden did not have quite Lord Carteret's grace, but he carried himself well and could be counted on to provide a diverting commentary as they moved through the figures of the dance. If Philippa, her mind still on her interrupted conversation with Mr. Ashton, was not quite as diverted as was usually the case, it was not apparent. At least, she did not think it was, until the waltz came to an end and Marsden said unexpectedly, "It's growing abominably hot in here. Should you mind foregoing the next dance and taking a turn about the garden?"

It did not seem overly warm to Philippa, but she gave her consent and permitted him to lead her out of the ballroom. It was, she thought later, one of the sillier things she did in the course of the evening.

The Marquis of Carteret looked around the ballroom, trying to locate Miss Davenport. It was most important that he do so, for he had something very particular to say to her. He meant to ask her to be his wife.

Lord Carteret's doubts about Miss Davenport had come to an end. At least he had decided to ignore them. Miss Davenport would have to be firmly steered away from the unsuitable ideas and company into which her compassion often led her—what Anthony was willing to humour in a flirt he would not tolerate in a wife—but the surest way to do so was to provide her with a husband, a position, and children to occupy her thoughts.

He had reached this decision on the previous afternoon, after calling in Green Street and—as seemed to happen with increasing frequency these days—finding Elliot Marsden already with Miss Davenport. Lord Carteret badly wanted confirmation that he held the preeminent place in Miss Davenport's heart, the sort of confirmation that would be given by the presence of the Paget betrothal ring on her finger.

Though skilled in amorous pursuits, Anthony had never given much thought to the art of proposing marriage. But when he bent his mind to it, the Warwick House ball seemed an appropriate occasion. The setting would be elegant—Anthony had never been to a Warwick House entertainment, but Livia Warwick was said to be an excellent hostess—Miss Davenport was certain to be in her best looks, and surely he would be able to persuade her into the garden for a few minutes and lay his hand and heart at her feet.

That was his plan, and at first it seemed as if it was going to fall out rather well. Livia Warwick had filled her ballroom with masses of white jasmine and trailing greenery, creating a setting as romantic as he could have wished, and when he caught a glimpse of Miss Davenport on the opposite side of the room, he saw that she looked enchanting.

Then, just as Carteret had begun to make his way toward Miss Davenport, he was set upon by Georgina Nelliston, who complained that he had been neglecting her abominably. It was high time he gave Georgina her *congé,* but this was hardly the appropriate place. Out of deference to what had once been between them, he could not cut her or refuse when she asked him to procure her a glass of champagne. Anthony performed this office, silently cursing the crowds, only to be informed on his return, with the sweetest of smiles, that Mr. Davies had already provided her with the required refreshment. Anthony cast a look of dislike at the innocent Davies and took himself off, his obvious bad temper adding to Georgina's enjoyment of her small revenge.

By the time Anthony once again managed to locate Miss Davenport in the crowded ballroom, she was waltzing with Marsden. The marquis stationed himself on the edge of the dance floor, determined to wait his rival out. He relieved when the couple left the floor, but then, to his annoyance, they made for the gallery. Anthony considered following them, then decided against it. Past experience told him that Marsden was unlikely to retire from the field of battle, and a quarrel between her suitors would not predispose Miss Davenport to a proposal of marriage.

Chafing at the enforced delay, Anthony began to move about the ballroom. His eye lit on Edwina, surrounded by the usual crowd of admirers, most of them wearing idiotic expressions. He was going to have to have a talk with Edwina in the very near future. It was not an enjoyable prospect, but as long as he was forced to cool his heels waiting for Miss Davenport, he might as well get it over with.

Anthony broke through the crowd around his cousin without difficulty. One of them, he noted, was his host's younger brother. Explaining that he had something to discuss with his cousin, Anthony asked Harry Warwick if there was some place where they could be private for a few minutes. Very much on his dignity, young Warwick directed them to a small room at the back of the house.

With a smiling Edwina on his arm, Anthony made his way out of the ballroom, wondering for the first time exactly how he was going to tell his cousin that it was nothing personal, but he couldn't possibly make her his wife.

Philippa remained silent as she and Marsden moved along the gallery, down the stairs thronged with late comers, and along the hall to the back of the house. The garden had been illuminated for the comfort of the guests who wished to escape

211

the heat and crowds indoors. A group of young men were standing on the terrace, several couples were strolling on the walks, and there was laughter from the shrubbery beyond.

"I don't think I've heard you complain of the heat before," Philippa remarked to Mr. Marsden.

"No? Very likely not. It does not in general trouble me. But I had to have some excuse to speak with you more privately." Mr. Marsden guided her down the terrace steps and onto a gravel walk.

"Large balls do not lend themselves to private conversation," Philippa returned, following him without demur.

"No, but I've had the devil of a time finding you alone these past days. Carteret seems to positively haunt the house. I can only be thankful that he arrived after I did this evening."

"No doubt Lord Carteret had to accommodate his stepmother," Philippa said, turning her head so she could observe Marsden's reaction to this mention of his patroness.

There was none, at least none that she could detect. "Very true," he agreed cheerfully. "There are, it would seem, ways in which I am more fortunate than the marquis. Though, knowing Carteret, he's liable to come strolling through the shrubbery at any moment." They had reached a point where no one was within sight, although they could still hear strains of music from the ballroom above. "I think a prudent man would take advantage of his good fortune while it lasted. Would you say that I am a prudent man, Miss Davenport?"

"You are certainly a shrewd one, Mr. Marsden," Philippa said with a smile.

"It's much the same thing," said Elliot Marsden, drawing her into his arms and lowering his mouth to hers.

Philippa did not struggle, at first because she was too shocked, then because she did not want to. The volume of Lord Rochester's poems which she had found in the library at the inquisitive age of thirteen, the copy of *Les Liaisons Dangereuses* which she had devoured two years later, her mother's matter-of-fact explanations which had caused Juliana and her to blush and giggle with embarrassment, none of these had prepared

Philippa for her response to her first kiss. It was as if a part of her, suppressed long ago when she first faced her failure on the Marriage Mart, had suddenly welled to the surface, all the stronger for having been held in check so long.

Her mind was filled with images: her mother and Lord Braithwood embracing at their wedding; Gerry and Francesca standing in the doorway of the bedroom which, contrary to convention, they always shared. Bedrooms. Beds. A great deal of one's life was spent in bed, and if one was married this time was not spent alone. There was, Philippa realized, considerably more to marriage than companionship and raising children and running a house.

Yet though the sensations Mr. Marsden was evoking were intoxicatingly delightful, and though Philippa had unconsciously wrapped her own arms around him, it was clearly Elliot Marsden who was in control. The kiss was very like the man himself: exciting and overpowering. Philippa did not easily surrender her autonomy, and it was the sense that she was fast losing all personal dominion which at last caused her to protest.

Marsden released her immediately, though he continued to hold her with his eyes. "Miss Davenport—Philippa—"

"No." Philippa put up her hand involuntarily. "Please take me back to the ballroom, Mr. Marsden. I'm not angry," she added quickly. "Or about to have a fit of the vapours. But don't say anything more. Not now. Not yet. Please."

"Of course." Marsden smiled, his gaze unwavering, and offered her his arm. Philippa took it, her eyes fixed on the path ahead. She had feared it would be an evening of complications, but Elliot Marsden had introduced one that was entirely beyond her realm of expectation. She wanted above anything to escape to the privacy of her bedchamber and attempt to sort out her feelings, but it would be several hours before she could do so.

It was only as they were about to reenter the ballroom that she realized that, while this would no doubt be the greatest complication of the evening, there was no guarantee that it would be the last.

213

Chapter 14

Lady Edwina Thane was not normally forced to employ any arts to attach a gentleman, but in Anthony's case she was worried enough to make an exception. She had noticed that Philippa Davenport was looking surprisingly well this evening, but she knew the woman was no match for her. Now that she had Tony's attention she meant to put the opportunity to good use. She preceded him into the small parlour to which Harry Warwick had directed them and turned to give Anthony her most ravishing smile.

"I've never known you so importunate, Tony. What is it you wish to speak to me about?"

Anthony closed the door and studied his cousin. She was wearing a gown of ivory poult-de-soie, the skirt ornamented with satin rouleaux in the same shade, the bodice softened with Brussels lace. Her luxuriant dark tresses were dressed high and pinned with flowers of ivory silk. The only colour was provided by the necklace, earrings, and bracelet of diamonds and rubies set in gold which had belonged to Catherine and Aurelia's mother, and then to Catherine, and then had been presented to Edwina on her twentieth birthday. The jewels outshown Miss Davenport's ruby earrings by far. Edwina herself most certainly outshown Miss Davenport. Anthony did not regret giving her up in the least.

"Edwina," he began, "you must know that our families—that is, Aurelia and your mother—" He plunged into it. "There's been some talk about our marrying."

"*Talk?*" Edwina gave a laugh designed to cover her rising unease.

"Yes. But contracting people in the cradle—that's all rather gone out of style. And it wasn't in the cradle anyway, was it?" Anthony had once been informally betrothed to her errant sister Demetra. Edwina did not enjoy the reminder. "We're both adults," he went on, "and we do not lack understanding. There's no reason we shouldn't decide these things for ourselves."

Decide for ourselves? Could he possibly be on the verge of a proposal? Or was he saying—

"I think you'd better tell me what it is you're trying to say, Tony," Edwina said sweetly, her smile kept carefully in place.

In his nervousness, Anthony had paced the short length of the room. Now he turned to face her. "Oh hang it all, Eddy," he said in tones which harkened back to childhood, "you're not in the least in love with me and I'm not in the least in love with you. There's no earthly reason we should tie ourselves to each other just to suit a pack of interfering relatives."

"You're referring to my mother and my aunt." Edwina was no longer smiling and her voice was not in the least sweet.

"I can't think of two people whom the term suits better." Anthony laughed. He was inexpressibly relieved to have the burden off his shoulders, and he did not take warning from Edwina's tone and expression. "You could have any man in London you looked twice at. I don't know why you didn't rebel against having me foisted on you years ago."

"Perhaps because, unlike you, Tony, I take family obligations seriously. But then you've never cared much for obligations of any sort, have you?"

"Oh, come now, Edwina, you can't claim that I'm obliged to—"

"You clearly do not feel yourself obliged to do anything. Am I to take it from this that our betrothal is at an end?"

"There never was any real betrothal," Anthony said, "only the scheming of two—"

"Thank you, you have more than answered my question. I should, I suppose, be grateful that you did me the kindness of speaking with me before you offered for someone else. I collect you are on the verge of offering for another lady?"

"I am."

"Well." She gave a slight shrug. "At least my name is Thane and not Paget. Whatever ramshackle connection you choose to form—"

"How dare you speak that way of Miss Davenport!"

"How dare you embarrass me with your ridiculous little flirtation? How dare you brush me aside as if I were one of your *chères-amies?*" Edwina was now flushed with anger. "I did not think you were lost to all sense of honour."

"Edwina, be reasonable—"

"Reasonable? Would you be reasonable if you had been dealt such an insult?"

"No insult was intended."

"I make no doubt of it. You are obviously in no condition to spare so much thought for another person. Except your Miss Davenport of course."

"That's enough!" Anthony had forgotten what his cousin's tantrums were like. Clearly he had not been much in her presence of late. She had never been able to bear being denied anything—he recalled a similar outburst when she was not given the pony she expected. He hadn't known her heart was so set on becoming the next Marchioness of Carteret. But she would soon get over it. That she might be feeling some very real alarm about her own future did not occur to him, partly because Edwina had always had her pick of men, partly because he indeed had thought for little other than Philippa Davenport.

"I don't believe there is any need for further discussion," Anthony said coldly. "I am returning to the ballroom. May I escort you?"

"Thank you, I can find my own way. I have no intention of relying on you for anything in the future."

"As you wish," said Anthony and took himself off, determined to find Miss Davenport and speak to her without further delay.

But the ballroom seemed to have grown more crowded in his absence and he could not locate Miss Davenport immediately. Surely she could not still be with Marsden? If so, he was half of a mind to go after them and tell Marsden to go to the devil and then—

"Carteret, m'boy! Didn't expect to find you here. What ill wind blew you into this nest of Whigs?"

Anthony turned. It was Gordon Murray.

The first person Philippa and Marsden encountered when they reentered the ballroom was their hostess. Philippa was much relieved. Livia Warwick's crisp good sense was just the leaven she needed at this moment. To her further relief, Marsden stayed only long enough to exchange pleasantries with Livia before moving on. Determined to shut out all thoughts of marriage and its intimacies, Philippa set herself to saying how very much she was enjoying the evening, how splendid the house looked, and how entertaining she found the company.

Livia was remarkably sharp-eyed, but she did not seem to perceive that anything was amiss. All the same, Philippa wanted to keep control of the conversation. "I'm sorry Claudia isn't here," she said. Livia and Gerry's sister had recently given birth to her third child. "How is she? Francesca and Gerry had a letter last week, but perhaps you've heard something more recently?"

"Yesterday. She's very well, and quite relieved that it isn't twins this time. That would be a bit much for even Claudia's maternal instinct."

Philippa smiled. Devil take it! Babies had seemed a safe enough topic, only one inevitably started thinking of how they were produced. Livia had a child herself, a boy of about Linnet's age. The Warwicks' marriage had always seemed singularly happy. Surely Nicholas never made Livia feel overpowered as Philippa had felt in Elliot Marsden's arms?

Philippa glanced around the ballroom for a safer inspiration and her eye lit on the Marquis of Carteret. Dear God, she'd forgotten she'd have to deal with him tonight, too. Then she saw the man with whom he was conversing.

"What a splendid idea to invite Gordon Murray." Philippa was diverted. "I didn't even know you knew him."

"Nicholas has known him for years," Livia said. "But I must confess it didn't occur to me to invite him. Mr. Murray didn't know we were entertaining. He came by to give Nicholas some information for a speech he's making on the repeal of the Combination acts, so of course we asked him to stay. I didn't know you'd met him."

"Henry Ashton introduced us. I quite like him—Mr. Murray, I mean."

"So do I." Livia followed the direction of Philippa's gaze. "I see he's trying to convert Lord Carteret. Do you think he'll meet with any success?"

"I don't know," Philippa said honestly. "I hope he does. This isn't his first attempt. Mr. Murray met Lord Carteret at Sophronia Neville's."

"I see." If Livia was surprised that Carteret had been at one of her cousin's meetings, she gave no sign of it. She might, Philippa realized, be equally surprised by Philippa's own presence, for Philippa had never shown any particular interest in reform. This last thought depressed her.

"Did Henry introduce them, too?" Livia asked.

"No. Yes. I think they rather introduced themselves."

Livia smiled. "That sounds very like Gordon Murray." She saw that the marquis had now detached himself from Mr. Murray and was making his way toward them. "I think Lord Carteret is seeking you out. Am I right in thinking you don't wish to talk to him just now?"

"Very right," said Philippa with feeling.

"Well, I see that Harriet and Granville have arrived. I really ought to go and speak with them. Come with me, I'm sure they'll be delighted to see you."

Livia's perceptiveness had proved an asset rather than a liability. Philippa smiled again, this time in gratitude, and followed her hostess across the room.

Crispin was watching Claris waltz with Harry Warwick. He was not in the least jealous, for he knew Claris' feelings for young Warwick were completely unromantic, as were Warwick's for her. He knew too that, having already danced twice with his beloved, he could not with propriety stand up with her

218

again. Crispin would not for the world do anything which might attach the least breath of scandal to Claris' name. All the same, he would far rather watch her than dance with any of the other ladies present, all of whom seemed too silly, too serious, too tall, too dark, too not-Claris.

His attempt to introduce Claris to his mother had been a failure. Even the naturally optimistic Crispin could not possibly call it anything else. Claris had been a Trojan of course, as he had known she would be. It was Mama whose behaviour had been sadly deficient. Crispin, used to being able to talk his soft-hearted parent around, had been shocked at the vehement coldness of her demeanour. But then, she had had Aunt Catherine sitting beside her. Aunt Catherine had a sadly detrimental effect on Mama's finer feelings, particularly when those finer feelings related to Crispin's wishes.

He would have to fall back on his second plan and ask St. George to approach Uncle Horace about the betrothal. A few words dropped at discreet intervals and surely St. George would be able to bring Uncle Horace round. Beside, for all his crusty exterior, Uncle Horace was not insusceptible to pretty young women. Crispin had watched Edwina wheedle him and Claris was far more charming than Edwina. Crispin considered introducing Claris to his uncle this evening but decided against it. Something might go wrong. Aunt Catherine might interfere, and if Uncle Horace took Claris in dislike, then they really would be in a pickle. Better wait and let St. George put his hand to it.

Crispin had just come to this decision when St. George himself appeared at his elbow, a thoughtful expression on his face. Crispin began to appeal for his cousin's help, but before he could get beyond a few words St. George held out his hand and said, "Do you recognize this?"

It was a handkerchief, a delicate scrap of linen embroidered with gooseberries, hardly large enough to be practical. "Yes, of course," Crispin said without hesitation. "It's Claris'. I didn't know she'd lost it. She'll be very pleased to have it back, she's excessively fond of it. How did you happen across it?"

"I found it," said St. George succinctly, "in Warwick's room."

Crispin stared at him. "What the devil were you doing in

Nicholas Warwick's room?"

"Not Nicholas Warwick's, his younger brother's. Harry Warwick asked a few fellows up earlier in the evening and I went along to see what I could learn about him, considering the way he's been hanging around my sister. Not that Edwina would look twice at him but it's wise to be cautious."

"I daresay Claris dropped the handkerchief and Harry picked it up and was keeping it for her," Crispin said. "She's over here all the time. Colonel Scott is Mrs. Warwick's brother, you know."

"I know that Miss Ashton spends a great deal of time in Harry Warwick's company," St. George said carefully, his gaze straying to Claris and Harry on the dance floor.

"Lord, yes. She sees him as a sort of brother, and I must say I wish he was for he's a deal more agreeable than the one she's got." Crispin took the handkerchief, folded it, and stowed it in his pocket. "I'll see that she gets it. Thanks for picking it up, Quen. Harry's so preoccupied with Edwina I don't know when he'd have thought to return it."

St. George stood regarding his cousin for an instant and then gave a smile which seemed even more mocking than usual. "Happy to have been of service, old fellow. Please say the same to Miss Ashton."

"I will, though ten to one you'll see her before I do. I suppose I should have left the handkerchief with you. Claris said you're taking her in to supper."

"You don't mind?"

"Good God, no. What sort of jealous idiot do you take me for? It wouldn't do for Claris to spend the whole evening in my pocket. Anyway, I daresay we can make up a table."

"Certainly." St. George's attention seemed to have wandered. "Who is that singularly odd gentleman talking to Tony? The one who stands in crying need of a new tailor?"

"Where?" Crispin followed the direction of his cousin's gaze. "Oh, I daresay it's Murray."

"Murray? I don't think I'm acquainted with the family."

Crispin grinned. "I'm quite certain you aren't. He's some sort of pamphleteer or publisher or something. He came by to give Warwick some information and they asked him to stay to supper. Harry told me."

"I see. And what exactly does Mr. Murray publish?"

"Oh, complaints about wages, attacks on the government, you know the sort of thing," Crispin said carelessly. "He's a friend of Ashton's."

"If he's a friend of Ashton's and Warwick's, I can imagine the kind of thing he publishes very well indeed. All the same, I wouldn't have thought even a man like Warwick would let that sort of fellow mingle with his guests. I'd heard the Warwick House entertainments were eccentric, but I hadn't expected this."

"Makes Mama's and Aunt Catherine's entertainments look cursed flat, don't it?" Crispin said cheerfully. "Good God, what the devil's come over Edwina?"

Lady Edwina was seething. It had always rankled her that she had only been considered as a wife for Anthony after her elder sister eloped with another man. To have Anthony in turn reject *her* was more than Edwina could bear. She needed to vent her feelings on someone. Lord Buckleigh had disappeared into the card room with Mr. Hansford soon after their arrival, and in any case it would never have occurred to Edwina to go to her father with a problem. Her mother was still in the ballroom with Aunt Aurelia, though fortunately Mrs. Hansford had taken herself off. Edwina went directly to them.

Lady Carteret smiled at her niece with pleasure. She had seen Edwina leave the room with Anthony and she had the most pleasant forebodings. Perhaps Anthony was finally coming to his senses. Perhaps he had even chosen tonight to make his betrothal to Edwina official.

"Edwina, dear," said Lady Carteret. "What's happened to Anthony?"

"I wouldn't know, Aunt Aurelia. But if I were to venture a guess, I'd say he's very likely proposing to Philippa Davenport."

Lady Carteret gave a strangled cry. "Aurelia!" said Lady Buckleigh sharply, seizing hold of her sister's arm. "Control yourself. Edwina, stop scowling. You're a beautiful woman but

221

even beautiful women can't affort to neglect their appearance. Especially at times like these. Did Anthony tell you that was what he was going to do?"

"He made his intentions clear enough. I am to consider myself free to look elsewhere for a husband. I know my sister disappointed you, Mama, but I think you might have been a little more careful about securing my future."

"You won't get Anthony back by talking like a shrew," her mother advised her. "I knew it was a good idea to come here tonight. I'm so glad I asked the Hansfords to stay with us. It only shows that even one's dullest acquaintances can prove useful."

"I don't know how you can be so unfeeling," Lady Carteret moaned, searching frantically through her reticule for her vinaigrette. "With the entire future of the family at stake—"

"Bother the family." Edwina supplied her aunt with the vinaigrette, which had fallen into Lady Carteret's lap. "It can look after itself. What about *my* future?"

"That," said Lady Buckleigh, "is why it is imperative to remain calm. Whatever Anthony's intentions, he is not proposing to Philippa Davenport at the moment. I just saw her talking with Mrs. Warwick. Aurelia, you look faint—"

"I feel faint," her sister interjected, pleased and surprised that Catherine had for once taken note of her delicate constitution.

"I'm sure a glass of lemonade will do wonders for you. I am going to ask Anthony to procure one."

"I don't want a glass of lemonade, and I most certainly do not want Anthony to fetch one for me. I never want to speak to him again."

"Nonsense. You are going to speak to him a great deal tonight. We all are. Edwina, you are going to apologize to Anthony for losing your temper, as I make no doubt you did. You never learned proper self-control, though that is neither here nor there at the moment. If you see Quentin, tell him I wish to speak with him. We could use his help. We are going to see to it that Anthony is kept very busy indeed. Far too busy to go anywhere near Philippa Davenport."

*   *   *

222

Livia was called away after she and Philippa had spent some minutes conversing with Harriet and Granville Leveson-Gower, but before long Nicholas Warwick appeared at Philippa's side and asked her to dance. When they left the dance floor, he insisted on presenting her to Sir John and Lady Raeburn who were down from Shropshire visiting their eldest son who was now sitting in Parliament. Philippa had always appreciated Nicholas and Livia, but she had never realized just how helpful they could be.

Had she been privy to more information she might have been equally grateful to the Thane family, for between Lady Buckleigh's orders to procure lemonade for the afflicted Lady Carteret, Lady Edwina's words of apology—which took some time, though they were uttered through clenched teeth—and St. George's manoeuvres which forced the marquis to dance with Miss Bennington, there was quite as active a campaign to keep Carteret away from Philippa as there was to keep Philippa away from Carteret. As for Elliot Marsden, he had apparently decided it was prudent to allow Miss Davenport some time to herself. Miss Davenport was grateful.

Just before supper, Claris detached Philippa from the Raeburns. "Who's taking you down to supper?"

"No one yet," Philippa said briefly and was spared the necessity of saying more by the timely arrival of Henry Ashton.

"Gordon's in his element," Henry informed them. "He's been lecturing Lady Holland on the Opposition's failure to address the problem of children born out of wedlock."

Philippa looked at him in horror. It was no secret that Lady Holland had had a child out of wedlock herself.

"Oh, it's all right," Henry assured her. "She thinks he's most amusing. I shouldn't be surprised if he finds himself invited to one of her dinner parties."

"He talked to Lord Carteret for some time," Claris volunteered, looking at Philippa. "I think it's splendid that Lord Carteret likes Mr. Murray so much."

"The marquis is always in search of novelty," Philippa said dryly.

Henry raised an eyebrow.

"Oh, look," Claris said, "here's Lord St. George coming to

223

take me down to supper. Don't frown, Henry, I wouldn't like Lord St. George to challenge you to a duel too. Crispin tells me he's a capital shot."

Philippa smiled but her mirth was short-lived, for as she watched Claris go off on Lord St. George's arm she somehow missed the approach of Elliot Marsden. Before she had time to frame a response he was asking to take her down to supper.

Why, oh why, hadn't she had the sense to secure a supper partner earlier in the evening? It was most vexatious. It couldn't be helped now, of course, only what was she to say—

"You've already had Miss Davenport to yourself for entirely too much of the evening, Marsden. Go away, there's a good fellow. Miss Davenport is going down to supper with me." The Marquis of Carteret had at last escaped his interfering relatives and was determined to waste no further time.

Marsden turned to Carteret, grey eyes meeting grey. They were of a height, Philippa realized. She had never seen them standing quite so close together.

"Surely that is something Miss Davenport should be allowed to decide for herself," Marsden said, not yielding an inch.

"Very well. Miss Davenport?"

Philippa smiled sweetly at the two men. "I'm afraid you're both too late. I've been promised to Mr. Ashton this half-hour and more. Mr. Ashton?" She gave him her arm. "We should go down before all the tables are taken."

"Of course." Henry took Philippa's arm and nodded at the disappointed lovers. "Marsden, Carteret, I daresay we shall see you later in the evening. Sorry to have stolen a march on you."

"Don't you dare," Philippa said when they were out of earshot and moving toward the gallery, "say anything, certainly not anything clever."

"Certainly not," Henry agreed. "You didn't say anything clever about Miss Myerson."

"Yes, but that was different."

"Was it?"

"Of course it was. Louisa Myerson is a fool."

"I have to agree with you there. But why does that make it different?"

Philippa eyed him frostily. "You don't like Louisa Myerson," she said.

"Not especially," Henry agreed. "Am I to take it that it was your liking for Lord Carteret and Mr. Marsden which made you wish to avoid their company this evening?"

Philippa continued to walk in silence, staring straight in front of her. "I'm sorry," Henry said, in a different tone, "that was impertinent. I'm delighted to be of service, whatever the reasons. I certainly have no right to inquire into them."

Philippa sighed. "Now I shall have to be grateful to you. That is excessively awkward, for I don't seem to be very good at it. But at least the obligation is not all on one side. I did give you a chance to steal a march on Lord Carteret and Mr. Marsden."

"And why exactly, Miss Davenport, should I be grateful to you for that?"

"I can't imagine," said Philippa, "you've always shown yourself so very fond of both of them."

The supper rooms were already beginning to fill. Philippa saw Claris and Lord St. George almost at once, sharing a table with Lord Christopher and Lady Helen Langdon, and Mary Fairchild and a young man whose name, Philippa thought, was Tutford. Philippa cast a sidelong glance at Henry.

"No," he said firmly. "I may be an overly protective brother, but not to the point of spending supper listening to St. George's witticisms." He steered her toward the table in the centre of the room which, many of the guests having yet to make depredations upon it, still bore the appearance of a work of art. Three epergnes surrounded by sprays of jasmine provided the focal point. Around and between them was the expected profusion of food, artfully placed so that no two similar dishes stood side by side. It was the arrangement, the cut vegetable flowers garnishing the cold tongue and sliced ham, the delicate pink of a lobster salad contrasting with a vanilla cream, which mattered far more than the quality of the dishes themselves, though Philippa knew from experience that the Warwicks had an excellent cook.

As she and Henry filled their plates, Philippa caught sight of Gordon Murray, champagne glass in hand, holding forth to a group of interested and illustrious persons. Lady Edwina came

225

into the room with the Earl of Deavers, an eligible parti whose attentions would have gratified most young women. Lady Edwina did not appear gratified.

Henry and Philippa made for a table in the far corner where Lord Palmerston, having decided to give his beloved Emily a taste of her own medicine, was flirting with Francesca. Francesca responded to his smiles and returned his banter, but, as Emily knew perfectly well that Francesca was still head over heels in love with her own husband, Palmerston did not find the exercise very satisfying and was quite willing to have Henry and Philippa join them.

Francesca did not seem surprised to see Philippa with Henry, which probably meant that Livia had warned her something was amiss. At least Francesca could be counted on not to ask awkward questions. And Palmerston was too preoccupied with his own romantic difficulties to take any interest in Philippa's.

They were soon joined by Colonel Ralston, a friend of Gerry's, and his pretty new wife. Conversation was lively. Philippa toyed with a slice of boiled chicken in Béchamel sauce and a blancmange which was satisfyingly bland, smiled a great deal and said very little. Nicholas stopped and exchanged a few words with them. Livia sat down at their table for a short time, snatching some rest. Philippa doubted if she and Nicholas had had time to eat more than a few mouthfuls all evening.

As they were lingering over coffee, Emily Cowper came up to the table on Gerry's arm—he was one of the few men in London whom she could be certain would not make Palmerston jealous. Emily smiled impartially at the company, then laid a hand on Palmerston's shoulder.

"Dear Harry. I haven't seen you all evening. It's been such a bore."

Palmerston looked up at her for a long moment, then smiled and covered her hand lightly with his own. All was clearly forgiven. Emily and Gerry drew up chairs and Francesca sent her husband a grateful look.

Used to the vagaries of Emily and Palmerston's affair, Philippa continued abstracted. Despite her resolve to wait until she was safely in her own room, she was allowing her

226

mind to dwell on those moments in the garden with Elliot Marsden and how they might have been different if Lord Carteret and not Mr. Marsden had held her. Her thoughts were interrupted by an outraged cry from the centre of the room.

Emily's eyes widened, Francesca gasped, and Gerry muttered, "Hell, this is just what Livia and Nicholas need." At first Philippa could not see what was happening. Then Colonel Ralston leaned back and she had a clearer view. Lady Edwina Thane had sprung to her feet and was clutching her wrist as if she had been wounded. A cut glass? A carelessly dropped knife?

"My bracelet!" Lady Edwina shrieked. "It's gone! It's been stolen!"

The room, which had been bubbling with innumerable conversations a few moments before, was suddenly silent. Philippa, to whom Lady Edwina had always seemed the epitome of cool—if not chilly—elegance, was amazed at this display of unbridled passion. But then she had never seen one of Lady Edwina's tantrums, which were generally confined to the family circle. And she did not know the provocation Lady Edwina's volatile temper had already received that evening.

Most of those in the supper room sat very still, watching in shock or fascination or sometimes both. Lady Edwina's supper partner, Lord Deavers, dropped to the floor and began to search for the bracelet, showing valiant disregard for the effect on his elegant attire but doing nothing to calm the hysterical Edwina. Lord St. George rose, then gave a slight shrug and sat down again. Crispin put his head in his hands. Elliot Marsden slipped quietly from the room, unnoticed by any but Philippa. By this time Nicholas and Livia had hurried through the doorway from the second supper room. Nicholas assured the distraught Lady Edwina that he would turn the house upside down once the ball was over.

"Once it's over!" Edwina exclaimed.

"I'm afraid a search wouldn't be very effective with so many people in the house," Livia said soothingly. "As soon as things are quieter we'll ask the servants to—"

"The servants," Edwina said scornfully. "The servants should be searched!"

Many of the staff had been with the Warwicks for years, thanks largely to exemplary treatment from the family. Nicholas and Livia exchanged glances. "We will speak to them," Nicholas said on a note intended to end the matter.

"And the musicians?" Edwina persisted.

"Of course," Livia promised her. "I'll talk to them myself."

"They should not be allowed to leave the house until their persons have been searched. No one should."

Nicholas went very white, a sign to those who knew him that he was controlling his own temper with an effort, though his voice remained even. "I cannot possibly ask that of a guest in my home," he said.

"Even when there are so very many odd guests present? You cannot vouch for all of them, Mr. Warwick. And if you will invite such people to your house—"

"If I invite anyone to my house you may be assured that he or she is not a thief."

Lady Edwina would no doubt have continued to protest, but she was forestalled by a voice from a nearby table. "I collect the lady is referring to me." Gordon Murray pushed back his chair.

Philippa gave a stifled exclamation and heard Henry draw in his breath. Oh, Nicholas, Francesca thought, don't, whatever you do, don't lose your temper.

"Murray," said Nicholas firmly, "I will not have—"

"Please don't trouble yourself, Mr. Murray," Livia said at the same time, moving toward him. "There is no need—"

But Murray had already risen and was coming forward. "No trouble at all, Mrs. Warwick," he said genially. "I'm happy to oblige Lady Edwina."

Under the interested gaze of the room's occupants—and several others who were crowding the doorway from the adjoining chamber—Murray proceeded to empty the contents of his pockets onto Livia's fine damask tablecloth: a pencil stub, the remains of a hastily snuffed cigar, a none too clean handkerchief, a few coins, and several battered scraps of paper which, he explained, contained jottings for various articles.

"Daresay you'd like to have a look at my coat yourself," he said when the pockets had been emptied, and proceeded to strip off the garment.

Someone gave a drunken laugh, abruptly silenced. Nicholas' lips were tightly compressed. Livia laid a hand on his arm. Henry rose and crossed quickly to Murray's side. "Gordon," he said, in a voice meant only for his friend's ear, "Gordon, stop. You're only making it worse for the Warwicks."

Murray seemed to see the sense of Henry's advice and shrugged the coat back onto his shoulders. Lady Edwina did not appear equally ready to end the scene, but before she could say anything further, Elliot Marsden returned to the room accompanied by her mother, her aunt, and Lord Carteret.

When first informed of her daughter's distress, Lady Buckleigh had thought that Edwina was creating a diversion to distract Anthony. A glance sufficed to assure her that her daughter was in earnest. Still, it made a splendid excuse to get Anthony out of the house before he had a chance to propose to Miss Davenport. Lady Buckleigh offered her apologies to her host and hostess and said she would take her daughter home. Lord Carteret would escort them, and Lord St. George would explain matters to the rest of their party.

Lady Edwina did not wish to leave with her bracelet unaccounted for, and she especially did not want to leave with Anthony, but she had spent much of her energy and could not stand against so many people. She followed her mother and aunt from the room, though she gave an angry sob and declined to take Anthony's arm.

Philippa let out a relieved sigh. Francesca rose and went to speak with Livia.

"Well," said Emily *sotto voce*, "I must say it's rather nice to see someone other than Caroline making a scene."

Emily's remark helped break the tension at their table. There were some smiles (though no outright laughter, for Caroline Lamb was seated on the opposite side of the room, surveying the scene with her large sad eyes) and conversation was resumed. A few moments later Henry rejoined them.

"Thank you," said Philippa, as he slipped into the seat beside her.

"I did little enough."

"You helped keep a difficult scene from growing worse. As I

recall, this isn't the first time you've done that. You're a very resourceful man, Mr. Ashton."

"So it's 'Mr. Ashton' again is it? I thought I'd progressed to 'Henry.'"

Philippa looked at him in puzzlement. Henry smiled. "I don't wonder it slipped your mind. You were occupied with more pressing matters at the time."

He had to be talking about the duel. Philippa could not recall using his given name on that occasion, but she took his word for it that she had. She was rather pleased with herself for having done so, and with him for having remembered it. "Henry then," she said. "Will Mr. Murray be all right?"

"Gordon? He's right as a trivet."

"I thought, underneath the show, he was rather angry."

Henry surveyed her for a moment. "You're very observant, Miss Davenport. Yes, I think he was angry. But Gordon's a pragmatist. He wouldn't have expected better treatment from someone of Lady Edwina's type."

This last statement had an uncomfortable ring. "What type is that?" Philippa asked.

"A wealthy, bored, spoiled young woman who's been raised to have nothing but contempt for those who aren't part of her small world."

"I see. And do I also fall into that category?"

"*You?*" Henry seemed genuinely surprised. "No, Miss Davenport, you most certainly do not."

"Thank you, Henry. And my name," said Philippa, "is Philippa."

"Philippa." Henry smiled.

Chapter 15

Philippa tumbled into bed at five and fell into a deep, exhausted sleep, only to be awakened by the cries of the cress sellers not long past six. Unwilling to face the day, she turned her face into the pillows, but sleep returned only in fits and starts. Marsden's face was before her eyes, his voice was murmuring in her ear, his touch suffused her whole body. She could not tell if this was the stuff of recollection or of dreams and at last, her bedclothes in a tangle, she forced herself into consciousness and sat up. Being kissed had proved much more momentous than she expected.

Philippa had not had much experience with men, and she had never been stirred in quite that way before. Kissing, she decided, was something she would like to explore. Her response to Elliot Marsden's kiss had been quite excessive, but she thought it might be general rather than particular. A kiss from Lord Carteret, for example, might provoke just such delicious and disturbing sensations as those she had experienced last night. It was to avoid thinking about this possibility that she had refused to go into supper with him. It might even be possible—heaven forfend—that she would react so to any man. Well, to any presentable man. How on earth did a young woman know when she was truly in love? Did she kiss a great many men and then choose the most exciting? Or was it possible that it did not matter very much which man one chose, at least for that secret part of one's life that was centred in bed?

Philippa debated ringing for tea, then decided against it. At the moment she could face absolutely no one. She got out of bed, pulled aside the curtain to let in the light and peered into the glass on her dressing table. Her face was flushed, her hair was plastered in damp strands over her forehead, and there were deep blue circles under her eyes. Philippa dropped the curtain and ran back to bed. She would have to get more sleep or she would not be fit to be seen. She turned the pillows, straightened the covers, and climbed into bed.

Still sleep would not come. Marsden had receded to the edge of her mind, but Carteret had taken his place. She thought of his quickly masked chagrin when she had denied him her company at supper. Then she thought of the appalling scene when Lady Edwina discovered the loss of her bracelet. Philippa ought to be grateful to her, for the commotion had taken Carteret out of the house at a time when Philippa did not think she could face him, and it had given her occupation for the rest of the evening.

Not all of the guests had been privy to Lady Edwina's astounding display of temper—for that, Philippa suspected, was all it was—but word of the event spread rapidly and gave an extra fillip to the evening. Livia Warwick had enlisted Francesca and Philippa and the three women had spent the remainder of the evening deflating the more preposterous rumours and deftly turning conversations.

Nicholas Warwick, Gerry, and Henry had done much the same in the rooms where the older men were gathered. Lord Buckleigh of course was informed, but he showed surprisingly little interest in his daughter's misfortune, remarking only that she was forever up in the boughs about one thing or another and it served her right for being so demn'd careless with her belongings. Then he turned his attention back to the cards which were giving him a particularly good run of luck.

Edwina's brother St. George was not turned off so easily. He might have created some difficulty had not Nicholas treated him with such obvious courtesy and concern, and shown such competence in his arrangements for a discreet search of the rooms and careful inquiries among the servants, and the viscount could find no further cause for complaint.

It was on these recollections that Philippa at last fell into a quiet sleep, waking some two hours later much refreshed. The house was quiet and she breakfasted alone. Even Colonel Scott, she was informed, was still abed. She decided to take Hermia for a walk, but found that her dog had already left the house on an errand with one of the footmen.

Philippa was too restless to work. She could not take refuge in conferring with the housekeeper, since she had turned all such chores over to Francesca. That left only Linnet. Philippa climbed the steps to the nursery gratefully. The uncomplicated little girl would soon put her own problems in perspective.

She sent Adèle off to have another cup of tea and spent a pleasant half-hour on the floor playing with the child. When the delights of chasing a ball began to wane, she put Linnet on her hip and carried her downstairs, thinking to find fresh distraction in the garden.

They were still there when Tuttle came to inform her that Mr. Marsden had called and, despite the earliness of the hour, insisted that he see Miss Davenport and begged to have his message delivered.

Philippa was immediately depressed. She had not sorted out her feelings for Elliot Marsden, and it was too bad of him to press her so soon after their encounter of the evening before. Then it occurred to her that he might have some message about the affair of Lady Edwina's bracelet. When she had finally left Warwick House it had not yet been found, and the Warwicks had clearly been disturbed by this fact. "It's all right, Tuttle," she said. "Show him into the jade saloon, I'll be there directly."

She picked up Linnet, wiped the dirt from her mouth, persuaded her to relinquish the fistful of thyme she had plucked from the herbaceous border, and carried her to the room where Mr. Marsden was waiting impatiently for her arrival.

"Forgive me," he said with a disarming smile, seeming oblivious to the child in her arms, "I know it is early and you do not want to talk to me, but there are things I must say to you, things you must know about me, and I dare not put it off any longer. Say that I may speak."

So it was not about the bracelet. She saw the look of appeal and uncertainty in his eyes—she had never before seen this trace of vulnerability in him—and she was oddly touched. She put Linnet down on the floor and the girl stumbled awkwardly toward the sofa where the fringe of a forgotten shawl promised to be interesting.

"Of course you may speak," Philippa said with what warmth she could muster. She sat down and directed him to a nearby chair.

"What I have to say is for you alone, Miss Davenport."

She was amused. "We are alone, Mr. Marsden."

He sat down then and leaned toward her as though he was about to speak, but Philippa had turned away, distracted by Linnet who was reaching for a china bowl on a nearby table. She turned her around and the child toddled over to Mr. Marsden, a smile breaking over her face as she stared up at him. He glanced briefly at her, but gave no evidence of actually seeing the little girl. Balked, Linnet dropped to the floor, turned round, then stood up and walked back to Philippa whose own face glowed in response to the little girl's smile.

"Miss Davenport," Marsden said, between amusement and exasperation, "I would like your undivided attention."

She knew then that she was using Linnet as a shield. Very well. He was determined, and she would have to deal with him sooner or later. Better now and have it done with. "I'll ring for someone to take the child," she said.

They waited, not saying very much, and Philippa devoted herself once more to Linnet. When Adèle had been fetched and Linnet had made a proper wave of farewell, Philippa turned at last to her would-be suitor. She would not insult him by pretending this was a social occasion or by offering him refreshment or chit-chat. So she faced him in silence, telling him by her attitude that she was ready to listen to whatever he might choose to say and would hear it, if not with approbation, at least with consideration.

Now that he had obtained his immediate objective, Marsden seemed uncertain how to begin. "I would not for the world offend you," he said. "I promise there will be no repetition of the scene last night. I don't know what infernal demon possessed me then, but I swear I could not help myself!"

234

This she could not let pass. There had been nothing impetuous about that kiss. "Mr. Marsden, I am not accustomed to being kissed in the middle of a ball"—unfortunately, she was not accustomed to being kissed at all—"but I am strongly of the opinion that you knew very well what you were doing."

Her eyes told him this was not a serious rebuke and his face broke into a rueful smile. He had a kind of rough honesty and could sometimes laugh at himself, which served to temper his habitual arrogance. "Ah, but it was a pleasant moment," he said. His smile deepened and she found herself responding in kind, then hastily schooled her features. She noted how the slight cleft in his chin echoed the line that already marked the space between his brows. He was not as handsome as Carteret, but he had his own kind of charm.

"I make no secret of my feelings for you," he went on, "but I will not speak of these. Not yet. I must tell you some things about myself and I hesitate to do so, for I fear I shall forfeit whatever regard you have for me."

The remark was well calculated to bring forth instant denial, but Philippa did not fall into the trap. "Mr. Marsden, I will endeavour to do you justice."

"It is not justice I want, Miss Davenport, it is charity."

"I make no promises," she said, "but do not keep me longer in suspense."

He did not immediately answer but stood up and began to walk about the room. What on earth did he intend to say that gave him so much trouble? He was hardly a man who lacked assurance. She recalled Henry's accusations. It must have something to do with Lady Carteret.

He came to rest behind his chair, grasping its back like a shield, and began as she expected, speaking of the trial and his acceptance of the brief from the marchioness' solicitor. "I do not deny that I was anxious to serve her," he said, "though the case was not to my taste. I believe people overvalue that precious bauble reputation. But Lady Carteret holds a considerable position in the world, and the association, I knew, would do me no harm. This much of course you know. But what you perhaps do not know is that I have been acquainted with Lady Carteret for some years, and she has extended me many kindnesses."

It was as Henry had suspected. Philippa thought with dismay of her scene with him in the library just over a week ago. And yet, he had had no cause to interfere in her life and his being right did not alter that fact.

She could not conceive what would have led Lady Carteret to take notice of Elliot Marsden, despite his undeniable talent and his personal attractions. A momentary thought of the kinds of services Lady Carteret might have thought worth repaying crossed Philippa's mind, but she shoved it aside as unworthy.

"You will not think well of me for what I must now relate," he continued, looking directly into her eyes. "When Lady Carteret recently asked me to perform a service for her, I did not feel I could refuse. I cannot tell you my reasons—you must simply accept that I am tied to her by past obligations—but they do not bring dishonour either to her or to myself."

Philippa sensed what might be coming, though she prayed it would not be so. "And that is why you found it necessary to walk a dog by the Serpentine." It was not a question.

He nodded. "I could say that our passages in court had piqued my interest, but you would not believe me. And you might be right, for I do not honestly know if I would have acted so on my own account." He was silent for a moment, seemingly lost in thought, but when he spoke again it was in a rapid, matter-of-fact voice. "Lady Carteret had observed her stepson's interest in you, Miss Davenport, and she asked me to put a stop to it."

Their eyes met and held. "And you undertook to provide me with distraction?"

He seemed more relaxed now, and a faint smile played about his lips. "She gave me no specific instructions. She feels things keenly, as you have no doubt observed, but her understanding does not allow sustained thought. I did not in all honesty know how I would go about the task, but I did know that I must first make your acquaintance."

There was silence in the room. Philippa was aware of the ticking of the clock which sounded preternaturally loud. Marsden's engaging frankness when he first came to Green

Street, the way his eyes followed her when she entered a room, the way he found his way to her side whenever they happened to meet, indeed the odd frequency of the meetings themselves were all part of his plan to detach her from Lord Carteret. He had not been attracted by her sparkling wit and certainly not by her nonexistent beauty.

Philippa was not surprised, but she was bitterly disappointed. She understood Carteret's interest. He was bored and aimless and took a perverse delight in doing something novel. But she could have sworn that Elliot Marsden had seen beyond the surface and found her worthy of his interest. His confession was an odd prelude to what was certain to be a proposal. Perhaps, as on their first meeting after Hermia's romp in the park, he was about to be devastatingly frank and tell her that, though he liked her well enough, he was actually after her money. Philippa suppressed a sigh and looked up to find Marsden's eyes upon her.

"It wasn't that simple," he said, as though he knew what was passing through her mind. He sat down opposite her once more, leaned forward in his chair and possessed himself of her hands. She withdrew them quickly. He raised a palm in acknowledgement of her action. He would not touch her. "I am a busy man, and I have not been hanging out for a wife. Even," he said, his eyes steady upon her, "a rich one."

She could not meet their naked intensity and she lowered her own.

"But," he continued, "I confess that I tried to attach you with no more than my obligation to Lady Carteret in mind. Or if not to attach you, then to make you aware that you had some choice in how you gave your heart."

"And if I had given you my heart?" she challenged him.

He smiled. "I knew from your book that you are cautious with your heart. I had no fear of breaking it. Philippa Davenport is not a woman to be taken in readily by any man."

It was so just an observation that Philippa had to smile. "But," she said, "you have somewhat bruised my *amour propre.*"

"Then let me restore it at once. I have never believed Carteret to be wholly serious in anything he does, but I have

237

grown jealous of him nonetheless, jealous of your regard for him, jealous of the time he spends in your company. Jealous," he repeated in wonder, "of a man such as that."

He did, she thought, insist upon it more than was necessary. She wondered at the bitterness of his tone—surely she could not be the sole cause of such feelings—but the thought escaped her notice in what followed.

"And that, my fair friend, is when I knew I had been truly caught. How on earth did you do it?"

So it was now her fault. She had to laugh at his impudence. But his eyes told her he was in earnest.

"I went to Lady Carteret," he said, "and told her I could no longer be of service to her. I told her on the day we met outside your friend Murray's office. What I did last night, what I say to you now, is between you and me. It has nothing to do with the marchioness."

So he was prepared to break with the woman who had been his patroness. For break with her he must if he pursued an attachment to a woman Lady Carteret despised. Perhaps at this stage in his career it was not a great sacrifice. And yet it seemed to Philippa that there was some nobility in his action, as though he had wiped clean a slate that had been smudged by unworthy motives. Was she reading him right? Or was it merely that he was so persuasive?

"I have little enough to offer you now," he went on, "but I have a future. We suit, Philippa Davenport, you and I. You are not wholly indifferent to me or you would not have suffered my impertinence thus far, and I am far from indifferent to you. I want you to be my wife."

At last. Her very first proposal. Or the first to which she had dared attend, for she had to admit that Percival Long had been about to blurt out some such thing at one of Mama's receptions, and she had been forced to flee the room to stifle a fit of the giggles. But then she had been scarcely eighteen and not nearly as adept at turning away nascent interest. Was that why her tongue had grown so sharp, to ward off the men who could never capture her interest, to guard against the disappointment of not being good enough for those she found attractive? What would have happened had she met Elliot

Marsden when she was eighteen, or twenty?

"You do not then hold my fortune against me?" She threw it at him, though her tone was light.

He returned it in kind. "I welcome your fortune, Miss Davenport, as I welcome your person. Though were you penniless, I should insist that we wait, for I am not yet ready to assume the burdens of a family." His eyes were bright, but some of his confidence had gone. He was not sure of her response.

Nor was she. "I do not know what to say. I truly do not know," she repeated, laughing helplessly. "You must give me time, Mr. Marsden, for though I enjoy your company, I am not like most women. I have not been hanging out for a husband. Mama has taught me that the married state can be a happy one, but I am not at all sure it is for me."

He began to protest, but she silenced him. "Please, no more. I will think on it."

He hesitated, then rose and prepared to take his leave. But at the door he seized her hands once more and held them close. "I need you. You make me better than I am. Believe that I would try to make you happy." He kissed her hands ardently and was gone, leaving Philippa's cheeks burning.

Was he a rogue or was he sincere? She could not decide, and perhaps it did not matter. Unfit to meet even the eyes of the servants, Philippa fled back into the garden.

By the time Francesca and Claris made their way downstairs, Philippa had recovered her poise and was able to join them in the breakfast parlour where they had the delight of talking over the ball and Lady Edwina's hysteria and the absurd spectacle of Mr. Murray emptying out his pockets before her. Claris was of the opinion that the lady had had a row with Lord Carteret— her sharp eyes had caught them returning from their tête-à-tête—which accounted for her frenzy over the bracelet. Francesca was beginning to gain respect for Claris' observations, and she suspected that in this case Claris was not far from the truth. But this bit of gossip did not long engage Francesca's attention. She was worried by their failure to find

239

the bracelet the night before and insisted on reviewing everything that had been done to retrieve it, and what should be done again, and what further steps they might take.

Gerry had already left for Warwick House and Francesca said she would follow him there. Philippa and Claris immediately offered to accompany her. "Unless you think we will be in the way," Philippa said.

"Not at all. If heads and hands can be of help, then the more the better." Francesca took a last swallow of coffee. "Let me just have a quarter-hour with Linnet and I shall be with you."

She was on the point of rising when Tuttle came into the room to announce that Lord Carteret was in the hall and, if it was not too early, he would like to speak to the ladies. Francesca did not stand on ceremony. She asked Tuttle to show him into the breakfast parlour and settled back in her chair. "He may have something to tell us," she observed. "I pray the girl has found the paltry thing."

Though Anthony was not accustomed to being received in this informal way by ladies of fashion, he had the knack of being at ease wherever he was. Or almost wherever, Philippa reflected, for he had looked distinctly out of place in Miss Neville's drawing room and in Mr. Murray's office. He accepted a cup of coffee and sat back in his chair, crossing his admirable legs. "I have come to make apologies for my cousin's behaviour last night," he said, "and I hope you will convey them to Mrs. Warwick. I hesitate to call on her myself. She may be much occupied today. And in any case," he added, setting down his cup, "Edwina should do it herself. There was no excuse for her behaviour. She was prone to tantrums as a child, though I thought she'd grown out of them by this time." Anthony picked up his cup and swallowed the rest of his coffee. Any lingering doubts about the wisdom of his declaration to Edwina last night had been swept away by the force of the passions she had displayed. The woman would make her husband's life a living hell.

Claris leaned forward eagerly. "Then Lady Edwina did not find the bracelet on her person? She could not recall where she might have dropped it?"

Anthony shook his head.

"What a splendid mystery! For you must know that it was never discovered last night. They searched and searched, though ever so discreetly. I think St. George did not feel the Warwicks were doing all they could, but I assure you that they were, and I told him so, several times. He does have a way of glowering when he thinks no one is looking, I am certain he is not really as bored as he pretends. Do you think he has a character like his sister's?"

Francesca sent Claris a look of warning.

But Anthony did not take offence. He saw both Quentin and Edwina with the clarity of childhood's eyes. Little Miss Ashton was dead right. "Something like," he drawled. His eyes turned to Philippa with an unspoken question.

Francesca saw it and stood up. "Thank you for coming, Lord Carteret. Now if you will excuse me, I must see to my daughter. Miss Davenport will talk to you. Claris, come, you have things to attend to." And before he had time to rise from the table she had swept the surprised Claris out of the room.

Anthony smiled. "And do you too have things to attend to, Miss Davenport?"

"I was planning to return to my book," she said smoothly, knowing full well that she was going to accompany her cousin to the Warwicks' and could in any case not bring herself to write today. Damn Francesca! "But I need not do so just yet. Would you like some more coffee?"

He shook his head. "I rather thought you were avoiding me last night."

"And why should I do that, Lord Carteret?"

"I don't know," he said simply. "I was hoping you would tell me."

She forced herself to meet his eyes. "You mistake me, sir. I believe you were much occupied yourself."

That, Anthony reflected, was true. He had not thought of it at the time, but there had seemed a concerted effort to keep Philippa Davenport out of his reach. He must make use of his time now before she once more eluded his grasp.

The door opened and a maid appeared, then quickly vanished as she saw that the breakfast parlour was still occupied.

241

But not here. He looked up and saw the doors that led to a small terrace and thence to the garden. "Could we walk awhile outside?" he said. "The day is fine."

Philippa surveyed the wreckage of the breakfast table, the scattered crumbs, the egg yolk congealing on the cups, the drops of coffee which stained the linen. Better to deal with Carteret in the open air. "Of course," she said brightly and led him outside.

They strolled for a while in silence. Philippa began to be easy. After Elliot Marsden, Lord Carteret seemed blissfully restful.

He stopped to inspect a bed of larkspur just coming into bloom. "You're very close to your family, aren't you?"

What an odd thing to say. Philippa had a sudden vision of a young Anthony Paget, handsome and aloof and quite lonely. It was a side of him she had not before imagined. "We are all fond of one another," Philippa acknowledged, "though we are not much alike."

"I've had little enough incentive to extend my own," he said with a trace of bitterness. "My mother, of course, I don't remember, but my stepmother is a vapourish female with the brains of a goose, her sister is a gorgon, and my cousin thinks only of herself. To tell the truth, women rather bore me. Or at least," he added, for he was trying to be honest, "they do so after a time." He stopped and looked down at her. "You do not bore me, Miss Davenport. I don't think you ever could."

She had not thought he would go so far, but now that it was at hand she found she was not afraid to hear what would follow. And that, she told herself with secret amusement, is what comes of getting practice.

So she stared calmly into his face, enjoying the sight of the straight nose and the parted lips and the fine grey eyes. With a gentle touch his hand traced the line of her jaw and her throat and came to rest on her shoulder. Her lips parted expectantly, but she was unaware of their response or of her body swaying inexorably toward his own.

His kiss was a long time in coming. His hand moved slowly from her shoulder down her back, causing the most delicious shudders to run coursing through her frame, while his other hand moved up to turn her chin to a more convenient angle, then found its way around her neck to ensure that she would not escape. Had she wanted to do so, which she distinctly did not. His head bent to hers at last and his lips were placed gently on her own. Gently, and tentatively, and then with a growing firmness that held promise of the fervour he was keeping in reserve.

Philippa lay back in Lord Carteret's arms and let herself be thoroughly kissed. It was, she thought, most satisfactory, perhaps more satisfactory than the demanding kiss Elliot Marsden had given her the night before. As with Marsden, Philippa was not sure she quite liked the sense of being a passive recipient of this attention, but it was undeniably pleasant, and she opened her eyes reluctantly as it came to an end. Carteret drew a little apart, though his hands still possessed her shoulders. If he had enjoyed the kiss as much as she, he gave no sign, but then for him it was less of a novelty. She wondered if anyone had been watching from the rooms upstairs.

He dropped his hands at last. "I think it should be soon."

She had turned away, conscious of the warmth of her cheeks and the smile that came unbidden to her lips, but at this she looked into his face. "I beg your pardon?"

Anthony was taken aback. That kiss had been a declaration and her willingness to accept it had been a pledge of her own intent. Once again Anthony had the sense that he was not being taken seriously. He controlled his annoyance and tried to make light of it. "Are you trifling with me, madam?"

"I believe you are trifling with me, sir."

"You allowed me to kiss you," he pointed out.

"Yes," she admitted, "I did. To tell the truth, I wanted to know what it would be like." She looked up at him. "It was very pleasant."

She was not following the rules, and Anthony was bewildered. He struggled to bring the conversation back to solid ground. "Miss Davenport, I have asked you to marry me."

There it was, another proposal. She had done her best to head him off. Why could he not have left it as it was? His kiss was quite enough to think about. "Then I did not understand you, Lord Carteret." She plucked a leaf from a nearby tree and smoothed it between her fingers. "You are certainly not obliged to offer for me because you took a liberty I was very willing to give. I confess I have not had much experience of men. I should not have let my curiosity overcome me."

Anthony did not find the remark amusing, and Philippa was suddenly contrite. She had been mocking him, if only to protect herself. She did not wish to turn him down, and she certainly could not accept him. Not yet. Not until she better understood her own mind and heart. "I'm sorry," she said, and her face was now wholly serious. "I do like you, I enjoy your company, but I cannot listen to a proposal of marriage."

"Why not, in God's name?" Anthony had never before offered for any woman, but he knew his own worth. By person, by education, by breeding, by all the favours of fortune he stood far beyond the general run of eligible bachelors. He doubted there was another young woman in London who would hesitate to become the Marchioness of Carteret. What did Miss Davenport want?

She did not answer, but her face betrayed her confusion. Anthony was seized by a sudden doubt. The image of Elliot Marsden sprang to mind and he was flooded with jealousy. It was bad enough that his stepmother had taken up the upstart barrister, but to have him pursue the only woman Anthony had ever taken seriously . . . "Are you promised to someone else?"

"No, no, I assure you!" Philippa flushed. She could not tell him about Marsden's proposal, and in any case Mr. Marsden was not the reason for her hesitation. "It is only—" she began unhappily, then broke off, unable to express, let alone understand, her feelings in the matter.

Anthony's jealousy subsided. It occurred to him that he was not used to tender passages with inexperienced women. Perhaps he had pushed her too quickly. "You are frightened," he said. "Do not be. I will not press you more now. Say only that you will think on it."

"I will think on it," she promised and smiled her gratitude for his understanding.

His self-esteem restored, Anthony took her hands and kissed

them lightly. He would give her all the time in the world. In the end, Philippa Davenport would come round.

After Carteret's departure, Philippa returned to the house and made her way slowly up the stairs. She would have to come to some decision on the question of marriage. Having two choices in the matter did not double the problem, but it made its resolution somewhat more urgent. One might keep one suitor dangling without impropriety, but to keep two might open her to accusations of greed by the rest of her sex.

On the whole, she rather thought she would opt for marriage. The discovery of the—well, frankly, animal side of her nature had been a surprise and a delight. Not that she had not had such yearnings before, but they had been diffuse and she had always been able to keep them well under control. She stared down at the cool empty hall below and remembered the years of her growing up, the looks that passed between her parents when they thought they were unobserved, the special glow on Ianthe's face when she returned from her wedding journey. The problem was that there was such a lot more to marriage than one's animal nature. Of course the indulgence of this nature led to children, and the last few weeks with Linnet had quite convinced Philippa that she would like to have some of her own. She sighed. She would have to think it out very carefully.

Still, she was rather pleased with herself for having negotiated that amorous passage with Lord Carteret, and it was in a cheerful frame of mind that she continued up the stairs to join Francesca and Claris and prepare to walk the few blocks from Green to South Audley Street.

They found Livia Warwick in the hall, giving directions to two of the maids. There was an air of activity and purpose about the house, though they saw no one else save Parkhurst, the Warwick butler, who betrayed no sign that the day was other than an ordinary one.

Livia came toward them with outstretched hands. "I'm so glad you have come. Nicholas has a meeting, but he'll be back soon. We're turning the house upside down, but so far there's no sign of that wretched bracelet. I'm coming to believe she left it at home on her dressing table and is afraid to tell us after the row she caused, but Harry swears he saw it on her arm. He's beside himself. He so wanted Lady Edwina to think well of him, and he would have been no use at all if Jack hadn't arrived and pointed out that he'd gain credit with the lady if he found the thing and returned it to her. Since then he's been in an absolute frenzy turning out rooms, but all we've discovered is a stray boot, several books that turned up in the kitchen, and an earring I've been missing for the past month. Come into the library, I've hardly been able to think about it sensibly, and I need to talk." She was as agitated as Francesca had ever seen her. Livia was usually a model of calm good sense.

Francesca passed on Lord Carteret's message. Livia could not hide her disappointment. "I feared as much. It does begin to look as though it was not simply misplaced. Gerry's organized a search of the garden. He says that if it *was* stolen, the thief might have hidden it anywhere, hoping to retrieve it at a later time. Gwendolen is helping him. She's thrilled, of course, it's the most exciting thing to happen to her since the time she followed me all the way to Jack-in-the-Hole and put a stop to Gerry's duel with Mr. Merriman."

The women settled in the library to talk the problem out, interrupted by questions from Parkhurst, who was organizing the search of the house, and reports from Harry and his friend Jack, who were doing it all over again. Livia was forced to deny herself to at least three callers eager to gossip about last night's events. She told Parkhurst that she would see absolutely no one.

When the library door opened once more, Livia turned to it impatiently, but her look quickly changed to one of alarm. It was Henry Ashton and his face was quite white. He gave his message without preliminaries. "Gordon Murray is in custody."

There was a collective gasp. "But that's absurd!" Philippa was really angry. "He turned out his pockets for everyone to see. He's the one person who shouldn't be suspect."

"It makes no difference." She could hear the weariness in Henry's voice. "An officer was sent to search his rooms. He found Lady Edwina's bracelet in the humidor."

Chapter 16

Henry was so obviously distressed that Claris ran and put her arms around him. He seemed scarcely aware of her presence.

Livia had risen in shock and dismay. "I won't believe it of him."

Francesca pursed her lips. "Careless," she said, "and much too obvious."

"Of course." Philippa's acquaintance with Murray was slight, but she had taken his measure and was absolutely certain. "It was put there to discredit him. And the question is—"

"Who?" her cousin finished.

Henry had reached this conclusion when he first heard that Murray was taken. He knew that an act of theft was completely out of character for Murray, but he was gratified that the women so quickly echoed his own sentiments.

"The first question," Livia said, "is what is being done? Does he have counsel?"

"He's not yet been charged. Where is Nicholas? I must see him."

"He'll be back soon, Henry. Please sit down, tell us what happened."

Henry could not sit. He ran his fingers through his hair, which was already more disarranged than usual, and began to pace the floor. He was outraged by what had been done to his friend, but there was little he could do immediately and the

247

inactivity was galling. "I don't really know what happened. I haven't been able to see Gordon. The little I do know I had from the printer who owns the shop below. He had it from the lad who works for him. A police officer came round about one asking for a Mr. Murray. Gordon had gone out and the boy told him so, but the man went upstairs anyway. Jemmy—that's the boy—heard him moving about. The officer doesn't seem to have cared who heard him. Then it was quiet, so Jemmy assumed the man had sat down to wait. When Gordon came back about a half-hour later, Jemmy thought to warn him, but Gordon only laughed and said he'd had dealings with the police before. When he came back downstairs, the officer had him by the arm. Jemmy said he didn't seem upset, only puzzled."

Philippa was thinking rapidly. "An information must have been laid against him. But by whom? The bracelet was only missed last night, and one would think the Buckleighs would have had the courtesy not to report its loss until Livia and Nicholas finished searching the house. Lord Buckleigh didn't even seem disturbed when he heard about its disappearance. So it must have been the thief who went to the magistrates."

Henry considered. "Not necessarily. Anyone present last night could have done so, anyone who might have taken exception to Murray's presence. He doesn't fit in, and he made quite an impression."

Philippa saw again that ridiculous scene when Gordon Murray turned his pockets inside out to calm Lady Edwina's hysteria. "But no matter who informed the magistrates, someone put the bracelet in Mr. Murray's rooms." Her brow furrowed. "No one knew he was coming last night, so it must have been an impromptu crime. Or perhaps the theft had nothing to do with Mr. Murray at all, but the thief panicked. Perhaps he realized that he—or she, to be fair—had been seen and tried to implicate Mr. Murray to divert suspicion. He'd be a safe target."

"Plausible," Henry admitted, "but dangerous. The thief might have been seen going in or out of Murray's rooms. It's a high risk to take when there are easier ways of saving your skin."

"I think Mr. Murray had a mortal enemy at the ball who

seized the chance to bring him down," Claris contributed.

They laughed, but Livia soon grew serious. "I suppose you've realized that the target might be Nicholas." It would not be the first time that someone had tried to discredit her husband. She found herself thinking of Oliver Merriman—a perfectly charming gentleman for whom she had once felt a somewhat sentimental attachment—who had once attempted to ruin Nicholas Warwick.

Francesca met her eyes and nodded. "That widens the field. Mr. Murray's enemies and Nicholas' as well. It will be difficult but not impossible. Livia, do you have a list of the guests? We can begin with that, and then we must consider everyone else who was in or about the house for any other reason. If we cannot find a likely suspect that way, we can conclude it was a panicked thief who cared only for his own skin. And that will widen the net."

"But there is something we can do first," Philippa added, "and it will make our task easier. There had to be opportunity. When was the last time the bracelet was seen on Lady Edwina's arm, and where was she after that point? Where did she sit, or walk, with whom did she talk or dance? There must be dozens of people who might have done it, but surely there are some who could be ruled out."

"Then we should ask Harry," Claris said, "for I swear he did not take his eyes off Lady Edwina all the evening."

Livia looked stricken. Her young brother-in-law was at that moment turning over every room in the house with the assistance of his friend Jack who, she hoped, was seeing that everything was put back more or less in its place. And Gerry was out in the gardens, supervising an exhaustive search of the grounds by the footmen, the stableboy, and Nicholas' daughter Gwendolen. She rose and went to the door. "I'll get the list," she said, "and I really think I'd better call off the hunt. After all the miserable bauble has been found."

A luncheon of sorts was put together and they all sat around the table in the breakfast parlour which, like that in the Davenport house, faced the garden and let in a lot of light. They were joined by Harry and Jack and then by Gerry and a disheveled Gwendolen. And there, with sheafs of paper and a list of guests, they tried to lay out exactly what had transpired on the previous evening. There was a tendency to talk all at once and some outrageous possibilites were bandied about, but when the plates had been pushed away Henry brought the group into some semblance of order and they considered the question of opportunity. When they were done, they had ruled out no more than a third of the guests, for people had moved freely thoughout the house during the evening. And, as Henry concluded bitterly, if more than one person was involved, almost anyone might have done the deed.

"But not almost anyone *would* have done so," Philippa pointed out. "Some, like Mr. Murray, would never stoop to such a course, and some would have no reason to try. So all we need to know is who are the people of questionable morals and light fingers, with pockets to let or with a grudge against either Mr. Murray or Nicholas. Or," she added, as a new possibility occurred to her, "against people like Mr. Murray. For you must admit that while his presence was a tonic to most of your guests, Livia, there was some muttering about asking such a man to stay on to supper. Even many reform-minded members of the *ton* are not anxious to move equality ahead quite so precipitately."

Henry gave her an appreciative look. It had occurred to him that Murray, if he was indeed the target, had been so in the general sense rather than the particular.

They talked some more and finally moved away from the table. They had agreed on a probable account of what had happened. Lady Edwina must have dropped the bracelet accidentally—hadn't someone heard her aunt say that the catch was loose?—and it had been found by a person unknown who pocketed it, perhaps only for mischief's sake, perhaps because it might fetch a fair price. Lady Edwina's hysterical, accusatory glance at the Warwicks' strange guest and Gordon Murray's flamboyant turn-out of his pockets might have given the thief an idea—either then, if he was only up to mischief, or later, if he found the bracelet difficult to dispose of.

There was still a great deal they did not know about the events of the evening. They all had tasks. Harry and Jack were to call on Lady Edwina and try to narrow the time of loss further and to account for the people they now suspected. Livia and Francesca would pay some discreet calls for the same purpose, and Gerry would talk to his fellow officers who had been present that evening. Philippa had her own set of acquaintances to question. Gwendolen, who moved freely below stairs and was on good terms with all the household staff, offered to find out what the servants might have heard or seen during the evening. Claris said she would consult Lord Christopher, pointing out that Lady Edwina was his cousin and he should take an interest in the matter. This earned Claris a hard look from her brother, but he was preoccupied with the problem of how the thief had gained access to Murray's rooms and did not try to dissuade her.

Gerry left for the War Office, promising to return that evening. Livia took Francesca upstairs to look in on her little boy, and the others began to discuss everything all over again. Henry said he would wait for Nicholas in the library and asked to be told when he had returned.

Philippa followed him there. He did not see her immediately and she watched him in silence. His face was drawn with weariness, but his anger burnt like a flame. "May I come in?" she asked.

He looked up and nodded. "There's so much I want to be doing. It's hard to wait. Please," he said as she hesitated, "I'd like to talk."

Philippa closed the door behind her. "I have an idea. I did not want to talk about it in front of Francesca and the others because it involves Lord Carteret, and we agreed, did we not, that we would not talk about the duel."

A shadow passed over his face at the mention of Carteret's name—or did she imagine it?—but the urgency of her communication carried her past the moment. "Lord Nelliston."

Henry looked at her in surprise. "He was playing cards all evening."

"Are we certain? Yes, I know that's what Gerry said. It's a convenient phrase, we use it when in fact it is not strictly true. A man will get up and go outside to smoke or to relieve himself or simply because his legs are stiff and he must needs be moving about. And yet his friends will say he spent all the night at the table."

"I grant you the possibility," Henry admitted. Nelliston had impressed him as an ineffectual bully and something of a coward, but he seemed a man driven by his obsessions. "You're thinking of the pamphlets, I suppose?"

"Yes, Lord Christopher said that Nelliston was livid and that, when Carteret wouldn't tell him the name of the author, he vowed he would take care of it later."

"He would have had to learn of Murray's connection with the pamphlets. It seems unlikely."

"But it need not have happened that way," Philippa urged. "He may have only noted the connection between Mr. Murray and Lord Carteret. I saw them speaking together last night, and if I did, a hundred people might have done so and talked about it to a hundred more. Nelliston could have guessed that Murray had something to do with the pamphlets. And then, I believe he truly hates Lord Carteret and would do anything to cause him hurt."

Henry nodded. "I doubt that Nelliston would even think of such an action in the ordinary course of things. He's a far from subtle man, but if he felt pressed enough . . ." He gave a short laugh. "I can hardly see him walking down Portpool Lane and skulking in a doorway watching for Murray to be gone. But you're right, hatred is a powerful sentiment and makes men do strange things. And he could have had an accomplice." His manner was suddenly brisk. "I'm going to Portpool Lane as soon as I've seen Nicholas. Someone must have brought the bracelet there, and someone is bound to have seen him. Or her. If Lord Nelliston is involved, we'll tie him to it."

"Then," she asked, obscurely disappointed that she was not to be involved, "is that all?"

"It's quite enough. Would you have me confront him at his home? or his club?"

"No," she admitted, "but something might be learned. Not from him directly, but from his wife."

Henry was startled. "You know her well?"

"I scarcely know her at all. But Lord Carteret does. They say," she said, a hint of laughter in her voice, "that he knows her very well. I assume that's why Lord Nelliston was so annoyed."

Henry knew of the stories about Carteret and Georgina Nelliston, but he had assumed that Philippa did not. "So you propose to call on her?"

"Oh no," she said, "though I would do so if there were no other way. I'll ask Lord Carteret to do it. I'm sure he has ways of finding out anything he wants from Lady Nelliston."

For a moment Henry forgot Gordon Murray's plight. The young woman facing him with such composure, the woman who had been receiving the addresses of an eligible peer with every evidence of pleasure, had just informed him that she proposed asking her suitor to cosset his mistress into revealing information about the man he had made a cuckold.

She returned his look calmly. There was just a glint of triumph in her eyes. Philippa Davenport was not to be left out when things of moment were afoot.

Over the next few days, the group that had met over luncheon at Warwick House came together severally to exchange information and encouragement. Francesca was the hub. She was as often in South Audley Street as in the Green Street house, and she refused to let spirits flag. This last was important, for though their inquiries enabled them to rule out some of the guests as suspects, they could not positively associate anyone with the deed.

Gordon Murray had been taken before a magistrate and evidence given against him. Lady Edwina, supported by her mother, was called on to identify the bracelet. It had belonged to her grandmother, she said, and she was very glad to have it back, but one of the rubies, a fine stone, was missing. Indeed, they were all fine stones, but this one, located in the centre of the bracelet, was most noticeable, and Lady Edwina was nearly as distraught over its absence as she had been over the original theft.

Lady Buckleigh was almost as upset as her daughter and demanded that that man Murray be required to produce the missing stone. Murray denied purloining it, but since he had already denied the theft of the bracelet, this did little to solve the riddle of the stone's disappearance.

When she heard of this exchange, Philippa suggested that,

when the bracelet had dropped from Lady Edwina's arm, the force with which it struck the floor had loosened the stone which then rolled out of sight and escaped the notice of whoever had later taken the bracelet. This precipitated another search of Warwick House in the hope that the stone might be recovered and the Buckleighs placated. The search resulted in a good deal of disorder and some short tempers, but the stone remained unfound. Harry became morose and was observed to drink more than was good for him. The normally outgoing Gwendolen shut herself in the library with a copy of *The Bride of Lammermoor*.

Murray had been committed for trial and was now in prison where Nicholas' money and Nicholas' influence contrived to purchase him some semblance of comfort. Well supplied with pen and paper, he was producing a series of acerbic articles that rapidly found their way into print. Henry was with him daily and reported that his spirits were high and he might even be said to be enjoying his current notoriety.

Nicholas ferreted out the story of who had given information against Mr. Murray. Lord Sidmouth, a friend and colleague of Lord Buckleigh's, had come by Buckleigh House the morning after the ball to breakfast with the earl. Lady Buckleigh had laid the matter of the bracelet before Sidmouth, and either she or St. George—Lady Edwina had not appeared that morning—mentioned Murray's presence and his peculiar behaviour in the matter of his pockets. Lord Sidmouth was a suspicious man. He was also Home Secretary, and the magistrates in the Public Offices and their police officers came under his direction. Sidmouth feared rebellion and he despised men of Murray's stamp. It was he who ordered the search of Murray's rooms.

So it was not the thief who had implicated Gordon Murray. But Henry pointed out that the thief must have planned to do so or there would have been no point in hiding the bracelet in Murray's office. And it was the thief they must find in order to clear Murray of suspicion.

Mr. Collingwood, Nicholas' solicitor, reported two or three days later that the brief he had prepared for Mr. Murray's defence had been returned by the barrister, Sir Rebington

Smythe, because of family business that made it impossible for the latter to appear. Philippa immediately sent for Elliot Marsden who assured her that this was all for the best since Sir Rebington's wife had run off to Bath with a fashionable preacher of magnetic presence and questionable morals, and the barrister was too distraught to make a creditable appearance in court. Philippa immediately urged him to undertake Murray's defence himself. Marsden, with strong reason to appear well in her eyes, said that he would be happy to oblige her, but the choice was Mr. Collingwood's. Philippa talked to Nicholas who conferred with the solicitor. Mr. Collingwood listened gravely, but said that he would prefer a more experienced man. He promised to keep Mr. Marsden in mind.

The theft caused a minor ripple in the sea of scandal that was the main preoccupation of the *ton*. The overriding question was, "Who is Gordon Murray?" On hearing that he was a writer or publisher or something of the sort, and a radical one at that, people were likely to murmur that they wouldn't have expected to find Lord Buckleigh's daughter in that kind of company. But when it was known that the event had occurred at Warwick House, people remembered that Warwick's wife was a harum-scarum sort of creature who had made a very improper first marriage and that Warwick himself was known to have dangerously advanced views.

The theft had a greater impact in political circles, owing chiefly to Lord Buckleigh's position in the majority party and that party's resolute opposition to men like Gordon Murray. A question was raised in the Commons, and Nicholas was forced to take the floor and remind his fellow members that, though there had been a charge, there had not yet been a trial. In the upper chamber, the Duke of Waterford made a speech in which he suggested that the theft was actually a political statement and was meant to be discovered. The act, he said, threatened the entire concept of private property. At the War Office, Lord Palmerston called Colonel Scott into his office for a private consultation. He had heard some ugly comments from the other ministers. He would like to help, but he would appreciate it if someone told him what the devil was going on.

Philippa meanwhile put into motion her effort to trace the movements of Lord Nelliston. Carteret had come to her immediately after hearing of Murray's arrest, perhaps, Philippa thought, to give vent to his contradictory feelings. For while he quite liked Gordon Murray and was disposed to think well of him, his confidence was shaken by what seemed evidence of Murray's incontrovertible guilt.

Philippa quickly resolved his dilemma. Mr. Murray, she said in a voice that did not brook any possible dissent, had not taken the bracelet. Therefore someone else had. And that someone had taken it to Mr. Murray's rooms and placed it in his humidor for the police to find, with the object of discrediting either Mr. Murray or his friends.

Anthony had asked Philippa to be his wife. He could refuse her nothing and certainly not his belief, so for the moment he fell into her way of thinking. Besides, it vindicated his initial impression of the publisher, and he rather prided himself on his ability to judge men as well as horses.

Philippa then laid before him all that had been said and done at Warwick House on the day after the ball. "There is one possibility we did not discuss," she added, "because I did not like to refer to your quarrel with Lord Nelliston. Your brother told us he was furious when he saw the pamphlets at White's."

Anthony was disturbed by the implications of this remark. "Surely you do not believe that I would have told Nelliston about Murray's connection with the pamphlets? That I would have told anyone at all?"

"No, of course I do not. But that wouldn't have been necessary, you see. Lord Nelliston might have seen you in conversation with Mr. Murray at the ball. If he's a clever man, that's all it would have taken."

Anthony would not grant Nelliston wit, but he admitted the man had a kind of dogged determination that might serve as well. "I don't doubt he'd gladly see Murray hanged just for the kind of man he is," he said, "though I can hardly imagine him going upon the sneak in Portpool Lane."

Henry had said much the same thing, but Philippa could not let the idea go—Nelliston was the one person who they knew had cause to wish Mr. Murray harm. Besides, Philippa had to admit that she wanted very much to be right. "I grant Lord Nelliston seems an unlikely prospect," she said, "but surely he should be considered. We know that he has no use for men like Mr. Murray, and he is certainly no friend of yours. He might have seen this as a way of bringing disgrace upon you."

Anthony smiled. "I doubt that Nelliston could bring disgrace upon a Paget." Then he turned thoughtful. "There would be little to gain by confronting him directly."

"We could at least trace his movements on the morning after the ball. He would have had to make inquiries about Mr. Murray to learn where he might be found, and then he would have had to go to Portpool Lane, or at least find someone to undertake the commission for him. Someone unsavoury," she went on, seeing with a storyteller's eye just how it might have happened. "He would not like to trust a friend with what he had done, lest the friend refuse him or threaten exposure, and he would hardly want to put himself in the power of one of his own servants. If we knew where he went directly after the ball and on the following morning, if we knew with whom he spoke—"

She broke off, trusting he would offer that which she wished him to do.

"You would like me to ask among his neighbours and acquaintances?"

"Yes," she said with a touch of impatience, "but later. I rather thought you might begin with his wife."

She had brought him into the garden, forgetting that the place might rouse associations unrelated to her present cause. They had been walking slowly down one of the paths, but at this he stopped abruptly. "I believe you are acquainted with her," she continued, "and if you pay her a visit she may be quite likely to tell you what we need to know."

Anthony stared down into her upturned face. She was regarding him calmly, and in that moment he was certain she knew everything that was rumoured about his affair with Georgina Nelliston. Philippa Davenport was a remarkable young woman.

"I will do whatever I can," he promised, "and I will come to you as soon as I have anything to report." He smiled and raised her hand to his lips, thinking all the while that it was a confounded nuisance she knew about Nelliston's wife. He had been avoiding Georgina, but now he would have to call upon her and be charming and perhaps even more. And all without telling her why he was interested in her husband's movements. It would be awkward. Perhaps a small gift? Georgina was fond of jewels. On these reflections Anthony took his leave.

Philippa saw him go with satisfaction and relief. Lord Carteret had shared her concern about Mr. Murray—as indeed Elliot Marsden had done—but both men were slow to take initiative. In this matter, at least, they showed none of Henry's quickness or energy. Henry sought her out daily to report his progress, or lack of it, and to hear what she had done. It was a temporary partnership, of course, but it overrode the discord that always seemed to rise between them, and Philippa looked forward to their meetings.

She never learned exactly what passed between Lord Carteret and Lady Nelliston. Georgina told her sometime lover that her husband had left the ball at three in her own carriage and gone directly home where, having won heavily and being in a good humour, he had inflicted his company upon her for the better part of two hours. She was sure he had slept soundly for most of the morning. She knew that he had left the house on foot at half past eleven, and she did not see him again that whole day. On further inquiry, Anthony learned that Nelliston was seen entering White's at a quarter to one. The servants averred that he remained there till at least four o'clock, by which time Gordon Murray was in custody.

It was, Anthony told Philippa, just possible. Nelliston could, of course, have sent a servant with the bracelet, or he could have done the deed himself in the hour and a quarter of time that, despite Anthony's repeated efforts, remained unaccounted for. But there was no positive proof, and for the moment their inquiries about Lord Nelliston were at a standstill.

Philippa had greater hopes for what Henry might uncover in Portpool Lane, but here too she was disappointed. The printer himself had been absent much of the morning Murray was taken into custody, and Jemmy, the thin, ferret-faced lad whom Philippa remembered from her earlier visit, had disappeared shortly after being questioned by his employer.

Henry made inquiries among the neighbours. Murray had been seen to leave his lodgings at something past ten o'clock, and the police officer had arrived about one. Between these hours a number of people had visited the premises, and Henry had painstakingly tracked down and accounted for each of them. None had been anywhere in the vicinity of Warwick House, and none seemed a likely candidate for a commission from any person who had been there. Henry had bills printed offering a reward for information and distributed these widely. With the promise of money, many people came forward, but none had anything new to contribute.

Henry continued to search for Jemmy, hoping the boy might have actually seen the person who brought the bracelet to Murray's office. He had nearly despaired of tracking him down when he caught sight of him in an alley and gave chase. The boy was clearly frightened and very hungry. Henry provided bread and soup and a gentle tongue. Jemmy quieted under this treatment. He had, it appeared, thought that the police officer would come looking for him as he had for Mr. Murray. When Henry assured him that the police had larger game in mind, Jemmy agreed to return to the printer who was in sore need of his services.

Better yet, the boy had information. He had seen a caller, not long after Mr. Murray left the building. The man had run quietly up the stairs and Jemmy caught no more than a glimpse of polished boots. He was curious and watched for the man's return, and in less than five minutes the caller came down the stairs again.

Philippa, to whom Henry was relating this, could not bear the suspense. "Who was it? What did he look like?"

"A gentleman, or so Jemmy claims. The boots, you see, and the kind of air that says he is above his surroundings. His description is more problematic. Not young, but not too old. Given Jemmy is no more than twelve, that could mean anyone from twenty to forty years of age. The man was well-built and wore a hat, so Jemmy could not see the colour of his hair and precious little of his face. He wore light pantaloons and a dark coat—Jemmy cannot say more than that. But his waistcoat was striped yellow and of some fine material. It was shiny, Jemmy says, and may have been embroidered. Next to the boots, it appears to be the man's most memorable feature."

"It does not sound like Lord Nelliston," Philippa conceded reluctantly.

"No, and anyway the time was wrong. But it might have been someone he sent."

She laughed. "So all we need to do—"

"—is find a man who owns a yellow waistcoat."

"That should not be too difficult." Her bright voice belied her disappointment.

"Right," he agreed. "We'll tell the others and begin our search again. And if that gets us nowhere, I can always try the tailors."

"Perhaps you can reach Gerry or Nicholas. No one else is about today. Francesca's gone down to her house at Petersham and Livia and Gwendolen went with her. And Claris is driving to Cranford with Lady Edwina and her brother." As she said this last, she looked at Henry with some curiosity. Cranford was St. George's country house, and Claris had been asked to make one of a small party at a luncheon he and his sister were giving.

Henry had been surprised by the invitation. He did not like St. George, but he did not try to dissuade Claris from accepting it. For Murray's sake, he did not want to further offend Lady Edwina. "Rather grand company for my little sister," he said dryly, "but I think Claris is up to it. In any case, it will do her no harm to see more of society, even of such society as St. George and Lady Edwina. She will not be awed by them, and they may help her to know her own heart."

It was a strange statement, coming from Claris' brother. Was he admitting the possibility that her attachment to Lord Christopher was genuine? And would Henry then sanction such a match, always supposing that Lady Carteret dropped her own opposition and Lord Buckleigh, who was the young man's guardian, gave his approval?

These speculations were cut short by the entrance of Tuttle who informed Philippa that Lady Edwina Thane was in the hall and begged to see Miss Davenport as quickly as possible.

Philippa stared at him in shock. She knew for a fact that Claris had driven off two hours ago with the Viscount St. George and that his sister had been in the carriage. Or had she? She told Tuttle to show her visitor directly into the library and rose to meet her.

Lady Edwina was as immaculately groomed as ever, but the periwinkle ribbons on her charming bonnet of Dunstable straw seemed to have been tied rather hastily, and her manner was almost agitated.

"Miss Davenport," she said, stepping quickly into the room, "thank goodness I have found someone at home. I had hoped to see Lady Francesca, but I am told she is away for the day. Mr. Ashton, I'm very glad to find you here as well."

"Please sit down, Lady Edwina," Philippa said, her tone made far more cordial by Edwina's evident concern. "May I offer you some tea?"

Edwina shook her head, but she accepted a chair and seemed in some measure to collect herself. She transferred her gaze to Henry. "Your sister, Mr. Ashton, is attending a luncheon my brother is giving at his villa this afternoon."

"She is attending a luncheon given by both you and Lord St. George," Philippa interposed. "I saw him call for her this morning, and Claris understood that you were in the carriage. What has happened?"

Edwina twisted the strings of her reticule in evident agitation, but her voice was perfectly direct. "My parents have gone to Berkshire for a few days to see my younger brother and sister, and I have been staying with Lady Carteret. My brother was to call for me there this morning—Lord Christopher was driving down with a friend and left the house early—and I waited for him an unconscionably long time. At last I was brought a note by one of the servants. My brother informed me that my presence was not required at luncheon and would, in fact, be 'deuced inconvenient.'" She looked at each of them in turn. "Quentin is my brother, but that is all I can say for him. I'm driving down immediately to repair any damage that may have been done, and I will bring your sister back with me. Her reputation at least will not suffer."

261

Chapter 17

"But—Good God," Philippa exclaimed, "he's Lord Christopher's own cousin!"

"This is not time to cavil about family obligations, Philippa." Henry was already on his feet. "You have a carriage, Lady Edwina?"

"Waiting in front." Lady Edwina rose as well. "You may rely upon my coachman's discretion."

Henry nodded briskly and moved toward the door. "Philippa, when Gerry or Francesca gets back, explain that I—"

"Don't be an idiot, Henry." Philippa sprang to her feet. "I'm coming with you. Only give me a moment or two. I must leave word for Francesca and Gerry."

Henry merely nodded and opened the door. Philippa darted into her study and scribbled a hasty note. There was no time to worry about such niceties as pelisses and hats, but fortunately she had brought a worsted shawl downstairs on a cool morning some days ago and had neglected to return it to her bedchamber. She threw it over her shoulders and hurried into the hall after Henry and Lady Edwina.

A glance at Henry's face told Philippa that he had used the brief respite to heap the blame for his sister's predicament upon his own shoulders. She was torn between a desire to offer comfort and an equally strong desire to shake him for wasting his energy so fruitlessly.

Henry had at least had the sense to ring for Tuttle. Philippa delivered her note to the butler, who gave her the briefest of smiles and opened the front door. Without further ado, Lady Edwina, Philippa, and Henry hurried down the front steps to the waiting carriage.

When the Viscount St. George had called for Claris earlier in the day, he gave Claris and Philippa to understand that his sister was outside in the carriage. But when Claris stepped out of the Green Street house she saw no sign of Lady Edwina. Nor did it appear that St. George expected her to join them, for he had brought his curricle which was scarcely comfortable for three.

Claris looked at the viscount with wide blue eyes which held no hint of accusation but were filled with inquiry.

St. George responded with a charmingly apologetic smile. "I must confess to a slight deception. My excuse is my ardent desire that nothing prevent you from attending my luncheon. I feared Miss Davenport might worry about the forms. My sister, as you perceive, is not with me, but I expect her to follow directly. She had a commission to execute for my aunt. There is no impropriety in the situation, but if you dislike it, of course you need not come."

Claris hesitated. It was perhaps a trifle unconventional, but St. George was Crispin's cousin and Crispin was Claris' betrothed. Besides, Lady Edwina would be not far behind. And Claris had no intention of missing a party at which Crispin was to be present, or of offending St. George, who had assured Crispin that he would do his utmost to win Lord Buckleigh's consent to their betrothal. Claris smiled prettily, gave St. George her arm, and said that of course she did not object.

The prospect of an hour or more alone in the viscount's company did not fill her with joy. St. George was a good-looking man by any standards, he wore a beautifully cut coat and a very smart waistcoat of black-striped valencia, and he drove a quite elegant curricle drawn by a handsome pair of dapple-greys, but Claris was indifferent to the charms of the viscount, his carriage, and his horses alike. She did not think he could come near to matching Lord Carteret—on whom, she

263

was convinced, he modelled his appearance—and she had not been speaking idly when she asked Carteret if he thought St. George's temperament was similar to Lady Edwina's.

Still, he was Crispin's cousin, and Crispin was excessively fond of him, and he was going to help secure their future. Claris unfurled a lace-edged parasol and prepared to derive what enjoyment she could from the occasion.

The viscount entertained her with the latest *on dits,* and a witty commentary thereon, as they drove out of London. He was an amusing companion and Claris was beginning to enjoy herself when the viscount remarked unexpectedly that he was grateful to his sister.

"Yes?" Claris had not seen any sign of Lady Edwina but then her carriage was probably not as fast as her brother's.

"You see, dearest Miss Ashton," St. George explained, "I am delighted to have you to myself for an hour or so. Cris is so devilish possessive."

"That," said Claris, adjusting her parasol so that it lay between them, "is the privilege of a betrothed, Lord St. George."

"Ah, but he is not your betrothed yet, is he?"

"As far as Crispin and I are concerned, he is," Claris said firmly, "and that is all that truly matters."

St. George laughed but let the matter drop. Claris kept a firm hold on her parasol. She was not really disturbed, for St. George always treated her in this teasing, half-flirtatious manner—though he had never before hinted that her betrothal to Crispin was not an accomplished fact. Still, it was not as if she did not have plenty of experience keeping young men in line, and in any case they would soon be at the villa where a perfectly respectable party would be assembled. Crispin himself would be there, and no doubt several other young men and women of his set, as well as Dorothy Milford, who was little older than the others but whose married state rendered her a suitable chaperone.

Cranford had come to the Thane family through marriage a couple of generations ago and had been turned over to St. George on his twenty-first birthday. It was not particularly large or grand, and its solid classical symmetry was at odds with the Gothic flights of fancy now fashionable, but somehow, Claris thought, as St. George pulled up his horses in the drive, it suited the viscount.

They were greeted at the front door by an elderly man with a gruff voice and bent back whom the viscount addressed as Luscombe. Luscombe informed his master that some of the guests had already arrived and were to be found on the terrace and that it had been mortal hard carrying the table and chairs out to the lawn, though of course if his lordship chose to dine outside instead of in his own dining room—which, incidentally, had been good enough for his father—then of course it wasn't his place to ask questions. St. George ignored these complaints and said that he must see to his guests. He asked Luscombe to show Miss Ashton to the yellow bedroom where she could freshen up. Mrs. Luscombe, who served as both cook and housekeeper, was understandably occupied in the kitchens. Luscombe conducted Claris up the main staircase—muttering that he was too old for all this climbing up and down—and left her at the door of the yellow bedroom. Claris entered and found a woman seated at the dressing table, carefully rearranging her glossy brown ringlets. She turned at Claris' entrance, smiled, and introduced herself as Angela Thorpe.

Miss Thorpe seemed little older than Claris and, though she wore a very stylish frock, her manner was unaffected and friendly. Claris responded warmly and was feeling quite cheerful by the time she and Miss Thorpe had finished repairing their toilets. There was no sign of Luscombe when they returned to the ground floor, but Miss Thorpe, who seemed quite familar with the house, led the way to the terrace.

St. George was not a stingy host. The company were all supplied with glasses of champagne, and a bottle stood cooling in a bucket of ice in the shade. On the sloping lawn below, a table had been set for luncheon with the appropriate profusion of silver, crystal and bone china. To Claris' disappointment, Crispin had not yet arrived, but in addition to Lord St. George two young men and two young women were present. The men she recognized as the Hon. Oscar Metcalfe and Archibald Baxter, Baron Trevelyn, both friends of Crispin's. One of the ladies was Mrs. Milford, a plump brunette in her early twenties whose husband, Colonel Milford, was in the Horse Guards and many years her senior. Claris had seen her in Trevelyn's company on several occasions and had a fairly shrewd idea of the nature of their relationship. Not that it disturbed her. After all, her vouchers to Almack's came from Emily Cowper.

The other lady was a slender, ethereal young woman of nineteen or twenty, dressed in a gown of sheer ice-blue muslin and a straw bonnet ornamented with a white lace veil. The ash-blonde curls peeking from beneath her bonnet and her pale complexion and fragile features made Claris suddenly feel excessively robust, but she was not given to jealousy and was quite prepared to be friendly. However, unlike Miss Thorpe, the woman, whom St. George introduced as Maria Doddington, seemed rather cool, though perhaps it was merely that her manner was more reserved.

Miss Thorpe went to sit beside Metcalfe with whom she was evidently well-acquainted—strange, Claris thought, for she had never heard Crispin mention her—and St. George handed Claris to a seat on a low-backed settee. The viscount then supplied Claris and Miss Thorpe with champagne and, having seen to the comfort of his guests, disposed himself beside Claris. Claris sipped her champagne and asked what had become of Lady Edwina. St. George laughed and tossed a hand carelessly in the air.

"I have long since ceased attempting to understand my dear sister's whims. No doubt while executing my aunt's commission she caught sight of a perfectly ravishing bonnet or parasol or some such thing. Ten to one she'll arrive in the middle of luncheon with a carriage full of boxes."

Though Claris had no great love for Lady Edwina, this last statement did not ring true. Spoiled and temperamental Lady Edwina might be, but Claris did not think that any daughter reared by the Countess Buckleigh would so neglect her social duties. She glanced around at the others. Miss Thorpe grinned at her. Miss Doddington was pouting prettily. Metcalfe and Trevelyn, normally cheerful company, looked rather uncomfortable. Mrs. Milford appeared amused about something, but perhaps that was merely the effect of the champagne.

St. George settled himself more comfortably on the settee

and started talking about the current season at the opera. Claris began, for no discernible reason, to feel uncomfortable again and waited impatiently for Crispin's arrival. But when Luscombe at last appeared it was not to announce more guests but to say that luncheon would be served directly. St. George rose and offered his arm to Claris. In answer to her unspoken question he remarked that he hadn't the least idea what had happened to his sister or to Crispin and Thornton, who were supposed to be driving down together, but he had no intention of allowing the meal to grow cold in order to accomodate them. Claris had no choice but to accept the viscount's arm and allow him to lead her down the steps to the lawn.

The party arranged themselves around the luncheon table, St. George seating Claris on his right. Luscombe brought out a first course of eel soup and potted lobster. More champagne was poured. Mrs. Milford told a long, gossipy story which became increasingly *risqué*. Claris did not find the story objectionable, but she knew it went beyond the bounds of what anyone—and most particularly a chaperone—should discuss in the presence of unmarried young women. She looked at Miss Thorpe and Miss Doddington to see if they shared her concern, but Miss Thorpe was smiling in genuine amusement and Miss Doddington was still pouting.

Claris turned to her host. He was watching her, and she thought she saw an odd, almost measuring look in his eyes. But as he met her gaze, he gave a practised, charming smile and she could not be sure whether or not she had imagined the earlier expression. Claris returned the smile sweetly and turned her attention to her plate. The food at least was excellent. She would enjoy it and as soon as Crispin arrived she would ask him to take her back to London. Crispin could be counted on not to fail her.

As her carriage pulled out of Green Street, Lady Edwina looked at Henry and Philippa, murmured, "You must forgive me. I fear I am too angry to speak with any moderation," and turned her gaze to the window. She was furious with her brother, both for his behaviour and for involving her in it. But though she looked forward with some satisfaction to the coming confrontation—for as long as she could remember she had wanted to see Quentin put in his place—she found her thoughts taking quite a different direction.

It was odd to be sitting here in her aunt's carriage beside the woman who had taken Tony from her. Lady Buckleigh, nothing if not a pragmatist, had already begun to cast her eye about for a new husband for Edwina and had advised her daughter to do the same. Once the shock of rejection began to wear off, it had occurred to Edwina that for the first time she was free to look about her, to consider the attractions of eligible gentlemen, and to think about just what qualities she desired in a husband. It had not taken her long to realize that Tony was lacking in many of these. For all his charm, he was not an ambitious man. He would never seek any power beyond that to which he had been born. And power, Edwina discovered, was what she wanted. Like Tony, she had been born with an assured place in society. Power she would have to attain through her husband. She thought of all this and re-called the condescending way Tony had treated her when she was in the schoolroom, and decided that Miss Davenport was welcome to him. Though perhaps Miss Davenport deserved better.

Philippa would have been startled to learn that she and Lord Carteret were the subject of Lady Edwina's reflections. She could spare thought for little other than Claris' plight, but when she looked across the carriage and saw Henry's expression, she pushed aside her own guilt and concern.

"Henry," she said quietly but firmly, "whatever happens you mustn't blame yourself. You couldn't possibly have foreseen this."

"On the contrary," Henry returned, staring at his hands, "I should have suspected his attentions to her from the outset. That I did not, that I was too preoccupied—but that is my affair. You have already been burdened enough."

Philippa eyed him shrewdly. In an odd way it was comforting to know that Henry was in an even worse state than she was herself. Guilt was a ruinously wasteful emotion and Henry must be coaxed out of his forthwith. Or perhaps coax was the wrong word. This was no time for sweet reasonableness, and in any case sweet reasonableness wasn't Philippa's forte, especially where Henry Ashton was concerned.

"You sound," Philippa said, "like a high-flown hero in the sort of novel which you seem to despise even more than you despise my writing."

This did rouse Henry from his brooding, though not for the reason she had intended. "Who said I despised your writing?" he demanded, meeting her gaze.

"You did," Philippa informed him. "In print. But that is neither here nor there at the moment. There was no earthly reason for you to suspect that Lord St. George's attentions to Claris were anything but honourable. I own I don't much like him myself, but I certainly never thought him the sort to attempt liberties with any respectable young woman, let alone the girl his own cousin hopes to marry."

"Ah, but that's just it." Henry's voice was taut with bitter mockery. "I imagine it is precisely because Lord Christopher hopes to marry Claris that Lord St. George took it upon himself to show his cousin that Claris is a common little baggage unfit to grace their family."

Philippa stared at him. "But that's absurd," she protested. "It's not as if Claris is—"

"Truly of low descent? St. George's definition of low descent must differ from your own."

"I would find his behaviour inexcusable whatever Claris' birth. You must know that."

This got through to Henry better than anything she had said thus far. "I do know it," he returned far more warmly. "You must forgive me. I am not myself, but that gives me no right to speak so harshly."

Philippa smiled. "Harsh is scarcely the appropriate word, considering the tone you and I frequently take with each other. You may be right about Lord St. George, though I still don't see how any of us could have guessed he had taken such exception to Claris. He and Lord Christopher appear to be close friends."

"What's that to say to anything?" Henry demanded. "St. George is only echoing the attitude taken by Lord Christopher's own mother, though I give Lady Carteret enough credit to think she would not approve his solution. Perhaps now you can appreciate how impossible my sister's life would be if she married into that family."

"Difficult but not impossible," Philippa said firmly. "Claris is a very enterprising young woman. And even you admit that Lord Christopher has more sense than you had given him credit for."

"I don't deny that I misjudged him in the past," Henry admitted. "And I don't deny that his feeling for Claris and hers for him seem more genuine that I at first supposed. But youthful attachments are notoriously short-lived under the best of circumstances, and I doubt theirs could survive the weight of his family's odium. Though after today the question may be moot."

Philippa had been concerned only with the danger to Claris' person and reputation. She had not considered the effect on Claris' romance. "Lord Christopher is a man of honour. He would stand by Claris," Philippa insisted.

"Lord Christopher is a conventional young man," Henry returned. "It remains to be seen if he will believe the girl he has loved a few short weeks or the cousin he has admired all his life."

Philippa had no answer for this. She leaned back and saw Lady Edwina out of the corner of her eye. They had both forgotten her presence and though they had been speaking in lowered voices and Edwina had given no sign of response to their conversation, it should not have taken place in her presence. They fell silent once more and Philippa was left to think of Claris and Lord St. George and what might be happening at the viscount's villa and what she and Henry and Lady Edwina would do when they got there. A disturbing possibility occurred to her. She looked at Henry. He was a sensible man, but even sensible men had been known to behave idiotishly.

"Henry," Philippa said, "when we get there, however angry you are, however much it seems the appropriate thing to do, it wouldn't be in the least helpful, you know."

Henry had fallen to staring at his hands again, but at that he looked up. "What wouldn't be in the least helpful?"

"Challenging Lord St. George," Philippa said.

Henry stared at Philippa. Lady Edwina turned from the window for the first time since they had left Green Street. "Not only would it not be helpful, Mr. Ashton, it would be far more than Quentin deserves."

To Philippa's surprise and relief, Henry began to laugh, though the sound was without mirth. "It would certainly not be in the least helpful. You should know I would not behave so foolishly."

"Some men would think it the gentlemanly thing to do," Philippa observed.

At that Henry spared her a brief smile. "You need have no fears, Miss Davenport. In Lord St. George's eyes, I am certainly no gentleman."

Claris took another spoonful of tansy pudding and kept her eyes demurely lowered so she would not have to meet her host's gaze. During luncheon Lord St. George's party had grown slowly but steadily less decorous. Mrs. Milford, who had a way of tossing down her champagne as if it were water, was now giggling at everything that was said; Trevelyn had ceased to look uncomfortable and told a decidedly improper joke; Metcalfe was still unusually quiet, but by the time the meal came to an end, his arm had stolen around Miss Thorpe's waist. Miss Thorpe, far from objecting, was leaning comfortably against Metcalfe's shoulder.

St. George's manner had been perfectly correct, but though Claris avoided looking at him as much as possible, she was acutely aware that his eyes were on her much of the time. Only Miss Doddington remained completely subdued and was seldom even disposed to smile.

Mrs. Milford was attempting to relate another story, but she had been overcome by the hicoughs as well as the giggles and was unable to get out more than two or three words in a row.

"Come on, Dolly," Trevelyn said, rising and holding out a hand to her. "What you need is a turn around the shrubbery."

For some reason this remark made Mrs. Milford giggle more than ever, but she rose unsteadily and permitted Trevelyn to guide her across the lawn. They had not been gone long before Miss Thorpe exchanged glances with Metcalfe and said it was growing cold and she wanted her shawl. She and Metcalfe rose and walked into the house together, their arms still intertwined.

Claris was sorry to see them go. Despite her growing suspicions about Miss Thorpe's lack of gentility, the other woman had been a friendly face and Claris had felt she could look to her for support. She had the dreadful suspicion that Lord St. George was going to make some suggestion that would entail her accompanying him into the shrubbery or the house or some other private place, but apparently the viscount had no intention of leaving the table. When Luscombe came to clear away the last of the dishes St. George asked for a bottle of claret.

Deciding it was best to keep the viscount occupied until Crispin arrived, Claris began to chatter in her most artless manner. Miss Doddington was of little help, but St. George was quite prepared to be sociable. Like the others, he had drunk a good deal during luncheon—after her second glass of champagne Claris had requested and been given lemonade—but unlike Mrs. Milford he showed no sign of it. Unless it made his hand rather unsteady. That perhaps was why, when Luscombe—complaining about the effect of so many trips to and from the house on his aged legs—brought the decanter of claret, the viscount's hand faltered and a large quantity of wine splashed onto the skirt of Claris' white tamboured muslin.

"My dear Miss Ashton," St. George exclaimed, righting the decanter, "a thousand apologies. You must excuse my infernal clumsiness." He turned to Luscombe who was still hovering behind his chair. "Tell Mrs. Luscombe her services are required immediately. Maria, take Miss Ashton upstairs so she may put aside her wet frock."

Claris protested that she was very well as she was, but St. George would hear none of it. She must not be allowed to catch a chill—Crispin would never forgive him. And the dress must be attended to before the stain set. Mrs. Luscombe was a wizard at such things and would soon have her put to rights. Claris, whose frock was indeed exceedingly damp, had little choice but to acquiesce. A cool and silent Miss Doddington guided her inside, up the central staircase, and to a door across the corridor. Then, seeming to feel her duty was done, she left, murmuring that Mrs. Luscombe would be with her directly.

It was not the yellow bedroom. The mahogany furniture and dark blue drapery had a decidedly masculine look and Claris strongly suspected that she was in Lord St. George's own chamber. She ought to march downstairs and demand to be taken back to London forthwith, but that would create a scene and a scene was just what she did not want to create. St. George, whatever else he might be, was still a member of Crispin's family.

She was standing by the fireplace, conveniently close to the poker and tongs, when the door opened to admit not the viscount but a plump, smiling woman who was evidently Mrs. Luscombe. The housekeeper fussed sympathetically over Claris, helped her out of her frock, and insisted she put on a voluminous silk dressing-gown—Lord St. George's no doubt—so she did not catch cold. Claris' petticoat and drawers were also stained, but she firmly declined Mrs. Luscombe's offer to clean them as well.

When Mrs. Luscombe had departed with the dress, promising to have it as good as new in no time, Claris inspected herself in the cheval glass and decided that the dressing-gown covered far more of her than her frock had done. For once she was grateful that her full figure necessitated a corset. She hesitated a moment, then reached for her bonnet and tied it firmly under her chin. And thus armoured, she sat down in a straight-backed chair near the fireplace and settled herself to await Mrs. Luscombe's return.

She had almost begun to believe that her apprehensions were groundless, when there was a light knock at the door. "Miss Ashton?" St. George asked politely. "May I come in?"

She could have refused. But the fact that he had asked argued that it might be safe to acquiesce. Conversely, if she refused, he could come in anyway. So she gave her assent and the viscount entered the bedchamber, looking not the least like a man bent on seduction.

"Mrs. Luscombe will be along with your dress in a bit," he informed her. "She's set it to dry in the sun. I thought I'd keep you company. Penance for being so clumsily responsible for the accident in the first place. Not that talking with you is penance, of course." He advanced into the room and leaned against one of the bedposts. "Besides, I want to speak to you about my father."

"You had plenty of opportunity to do so on the drive down here," Claris reminded him.

St. George smiled. "I had hoped to talk to you and Crispin together. But I consider Crispin has forfeited all rights to hear the news first by being so shockingly late."

He moved toward her chair. Claris eyed him warily and started to rise.

The viscount stopped and regarded her for a moment, then began to laugh. "My intentions are strictly honourable, future-cousin—though I won't say there aren't times when I envy Cris. You will be pleased to know that it may be possible to obtain my father's consent. I put the matter to him before he left town and he was not unsympathetic. However, there are certain conditions—" But here the viscount broke off, hearing the sound he had been waiting for in the hall below. His explanation would have to be cut short. "Allow me to be the first to welcome you to our family." He stepped forward, took Claris by the shoulders, pulled her to her feet—causing the dressing-gown to slither loose to her waist—and placed his lips lightly over hers.

Dutifully obeying orders from Lord St. George, the Hon. Hugh Thornton, with the help of his groom, contrived an accident to his carriage which kept Crispin and him cooling their heels at the Boar in Sutton for two hours. Thornton feared Crispin would propose abandoning their trip to Cranford altogether, a ruinous course of events, for St. George had stressed that, important as it was that Crispin be delayed, it was equally important that he eventually reach Cranford. But on this head Thornton need have had no fears. Crispin was not about to absent himself from any entertainment at which Claris was present. The moment the axle was mended he fairly dragged Thornton into the carriage, insisted on taking the reins himself, and drove at a pace which caused Thornton to feel some concern on his pair's account.

They reached Cranford at half past three. Again following St. George's instructions, Thornton told Crispin to go on ahead and make their apologies to their host while he saw to the stabling of the horses. Used to looking on his cousin's home as very little different from his own, Crispin let himself in the front door and started for the terrace but was arrested by a light feminine voice.

"Lord Christopher."

Crispin turned and saw a woman standing in the drawing room doorway. "Maria! Good God, what the devil are you doing here?"

Maria Doddington put her chin up. "I live here," she said succinctly. "Some of the time."

"Not when my cousin is entertaining respectable females," Crispin returned grimly, taking a step toward her. "What in God's name is going on here?"

Maria gave a graceful shrug—she had once been quite a talented opera-dancer. "You should know your cousin well enough to realize he never tells me anything. He's upstairs in his bedchamber. He said to send you up as soon as you arrived."

Not waiting to hear more, Crispin crossed the hall, bounded up the stairs, stalked across the corridor, and flung open the door to St. George's room. His cousin was standing by the fireplace embracing a young woman who appeared to be clad only in her petticoat and bonnet. The woman's face was obscured, but Crispin had no difficulty in determining her identity. Before he could speak, St. George released the woman and turned to his cousin with his habitual mocking expression.

"Damn you, Cris," he said lightly, "you do have a way of entering a room at the most inconvenient times."

Henry handed Lady Edwina down from the carriage in the circular drive before Cranford and turned back to assist Philippa, but found she had already sprung to the ground.

"Whatever happens," he said, "the important thing is to get

Claris away from here as quickly as possible and not give St. George the satisfaction of creating a scene."

"I only lose my temper with fellow writers," Philippa assured him and followed Lady Edwina up the steps.

Without hesitation, Edwina conducted Henry and Philippa across the empty hall and up the staircase. A door across from the stairhead was open and they heard sounds of a scuffle. Henry reached the door first, in time to see Lord Christopher Paget push his cousin against the dressing table and proceed to throttle the life out of him.

"Henry!" Claris shrieked from the opposite side of the room. "Thank heavens you are come! Stop them before they kill each other!"

As she spoke, St. George struck back and the two young men fell to the floor, together with several toilet articles which crashed and splintered around them. Seemingly not disconcerted by the fact that it was Lord Christopher and not his sister whom he was called upon to rescue from Lord St. George, Henry stepped into the room, seized Crispin, who happened to be on top at the moment, by the shoulders and hauled him to his feet. Philippa and Edwina remained in the doorway, concluding interference would be of little use at present.

"Damn you, Ashton," Crispin said, shaking free of Henry's grip, "stay out of this, it's my affair!"

"Not if it concerns my sister," Henry said firmly.

"You can deal with St. George when I'm done with him," Crispin offered generously. "If there's anything left." He lunged for his cousin again. Henry restrained him.

"No, no, Crispin!" Claris ran forward, her white silk bonnet bouncing against her shoulders and the dressing gown falling loose once more. "You misunderstand!"

"Precisely." St. George had taken advantage of Henry's interference to scramble to his feet. "Pray ask Miss Ashton if she was unwilling."

"Of course I wasn't unwilling," Claris returned, pulling the dressing gown back over her shoulders. "Lord St. George was only welcoming me to the family."

The viscount gave a dry laugh. "You may call it that if you like. My account might be rather different, but I leave it to you,

Cris, to decide whether you will believe Miss Ashton's account of the events or mine."

"You despicable little toad," Crispin spat, with all the hurt and anger of the newly disillusioned. "As if for one instant I would believe your word over Claris'! I don't know why you brought her here, Quentin, but by God you are going to answer to me for it!"

"Crispin!" Claris cried.

Henry glanced briefly at the doorway and met Philippa's eyes, the ghost of a smile in his own. "Don't be a fool, Paget," he said with quiet authority. "Do you want to ruin Claris completely?"

"I want to thrash the man who tried to ruin her," Crispin retorted, straining against Henry's hold.

"Then for God's sake don't create more of a scandal by putting a bullet through your cousin at dawn on Putney Heath. Or letting him put one through you. He's not worth it."

With this at least Crispin could agree. If Henry's arguments had not dimmed his anger perhaps they had helped to restore his control. He hesitated, eyeing his cousin with contempt.

Edwina took advantage of the momentary lull. "I'm so sorry, Quentin," she said sweetly. "Have I missed luncheon entirely?"

St. George turned to the doorway, aware for the first time of his sister's presence. "Damn you, Edwina," he said furiously.

"Oh, come, Quentin," his sister chided, "I know I was hours late, but surely that's a bit excessive."

Philippa meanwhile had crossed the room, carefully avoiding the three men and the shards of broken glass which littered the floor, and put an arm around Claris.

"Where's your frock?"

"Mrs. Luscombe has it," Claris said, her eyes on Crispin. "I think."

"Mrs. who?"

Before Claris could answer or Crispin could make a further move, the door opened to admit Oscar Metcalfe, minus coat, waistcoat, and cravat, his shirt only partially tucked into his trousers, and Angela Thorpe who, like Claris, was dressed in her petticoat, except that she had thrown a large shawl around her shoulders.

"What the devil's going on in here?" Metcalfe demanded. "We thought someone was being murdered from the sound of it."

"Unfortunately you were mistaken." Crispin turned a hard gaze on his friend. "How much did you know about this?"

Metcalfe gulped. He hadn't liked Miss Ashton's presence at the party from the beginning, though it never would have occurred to him to question St. George.

"Never mind that now," Henry cut in. "Let us be charitable and say there has been a series of misunderstandings. To avoid further misunderstandings, let us assume that Lady Edwina and Miss Davenport and I have been here the entire afternoon and that following luncheon we escorted my sister back to town, as we are now about to do."

"And what," Lord St. George inquired, in a fair semblance of his usual tones, "if some of us find we recall the events rather differently?"

"Then," said Crispin, relishing the chance to attack, if only with words, "I shall lay the whole before Uncle Horace. It will be my word against yours, but I don't think you would be wise to chance it."

"Nor do I," said Edwina, "especially as it will be my word as well as Crispin's. And there are one or two other things I can tell Papa about into the bargain."

St. George was not a coward, but his father had the power to stop his allowance. Crispin's and Edwina's threats were clearly effective.

Henry glanced at the viscount, then turned to Metcalfe and Angela. "How many others are here?" he demanded.

Metcalfe was staring fixedly at the floor, but Angela, who had quite enjoyed seeing St. George put in his place, said promptly, "Only Maria and Lord Trevelyn and Mrs. Milford."

"Maria's downstairs," Crispin put in. "I didn't see Trevelyn or Dolly Milford—"

"They're—" Angela hesitated.

"In the shrubbery," Claris volunteered.

Philippa choked and thought that perhaps Henry was struggling with a similar flash of amusement.

Crispin was in no state to find anything remotely humourous. "Thornton's here too," he said briefly. "I'll speak with all of them. But,"—he turned back to his cousin—"I'm holding you responsible for their silence. Metcalfe's and Angela's too. If one word of this leaks out, no matter what the source, I will go to Uncle Horace. In fact, I strongly advise you to remain in the country for a time, Quentin, lest the sight of you causes me to forget myself and go to my uncle anyway." He looked at Claris and his expression softened. He made a move toward her, then checked himself and turned to Metcalfe. "Come on, Oscar. Let's go find Thornton and Trevelyn and I'll tell you the whole. Then you can do as you wish, though I don't fancy you'll relish staying under my cousin's roof much longer."

St. George watched the door close behind the two men and Angela. "Out of courtesy to Mrs. Luscombe," he said with exquisite politeness, "you might do me the favour of telling me how many of you intend to remain for dinner."

"I can't speak for the others," Henry returned, equally politely, "but my sister and I have no intention of sitting down to table with you tonight. Or on any other occasion."

"Nor do I," said Philippa.

"Even Mrs. Luscombe's culinary wonders couldn't tempt me," Edwina assured him.

"As you wish." The viscount inclined his head. "In that case, if you will excuse me, there are some matters I must attend to. Ladies, your servant."

As the door shut behind the viscount, Philippa turned to Lady Edwina. "I hate to seem impertinent," she said, "but you must know the house better than I do. Do you think you could possibly locate Claris' frock?"

With Philippa's assistance, Claris emerged from the bedchamber fifteen minutes later presenting a reasonably creditable appearance. Crispin was still with his friends, and Lady Edwina had gone to have a final word with her brother, but they found Henry waiting for them in the hall.

"St. George didn't really do anything improper, you know," Claris said unexpectedly as the three of them stood by the front door. "He was merely trying to make it look as though something untoward had happened so that Crispin wouldn't want to marry me."

Henry looked at her sharply.

"Of course I knew that's what it was about," Claris said in response to his expression. "That is, I didn't at first, though I knew something was odd, but when Crispin came in it all became painfully clear, only of course I couldn't say so in front of Crispin because he was violent enough as it was. Now that I think of it," Claris continued thoughtfully, "I'm quite certain St. George tried something similar once before."

"What?" said Philippa and Henry, almost simultaneously.

"Well, not so bad, but the same sort of thing," Claris amended. "It was at the Warwicks' ball, before all the fuss with Lady Edwina. St. George gave Crispin my favourite handkerchief—you know, Henry, the one embroidered with gooseberries that Mama gave me just before I left for London—and said he'd found it in Harry Warwick's room. He must have meant Crispin to assume the worst, but Crispin's such an innocent he just thought Harry had picked it up and was keeping it to return to me."

To his own surprise, Henry found that he was laughing. "How very unoriginal," he said. "On top of everything else, the man's a plagiarist."

"In all fairness," Philippa pointed out, "Shakespeare was too." She was grinning.

"Well, yes," Claris said, "it is rather funny, isn't it? Only I don't think we dare say so in front of Crispin. He does tend to take these things rather seriously."

Crispin and Edwina returned to the hall a few moments later. Far from spreading rumours which would damage Claris' reputation, Crispin said, Metcalfe and Trevelyn and Thornton were more likely to refuse St. George's hand at their next encounter. Even Dolly Milford, Edwina added, had seen sense. She did not elaborate. Philippa wondered if any threats concerning Colonel Milford had been involved.

They were all silent during the journey back to town. Crispin and Claris seemed content to smile dreamily at each other across the carriage. Philippa and Lady Edwina stared out their respective windows. Henry too felt little desire to talk. There was much on which to think. Young Paget's behaviour, if a trifle foolhardy, had certainly shown that his feelings for Claris were all the most devoted brother could wish for in a candidate for his sister's hand. And he had been surprisingly ready to listen to reason. In fact, Henry began to wish very much that the young man were a little older, or came from a slightly more compatible family, or anything that would make the match less impossible than it obviously remained.

But as they left Cranford behind, Henry found that it was not Lord Christopher or Claris or even St. George who occupied his thoughts. It was Philippa Davenport.

Odd that, for Philippa hadn't really played a central role in the day's events. Not that she hadn't handled herself superbly of course. She had rather a way of handling herself superbly in crises. Henry thought of her attempt to jolt him out of his morose humour on the drive down. That had taken considerable strength, for she had been as shaken as he. It confounded the mind to think that a woman of such quality might shackle herself to Elliot Marsden or the Marquis of Carteret.

Henry realized that he had clenched his hands tightly together. He was filled with the burning hostility which seemed to possess him whenever Marsden or Carteret was present. Or even thought of. It was only natural, of course. Marsden was an ambitious sycophant and Carteret was an idle fribble. Strange though, such qualities in other men were as likely to arouse his ridicule as his enmity. No, enmity wasn't quite the right word—Henry had a reputation for using words with care. This was a more specific emotion. Not enmity or hostility but . . . jealousy.

Henry unclasped his hands. The air seemed suddenly very still. He looked at the three women sitting on the opposite side of the carriage. Lady Edwina had managed to maintain her modish elegance, and Claris, despite a somewhat damp frock, had put herself to rights remarkably well, but the afternoon had left its mark on Philippa. Her hair was more down than up and, other than pushing the loose stands behind her ears, she had made no effort to repair it. Her gown was rumpled and her face showed signs of strain—far more than Claris' did. Henry was aware of a sudden desire to move across the carriage and gather her into his arms. A strange impulse, for with all the many feelings Philippa Davenport aroused in him, he had never before wanted to comfort her. When he thought of Philippa it was not of her vulnerability but of her acerbic wit. And her laughter. It was a gift that, being able to laugh. She was better at it than he was. And then there was her mind. Her hard, bright mind. And the gentleness underneath.

Jealous. If he was jealous, there must be a reason. Henry drew a breath and faced what would have been obvious long before had it not been so astounding. He was in love with Philippa Davenport.

Chapter 18

Gerry returned to Green Street shortly after five. Tuttle, who seemed uncharacteristically anxious, promptly presented him with Philippa's note. The contents were brief. Philippa and Henry had been called away and it was possible that neither they nor Claris would return to London in time for dinner. No one should be alarmed by their absence. Gerry was not given to fanciful speculation, but he was disturbed by the connection between Philippa and Henry's departure and Claris' engagement. When further questioning of Tuttle elicited the information that Lady Edwina—who, Gerry recalled from conversation at the dinner table on the previous evening, was supposed to have accompanied Claris and Lord St. George—had left with Henry and Philippa, Gerry was able to arrive, if not at the truth, at something remarkably close.

It was at this point that Francesca, having delivered Livia and Gwendolen to South Audley Street, returned from her own expedition to the country. Gerry dragged her into the library and thrust Philippa's note into her hands.

"I'm more than half-inclined to set off for Cranford myself," he told her.

"No, Gerry." Francesca scanned the note quickly. "Someone ought to be here when they return. Or in case they send word."

"You'll be here."

"I might need your help."

"Doing it much too brown, my girl," Gerry protested, but

the argument was cut short by the entrance of Philippa herself, closely followed by Lady Edwina, Claris, Lord Christopher, and Henry.

The story of the day's events—Crispin and Edwina refused to soften the account in the least—left Gerry enraged and Francesca coldly furious, but it was apparent to both that there was little more to be done. Claris had come to no harm and any further action against Lord St. George would only risk damaging her reputation.

Francesca extended a dinner invitation which Crispin promptly accepted. To Philippa's surprise, Lady Edwina did as well, saying she could send her coachman back to Cavendish Square with a note for her aunt. To Philippa's even greater surprise Henry declined to remain for dinner and took himself off almost immediately. Though he said everything that was proper to Lord Christopher and Lady Edwina, his manner was almost abrupt and he did not even spare Philippa a smile. Philippa put it down to the strains of the day, but it cast a cloud over what otherwise proved to be an unexpectedly pleasant evening, culminating in a noisy game of billiards.

Edwina's tact and Crispin's anxiety about the day's effect on Claris led them to make an early departure. Philippa found she was quite exhausted and climbed into bed with relief. She awoke somewhat later than usual, with a vague sense that there was something she had to do. The feeling persisted throughout her morning walk with Hermia, though try as she might she could not recall what it was. Her novel was going reasonably well, and though she was concerned about Mr. Murray, there was little more she could do to help him at present.

She was still puzzling the matter over when she walked into the breakfast parlour. The room was empty, but she saw Francesca and Linnet in the garden. Philippa waved to them, helped herself to toast and coffee and reached for the *Morning Chronicle*. Five minutes later the answer came to her. Of course. Marsden and Carteret. They were being very patient, but they expected answers. They deserved answers. And she could no longer claim to be too busy with Mr. Murray's affairs to have time to think about her own.

Philippa swallowed the last of her coffee and went out into

the garden. It was a warm morning and Francesca was sitting at a wrought iron table writing letters. Linnet was perched on one of the ornamental rocks which bordered the flower beds, wriggling her feet in the dirt and watching a pair of sparrows with great interest.

Francesca looked up from her letter and smiled, then noted her cousin's expression. "You're frowning. Is it about Mr. Murray? I know how vexatious it is to have to wait, but I am sure every effort is being made—"

"I know," Philippa said, sitting at the table opposite her cousin, "and it is vexatious, but that's not the trouble. Do you remember a couple of weeks ago when we talked about Mr. Marsden and Lord Carteret and you asked my why I didn't wait until the time came and see how I felt?"

Francesca nodded.

"Well," said Philippa, "the time's come."

Francesca set down her pen. She did not appear particularly surprised. "Marsden or Carteret?" she asked, her voice composed.

"Both," said Philippa forlornly.

"When?"

"The day after the ball at Warwick House. I would have told you earlier," Philippa added quickly, "but with all the business with Mr. Murray it—slipped my mind."

"Slipped your mind?"

"I suppose it would be more accurate to say that I pushed it out." Linnet had toddled over to Philippa's chair and stood grinning up at her. Philippa smiled back and tousled the child's blonde hair.

"Have you rejected either of them?" Francesca asked.

Philippa shook her head.

"Or accepted one of them? Or both of them?"

"I'm not quite *that* idiotish. I said I needed time to consider. Well what else was I to do," Philippa asked defensively, "when I'm just as confused as ever?" And much more unsettled, she added to herself, remembering the very different but equally perturbing kisses she had received from the two gentlemen. But somehow she could not bring herself to discuss that with Francesca.

"Henry was right about Mr. Marsden," she said instead. "Lady Carteret asked him to do something to prevent Lord Carteret from making the mistake of his life and marrying me. Mr. Marsden told me all about it."

"Before or after he proposed?"

"Just before. He said Lady Carteret's wishes don't signify anymore, that he truly wants to marry me for myself."

"Do you believe him?"

"I don't know. Sometimes I'm not even sure his reasons matter, assuming we could be happy together."

Francesca reached down to pick up Linnet. "Could you be?"

"I don't know," Philippa said again. "It's so unfair! If it were a book, I could write one of my heroines out of a situation like this with no trouble at all." But perhaps, her thoughts went on, that's because I don't really understand love, no matter how cleverly I write about it.

"Well," said Francesca, smoothing Linnet's dress, "why don't you?"

"Why don't I what?"

"Write about it."

Philippa stared at her cousin for a moment, then suddenly smiled. "Francesca, you're brilliant. I don't know why I didn't think of that myself."

"Do you think it will work?"

"I haven't the least idea, but it's certainly preferable to brooding. Thank you a thousand times." She pushed back her chair and rose. "I'll be in my study. Probably for hours."

"Remember what else I said the last time we talked before you send a hasty summons to Cavendish Square or Temple Lane," Francesca advised.

Philippa stopped and turned back to her cousin. "Be absolutely sure of where my heart lies. I'll do my best, Francesca. But I'm beginning to think I'd settle for the smallest degree of partiality."

"Perhaps," said Francesca quietly, "it doesn't lie with either of them."

"Don't," Philippa exclaimed, in only partly feigned horror. "I've quite made up my mind that I want to marry. It has to be one or the other."

Francesca made no reply, but Philippa's mind was already filled with the task of translating her problem into fiction. She walked swiftly back toward the house, smiling absently at Gerry who had just come outside.

Used to Philippa's abstraction, Gerry grinned and continued into the garden. Francesca had returned to her letter, but Linnet, now sitting on the gravel walk, greeted him with a delighted gurgle. Gerry scooped up his daughter and swung her into the air.

"Hullo, minx. What have you been up to?"

"Nothing," said Francesca whose eyes, Gerry noted, held more than a trace of concern. "She's been an angel. Wait about twenty years. That's when we'll have to start worrying about her."

Philippa stared out of her study window and watched the Scott family, while the ink dripped from her quill and splattered against a clean sheet of paper. Where could she possibly begin? And with whom? It was Marsden who had proposed first, by an hour or so. But it was Carteret who had first begun to court her. And it was Carteret, she realized, whom she understood best, while Marsden remained largely an unknown quantity, albeit a most intriguing one.

Yes, she would begin with the marquis. And the setting? Of course, where else to begin writing about a marriage? With the wedding. She reached for a fresh sheet of paper, redipped her pen, and began to write, trying to let the words come without stopping to think.

Philippa listened to the voice of the bishop droning on and told herself that one really should not be bored at one's own wedding.

Philippa stared down at the words she had just penned. That was not at all what she had intended to say. Of course, bishops did rather tend to drone, and her mind had certainly wandered at other weddings—she'd reorganized a whole chapter during Ianthe's. Perhaps it was only natural that she should be impatient to have the formal business of her own wedding over and done with. Especially, she realized, if it was the sort of wedding she would be compelled to have as the future

Marchioness of Carteret, a very different sort of affair from her sisters' marriages in the Green Street drawing room.

Her future husband stood beside her, looking unusually solemn and almost remote. On her other side stood her bridesmaids, Claris and young Gwendolen Warwick and Edwina Thane. Philippa had felt quite charitable toward Lady Edwina ever since the incident at Lord St. George's villa, but she was aware of an uncharitable wish that her betrothed's nearest unmarried female relation was not quite so strikingly beautiful. It was especially daunting as the pale lilac chosen for the bridesmaids became Lady Edwina so admirably, while Philippa herself felt overpowered by the mass of white satin and point lace.

Oh no, not something so elaborate, Philippa objected, lifting her pen. I'd look a fright. I wouldn't be so silly.

Why had she let Madame Dessart convince her that a simple ivory silk was too plain for the new Marchioness of Carteret?

Why indeed? Of all the poor-spirited— Do stop interrupting and get on with it, Philippa admonished herself. Oh, very well, there was more to weddings than dresses and droning bishops. Weddings were family affairs, and she was very fond of her family.

It was comforting that her mother and sisters and Francesca and all their various husbands were gathered in the pews just behind her. Of course, Lady Carteret and the Buckleighs and Lord St. George were there as well, but they too must now be counted part of her family, and surely in a few months they would all be getting along spendidly. She did rather wish that her stepfather, Lord Braithwood, had not denounced Lord Buckleigh quite so vehemently in the House of Lords last night, but they would have to learn to put politics aside at family gatherings. The gentlemen could always discuss horses, and there must be some subject Mama and Lady Carteret and Lady Buckleigh had in common. Lady Edwina was proving quite human. As for Lord St. George—

Philippa stopped writing and stared dissatisfied at the paper. The wedding had been the wrong place to start. Best to skip over the oppressive formality of the marriage ceremony and move on to the wedding journey. Would they go abroad? No, something told Philippa that the marquis would first wish to go to Carteret Park. They would arrive that evening and then—

No. She might be shirking an important part of her married life, but she could not bring herself to carry this exercise as far as the nuptial chamber. Besides, she lacked the practical knowledge to describe the scene with any degree of accuracy. She would move to a time in the future when she and Carteret would have settled into a comfortable routine. How would a typical day in their life begin?

Philippa Frances Paget, Marchioness of Carteret, entered the breakfast parlour of Carteret House on a brisk morning in the spring of 1825 to find her husband already at the table, casting an eye over the Morning Post.

The *Morning Post?* Surely she would have persuaded him to take the *Chronicle* after six years of wedded bliss. Philippa began to alter the name of the paper, but a sterner voice warned her that it was her first instinct which was important.

"Good morning, my dear." He greeted her with one of his lazy smiles and rose to give her a good morning kiss; it was a perfunctory embrace, not at all like the gentle, practised salute that had so excited her that first time in the garden. The marquis then returned to his plate and his paper and the marchioness poured herself a cup of coffee, though she had breakfasted several hours before. It was her custom to rise early in order to write.

"I trust you had a pleasant evening, Carteret," she said, sitting down opposite—

Carteret? What the devil was she calling him that for? Of course, some women addressed their husbands thus, but Mama had certainly never called Papa "Davenport," any more than she called her new husband "Braithwood." Philippa wondered what would she call Carteret if he was her husband? "Anthony?" or "Tony," as Lord Christopher addressed him? Both sounded odd, but no doubt, were they really married, one would come easily to her lips.

"Oh, tolerable enough," Carteret returned. "And your own evening? How was the play?"

"It was an opera and not above average." The marchioness regarded her husband with resignation. He had returned some time after she had and had not visited her chamber. In fact, he hadn't visited her for rather more than a week. It was not, the marchioness told herself, that she expected absolute fidelity, but she did wish her

husband would give her her share of attention.

Not expect absolute fidelity? Of course she would expect it. But, Philippa realized, many wives must not or if they did their expectations were certainly not met. Would Carteret remain faithful after six years of marriage? She did not doubt the sincerity of his feelings for her now, but he was a man frequently subject to boredom.

"Have you seen my copy of the Chronicle?" *the marchioness inquired.*

"I believe Nesselbank placed it on the sideboard, but pray leave it until I have gone. I have no wish to listen to a reform lecture over the breakfast cups, even from so charming a reformer as yourself."

Philippa glared at the sheet of paper before her. What a condescending thing to say! The marquis stood in crying need of a good setdown. What had happened to the man who had attended a meeting at Sophronia Neville's and distributed Mrs. Robinson's pamphlets at White's? True, he had perhaps done these things merely to get her attention, but surely once they were married she would be able to coax him along in the right direction. . . .

Six years of marriage had inured the marchioness to this sort of remark, so she returned no reply other than a slight smile.

"Speaking of reform," the marquis continued, adjusting a fold in his neckcloth, *"I wish you hadn't asked that Robinson woman to call. And as for taking her up to the nursery and exposing Tony and Belinda to her presence . . . Your kind heart does you credit, Philippa, but you mustn't allow it to interfere with the welfare of our children."*

"I would not," the marchioness said firmly, *"do anything to interfere with the welfare of our children."*

"Of course you wouldn't, my dear. I knew you'd understand as soon as we talked about it. By the way, I finished The Prime Minister's Indiscretion *yesterday. I quite liked it."*

The marchioness brightened at this praise of her latest novel and allowed the issue of Mrs. Robinson to drop. "Thank you, darling."

"But perhaps you went a trifle far in the portraits you drew of his majesty's government."

No, thought Philippa, I wouldn't. Not again.

"They were entirely fictional," the marchioness protested. *"I was most careful to leave out scars or moles or anything that could*

possibly be mistaken for an allusion to someone I met at a house party when I was eighteen."

Lord Carteret was disposed to smile briefly, but said, "No one thinks they represent individuals, my dear. But the collective picture you paint is somewhat disturbing."

"Oh, dear. Didn't you find it amusing?"

"Very amusing. That's the point. Stop and think for a moment, Philippa." The marquis' tone was almost pleading. "In times like these, people in our position need to support the government, not ridicule it."

"In times like these," the marchioness returned tartly, "the government needs to be ridiculed more than ever."

Oh, good for you, Philippa thought.

"But not by you," the marquis said. "I wish you would remember that you are no longer Philippa Davenport. When you married me you took on certain responsibilities along with your coronet."

"Are you asking me to stop writing?" the marchioness demanded, a sparkle in her eye and a challenge in her voice.

"Of course not, dearest. I only wish you would confine yourself to more womanly subject matter, as you did in your earlier books."

Philippa was too annoyed at this husbandly interference to wonder at the change she had assumed in her own writing.

"Worthman's having some people up at the end of July," the marquis said, temporarily abandoning his wife's novel, though his wife had no illusions that this was the last she would hear of it. "I thought we could go there for a fortnight or so when we leave London."

"Oh, must we?" the marchioness asked. "I'm sorry, I didn't mean that the way it sounded," she amended hastily. "But we're already going to Buckleigh Place in August and the children have been looking forward to some time at Carteret Park—"

"There's no reason Tony and Belinda shouldn't go to Carteret. Worthman doesn't have a great deal to say to a three-year-old, even if Tony is his godson."

"We can't send them to Carteret alone."

"They'll hardly be alone, Philippa. They'll have Nurse Bruton and Mademoiselle Vicennes and the under nursemaids, and Aurelia is just next door in the Dower House."

The marchioness sent her husband a speaking look. The marquis had the grace to look uncomfortable. "*I own I don't much like the way she fusses over Tony,*" he admitted, "*but it wouldn't do any harm for her to teach Belinda some manners. Our daughter is a regular hellion, my dear.*"

"*Why don't you go to Lord Worthman's,*" the marchioness suggested, "*and then join the children and me at Carteret Park. I could use some quiet to work on the new novel.*"

"*Damn it, Philippa!*" The marquis exploded with sudden force. "*Are your precious books really more important than all your other duties?*"

"*You can't say I neglect the children,*" the marchioness retorted, stung by his words.

"*I wasn't thinking of your duties as a mother. I was thinking of your duties as a wife.*"

Philippa chewed the tip of her pen. Did Carteret perhaps have a point? It was true that her writing took a great deal of her time. Perhaps it took up too much to allow her to be a very good wife to anyone. On the other hand—

"*You might have accompanied me to the opera last night,*" the marchioness suggested. "*Or taken me along on your own engagement.*"

At that Lord Carteret laughed. "*My darling Philippa, I could hardly have taken you to White's. And as for foregoing an engagement with my friends in order to escort you to the opera—well, it wouldn't do for it to be said that I lived in my wife's pocket, would it?*"

Philippa flung her pen down in disgust. What had happened to the fun-loving Carteret who, whatever his faults, was always entertaining?

No doubt the portrait she had drawn was exaggerated—her sense of the ridiculous could not resist going to extremes for comic effect—but it contained more than a grain of truth. Carteret was very engaging when he flirted with her, but men in his set did not flirt with their wives. After they married he would very likely expect to continue to live much as he always had. But Philippa did not think he would accord his wife the sort of freedom that Peter Cowper accorded Emily. Not only would Carteret expect fidelity from his wife, he would expect her to give him her attention when called upon. And he would, of course, expect her to keep up her position as the

Marchioness of Carteret. If they married, she would have to work hard to change his ideas about what constituted appropriate behaviour for respectable women and to counteract his share of the Paget family pride which was larger than she had realized. It reminded her rather of the situation in *Pride and Prejudice*. A pleasing image, but she wondered if her efforts would be as successful as Elizabeth Bennet's, when all the weight of tradition, family, and society would be working against her.

Feeling depressed, Philippa decided to abandon the marquis for the moment and move on to Elliot Marsden. He at least had little use for family—in fact, he rarely mentioned his deceased parents, or even his brother, seemingly his only living relative—and he certainly saw the hypocrisy in society's conventions. What would a morning be like at their breakfast table? Or no, she must be fair and allow him the same opportunities as Lord Carteret. What sort of wedding would they have?

Philippa reached for a fresh sheet of paper and let her imagination take over once again.

The day following his extraordinary discovery about the state of his heart, Henry's spirits alternated between a sense that it was sheer joy simply to be alive and in the same world as Philippa Davenport and fits of depression as he realized that Philippa did not return his regard, that she was no doubt on the verge of committing herself to the shallow Carteret or the scheming Marsden, and that, even were she not, marriage between the penniless son of an obscure Dorset parson and a wealthy young woman connected to some of England's best families was sure to be a disaster.

He repeated this litany of objections at frequent intervals. Sooner or later he would see sense and put Philippa—Miss Davenport—firmly from his mind. But whenever he thought he had done so, she managed to intrude on his thoughts by the most circuitous of routes. He saw something in the morning paper the ironies of which only she would fully appreciate. He wondered what she would think of the page he had just written. The voice of the young singer who occupied rooms next to his recalled Philippa's singularly lovely voice and then her equally lovely person, of which he had foolishly never taken sufficient notice.

His work was a disaster. Jeremy was showing a distressing tendency to dwell on the charms of Lady Eleanor, who was supposed to be his adversary, not his beloved. When he gave up trying to write and began to review the earlier chapters, Henry found that Jeremy's feelings for Eleanor had been drifting in that direction for some time. He had been as blind to what was happening to his characters as he had to what was happening to himself.

As the afternoon wore on, Henry pushed his novel aside in disgust and took himself off to Warwick House. He would see if Nicholas had learned anything of profit to Murray's case. A brisk walk and some conversation about a problem which at least had a tangible solution should help give his thoughts a more appropriate direction.

When he arrived in South Audley Street, he found that Nicholas was out. Livia and Gwendolen received him warmly but had no news. Livia did her best to be cheerful and Gwendolen entered into the mystery with an enthusiasm which would have been diverting had it not somehow reminded him of Philippa's ready eagerness to attack a problem.

Gerry came in while they were talking, also seeking news of Murray. Livia, who had been interrupted in the midst of giving Gwendolen lessons and who also had a young son to see to and an evening engagement for which to prepare, asked Gerry to look after Henry and took a reluctant Gwendolen back to the schoolroom.

Gerry suggested they wait until Nicholas returned home and Henry acquiesced readily. He welcomed company and any excuse to keep himself occupied. He knew that Philippa would expect him to call in Green Street to discuss the latest news, as he had done each day since Murray's arrest, but he could not bring himself to face a private interview with her. Not yet. This way he had a perfectly legitimate reason to postpone his visit. Perhaps he could even send a message with Gerry and avoid seeing her altogether.

Livia had ordered tea and Henry was already supplied with a cup. Gerry poured one for himself and settled back in a rosewood armchair. Henry forced his thoughts away from Philippa and asked after Claris.

"She was setting off on a shopping expedition with the Weston girls when I left the house. She seemed in capital spirits. If you ask me, she came through yesterday better than any of you." Gerry smiled. "Sisters are a great responsibility, aren't they? I must say I'm grateful I was out of the country most of the time mine were getting into scrapes."

"Claris is the only one of mine who's giving me any trouble. Of course, she's also the only one who's had the opportunity to do so. In our village, it would be difficult to find a scrape, let alone get into it."

"Do you miss it?" Gerry asked. Henry didn't talk much about his home.

"Occasionally. Though I was ready enough to leave when I went up to Oxford. And ready enough to come down to London when I left university. Off I marched, pen in hand, ready to take the world by storm. No, actually I wasn't thinking along nearly such grandiose lines. I was content just to have a look at the place. The truth is, Gerry, I had the devil of a time taking myself seriously."

"As a writer?"

"Especially as a writer. I used to envy Paul for being so damned self-confident about his painting."

"Self-absorbed might be nearer the mark." Gerry grinned. Paul Redmond, who had once shared lodgings with Henry, had recently married Gerry's youngest sister, Diana. Gerry suspected that Paul's departure for Paris three years ago had helped Henry take his own work more seriously, though it also must have left him lonely.

"At all events," Henry continued, "I didn't think anyone would actually want to publish *Robert Levering*. And when someone did, I suppose I began to take myself too seriously."

There was perhaps an element of truth to this, but what Henry had neglected to say was that his father had died shortly after *Robert Levering* appeared in print. Henry had been forced to grow up very quickly. "It isn't easy to suddenly be responsible for one's mother and sisters," Gerry said.

"Oh, I don't know. My sisters were thoughtful enough to fall in love with men who were willing to take them with practically no dowery. All but Claris. No, don't say it!" Henry flung up a hand. "Lord Christopher would very likely take her without any dowery whatsoever. It doesn't change anything."

Gerry laughed. "I've no desire to land in the middle of that quarrel." He watched Henry for a moment, then added, a shade too casually, "Speaking of quarrels, it seems you were right about Marsden. He was acting on Lady Carteret's instructions, at least initially."

"Don't tell me you've been making inquiries about him, too?"

"After Philippa's reaction to your efforts? Hardly. Marsden confessed."

"To you?"

"To Philippa."

"The devil." Henry set his cup down with deliberation. "The man is damnably clever. Did she forgive all?"

"You'll have to ask Philippa about that. I had it from Francesca." Gerry was tempted to relate the other news he had had from his wife, but he knew that Philippa would regard this as a breach of confidence. Henry, she would say, had no right to be interested in who did or did not propose to her. Gerry was beginning to suspect that, whether or not he had the right, Henry was very interested indeed.

"If Marsden's confessed," Henry said thoughtfully, "he must really mean to offer for her."

"He may have come to genuinely care for her."

Henry gave a short laugh.

"He'd be labelled a fortune hunter, of course," Gerry went on, "but from all accounts Marsden wouldn't care about that."

"Some men would." Henry turned his empty cup around in his hands. "Gerry. Don't answer this if you don't want to—it's a damned interfering question and I've no right to ask it, but wasn't it—that is, didn't you find it difficult—"

"Didn't I find it difficult when I married Francesca and everyone thought I was a gazetted fortune hunter who'd snared an earl's daughter?" Gerry supplied cheerfully. "Yes, I did, hellishly difficult, especially at first. Not that it isn't done every day, you know. Almack's is full of fellows hanging out for rich wives."

"To shore up the ancestral estate."

"Quite. I imagine some of the stiff-rumped dowagers still regard me as an impertinent upstart, but that's more a matter of birth than fortune. It's one thing to offer a girl a coronet in exchange for her dowery. It's another matter if you haven't got anything but your face to recommend you and that recommendation's a bit dubious. It's all quite comical. It reminds me of something from one of Philippa's novels."

Henry seemed to miss this last. "Did it ever bother Francesca?"

"That people thought she'd been married for her money? No, Francie's made of sterner stuff than that. I think it's in the Lyndale blood—her father never pays any heed to what's being said about him either. I daresay it's on the maternal side as well," Gerry added. Francesca's and Philippa's mothers were sisters.

It was a fairly broad hint, but it drew no response from Henry. He was frowning. "Still, there must be times—I don't know how you manage so well," he said.

Gerry thought he detected a trace of the old Henry who had doubted his own worth. "Well," Gerry admitted, "I won't deny there are times when it's difficult, knowing she pays most of the bills. On the other hand, while I wouldn't say money makes for a happy marriage, you must admit the lack of it makes for many an unhappy one. I imagine I'd feel a good deal worse if I thought I'd dragged Francesca into a life of genteel poverty, and it's certainly comforting to know I don't have to worry about my daughter's future."

This was an aspect of the matter Henry had not considered. He returned his cup to the tea tray, a thoughtful look on his face. "I still think," he said after a moment, "that it takes two special people to make it work."

Gerry grinned. "I suspect that's true of marriage in any case. But I wouldn't have expected these sorts of doubts from you. You've always professed to believe in greater equality between the sexes."

"Certainly I do. What's that to say to any of this?"

"Think, Henry. You didn't bring Claris to London so she could marry a man with no more money than she has herself."

Henry stared at him for a moment, then began to smile.

"Exactly," Gerry said. "All my sisters went to considerable

lengths to find eligible husbands—that is, Livia went to considerable lengths to find one for Claudia and ended up getting one herself into the bargain, and Diana—well, Diana's always been different from the rest of us. She and Paul may not have a fortune, but they have their work in common. I suspect that's a great help."

Henry thought about Paul and Diana and then about the other couples. Francesca and Livia, he realized, also shared their husbands' concerns. He did not think Philippa would enter with equal enthusiasm into Carteret's life or Marsden's. But would she discover that before it was too late?

"Still," he said, "you can't deny that society looks differently on a woman who marries above her than on a man who does."

Gerry began to laugh. "Henry, since when have you cared for society's opinion?"

Henry gave a sudden, rueful grin. "An unfortunate lapse. Don't let it get about." He fixed his friend with a suddenly hard stare. "But it isn't my life we're discussing."

"No," Gerry agreed blandly, "it isn't. Care for some more tea?"

Nicholas returned home some ten minutes later to find Henry looking thoughtful but a good deal more cheerful than he had for some time, while Gerry seemed to be smiling in secret amusement. Nicholas thought they might have good news, but that proved not to be the case. He had little news of his own and that little was discouraging. They discussed possible courses of action for a time, none of which seemed productive, and then Gerry proposed to take Henry back to Green Street for dinner.

An hour ago, Henry had wanted to avoid Green Street and Philippa Davenport at all costs. But that was before his talk with Francesca's husband. That talk had changed a number of things. The future no longer seemed nearly as bleak. He did not know if he could ever capture Philippa's heart himself, but he could see to it that she did not throw herself away on Marsden or Carteret. This was no time to be idle. Henry began to whistle as he and Gerry set off down the street.

Chapter 19

What sort of a wedding, Philippa wondered, would she and Mr. Marsden have? Surely a less formal one than—

Philippa, who had expected to be married at home, was surprised when her betrothed expressed a marked preference for St. Margaret's, Westminster, and even more surprised at the interest he took in the guest list.

You shouldn't be, Philippa told herself. You know the man's ambitious. He's bound to think about his career, though the wedding does seem a little early to start.

Now, as she stood at the alter at Elliot Marsden's side, the pews behind her filled with her family and the most influential and distinguished members of her family's acquaintance, and listened to the voice of the bishop droning on—

That at least told her that her boredom had more to do with droning bishops than with Lord Carteret. And under no circumstances would she allow Madame Dessart to bully her into wearing white satin and point lace at this wedding.

So far so good. Would it be giving Marsden short shrift if she jumped six years into the future and examined their married life? Her hand was beginning to grow tired and she decided that it would not. She let her hand rest idle for a moment while she tried to visualize a typical morning in the Marsden household.

Mrs. Elliot Marsden, the former Philippa Davenport, entered the breakfast parlour of the Marsden house on a brisk morning in the spring of 1825 to find her husband already at the table, perusing the Morning Chronicle.

She had at least managed to turn Marsden into a self-respecting Whig. Philippa ignored her suspicion that Marsden's change of party loyalty might have more to do with expedience than belief.

"Good morning, my dear," said Marsden, half-rising from his chair and pushing aside his newspaper. The Morning Post *and* The Times *were lying beneath it.*

Philippa gave a wry smile. How very like Elliot Marsden to walk a line between both parties. She wondered briefly if the Whigs would have finally regained power by 1825, then told herself that the party's fate was not the reason for her attempt to peer into the future.

Mrs. Marsden returned the greeting and poured herself a cup of coffee. Both the Marsdens had risen early, for despite a late evening at the Cowpers, neither could afford to sleep half the morning away.

Not a bad start. Marsden had not given her even a perfunctory good morning kiss, but they had spent the previous evening together in congenial company, and she could count on her husband's companionship at breakfast.

Mr. Marsden swallowed the last of his coffee. "I must be off. I'm meeting with Canning and then going on to Brooks'. I have to look in at the House this evening, but I'll be back in time to escort you to Holland House."

Of course, he would have entered Parliament by this time. Life with Marsden the politican should be far more like the household Philippa had grown up in than life with Carteret the marquis. And while Marsden had been too preoccupied to give his wife a good morning kiss, he would also, Philippa thought, be too preoccupied to let his attention stray to other women.

Mrs. Marsden watched her husband rise from the table and thought again about the way he had flirted with Madame de Lieven on the previous evening. Elliot assured her that his heart was all hers and she did not doubt him, but she sometimes wondered at the lengths to which he would go in his drive for advancement.

Oh dear, she hadn't thought of that. There was more than one reason to have an affair. She had never considered that side of a political career. But a political career should have a positive effect on Marsden as well. Would he, like Papa and Nicholas

Warwick, pay visits to Sophronia Neville?

"*By the way, Philippa,*" *Marsden said on his way out,* "*I wish you wouldn't have that Robinson woman over again.*"

Mrs. Marsden regarded her husband with surprise and disappointment. "*Don't tell me you're afraid she'll corrupt the children, Elliot.*"

"*Good God, no. More likely the other way around. But it gives the wrong impression. Waterford remarked on it only last night. It's all very well for you to take an interest in widows and orphans, but the wife of a future cabinet minister should not be seen hobnobbing with a lot of rabid reformers.*"

"*Future cabinet minister?*" *Mrs. Marsden inquired.*

"*Naturally,*" *her husband returned smoothly.*

Naturally. Well, if she were a man and a politician it's what she would want. But not if it meant turning her back on people like Mrs. Robinson and Sophronia Neville and Gordon Murray.

"*And while we're on the subject,*" *Marsden continued,* "*I think perhaps we ought to have a talk about* The Prime Minister's Indiscretion."

"*Oh dear,*" *Mrs. Marsden exclaimed,* "*what has the silly man done this time?*" *In fact she was quite pleased by his remark, for her husband had been too busy to pay much heed to her recent novel.*

Mr. Marsden was disposed to smile briefly, but said, "*Some people don't care for the portraits you've drawn of his majesty's government.*"

"*Rubbish!*"

"*Far from it.*" *Marsden returned to the breakfast table and leaned upon it.* "*Philippa,*" *he said, his cajoling voice belied by the force of his expression,* "*you know the position I am in. I am not a Fox or a Lamb, with family credentials that can stand up to any scandal. I cannot afford to offend anyone for the sake of my future—our future.*"

Mrs. Marsden did not appear sufficiently swayed by this persuasively delivered argument. "*Are you asking me to stop writing?*" *she demanded, a sparkle in her eye and a challenge in her voice.*

"*Of course not, love. I only wish you would confine yourself to more frivolous subject matter—as you did in your earlier books.*

Speaking of our more immediate future," Marsden added, moving to the door once again, "the Grenvilles have asked us up in July. I accepted, of course."

"Oh, Elliot, you didn't! Have you forgotten we're promised to Mama and Kenrick?"

"I'm sure your mother and stepfather will understand. We can send the children to them."

"Send the children to them! Elliot, you hardly see Belinda and young Elliot when we're in town. If we send them away for the summer—"

"Philippa, I've already accepted the invitation."

"Then you can go to the Grenvilles' and the children and I will go to Mama's as planned. You can join us in a few weeks. That way I'll have time to work on the new novel—"

"Will you stop thinking about your damned books for two minutes together?" Marsden exploded with sudden force. "If you don't come to the Grenvilles' with me, the world will say that we have quarrelled. Philippa, I wish you would remember that a man in my position—"

Philippa flung down her pen. The man was insufferably high-handed. And he showed even less interest in his children than Carteret had done. But then, she recalled, Marsden had not melted to Linnet's charms, while Carteret had at least shown some interest in Bertie when he thought the child might be his own.

She had drawn another picture which was far from flattering. Of course Marsden had never pretended to be an idealist. His political goals were motivated by personal ambition, not a desire to reshape society. *You make me better than I am,* he had said to her. As in Carteret's case, the question was how well she could do her work.

But perhaps what disturbed her most about the stories was her assumption that both Carteret and Marsden would expect her to conform to their way of life rather than trying to build a new life together with her. Was this perhaps inevitable in any marriage? True, it was usually the woman who moved into the man's home, but she thought there was something different in her memories of her parents' marriage and in what she had observed of the marriages of her sisters and Francesca

302

and Livia.

She pushed aside the scribbled sheets with an impatient gesture. She would wait. She would tell them she could not possibly think of her own future until Mr. Murray had been exonerated. Perhaps that was cowardly, but it would give her time. And she desperately needed time. She was not yet ready to give up her suitors, but today's exercise had not exposed a secret partiality. It had only raised more troubling questions about both men.

"I don't know that I'm particularly perceptive, and you know I've never been a betting man," Gerry said to his wife later that evening, "but I'd wager you a monkey that Henry's in love with Philippa."

"Yes, of course he is." Francesca was seated at her dressing table, undoing the delicate paintwork she did each morning. "That's been evident for some time. I think he's just the man for her, don't you?"

Leaning in the doorway between the dressing room and the bedroom, Gerry regarded his wife with appreciation. "You really are a redoubtable woman, Francesca. How long have you been thinking about this?"

"Oh, it occurred to me years ago that they would deal together admirably, only when I introduced them somehow they took each other in dislike. Even then I had my hopes, because strong enmity often masks quite the opposite. And when Henry took such exception to Marsden and Carteret I began to grow suspicious."

"So did I. Poor chap."

Francesca turned to look at him. "Why poor?"

"Because, my darling schemer, while I agree that Henry's just the man for Philippa, Philippa's main concern, as you told me this morning, is whether to marry Elliot Marsden or the Marquis of Carteret."

"Yes, and I must admit she had me worried for a time, but I think she's going to come round quite nicely," Francesca said serenely.

Gerry had a good deal of respect for his wife's perceptions, but this was going a little too far. "I'll admit she and Henry are getting on rather better these days—" he said cautiously.

"A great deal better. As you once pointed out, they quite seem to enjoy quarrelling. That's always an excellent sign."

Gerry grinned. "As I recall, you and I used to squabble a good deal."

Francesca pulled a face. "Squabble is such an undignified word, Gerry."

"As I recall, we weren't very dignified."

"No," she agreed, reaching for another bottle, "we weren't. It was such fun." She began to rub her face with Balm of Mecca. "You may not have noticed, Gerry, but Philippa's been changing in these past weeks."

"I hate to disillusion you, my sweet, but I am not blind to the charms of other women. Of course I noticed. But I must confess I put it down to Carteret and Marsden's influence."

"If you mean that she's been paying rather more attention to her appearance, I daresay that may have something to do with Marsden and Carteret—or simply with the effect of being courted. That's all very well, but I was thinking of something more substantial."

"In that case I am quite out. What?"

"Henry took Philippa to a meeting at Sophronia Neville's," Francesca said, pulling the pins from her hair.

"Yes, I know." Gerry watched his wife's fair tresses cascade over her shoulders. "That was where she met Gordon Murray. I understand there was something of a row. What was it about?"

"Bastards, Gerry. The row was caused by a Mrs. Robinson who used to run the sort of establishment in which they're a frequent hazard of business. I understand some people took exception to the subject matter."

"But Philippa wasn't one of them."

"Certainly not." Francesca returned the pins to the appropriate box and picked up her brush. "She came back most enthusiastic and told me all about the benefits of sponges."

"Sponges?" Colonel Scott repeated blankly.

"They have more than one use, you know."

It took a moment more and then Gerry began to grin. "I'd

304

have given a great deal to see you handle it, Francie. Did you feign surprise or tell Philippa Mrs. Robinson wasn't the only one to know about such things?"

"There was no need. Philippa said she was certain I already knew all about it, but wasn't it a pity that more young women weren't properly instructed, and shouldn't there be something one could do about it."

"Practical Philippa. You might have told me some of this earlier," he added in an aggrieved tone.

Francesca stopped attending to her hair and threw him a glance over her shoulder. "Somehow when we're alone we always have more important things to attend to."

This remark caused Colonel Scott to abandon his nonchalant pose in the doorway. Francesca put up a restraining hand. "Careful, Gerry, if my perfume gets spilled again the servants will never forgive us! Besides, I haven't finished the story."

Gerry returned, reluctantly, to the doorway. "It had better be good."

"It's illuminating. After the meeting at Sophronia's, Henry took Philippa to visit Mr. Murray's office. I gather that visit was also rather eventful, though no one's given me the details. You know, Philippa's always been as reform-minded as the rest of the family, in a theoretical sort of way, but I don't think she's ever given it a great deal of thought. At least not until recently. But not only has she entered into Mr. Murray's defence with enthusiasm, yesterday morning she was talking about the Combination acts, and she had some rather hard questions for Nicholas the last time the Warwicks dined with us."

"She asked me about the disturbances in the north only a few days ago," Gerry said thoughtfully. "But none of this," he pointed out, returning to the original argument, "really tells us anything about how she feels toward Henry."

"It tells us he's had much more of an impact on her than her two acknowledged suitors," Francesca said, rising from the dressing table. "And it tells us she'd be far happier with him than with either of the others." She kissed Gerry lightly and moved past him into the bedroom. "I suppose you noticed the way Henry was looking at Philippa at dinner. Something happened today, I'd swear it."

"Something did. He talked to me."

Francesca stopped midway across the room, her brows raised. "About Philippa?"

"Not in so many words. He wanted to know how I manage to retain my self-respect when I married so far above myself."

"Oh, dear," said Francesca, dropping down on the edge of the bed, "I should have thought of that. Men can be so silly. I trust you were able to reassure him."

"I think so. I told him that after a bit one finds one can do quite well without self-respect."

Francesca reached behind her for a pillow and threw it at him. Gerry caught it neatly and advanced toward her, the pillow held before him. The ensuing scuffle left the pillow on the floor, but Colonel Scott and Lady Francesca both on the bed. There followed a rather long interval during which, whatever happened, nothing was actually said. Finally Francesca was moved to murmur reluctantly, "Gerry—darling, remember Mrs. Robinson—"

Gerry sighed and propped himself up on one elbow. "You don't think," he asked wistfully, "that Linnet might like a little friend to play with?"

"I think," said Francesca, putting her dressing-gown to rights and climbing off the bed, "that we should wait until she's old enough to make an informed judgement." She moved toward the painted screen which stood on the opposite side of the room, stopping to pick up the abandoned pillow and toss it back to him.

Gerry fluffed the pillow and returned it to its proper place. "If Henry declared himself, what do you think Philippa would do?" he asked.

"I don't know." Francesca sighed, admitting concern for the first time. "She wrote about her future with Carteret and with Marsden today, and she told me she wasn't very happy with either story. But she isn't yet ready to give them up. Of course, I don't think she realizes she has any other options. I tried to convince her that she should wait until she's absolutely certain, but women do tend to get rather desperate, you know."

"I disclaim all responsibility," Gerry said, removing his dressing-gown. "You should have proposed to me weeks earlier."

"Years, actually." Francesca emerged from behind the screen. "But that's neither here nor there. Philippa won't propose to Henry. On the other hand, Henry was at some pains to learn that everyone but Philippa will be from home tomorrow morning. Do you think he might actually declare himself?"

"I think he *might*," said Gerry. "The truth is, Francie," he continued, turning back the quilt and climbing beneath it, "for all Henry's brains, I don't trust him not to make a mull of it. I'd far rather have him by me in a tight spot than Carteret or Marsden, but I doubt he has their finesse when it comes to dealing with women."

"Of course he hasn't," Francesca agreed, slipping into bed beside her husband. "That's what makes him perfect for Philippa. Philippa would grow bored to death being treated with finesse and she'd drive any man mad who expected her to take him seriously."

"You needn't convince me, Francie. I agree it's a match made in heaven." Gerry laced his hands behind his head and stared meditatively at the green damask canopy. "The question is how to make *them* agree when, as far as I can make out, they have yet to agree about anything at all."

"Henry's a very enterprising young man."

"I know, but—"

"Gerry." Francesca twined her arms around her husband's neck. "Let's worry about it in the morning."

Henry arrived in Green Street at ten o'clock the next morning, determined to ask Philippa to be his wife. Thanks to judicious questioning at the dinner table on the previous evening, he knew that Gerry had a meeting, Francesca and Claris were going out to make some last minute purchases for the breakfast Francesca was giving in three days time, and Philippa meant to spend the day at home working on her novel.

Now that he had decided to put it to the chance, Henry was

less nervous than exhilarated. It might be a long campaign, but he would not allow Marsden or Carteret to vanquish him. And whatever the outcome of this morning's venture, at least he would no longer have to pretend in Philippa's presence.

Tuttle showed him into the library and Henry, too impatient to sit, stood by the window, thinking of the quarrels he and Philippa had had in this room, and how foolish they had been, and how Philippa's eyes sparkled when she was angry—

"Henry, how nice." Philippa stood in the connecting doorway from her study, dressed in the plain dark green dress she often wore when she was working, stray wisps of hair adorning her neck and forehead. He had clearly interrupted her at her writing, but she was smiling warmly—no, bewitchingly. "Is there some news about Mr. Murray?" she asked, closing the door behind her.

"About Gordon? No, nothing. Nothing new that is." Henry ordered his thoughts with an effort.

"I'm sorry. We're getting wretchedly short of time, aren't we? But then we went over all that last night. Are we going to be reduced to making the rounds of the London tailors and compiling a list of all the gentlemen who've ordered yellow waistcoats in the last year or so?"

Henry smiled, but before he could turn the conversation into a more appropriate direction, Philippa remembered her duties as hostess and asked if he cared for any refreshment. Henry declined. The most romantic proposal would, he felt, be marred by the presence of coffee cups. He then realized that it was incumbent on him to apologize for interrupting her at her work. By the time Philippa had assured him that she was delighted to see him, it had occurred to Henry that one had to work round to this sort of declaration gradually. He asked her how her novel was progressing.

"Quite well, considering all the distractions I've had. Though Anne and Nigel are turning out rather differently than I'd expected."

"I've been having the same trouble with Jeremy and Eleanor."

"Jeremy and Eleanor?"

"My hero and—I suppose she's my heroine. I rather think

I'm going to have to let Jeremy marry her after all."

"And let them both survive the book?"

"Oh, yes. I don't approve of killing off characters just to tie up loose ends. It's too conveniently tidy. Not a bit like life."

"And what about Amelia?"

"Amelia wasn't really important, not to the book and certainly not to Robert."

"And Eleanor is?" Philippa was curious. "Both to the book and to Jeremy?"

"Very much so."

It was an excellent opening, but before he could seize it, Philippa said, "It's surprising what characters can do without consulting one in the least, isn't it? Nigel has decided to stand for Parliament. I wouldn't have thought Anne would be interested, but she has quite entered into the spirit of the thing, which only goes to show that one's characters can be far more complex than one gives them credit for."

"Very true," Henry agreed gravely, trying to conceal how much her last words meant to him. "You aren't worried that your novel is becoming too serious?"

"Because I'm dealing with *politics?*" Philippa demanded, her eyes dancing. "Can you imagine a subject more ripe for satire?"

"It would be difficult," he admitted.

Philippa laughed suddenly, a delightful, infectious sound that made Henry momentarily forget his objective in the simple enjoyment of being with her. "You know," she said frankly, "I never would have thought we'd be discussing our work like this. There was a time when I wasn't even sure you acknowledged me as a fellow writer."

"I never denied your talent," Henry said quickly. It was no more than the truth.

"No, only my choice of subject matter. And I must confess that you were right—at least, I admit that I was too superficial in my treatment of it."

"Perhaps. But your writing has a certain—I suppose humanity is the best word—which my own quite lacks."

Philippa sat back in her chair. "Thank you, Henry," she said after a moment. "I believe that is the nicest thing you have ever said to me."

"A chastening estimate of my past behaviour." He drew a breath. "Philippa—"

"Henry," Philippa said at the same time, "if either Lord Carteret or Mr. Marsden calls, will you please stay here until he leaves?"

"Certainly," Henry agreed, surprised but not displeased. Could she at last be tiring of them?

"I suppose it's cowardly of me." Philippa sighed. "I shall have to face them sooner or later."

"I was under the impression," Henry could not resist saying, "that you faced them almost every day."

"Yes, but now I have to tell them about my decision. Or rather, that I haven't come to a decision yet."

Being nothing if not quick-witted, Henry was filled with an unpleasant apprehension which waited only for the confirmation Philippa was quick to give.

"I suppose you might as well know the truth," she said. "The rest of the family know—all but Claris, and I'd as soon she didn't, for she'd never give me a moment's peace."

"You may rely on my discretion. I take it that I am to congratulate you on having received two offers of marriage?"

"I might have known you'd work it out for yourself," Philippa said approvingly. "Though considering your opinion of the gentlemen in question, you can hardly expect me to take your congratulations seriously."

"Perhaps you'd find me more sincere if I congratulated you on having not yet accepted either proposal," Henry countered, with a lightness he did not feel. "Or are those congratulations not in order?"

"How could I think about something as important as marriage in the midst of Mr. Murray's trouble?" Philippa demanded.

"Easy, my girl. It's not me you need to convince." Although five more minutes and it might have been. It might still be. Should he say, as long as you're reviewing offers why not consider mine as well? It was not quite the proposal he had imagined, but—

"Very true," Philippa said, laughing. "But it is vexatious

310

that they should have spoken when I have so much else on my mind, though I suppose I can't really blame them, for they made their offers before Mr. Murray was arrested. Still, it's all gotten tiresomely complicated. I was excessively pleased when Tuttle told me it was you who had called, Henry. It's lovely to talk to just a friend for a change."

That settled it. It was somewhat—well, very—lowering to realize that Philippa regarded him simply as a friend, but at the moment she was apparently more in charity with her friends than with her suitors. It would be foolish to abandon the first state for the second, no matter how much one wished to express one's feelings. He would be patient. At least she had not yet accepted either of them. There was reason to hope. Philippa, Henry knew with sudden conviction, would not tie herself to a man unless—unless—

Unless she truly loved him. It was the one complication Henry had not foreseen. He had been afraid that, blinded by infatuation, Philippa would promise herself to Carteret or Marsden and live to regret her decision. He had thought he could save her from making that mistake. But he should have known she would give the matter careful thought. And if she accepted one of her suitors, it would not be because she was blind to his faults, but because she loved him in spite of them. And if that was the case, how could Henry possibly stand in her way?

Philippa watched the expressions flitting across his face and put them down to concern about Mr. Murray. "I know," she said. "Waiting is the very devil."

Henry met her eyes. "Yes," he said with a rueful smile, "it most certainly is."

Chapter 20

Raynley was a pleasant house set in the rolling green country near Petersham, not far from the river. As befitted a Lyndale it was large and well-appointed, but the easy-going earl cared little for formality. The furniture was old and comfortable and the grounds had been little improved, though the lawns were well-tended. A small stream meandered not far from the house, but it boasted nothing but frogs. The trees were old and fit for climbing or sitting under or hiding behind, but they had not been shaped to please the eye. The flower beds ran chiefly to gilliflowers and stock and sweet rocket. In the spring, white violets grew wild on the banks of the stream.

Francesca had been delighted when her father made her a casual gift of Raynley before she and Gerry left Paris. It was perfect for the entertainment she had in mind, a breakfast for no more than sixty people—well, perhaps a few more—with no more diversion than could be provided by archery and croquet and other lawn games and dancing in the late afternoon for the younger people who might care to stand up to music provided by a piano and two or three strings.

For her cousin's sake, Francesca invited Lord Carteret and Elliot Marsden—the more Philippa saw of them, the sooner they would pall—and for Claris' sake she invited Lord Christopher. Then for the look of the thing she felt obliged to ask Lady Carteret who in turn asked to be allowed to bring Lady Edwina. Fortunately, Edwina's brother was still in the country. Francesca had never been taken with his charm, but she had put his affectations down to youth and gaucherie. Until, that is, that disgraceful episode with Claris. Had Lady Carteret begged an invitation for him as well, Francesca would have refused him the house.

Francesca set out the day before the party with Philippa and Claris, carrying Linnet in her arms. Their maids and Adèle followed in a second carriage, together with the quantity of clothes required by three ladies for a stay of two days, as well as some table linen and several boxes of glassware that were being borrowed from the Green Street house for the occasion. The Davenport cook and two of the kitchen maids had left earlier in the day, armed with hampers of food that was not to be readily procured in the country. Gerry would come down with the Warwicks the following afternoon, and he promised to see that Henry left off his search for a yellow waistcoat long enough to join them.

As they neared Raynley, Philippa felt her spirits lighten. Hermia, asleep at her feet, stirred and sniffed the air. Linnet woke from her doze and became excited by the sight of a pair of geese waddling past the open door of a cottage. Philippa was eager for activity. If Francesca did not need her, she would take Hermia and go for a long walk through the grounds and beyond and forget her inability to help Mr. Murray and her inability to choose between her two suitors.

But in the event the three women were far too busy that day and well into the evening, and Philippa did not have time to think of anything beyond the placement of chairs and the counting of silver and napkins.

She rose very early the next morning and slipped out of the house and found herself perversely unable to think of anything but the rival merits of Lord Carteret and Elliot Marsden. She tried to recall her exact sensations when each man had held her in his arms. To her dismay, the memories tended to merge, till in the end she could recall only the delicious feeling of being held close in a man's arms and the warm scent of a man's breath as his face moved down to hers, darkening her vision and sending exquisite chills through her body as his lips pressed softly and firmly against her own. She stopped and closed her eyes, savouring the memory again, but try as she would she could not clearly see the man's face. What a ridiculous schoolgirl she had become, knowing not her mind nor her heart nor her treacherous body.

She thought of Claris' unquestioning commitment to her own lover. "Crispin is absolute perfection," she had said. "Of course, Henry says he will not seem so with time, and I know no one is ever quite perfect—I am not so myself, and Henry certainly has great room for improvement—but I will always think Crispin so, and that, after all, is the ideal foundation for marriage."

Philippa wished she could be at once as uncritical and as clear-eyed as Claris. She herself was all too prone to see flaws in people. Was that why she had never been able to fall truly in love?

She opened her eyes and looked about her. She had gone well beyond the boundaries of Raynley and stood now on a small rise, looking down onto a cluster of cottages. Hermia came running back and lay panting at her feet. Philippa crouched down and rubbed the soft cap of the dog's head, running her fingers into the folds where her ears sprang out to droop beside her muzzle. Hermia could live in the moment. Why couldn't she? And if she could not, couldn't she at least make her memories work for her? Now if she had a heroine who was very ready to be loved, and if that heroine had two very different but equally attractive suitors . . . Philippa clasped her arms round her knees, stared unseeing into the distance, and moved into a world of her own devising.

By two o'clock the first guests had begun to arrive, and by three the house and terrace and adjoining lawns were growing crowded. There were above a hundred people present, and most of them chose to be outdoors where the women's bright clothes and the ready laughter which was never given free rein in drawing rooms and saloons gave the guests the sense that they were participating in a joyous rustic festival.

Philippa was wearing a new pink-and-white striped percale with a small ruff, and she felt almost pretty. She moved easily among the guests, talking with friends and acquaintances and,

314

for Francesca's sake, keeping an eye on the servants who were passing through the throng with trays of champagne and lemonade. She had seen the Paget family arrive and had nodded to Lord Carteret but was pleased that he had not immediately sought her out. He was being unusually attentive to his stepmother, guiding her to a chair on the terrace, adjusting her parasol, and procuring her congenial company and a glass of champagne. Lord Christopher was being equally circumspect, though she could see his eyes searching the company for a sight of Claris. Claris, however, was some distance off, enjoying a game of battledore and shuttlecock with Gwendolen Warwick and two of the younger male guests. She could hear their cries and exclamations in the distance.

Philippa was less successful in avoiding her other suitor. She knew Mr. Marsden had been invited, but she did not see him until he appeared suddenly at her side, looking rather out of place in this pastoral setting. "May I walk with you," he said, "or are you bound on some domestic errand?"

She shook her head. She had just left Emily Cowper and her daughter Minny and was on her way to speak to the Richardson family whom she had not seen in several weeks, but that would keep. She took his proffered arm, thinking that she much preferred to stroll with her arms free, but conscious at the same time of his lean strength and the suppressed energy that was at once so attractive and so disturbing. As they walked along the bank of the stream and across the curved bridge that spanned it, she made inconsequential talk about the day and the place and the guests. But she need not have worried. He did not offer her gallantries but instead asked about Gordon Murray.

Startled, for at the moment Murray was far from her mind, she dropped his arm. Then of one accord they moved into the shade of a clump of oaks where they would be in less danger of interruption or of being overhead. Philippa described Henry's effort to find the person who must have visited Murray's office and hidden the bracelet and his search for the boy who had disappeared and the boy's description of the man with the yellow waistcoat. "So you see," she concluded, "there is nothing more to be done than find which of the Warwicks'

315

guests owns such a waistcoat or knows a person who does and might be willing to abet a felony."

He looked at her with genuine concern. "Don't be bitter," he said, "the case is far from hopeless. The very fact that such a man was seen must raise questions about Murray's guilt. I trust Mr. Collingwood has been informed?"

"I believe so," she said slowly. She had not before thought Jemmy's evidence much use to anyone by Henry and herself and the small band of Mr. Murray's friends. Mr. Marsden's statement gave her some comfort.

"Perhaps you know that he decided not to employ me in your friend's defence?"

Philippa shook her head.

"I'm sorry not to be able to serve you in this way, but I'm sure he has his reasons. I understand a brief had been sent to Sir William Demings. He's a competent lawyer and has more experience in such matters than I."

Elliot Marsden was not a modest man, and this last disarmed her. She thanked him warmly for his offer of help, then made to return to the party.

"Not yet," he begged. He placed a restraining hand on her arm. "There is something more I would say. No, don't be distressed," he added as she stiffened at his touch, "I will not importune you. I ask only if you have considered my offer, and if you have come to a decision."

He was unaccustomedly gentle and she could not take offence. It was three days since her unsuccessful attempt to solve her problem by writing about a future life with each of her suitors, but she had not yet told either of them of her resolve to put off her decision until Mr. Murray was freed. "I know you deserve an answer," she said, "but in all honesty I cannot yet give you one. The very day you spoke to me I learned of Mr. Murray's arrest, and I have been so preoccupied with the matter I can scarcely think of anything else."

She wanted to ask him if he meant to become a cabinet minister, and if he cared which party he served, and if he really would sleep with Countess Lieven to further his career. But instead she said, "I beg you, wait till it is settled. I promise to answer you then."

He looked as though he would have spoken, or kissed her hand, or perhaps taken her lips once more. She was conscious of a great longing to be kissed again and felt her body yielding to him. But he only smiled and, to her mingled relief and disappointment, led her back to the lawn where the other guests were congregated. "Perhaps I can be of more use this afternoon," he said before he left her. "I shall circulate among your cousin's guests and observe who is wearing a yellow waistcoat." He grinned. "I assure you I do not own such a garment myself."

Anthony made his way slowly through the grounds, pausing now and then to speak to the men he knew or to exchange flirtatious banter with the women of his acquaintance. He sipped a glass of chilled champagne. The quality was good. Lady Francesca did not stint her guests.

He wanted to talk with Miss Davenport, but she seemed to have disappeared. Then he saw her further off walking by the stream with a man whose back was somehow familiar. He smiled and answered a question from Lady Winfield, then excused himself and moved on. The man was Elliot Marsden. What was he doing here? But he knew perfectly well what he was doing here, Lady Francesca had asked him because of his interest in Miss Davenport.

Anthony took another glass of champagne from a passing servant, stepped out of the path of two young girls running across the lawn, and made his way toward the stream. The couple had crossed the bridge and were moving deliberately into the secrecy of a clump of trees. A wave of fury swept his long frame. He turned his back, his manner showing just the faintest trace of ennui. He would not intrude. He placed his empty glass on a nearby table and drained a full one which had been left there. And all the time his charming smile never left his face.

He was detained for a few moments by Lady Mountjoy, who had some hopes for her eldest daughter, and then by Felicia Whidbury, who had some hopes on her own account. Wanting to avoid any more such encounters, Anthony moved away from the house, down a grassy slope and onto a flat meadow where a straw target had been set up for those who would try their skill with bow and arrow. Half a dozen men were gathered there. Anthony watched them awhile, then removed his splendidly cut coat and tried his hand.

As was true of most of the manly sports, Anthony showed skill, strength, and considerable elegance of movement. The heft of the bow in his hand, the pull of his muscles as he drew back the string, the moment of intense concentration on the target, and the exhilarating release as the arrow flew through the air toward its mark, all did much to restore his good humour. He laughed a bit with some of the men and had a sort of match with young Ralph Dudley whom he bested with ease. Then a group of young women came by and claimed the younger men and the others drifted off. Anthony debated following them back toward the house or staying to perfect his skill with the bow. He had shot well, considering that he had not had one in hand for several years, but there was always room for improvement.

He decided to stay and had just nocked an arrow when he became aware of a new group of guests who had drifted out to the meadow in search of fresh diversion. He heard the husky tones of his cousin Edwina and, to his surprise, the answering voice of Elliot Marsden.

The arrow flew wide. He shook his head slightly and reached for another, and no one but Edwina could have told that he was angry. "I'm sorry, Tony," she said, in a tone which indicated the matter was of no consequence, "we spoiled your aim." Edwina was now tolerably composed in Anthony's presence and rather glad she was not betrothed to him, but she had not forgiven him for the humiliation he had inflicted on her at the Warwicks' ball. "Do you mind if we watch?" she asked, just the faintest trace of malice in her voice. "Or perhaps you would allow Mr. Marsden to try his skill against you, he tells me he was quite adept as a boy."

The two men measured each other with their eyes. Then Anthony nodded and Marsden stripped off his coat and hefted the bows, looking for one whose weight would match his strength. Edwina watched them with anticipation. She knew

318

they had been slightly acquainted for a number of years, and she suspected that neither had much use for the other. She also knew that they were rivals for the attentions of Miss Davenport. But she had never guessed at the depth of rancour now visible in their eyes. Was it all on Miss Davenport's account? Or were there other reasons?

Marsden, she suspected, was jealous of her cousin who in feature, and bearing could be considered his superior. Then there was the disparity in their fortunes. Marsden had had to make his own way, and it had given him a hardness, an edge that made him quite as formidable in his own way as Tony was in his. In fact, looking at them now as they waited for the gardener's boy who had been detailed to remove the spent arrows, she would have said that Elliot Marsden was every bit as attractive as the great Lord Carteret, and was perhaps the more exciting man. One could grow very tired of perfection.

She moved to get a better view and adjusted her parasol to shield her skin from the sun. Both men showed to advantage in their shirt-sleeves. A considerable crowd had gathered by this time, but their chatter died as the men made ready to shoot. Marsden went first, a good solid hit not far from the centre of the target. Anthony's following arrow was closer. There were murmurs of "Well done."

Edwina waited impatiently for the next round and to her delight the honours went to Elliot Marsden. After four rounds they were even. The men were pale with concentration, their faces shiny with sweat. "Three more?" Marsden asked. "The best of seven?"

Anthony gave a terse nod. He took the next round and Marsden the one after, so they were even once more. More people had joined the onlookers, and Edwina could hear the murmur of bets being made on the final round. She found Henry Ashton standing by her side, a bemused smile on his face. She had been thinking rather well of him ever since the episode at her brother's villa, and she turned to him with a smile. "Are you a betting man, Mr. Ashton?"

He shook his head. "Their styles are different, but there is little to choose between them. And you?"

"Oh," she said, not willing to put her desires into words, "I only wait on the outcome."

A hush came over the crowd. Marsden's arrow flew true and landed not a finger's breadth from the centre of the target. There was a general exhalation of air. Then Anthony stepped forward and took aim, his eyes fixed on that centre but his whole being concentrated in the arrow's tip. It sang in its flight, landing at the target's core.

But not quite. It was so close that several men ran forward to measure, then came back to report that a determination could not be made. It was close, but no closer than Marsden's arrow, and certainly no further away. All bets were off.

The men shook hands, if not willingly then for the look of the thing, and donned their coats and strolled back toward the lawn where most of the guests were gathered. Edwina congratulated her cousin and Mr. Marsden in turn, then took Mr. Marsden's arm as the onlookers departed.

Henry was about to follow, but the sight of the discarded bows roused memories of his home and afternoons spent nocking arrows for his sisters. Claris, he remembered, had shown some real aptitude for the game. He picked up a bow and set an arrow to the string. Just one, for memory's sake. He shot the arrow straight and true, and it came to rest at the centre of the target, right between Elliot Marsden's arrow on the left and Anthony Paget's arrow on the right. But save for the gardener's boy, who stared at him in wide-eyed admiration, there was no one to see him do it.

Word of the competition between Carteret and Marsden spread rapidly among the guests, most of whom were aware that both men had been paying court to Philippa Davenport, and Philippa found herself the object of whispered asides and veiled attention.

She was inclined to think the story rather funny. It would be quite splendid in a book. Then she berated herself for making light of the feelings of the men involved. It was on her account that they had become rivals, and she was making it worse by her refusal to decide between them.

She was not then unprepared when she saw Carteret making

his way leisurely and inexorably through the crowd toward her, and she went to meet him, ready to let him too have his say.

"Miss Davenport," he said, smiling down at her, "you have been elusive this afternoon."

"I have been paying off the arrears of courtesy." She took his arm, and they strolled through the grounds. "I have been neglecting my friends as well as my work."

"I pray you won't neglect me. I have fought valiantly for you this afternoon, but I confess I cannot bring any laurels to lay at your feet."

She did not pretend to misunderstand him. "I am rather glad you cannot. I do not like to see anyone contesting for me, and if they are foolish enough to do so, I would prefer there were no victor."

"Then you admit there is a contest?"

"I admit to no such thing!" The fact that he was right only added to Philippa's distress. True, she had two suitors from whom to choose, but she was beginning to think she would feel the same hesitation were there only one.

"You see, I thought that your reluctance to give me an answer might be related to your interest in someone else."

"I am interested in many people, Lord Carteret."

"Then—"

"And I cannot answer you yet." She sought for a way to tell him that she was attracted to his person but that perhaps this attraction was not enough, that she was unsure they would suit each other through the years. "I have not been able to think of it calmly, I have been too distressed about what has been happening to Mr. Murray."

She knew he could not answer that directly, but he made an attempt at raillery. "I would that you were not tranquil when you thought on it."

It was hard to be tranquil when she was looking into his eyes. "You have a most unsettling effect on women, Lord Carteret. It is quite unfair of you to take advantage of it."

That seemed to please him. "I would not be unfair, but my wishes are unchanged."

She grew serious then. "Marriage is a great step, especially for women. We do not readily give up our independence of action." It was, Philippa realized, the surrender of her autonomy to another's will that made her hesitate at marriage, even though her body longed to share in its delights.

He looked puzzled. "I have always thought that marriage enlarged a woman's freedom."

"In some cases, perhaps. If the woman's family has kept her close." She wanted to ask him if he was so very partial to the *Morning Post,* and if they would have to spend much time with the Buckleighs, and if he would really neglect her bed after six years of marriage. But instead she said, "For me, at least, it is difficult, and I need leisure to think on it. When Mr. Murray's affairs are settled, I will tell you. I promise." She smiled to lessen his disappointment and drew him back toward the terrace. Then, knowing herself a coward, she made some excuse and escaped into the house.

Ten minutes later she came back onto the terrace only to find herself detained by a question from one of the servants. This caused her to go in search of Francesca who was standing by the dining tents with Henry and several other people. She delivered her message, then fell into conversation with Henry, and after that it seemed quite natural that they stroll away together. They did not discuss contests with bow and arrow or commitments or her own future but conversed pleasantly on indifferent topics until she felt she was quite enjoying the afternoon.

She caught a glimpse of Claris standing with Lord Christopher on the little bridge that spanned the stream and remembered the convenient clump of trees into which she herself had retreated with Elliot Marsden earlier in the afternoon. She wondered if she should intervene, but the couple wandered into the safety of open lawn.

Henry had seen them, too. She noted the faint frown on his face and was annoyed that, after all they had been through with Lord Christopher, he still took exception to him. "Do you know what I've been reading?" she said. "*The Bride of Lammermoor.* I had it from Gwendolen Warwick who warned me that it was dreadfully sad."

He smiled. "And is it?"

"Quite Gothic, though the story is well-told. There's a young woman whose family will have nothing to do with the man she loves and forces her into a marriage with a man she does not."

He refused to be baited. "Not an original topic."

"A timeless one. The young woman's surname is Ashton."

"Is it?"

"And she has a brother named Henry."

He smiled. "How very extraordinary. By any chance does the young woman's name happen to be Clara or Clarissa or something of the sort?"

"No, it is Lucy."

"Close enough."

"Yes, it's much cleverer, isn't it?" Philippa said. "The names sound nothing like, but their meanings are close."

"I might have known your Latin would be sound."

"Yes, you might."

"Do you think I should sue the author for libel?"

She shook her head gravely. "In my experience, a libel suit is to be avoided at all costs. And in this case I fear it would not stand. Her older brother is more the villain. Henry is only fifteen and rather sympathetic."

"I have never intended to be otherwise."

"I'm sorry, I should not have teased you. She is your sister, not mine."

"But you're her friend, and I am grateful for it. Don't despair of me. I will not force her."

No, he would not force her, but he would prevent a match that Philippa was convinced would make for Claris' happiness. She envied Claris the certainty of her affections and her determination to be happy in her choice. She wanted it to come right. But there was so little time. "In a few weeks the Season will be over."

"And Claris will return to my mother. But not for long. Did you know Francesca has asked Claris to come back to her in the autumn? And if Gerry's sent to the Continent, they would like to take her with them."

Her eyes on the young couple in the distance, Philippa felt a pang at the idea of their separation. Still, Francesca's proposal was sensible, Claris would not be forced to commit her future, and if the attachment weathered time, they might be united in the end. "No, I did not know," she said, wondering that Francesca had said nothing of this to her, "but I am delighted. If Francesca had not asked to keep her, I would have done so myself."

So she was to lose not only her cousin, but Claris as well. And if Claris, then Henry. For Henry would no longer have a reason to call in Green Street. Philippa was unaccountably depressed. She would miss Henry Ashton.

Philippa and Henry were not the only persons to note Claris and Lord Christopher's tête-à-tête. Lady Carteret had kept a watchful eye on her son throughout the afternoon. Indeed, she had accepted Lady Francesca's invitation chiefly for that purpose, though her niece's obvious interest in attending the breakfast had played some role as well. She was seated now on one of the white wrought iron benches scattered about the lawns for the comfort of those fatigued by walking or simply standing about, and here she held her court, receiving the gallantries of a number of the older gentlemen in attendance, gossiping with the few women she numbered among her acquaintance—she was not on terms of intimacy with most of Lady Francesca's guests—and following her son's progress through the grounds.

When Edwina and Elliot Marsden strolled by, she called them to her side, dismissing Lord Sanderson, with whom she had been carrying on a discreet flirtation, and indicating that Edwina should take his place on the bench. "Do you see what Crispin's doing? I had so hoped he would be over his infatuation, but he persists in following the girl about. I cannot see what the attraction is. She is pretty enough, but the type is common and her manners leave much to be desired."

Edwina had no wish to quarrel with her aunt. In the past she would have pronounced the match quite unsuitable, but, after her brother's despicable behaviour toward Miss Ashton and

Crispin's heroic efforts to rescue her, Edwina was inclined to look favourably on their attachment. "Do not fret yourself, Aunt, it will do no good and will only give you lines in your forehead. Crispin does not like to be thwarted, any more than his brother does"—she remembered Tony's bad temper this afternoon with some relish—"and you will only make matters worse by trying to interfere."

Lady Carteret sniffed and her lovely blue eyes filled with tears. "I might have known you would not be sympathetic."

"But I am, I assure you," Edwina protested. "I am only trying to be realistic."

"Elliot, surely you understand. Tell me what I must do." The marchioness laid a delicate hand on Mr. Marsden's sleeve.

He was standing before her, rather wishing he were somewhere else. He had been uncertain of his reception ever since he told her of his intentions toward Miss Davenport, but it was clear from Lady Carteret's manner that she had taken no offence. She had no cause to, he reflected wryly, as his decision only furthered her own aims. How she would treat him after he married Miss Davenport was another question. "I can understand your concern, ma'am, but I think Lady Edwina's advice is good. You must buy time and trust to its efficacy."

Her hand clutched his arm and he removed it delicately. "No," he said, reading the intention in her eyes. He was not about to undertake another mission for the marchioness, no matter what his obligations. "I am much too old."

Lady Edwina watched this exchange with curiosity. She had not known that her aunt was on terms of such intimacy with the barrister, and she wondered at the reason. Then she thought of what her aunt had seemed to propose. It was not unlike what her own brother had undertaken, to disastrous effect, but she would not make her aunt privy to that disgraceful episode. And then it occurred to her that this might not be the first time her aunt had made such a request of Mr. Marsden. Did his pursuit of Miss Davenport have some devious intent? How enterprising of Aunt Aurelia! And yet she would have sworn the matter was not so simple. His ill will toward Tony seemed quite genuine.

Elliot Marsden was a more interesting man than she had

supposed. And having reached this conclusion, Lady Edwina determined to keep him beside her for the rest of the afternoon.

The objects of Lady Carteret's anxious eyes were aware of nothing but the pleasure they took in one another's company. Claris was very happy. Not only was she with the man with whom she planned to spend the rest of her life, Crispin had promised to go directly to Lord Buckleigh to get permission for their marriage; he should never have agreed to let his cousin speak for him, and he was well repaid for his reluctance to confront his uncle. Now he would face Lord Buckleigh's displeasure like a man, certain that the rational force of his argument would win his uncle over.

He had told her all this on the day following her rescue from his cousin's house. He was only prevented from carrying out his intent by the absence of his uncle and aunt.

Crispin told her this all over again as they walked slowly along the bank of the winding stream, oblivious to Lady Francesca's other guests. When they had temporarily exhausted the subject of what Crispin was to do to ensure their eternal felicity, the talk veered back to the disturbing behaviour of Lord St. George.

"I would never have believed he would play me false," Crispin said, shaking his head in bewilderment. "I admired him, you know. He always treated me kindly. He's not as old as Tony, and when we were growing up I think I saw rather more of him than of my own brother. I thought he liked me, too. What a fool I've been!"

Claris did not like to see her beloved so distraught. "I'm sure he does like you, Crispin, but he *is* older and that makes him think he is cleverer than you. At least that's the way it was in my family. I'm sure he thought he was doing it for your own good."

"As if he would know what that would be!"

"No, be sensible, Cris, think of how it appeared to him. A girl of no fortune and indifferent family."

"But no one cares for that sort of thing any more!"

"Well, of course, I know that and so do you, but St. George

knows very little of the world and so he's inclined to think his own corner of it more important that it is."

The description of his cousin as unworldly struck Crispin with all the force of a wholly novel idea. He turned it round in his head, but was distracted by Claris' next statement.

"And like all ignorant people, he's frightened of what he doesn't know. When he took me into supper at the Warwicks' he could talk of nothing but Mr. Murray's presence in the supper room. The Ashtons are good enough to sit at table with, if not to marry, but Mr. Murray is quite beyond the pale." Claris' laughter bubbled over. "He said he considered him a threat to the ruling class."

Crispin did not find this particularly funny. "I'm sure my uncle would agree, he talks like that all the time. I suppose St. George takes after him."

"He saw your brother in conversation with Mr. Murray at the ball and could not understand how Lord Carteret would allow it. 'Tony,' he said, using that drawling tone he affects when he wants you to notice him, 'has been showing a distressing lack of discrimination of late.' I don't think," she went on, "that he even approves of Philippa."

"That's different, his sister is involved." Crispin was still pondering over his new insights into his cousin's character. "Knowing what he's done, I can see how he came to do it. But until it happened, I would never have believed he'd try to ruin a respectable young girl. I wonder what he's actually capable of . . ."

They walked on in silence. Claris was thinking about Philippa and how splendid she had been in her defence of Mr. Murray. Then she recalled the conversation they had had over the luncheon at Warwick House the day after the ball. What was it Philippa had said? Someone with a grudge against people like Mr. Murray. Claris stopped to pick a daisy that had escaped the gardener's notice and stroked its petals thoughtfully. "Crispin, does your cousin own a yellow waistcoat?"

He did not at first grasp her meaning, and when he did he looked at her in disbelief. "Quentin steal his own sister's bracelet?"

"Yes, I know," she said hurriedly, for now that the idea had come to her she was eager to talk it out. "It probably fell, just as

327

we supposed, on the floor or in a corner of the sofa where Lady Edwina had been sitting. He picked it up, thinking to return it to her. But he did not see her immediately, and then Mr. Murray came in and he saw your brother talking to him and he asked you about him, and then he became angry because Mr. Warwick was treating Mr. Murray just like one of his other guests, and the more he thought about it, the angrier he became. And it all got mixed up with his feelings about me and how I wasn't worthy of his family and Mr. Murray wasn't worthy of Lord Carteret's acquaintance and the man was positively dangerous to people like himself. So he decided to take revenge."

It was a ridiculous story, but Claris made it seem plausible. "You think he had the idea then? When he saw Murray talking to Tony?"

"Or perhaps later, when Lady Edwina discovered her bracelet was missing. He may have forgotten about it till then."

"It would fit, you know," Crispin said. "Quentin made a great howl about the bracelet, and it's not at all in his usual style. He must have enjoyed it, everyone scurrying to placate Edwina. It put Warwick in an awkward position, but he wouldn't mind. He has little use for the family."

"Crispin. Does he have a yellow waistcoat?"

"What? Oh, yes, he does. White, with yellow stripes going round like this." He ran his hand across his chest. "A handsome thing, with horn buttons." He did not seem to consider the matter of great moment. "The question is, the missing ruby. He might have removed it deliberately, to make it look worse for Murray when the bracelet was discovered, or it might have come loose and be lying in a coat pocket. We'll have to go through his clothes."

Claris looked at the two large tents on the lawn below the terrace. The curtains had been looped up to allow the breeze to pass and she could see the tables covered with silver and china and huge baskets of flowers. Then she remembered another outdoor table, prepared for a smaller party. "You won't have to search his clothes, Cris. I know where the ruby is. He had it set in a pendant and gave it to Maria Doddington. I saw it round her neck at Cranford."

Chapter 21

After her talk with Henry, Philippa escaped from the crowds and made her way toward the front of the house. Her path took her within view of the stables. These had been the scene of frantic activity earlier in the day, but though a handsome array of carriages stood nearby and an even larger number of horses were tethered and grazing in an adjacent meadow, most of the grooms and coachmen had taken themselves off to the refreshment table set up for the servants.

As Philippa drew closer she saw that one of the carriages, a smart curricle, had a frisky pair of greys harnessed and ready for departure. Or had someone just arrived? Philippa stopped and regarded the curricle in idle curiosity, then caught sight of the couple about to climb into the carriage and began to run.

"Claris!" Philippa cried. "What on earth do you think you're doing?"

"Oh, Philippa, thank goodness!" Claris released Crispin's hand and ran forward to greet her friend. "Crispin and I have discovered that it was Lord St. George who stole Lady Edwina's bracelet and Crispin insists on going off to confront him immediately—he's still at Cranford, you know—and I really don't think he should go alone. Crispin, I mean. St. George can look after himself."

Philippa had quick wits and was adept at dealing with the unexpected, but this monologue left her momentarily bereft of speech.

"I know," said Claris, reading her expression, "you never

329

thought of it, and of course you couldn't have, for there was no reason to suspect St. George—"

"There was every reason." Crispin was standing impatiently by the horses' heads. "I should have realized it from the first."

"You only say that because you are put out with him, and I own I am as well, but of course that does not make him guilty of every crime possible, only it so happens that he is guilty of this one. At least, it seems excessively likely that he is, for he has the right sort of waistcoat."

By this time Philippa had managed to collect her thoughts. "If you have any evidence about the bracelet," she said calmly, "we should find Henry at once. Lord Christopher—"

"No." Lord Christopher's voice was surprisingly firm and he did not look at all angelic. "This is between St. George and me. I have lost enough time as it is. Claris, if you are coming—"

"You see," said Claris, pulling on Philippa's arm, "it's no use trying to dissuade him. Come with us, do, I'm sure you'll be able to contrive a much neater resolution than Crispin and I, for it's just the sort of thing you do so well in your books."

Thinking furiously, Philippa allowed Claris to propel her toward the carriage. If she went in search of Henry, Lord Christopher and Claris would be gone. Aside from the ruinous effect on Claris' reputation, she could not leave the girl alone to cope with the explosive confrontation which seemed about to occur between Lord Christopher and his cousin. Besides, if St. George really had stolen the bracelet it seemed likely that Lord Christopher would merely put his cousin on his guard and ruin their chances of obtaining proof to clear Mr. Murray.

She would have to go with them. But if she could not speak to Henry first, could she at least get word to him? "Only wait here two minutes longer," Philippa said, breaking away from Claris and darting toward the area where the horses were tethered. She was gambling on Claris' strength of will against Lord Christopher's impatience, but instinct told her it was a fairly safe bet.

Among the handful of coachmen and grooms who had been left to watch over the horses was a red-headed stableboy, a slight youth of about fourteen. His name was Owen, Philippa remembered. He was the nephew of the Raynley gamekeeper, and Francesca said he was a trusty lad. She called his name and, once he had been distracted from Mr. Warwick's magnificent bays, he hastened to her side. Without preamble, Philippa asked him to inform Mr. Ashton that she and Miss Ashtom and Lord Christopher had been obliged to pay a visit to the Viscount St. George at his country house, and would he please join them as soon as possible.

"Yes, miss," said Owen, his eyes shining at the scent of adventure. The Davenport servants who had come down from London for the breakfast had had some interesting stories about the doings in Green Street.

Scarcely waiting for Owen's nod of response, Philippa hurried back toward the curricle. She was relieved to find it still stationary—though, judging by Lord Christopher's expression, it would not remain so much longer—and she made haste to climb up and squeeze in beside Claris.

They started forward with a jolt, Lord Christopher urging the horses on to furious speed. "Now," Philippa said, "what is all this about Lord St. George stealing his own sister's bracelet?"

After his talk with Philippa, Henry found the breakfast curiously flat. Well, no, not curiously. He smiled wryly and, not being in the mood for social chit-chat, or for catching glimpses of Philippa and her two acknowledged suitors, he made his way to the far side of the stream. But at the edge of the stand of oaks he was pounced upon by Gwendolen Warwick who located a convenient log, spread her handkerchief on it to protect her frock, and proceeded to ask him some very specific questions about Mr. Murray and to propound several theories of her own about the bracelet's theft. One involved her father's rival, Oliver Merriman. Another particularly inventive one dragged in two cabinet ministers and a member of the royal family and caused Henry to glance quickly about them.

"It's all right," Gwendolyn said comfortably. "There's no one listening. I know about being discreet. Not that anyone would pay attention to me anyway. Where's Philippa?"

"I don't know," said Henry conversationally. "Somewhere among all the other guests, I suppose. Why?"

"Well, you spend a lot of time with her, don't you?"

Henry shot Gwendolen a hard look, but she was busily tracing a pattern in the ground with the toe of her white kid shoe. "I'm in Green Street much of the time," Henry said. "Ask my sister. She'll tell you I'm an overly protective brother."

Gwendolen smiled. "Brothers can be difficult, can't they? I'm glad little Justin's so much younger than I am. It's more likely to be me who's overly protective of him." Henry echoed her smile and congratulated himself on having managed the change of subject so smoothly. But the congratulations were premature.

"I suppose it's only natural for you and Philippa to get on so well," Gwendolen said thoughtfully, "both being writers and all, and both being friends of Mr. Murray. I was just wondering, since you're such good friends—do you think she'll marry Lord Carteret? Or that lawyer, Mr. Marsden?"

Henry stared down at the thirteen-year-old beside him. He really shouldn't be surprised. Nicholas was damnably acute, and Livia certainly had an influence on the child. "I mean," said Gwendolen, "their intentions are pretty clear, aren't they?"

"I don't," said Henry, not quite truthfully, "know anything about Marsden's or Carteret's intentions. Nor," he added, with perfect truth, "do I know anything about Philippa's."

"Well," said Gwendolen, stretching her legs out before her, "if you ask me, I don't think she should marry either of them. Oh, hullo, Owen. Are you looking for something?"

Owen had been very excited when Miss Philippa entrusted him with her message, but as he started off on the errand it occurred to him that he was not at all sure he would recognize Mr. Ashton. He stopped on the edge of the crowd, daunted by the number and elegance of Lady Francesca's guests, but fortunately he caught sight of Miss Gwendolen talking with a gentleman on the opposite side of the stream. Miss Gwendolen had a good eye for horses and a ready smile. Relieved, Owen determined to apply to her for assistance.

He was so intent on his mission that he barely glanced at the gentleman sitting beside her. When Miss Gwendolen asked if he were looking for something, he blurted out, "Yes, for Mr. Ashton."

"Then you've come to the right place," Miss Gwendolen's companion said, his tone amused but friendly. "You have a message for me?"

Owen looked at the gentleman and realized that of course this was the man who had arrived with Colonel Scott earlier in the day. The difficult part of his mission over, his excitement began to return. "Yes, sir, from Miss Philippa."

"Miss Philippa?" Henry's voice was suddenly sharp. "What's happened? Where is she?"

"Well, sir," Owen considered, "I think she's probably somewhere near Whitton by now. It took me a bit of time to find you."

"Are you telling me that Miss Davenport has gone off by herself in the middle of her cousin's breakfast?" Henry demanded, rapidly turning over possibilities.

"Oh, no, sir. She has Miss Ashton and Lord Christopher with her."

"She—never mind. There's more to the message? Where have they gone?"

"To visit the Viscount St. George," Owen said quickly, remembering the necessity for speed and missing the look of incredulity on Mr. Ashton's face. "I was to ask you to join them as soon as possible."

Henry had every intention of joining them, but Philippa's request for his presence made his spirits lighten remarkably. He looked at Gwendolen. The child might be too perceptive for her own—or rather other people's—good, but she knew when a matter was to be taken seriously.

"I'll tell Aunt Francesca," she said. "You'd best leave at once."

Like Philippa and Henry, the Marquis of Carteret was not in

a humour to enjoy the very amusing company which Lady Francesca had assembled. The archery contest with Elliot Marsden had left him seething with frustration, and somehow his inconclusive talk with Miss Davenport had only worsened his mood and deepened his resentment.

Carteret wanted nothing so much as to continue his contest with Elliot Marsden, preferably with his fists. As this was not an option at the moment, and as he doubted he would have the opportunity for another tête-à-tête with Miss Davenport today, Anthony was tempted to take his leave. A glimpse of his stepmother decided him. He was in no mood to cope with Aurelia, especially as he suspected that she hadn't quite given up hope of him and Edwina. Anthony glanced around for his brother who had driven down with him, but he was nowhere in sight. Impatient to be off, he determined to order the carriage and then take his leave of Lady Francesca and search Crispin out. If Crispin wanted to stay longer, he could always return to town with his mother.

When Anthony reached the meadow where the horses were tethered, there was no sign of his groom. He asked one of the Scotts' grooms to make his curricle ready and find Mugford. The man looked at him in surprise and said that Lord Christopher had driven off in the curricle some quarter-hour since.

"Lord Christopher drove off in my carriage?" Anthony repeated, more startled than angry. "Did he leave any message? Where was he bound?"

"There was no message, my lord. And he didn't mention his destination."

Something in the groom's manner told Anthony that there was more. "Was he alone?" the marquis demanded in a sharper tone.

The groom hesitated. He was beginning to see that the situation might be rather delicate and he was not sure where his loyalties should lie. "No, my lord," he admitted. "Miss Ashton and Miss Davenport went with him."

Damnation! Anthony did not need to ask further questions. When a young man made a secret departure accompanied by the young woman whom he was determined, in the teeth of pposition, to make his wife, the reason was perfectly clear. young idiot. Anthony had no objection to Miss Ashton—her rother had some queer ideas, but there was nothing wrong with the girl herself. She was a pretty little thing and Miss Davenport's fondness for her naturally disposed Anthony in her favour. He thought his brother rather young to put himself in fetters, but had he been Crispin's guardian he would probably have given his consent to the match.

But to an elopement—never! His own affair with Georgina Nelliston was one thing; running off to Gretna Green was something very different. Carteret was surprised that Miss Davenport would even countenance such a bit of folly, let alone accompany the runaway lovers. It was another example of her kind heart leading her to the most inconsidered actions. When he explained it, she would understand why the lovers must be brought back. And brought back they must be. Anthony was almost relieved at the call to action.

But first he would have to find a carriage. There was his stepmother's landau, but he would prefer something faster. If need be, he could borrow one of the Scotts' vehicles, though he did not fancy the time or the explanations that this would entail.

As he debated the question, he turned toward the stables and caught sight of Henry Ashton harnessing a pair of chestnuts to a sleek curricle—had Anthony been less preoccupied he might have identified both as belonging to Colonel Scott. As it was, he merely knew that he had found a carriage. He strode quickly from the meadow to the stables.

"So you've learned of it too, have you, Ashton? It must be stopped."

Henry continued adjusting the traces. "I'm sorry, Carteret. I'm afraid I'm quite in the dark, and I'm also in rather a hurry. What must be stopped?"

"Damn it, man, your sister has eloped with my brother. If you don't think they have to be stopped—"

"I doubt it," said Henry going around to the horses' heads.

"If you want to see your sister ruined that's your own affair, but I am not going to stand idly by while my brother embroils himself in a scandal." Anthony had at last found the quarrel he

335

had been spoiling for. If Ashton was not Elliot Marsden, he made a very decent substitute.

"I mean, I doubt they've eloped."

"One of the grooms saw them, I tell you. Driving off in my curricle."

"Oh, was it yours? I wondered what they'd done for a carriage." Anthony's tones had disturbed one of the horses and Henry stroked it reassuringly. "I don't think it's an elopement, Carteret."

"Then you have more faith in your sister than I have in my brother."

"I have a good deal of faith in Miss Davenport. She went with them."

"I know," said Anthony impatiently. "I was surprised she'd abet them, but she has a kind heart and you know how romantic women can be."

"In my experience they tend to be fearfully practical. Ever heard of a woman fighting a duel?"

This was a low blow but fortunately it was lost on Anthony. "Are you telling me you don't mean to go after them?" he demanded.

"I have every intention of going after them. Hence my need for a carriage."

"Good," said Anthony. "I'm coming with you."

Henry regarded the other man. With the exceptions of the Viscount St. George and possibly Elliot Marsden, there were few people whose company he desired less. Henry was certain his sister and young Paget hadn't eloped. Not only did he trust Philippa not to assist such an adventure, if she had done so she certainly would not have asked him to follow the lovers. And the lovers most certainly would not have made for St. George's house.

The most likely explanation—indeed, the only one that Henry could think of—was that Lord Christopher's temper had boiled over and he had decided to confront his cousin. The two women must have gone along to restrain him. In which case, Henry was forced to acknowledge, it might be helpful to have Carteret along. He had an authority over both Lord Christopher and St. George which the rest of them lacked and he was not unhandy with his fives. Henry gave a curt nod and sprang into the curricle.

"I imagine they'll head straight north," said Anthony, settling himself on the carriage seat as Henry took up the reins, "but we can stop and make inquiries along the way—"

"There's no need. They've gone to Cranford."

"To Cranford? What the devil for?"

"To call upon the Viscount St. George, I believe."

"St. George? Don't tell me he's in this, too?"

Henry hesitated. For Claris' sake, the fewer people who knew about St. George's quarrel with Lord Christopher the better. There was always a chance the situation would be in hand by the time they reached Cranford. If it was not, the truth of the matter would come out soon enough.

"As to that," Henry said, as they rolled down the drive, "you are in a better position to judge than I."

"By God, if he's spurred Cris on in this folly—what the devil's that?"

This last referred to a faint scuffling coming from beneath a rug on the floor of the carriage. Henry had a sudden foreboding. "I rather think we have feminine company, Carteret," he said. "She must have been trying to find a quiet place away from the crowds."

"She?" Puzzled, Anthony lifted the rug. Hermia licked his hand.

"No, Aunt Aurelia, I have not seen Crispin recently. But that's hardly surprising. There must be above a hundred people here. You have to admit Lady Francesca is a most accomplished hostess." Edwina regarded her aunt with barely concealed irritation.

"If Crispin were here," Lady Carteret said firmly, "I would be able to locate him. When you have children of your own you will understand these things, Edwina. Have you seen Miss Ashton?"

Lady Edwina shook her head.

Lady Carteret seemed almost triumphant. "I knew we should never have accepted the invitation."

"If we hadn't, Crispin and Anthony would only have come without us."

This remark was suspiciously close to the sort of thing Edwina's mother would have said had she been present and did nothing to improve Lady Carteret's temper. "You have no sympathy for me," she declared bitterly. "I had thought you at least would understand. He is your own cousin, and I am sure I have always looked on you as a daughter, not that I would ever try to take your mother's place of course, though I must say I have frequently thought that Catherine— Oh, Elliot, thank God." Elliot Marsden had just brought her a glass of champagne. Lady Carteret clutched at his sleeve. "Crispin has disappeared along with the wretched little Ashton chit. It is too bad of him but he is such a young innocent and whatever are we to do?"

Marsden bestowed a reassuring smile on the marchioness and rolled an inquiring eye at Lady Edwina.

"Aunt Aurelia has been unable to locate my cousin or Miss Ashton," Edwina explained, "and she fears something is amiss."

"I *know* something is amiss," Lady Carteret corrected with feeling. "You haven't seen Crispin, have you?"

"Not for some time, Lady Carteret. The gardens are quite crowded. But I'd be happy to have a look about if it would set your mind at ease."

"Oh, yes, Elliot!" the marchioness exclaimed gratefully. "I knew I could rely on you."

This last remark was intended as something of a setdown for Lady Edwina, but Edwina did not seem to notice and merely said that she too would make inquiries after her cousin. She was certain that Crispin and Miss Ashton could have done nothing more than slip away for a few private moments—and even then, she did not think they would have stolen more than a chaste kiss. Crispin had shown himself determined to protect his beloved's reputation.

But if Edwina did not owe it to Aunt Aurelia to find Crispin, she owed it to Crispin to warn him of his mother's mood. The incident with St. George had drawn Edwina and Crispin closer together and now that Edwina was considering her own choice of marriage partner, she was more inclined to support Crispin's freedom to choose his.

Marsden saw Lady Carteret comfortably settled in a chair on the terrace, then said that he would have a look by the archery field. Edwina volunteered to investigate the area near the stream.

But though she moved through the crowd for more than a quarter-hour, Edwina saw no sign of her cousin or his beloved. She was growing weary of the exercise and was relieved when Elliot Marsden touched her lightly on the arm and asked if he could speak with her. Edwina nodded and was amused when the barrister insisted on drawing her behind some shrubbery which afforded them a little privacy. "I haven't seen my cousin," she said, "but I daresay he just slipped away to have a few moments alone with Miss Ashton."

"I'm afraid it's more complicated than that." Marsden, from what Edwina saw, was perfectly serious, even grave. "I went to the stables and had a word with a lad who's employed there. He said Lord Christopher and Miss Ashton drove off some time ago."

Edwina's exquisite blue eyes widened in genuine surprise. "Alone?"

"No, they were accompanied by Miss Davenport."

This was even more surprising. "Did the stableboy know their destination?"

"Apparently they were going to your brother's country house."

"To Quentin's?" Edwina was now truly alarmed. "Mr. Marsden, believe me, this is not an elopement. But I think someone should go after them. My brother and cousin are not on the best of terms at the moment. They may come to blows."

Marsden had believed Lord Christopher and his cousin to be friends and had thought the viscount must be helping the young couple elope, but Lady Edwina was not a foolish woman and he took her words seriously. In any event some action seemed necessary and Philippa Davenport's involvement in the flight made Marsden eager to give chase.

"I'll go after them, of course," he said. "If you will explain the matter to your aunt—"

"I will do no such thing. I'm coming with you," Edwina

said firmly.

"My dear Lady Edwina, there is no need—"

"There is every need. This is a family matter and far more my concern than yours. We can take my aunt's landau."

"But someone must explain matters to Lady Carteret," Marsden insisted.

"We'll send her a message with one of the servants. Or you may speak with her yourself while I give orders about the horses."

This was the last thing he wanted to do, as Edwina knew perfectly well. On the other hand, he had no desire to be encumbered by a female, even an intelligent one. "Lady Edwina," Marsden said, controlling his temper with an effort, "if you will consider—"

"Of course," Edwina continued, "you may always ride down and leave me to take the carriage by myself, but I don't think that would be wise. You don't know the direction of my brother's house."

Even Philippa Davenport had never challenged Marsden so directly. "I'm sure I'll be able to find my way," he said coolly. "I understand it's in—"

"Edwina! Elliot! There is no need to argue. I have heard it all!" From her seat on the terrace, Lady Carteret had seen Edwina and Marsden meet and move into the shelter of the shrubbery. Fearing there was something they were keeping from her, she had immediately made her way toward them and for some moments had been standing unseen on the opposite side of the shrubbery.

Now that there was a definite action to take, Lady Carteret was quite capable of rational thought. "We must leave at once," she declared. "All of us."

Elliot Marsden bowed to the inevitable. "Of course, ma'am. I will see to the carriage."

Chapter 22

The curricle was not meant for three. Crispin drove with intense concentration and without heed to the labourers or geese that were put to startled flight by the sight of Lord Carteret's greys bearing down upon them. Only Crispin's skill avoided a rather nasty accident with an unsuspecting driver in a cart laden with cabbages.

Her arm around Philippa to save space on the crowded seat, Claris told her everything she knew that pointed to St. George's involvement in the theft of his sister's bracelet and its appearance in Mr. Murray's office. Philippa heard her with interest but with no real conviction until Claris described the pendant worn by Maria Doddington. That had the ring of truth—it was just the sort of insolent gesture a man like St. George would make—and she abandoned Lord Nelliston without a qualm.

Having reached this point, Philippa was free to turn her attention to Lord Christopher's driving. Claris had wisely not commented on it, but Philippa did not feel the constraint of affection and she asked him sharply to slow his pair so they could talk. He was in no condition to confront his cousin, and he would very likely ruin everything.

Startled by her tone, Lord Christopher complied, though his jaw was still tightly set and a deep line furrowed the perfection of his brow. "There is no need to talk, Miss Davenport. It's time for action."

"On the contrary, it's time for thought. What do you plan to

341

do precisely?"

"Have it out with him, of course. Make him own up to what he's done and put things right for Mr. Murray."

"He'll laugh at you."

"Not when I'm finished with him." The young man's tone was grim.

"He need only persist in denying everything," Philippa insisted. "No matter what state you reduce him to. And that will hardly help Mr. Murray."

Crispin looked uncertain for the first time since their flight had begun.

Philippa followed up her advantage. "He's a clever man. You'll have to take him unawares or he won't tell you anything. Use your wits, Lord Christopher. What do you suppose your cousin will think when we arrive uninvited? Considering what happened on our last visit, he's likely to find it very odd."

"Damn!" Crispin had not thought so far.

"You must have a plausible reason for calling on him. I'm afraid there's only one way for it. You'll have to apologize."

Crispin jerked at the reins involuntarily and brought the horses up short. "Apologize? Never!" He set the horses in motion again.

Philippa ignored this outburst. "Not of course that you in any way condone what he has done, but he *is* a member of your family and you're sorry for the breach the quarrel has made between you."

"But apologize—"

"Claris insisted that you do so."

Lord Christopher was silent. Philippa waited while he swallowed this particular pill. "And then?" Crispin said. "How do I get him to confess? For he must confess—"

"He must have reason to confess," Philippa said, rapidly inventing and discarding a dozen approaches to the viscount. "We have no tangible proof. None, that is, except the pendant."

"I'll confront him with the pendant."

"He could deny that too. I wonder if—Lord Christopher, could Lady Edwina identify the jewel?"

342

"I don't doubt it. Edwina has a passion for jewels, and I'm sure she knows her own intimately."

Claris spoke for the first time since Philippa had called Crispin to order. "Then you must simply steal the pendant and take it to Lady Edwina. Oh, Crispin, you're so clever!"

The young man visibly relaxed and the ghost of a smile played about his mouth.

Claris turned to Philippa with an anxious frown. "But suppose she cannot positively identify it?"

"It makes no difference, as long as she thinks it might be hers. That's the beauty of it. If Lady Edwina is convinced, she can go to the magistrates and persuade them to drop the charges against Mr. Murray. Then it won't matter whether or not Lord St. George owns up to the theft. At least," she added, for she wanted complete vindication for the publisher, "it won't matter as much."

And if Lady Edwina said the jewel could not possibly have come from her bracelet, then they were wrong about her brother's involvement and were back where they started. But that would not happen. Philippa was certain they were finally on the right track.

Lord Christopher was smiling, his eyes on an inward vision. He whipped up the team again and Philippa had to remind him that it really would not do to arrive at Cranford with the horses in a lather. It might put his cousin on his guard.

There was no one in sight when they drove up to Cranford. It was late afternoon, a lazy time when the day's heat hung heavy over the trees and the birds were still. Crispin turned the curricle toward the stables where he instructed the stableboy to unharness the greys and walk them about until they had recovered from the journey. Whatever his eagerness to have the visit done with, Crispin did not dare neglect his brother's cattle.

The boy was well acquainted with Lord Christopher and did not appear to have heard of the quarrel. Crispin tipped him lavishly and asked that the greys be reharnessed and the curricle held in readiness near the front drive in a half-hour's time.

Then, a woman on each arm, he walked toward the house.

The front door was ajar and there were sounds of activity from within. Puzzled, Crispin pushed the door open and stepped inside. His way was blocked by two armchairs, a tripod pedestal with lion feet, three lamps, a tabouret and a pier-table of carved and gilt wood. These objects had been pushed together in a single mass and then apparently forgotten. Crispin looked toward the back of the hall where the double doors to the drawing room stood open. He could hear mumbled words and then the sound of his cousin's voice raised in admonition. "Damn it, man, be careful!"

Luscombe and an elderly man whom Crispin recognized as the gardener came out of the drawing room carrying a French commode of painted bronze-green and gilt. It was an old piece and heavier than it looked, for the men were straining and Luscombe was swearing under his breath. St. George followed them into the hall and stopped abruptly at the sight of Crispin. An ugly flush suffused his face. "What the devil are you doing here?"

Crispin walked forward and, though it cost him dear to do it, held out his hand. "Hullo, Quentin. I've come to heal the breach."

The viscount stared, gave a shout of laughter, then took the proffered hand. "Come round to the garden. Maria's somewhere about. We'll have a drink." He put his arm on Crispin's shoulder and led him through the drawing room and onto the terrace, leaving Philippa and Claris to follow as best they could.

"I've not changed my mind, Quentin," Crispin explained. "And I intend to speak to my uncle as soon as he returns." He glanced at the elegant figure beside him and wondered what it was he had so admired. "What you did to Claris was despicable, but she bears you no ill will. She's an angel," he added, momentarily breaking out of his assumed character.

St. George snorted.

"And she does not want us to quarrel on her account," Crispin continued, seeing that they were in danger of doing so. "We've been friends for years, Quentin, I don't want to lose that. You gambled and you lost. Give it up. Leave it to your

344

father, we'll abide by his decision." This last was a blatant lie, but under the circumstances Crispin thought it justified.

There were some chairs on the terrace and a small table on which stood a glass and an empty bottle. A wilting bunch of larkspur lay beside them. St. George tossed these into the shrubbery with an oath. "Maria's forgotten the flowers. Luscombe!" He flung himself in a chair.

Crispin seated the women and his cousin raised a mocking hand in salute. It was the first time he had acknowledged their presence. "How do you do, Lord St. George," Claris said sweetly. Philippa thought it discreet to say nothing at all.

When Luscombe appeared at the door, St. George called for a fresh bottle. Crispin suggested that the ladies might prefer tea. His cousin reluctantly gave the order and told Luscombe to get Miss Doddington out of bed.

"I have not been in bed, Quentin, I have been mending a flounce." Maria appeared in the doorway where she stood poised for a moment of recognition. She was wearing a simple white jaconet with a sapphire blue sash. There was no sign of the pendant. She took a chair beside the viscount and looked with hostile eyes at his female visitors.

"You remember Miss Ashton, Maria. And Miss—ah—Davenport. They've come to take tea with us."

Maria grudgingly acknowledged the two women. She seemed out of sorts, her fragile prettiness blurred by some secret discontent. Crispin, who knew his cousin well, guessed that St. George, whose temper was uncertain when he was drinking, had not been kind these past few days and that Maria was chafing at her forced isolation in the country.

The viscount seemed amused by the ill-assorted group. Claris talked brightly of the breakfast from which they had just departed and Philippa, her social instincts roused, told two or three stories that she thought might amuse the viscount and his mistress.

Crispin demanded to be told why Quentin was in the process of rearranging all the furniture in the house. "The billiard table, Cris, don't you remember? Pity you won't be here tomorrow, you could try it out."

"But in the drawing room?"

345

"Why not? It's the largest room in the place. I've missed having one here. What else is one to do between the pleasures of the table and the bed?"

Crispin grinned, though he regretted the coarseness. Luscombe arrived with a fresh bottle and the tea tray, and while Maria was engaged in playing lady of the house, Crispin excused himself and went inside. Provided with a fresh glass, St. George did not even turn his head, and Philippa uttered a silent prayer that Lord Christopher would finish the business quickly so they could leave. She had momentarily exhausted her conversational resources and was reduced to talking about the Duchess of Kent's new baby.

"May I trouble you for the cream, Miss Doddington?" Claris could think of nothing else to say to the silent Maria. It did not seem quite right to ask whether she was enjoying her stay in the country or whether she was resting well after the rigours of the Season. She accepted the cream pitcher from Maria's hand and busied herself with her cup. "I do like it here," she said, "it's so quiet and peaceful."

This comment did not further the conversation. "Not but what I don't enjoy being in London," Claris went on doggedly. "There's so much to see and do. Have you been to Vauxhall, Miss Doddington?" Claris had no particular desire to go to Vauxhall, but it was a place she thought Maria might have visited. "I would adore to go, for I hear it's ever such a lark, but I don't think Lady Francesca would allow it." It occurred to her that the implied distinction between what was proper for her and what Maria might freely do was not a happy one. "But perhaps it's overrated."

"I'll take you to Vauxhall," St. George said in a lazy voice. "After all, we're to be cousins." His eyes, Philippa noted, were alert and his gaze was directed at Claris' lovely rounded bosom.

Philippa began to understand Henry's objections to the match. If she had not come to think quite well of Lord Christopher, she would have warned the girl against it on the grounds of his deplorable family. Claris was resourceful, but she would have to be careful in her handling of her husband's lascivious cousin.

Maria had also noted the viscount's look, and she bit her lip. It was not that she doubted her own attractions, but she knew

346

her lover was easily surfeited and might have begun to grow tired of her more delicate charms.

"If your father approves," Philippa said coolly, "and if Claris' brother can be brought round. He has never sanctioned the match, and in any case he is not eager for Claris to make a commitment while she is so young."

Claris turned to her friend, an exclamation of outrage on her lips, then smiled sweetly and looked down into her cup.

"Cris has been the devil of a time," St. George said suddenly. "What's keeping him?"

Philippa thought the same but could not think of a suitable reply.

"I believe he complained of the cramp when he was at the breakfast," Claris said, her eyes still downcast.

Philippa bit back a laugh. Claris was betraying her country origins.

St. George, however, was amused. Maria was not. She rose swiftly and said that she was going to her room to fetch her shawl. And before either Philippa or Claris could think of a way to stop her or an excuse for accompanying her, she disappeared into the house.

Philippa immediately launched into a rambling story about Lady Calder's daughter-in-law who had mislaid a China silk shawl given her by her husband's mother and prayed that Lord Christopher would reappear, but both he and Miss Doddington continued absent. Relief came at last from another direction. Philippa heard a familiar bark and a small brown-and-white dog tore up the terrace steps and jumped into her mistress' lap.

Henry had arrived. She did not know what had induced him to bring Hermia, but at the moment she did not care. She looked in the direction from which Hermia had come, willing Henry to appear. And because she expected Henry, it took her a moment to recognize the figure striding rapidly toward them. It was Lord Carteret and his agitation was evident. His eyes took in the three people seated on the terrace and came to rest on Claris. "Miss Ashton," he said in strangled accents, "what have you done with my brother?"

* * *

The two men had spoken little after they left Raynley. Henry concentrated on his driving and Anthony on his grievance. Anthony was outraged that Crispin had behaved in so irresponsible a manner. If he had to run off with the girl, he ought to have had the sense not to do it at a public gathering at which his own mother was in attendance.

Then there was their choice of St. George's house as a destination. Anthony thought Quentin wielded undue influence over his brother and would not put it past him to have a special license and a parson ready at the house so the young couple would not need to post to Gretna Green.

"Ashton," he said suddenly, "what do you know about this?"

"No more than you." Henry negotiated a sharp turn with a skill that evoked Anthony's approval. "One of the stableboys brought me a message from Miss Davenport. She had gone off with your brother and my sister, they were going to visit Lord St. George, and I was to join them there. Believe me, Carteret, I know no more than that."

"You don't think they go there to be wed?"

Henry slackened the reins. "Good God, man, do you think I would countenance such a thing?"

"No," Anthony admitted, "but St. George might."

"I have not given my consent to a betrothal. They're both much too young, and your family is opposed to it."

"My stepmother is, but she thinks no one is good enough for her son. *I* have nothing against your sister, Ashton."

"Good of you," Henry muttered.

"Can you think of another reason for such a witless act?"

Henry merely tightened the reins and set the horses at a faster pace, causing Hermia, who had been perched between the two men, to lose her balance. He put a hand on the dog to steady her.

Anthony had another thought and he looked sharply at Henry. He did not think Ashton was playing him false, but the man did not seem entirely forthcoming. "Did Miss Davenport's message give you the location of my cousin's house?"

Henry slid over the awkward moment. "Yes, near the Bath road, beyond Hounslow. When we get there, I'd be obliged if you'd direct me."

They said very little more till they reached Cranford where they drove directly to the stables. Anthony noted that his greys appeared to have come to no harm, and the stableboy was even then in the process of putting them back in their traces. So the couple planned to make their escape soon. "Leave them," he said, and his manner gave the boy no choice but to obey.

Anthony was no longer thinking clearly. He was convinced that a wedding ceremony was imminent and his only object was to find Crispin before he was irretrievably tied. He had forgotten Ashton and forgotten the dog till he heard the sound of her barking coming from behind the house. Quentin and the others must be on the terrace. Did they plan to hold the ceremony outdoors? It was just the sort of gesture that was all of apiece with this callow escapade. Anthony rounded the house, fully expecting to see his brother standing up with Ashton's little sister. But his brother was nowhere in sight, and Miss Ashton was peacefully taking tea with Miss Davenport and his cousin.

Or strictly, taking tea alongside his cousin, for St. George appeared to be going through a bottle of claret, and his careless pose did not suggest an attentive host. It was not the scene that Anthony had expected, which perhaps accounted for the ungenerous tone of his question. "Miss Ashton, what have you done with my brother?"

"How good of you to visit me, Tony." St. George's manner continued negligent, but he did not smile and his eyes were wary. "Ashton," he added, with a stiff nod toward Henry who had reached the terrace just behind Anthony. "Here I am, rusticating with positively no amusement, and today I've been blessed with two parties of visitors. I take it Lady Francesca's entertainment is deadly dull."

Claris would have protested, but Philippa cut her off. "Lord Carteret, Mr. Ashton, would either of you care for a cup of tea?"

Henry said that tea was exactly what he would like. He took a chair between Philippa and his sister and prepared to wait for a cue as to what was required of him.

Anthony stood uncertain, then walked up to his cousin.

349

"Where's Crispin?"

"Inside. Miss Ashton believes he may have the cramp."

"He's ill? I'll go and see." He started for the house.

"Oh, I'm sure that's not necessary, Lord Carteret," Claris said in her brightest voice. "It's probably just nerves. It took him on the way here."

This brought Anthony round. So the bridegroom was having second thoughts. He was going to feel much worse when his brother was through with him.

Philippa handed Henry a cup of tea, wondering why on earth he had brought Lord Carteret with him. And Hermia. They were both complicating matters. The dog was now sniffing around underneath the table. This earned her a casual kick from the viscount, and she yelped and retreated to the edge of the terrace where she sat regarding the group with reproachful eyes. Philippa tactfully ignored the incident. Perhaps Henry had not been able to keep them away. Carteret was clearly concerned about his brother—dear God, he must think it an elopement. Philippa searched for some words of reassurance, but there was no way to explain their precipitate dash across country as a mere social call. Nor could she invoke an effort to mend matters between Lord Christopher and his cousin, for Carteret knew nothing of the quarrel. They would have to play the farce out. "Won't you join us, Lord Carteret? I'm sure your brother will be out directly."

It was a sign of Anthony's distress that he did not look at the woman whom he longed to make his wife and merely shook his head. "What do you know about this, Quentin?"

St. George shrugged. "I? Nothing at all, my dear fellow. Cris decided to pay me a visit."

Anthony did not like being called "my dear fellow," least of all by his cousin who he was sure was lying. He looked round the garden. There was no sign of a man of the cloth, but perhaps he was expected later. Or perhaps Crispin had gone to fetch him. Anthony debated having it out with Miss Ashton, but his delicacy toward the sex forebade it. In any case, Ashton might object to having his sister bullied. He would have to wait for his brother. Crispin had never been able to withstand him and he would soon have the truth.

At last, unable to control his impatience, Anthony strode through the French windows, across the drawing room, and into the hall. There he was brought up short. The hall was filled with furniture and he remembered that the drawing room had been strangely empty. He looked about, searching for an explanation, and saw his brother coming down the stairs.

Crispin was in his shirt-sleeves, his hair was rumpled, his face was shiny with sweat, and he looked nothing at all like a prospective bridegroom. Unable to understand anything at all, Anthony gave vent to the second of his grievances. "Cris, what the devil do you mean by taking my cattle?"

When Crispin had gone into the house, he had known that he must finish the business quickly. He was not sure that Quentin believed his excuse for their visit, and his cousin was suspicious by nature. Fortunately, Luscombe was not in sight, and his wife was presumably in the kitchen. There seemed to be no other guests.

Crispin ran lightly up the stairs. Maria's room was at the back of the house, overlooking the garden. He moved silently across the corridor and shut her door behind him. Where would a woman keep her trinkets? He looked around. The bed was rumpled, articles of clothing were cast carelessly over the chairs, and the dressing table was covered with a sprinkling of powder and half-a-dozen bottles. And a leather box. Of course, her jewel case. Feeling very much a thief, Crispin opened the lid, and lifted out a tangle of chains and bracelets and earrings. He did not recall seeing the pendant on his earlier visit, but Claris had described it and he knew that the single stone had to be a ruby. He sifted carefully through the jewelry, then did so once again. The pendant was not there.

What next? He went rapidly through the drawers of the dressing table, lifting handkerchiefs and ribbons carefully so he would not leave a trace of his search. He could smell her scent, a light floral that was pleasant to the senses. Baffled and impatient, he turned to the wardrobe and then her trunk, but neither yielded up the treasure.

Think, he said silently, think, and he forced himself to stand

351

still. It was a recent gift, therefore she was likely to wear it often. But her neck had been bare when she came onto the terrace. Last night? Yes, that was likely. But why had she not put it away when she went to bed? Perhaps Quentin had told her it was valuable. A girl like that would take care of her valuables, she would be likely to hide it. Crispin felt under the pillows, looked under the bed, the chairs, the tables, lifted the rug.

Discouraged, he rose and brushed the dust from his knees. If she had gone to Quentin's room, the pendant might be there. But Crispin knew that his cousin preferred to keep his own territory free of the female sex. He would have visited Maria here, and here the pendant had to be. All right, perhaps she had not hidden it, perhaps Quentin had been importunate and she had not had time to put it away. But then, why hadn't she done so this morning? Crispin realized that he did not know a great deal about women.

Quentin had said she was in bed when they came. That seemed odd, he had not thought Maria an indolent girl. But suppose Quentin had taken her back there this afternoon? She might have removed the pendant then, but where in God's name had she put it?

He was taking the devil of a time. He moved toward the window, lifted the drapes away from the sill, and looked down on the terrace. Maria was rising from the table and walking into the house.

He had to get out of her room. Crispin clenched his fists in fury and frustration. Maria by the bed, Quentin pushing her down, pulling at her clothes. Perhaps she hadn't gotten around to the pendant. It would not be much in the way, not at first. But perhaps later, as she twisted and writhed—Crispin had not had much experience with women, but he was not an innocent—it would bind. He had an image of her hands behind her neck, struggling to free it, while Quentin, intent on other matters, failed to notice. Then her hands would fall and perhaps Maria too would find her own oblivion. With a movement borne of desperation and certainty, Crispin flung back the bedclothes. The pendant was there, in a fold of the sheet, looking curiously insubstantial, its ruddy warmth glowing against the white of the linen.

Crispin scooped it up and slipped it inside his coat pocket as he strode to the door. He closed the door quietly behind him and found refuge in the water closet just as Maria's step could be heard on the stairs.

His heart pounding, Crispin stayed quiet for a moment, conscious of a growing elation. He had done it. All that remained was to get Claris—and Miss Davenport, of course—and drive back to Raynley.

Priding himself on his attention to detail, Crispin made use of the facility, listened for the telltale rush of water, and stepped out into the hall and down the stairs. But as he neared the bottom, he was stopped by Luscombe. The commode, which had been abandoned in the middle of the hall, was to be moved to Lord St. George's room upstairs and Luscombe, complaining that his back was giving him trouble, wondered if Lord Christopher would be so good as to oblige. The gardener, a bent white-haired man a score of years Luscombe's senior, could not manage it on his own. Feeling it would be churlish to refuse, Crispin indicated his willingness to help. He stripped off his coat and laid it on the stair-rail, then went to the gardener's assistance.

The commode was heavy and some care had to be taken to manoeuvre it around the landing without damaging the walls. It was a full quarter-hour before Crispin emerged from his cousin's rooms and started down the stairs once more, intent on rejoining Claris and leaving Cranford as quickly as possible. But this resolution faded from mind as he looked down and saw his elder brother, his face convulsed with fury, waiting for him. "Cris, what the devil do you mean by taking my cattle?"

Philippa had grown increasingly concerned by Lord Christopher's absence, but she kept up a stream of inconsequential talk, willing St. George to stay in his chair and continue his copious consumption of what was undoubtedly a superior claret. She was relieved when young Paget finally appeared, but he gave no sign that he had been successful in his search. He had a hang-dog look, like that of a schoolboy found out in some pecadillo, but perhaps that was accounted for by the presence of his elder brother who followed close behind him. And why on earth was Lord Christopher in his shirt-sleeves?

Even St. George was startled. "Good God, Cris, what have you been up to? Were you ill after all?"

"Nothing to cause concern." Crispin glanced briefly at Claris and Miss Davenport, hoping his answer would cover whatever tale they had been telling. "I was helping Luscombe move your damn'—your commode," he amended, remembering that he was in the company of ladies. Tony's appearance had seriously upset him. "Luscombe's back wasn't up to it."

"Luscombe's a lazy rascal, there's nothing wrong with his back." St. George poured more wine and saluted Crispin with the glass. "But my thanks, whatever they're worth. Want some claret?"

Crispin shook his head. He had just become aware that he was in his shirt-sleeves. "I must have left my coat on the stairs. Just let me get it, then we'll have to be on our way."

"The devil with your coat!" Anthony turned his brother around to face him. "I want some answers!"

"I haven't heard the questions, Tony," the young man said in a cool voice. Then, seeing that this would only prolong his brother's quite justified rage, he took a more conciliatory tone. "I'm sorry about the greys—I assure you they came to no harm—but I had no transport of my own. If I'd known you were coming to Cranford, I wouldn't have taken them. Or," he added, tempting fate, "we could all have come together."

"There was no need to come at all." Anthony's voice oozed sarcasm. "I know you and Quentin are great friends, but you're with him every other day. I fail to understand the urgency of this visit."

"It was a lark, Tony, no more. And I guess not in the best of taste."

St. George began to laugh. "You'd best tell him the truth, Cris," he said when the spasms had died down, "he thinks it's an elopement."

Claris gasped and jumped to her feet. "Lord Carteret, you cannot believe Crispin would do such a shabby thing! Or that I

354

would consent to it!"

Anthony was bewildered. Her affront seemed genuine, and there had been nothing else to indicate an imminent flight or a ceremony of marriage. But then why had they come?

Crispin thought it prudent to take his cousin's advice. "Quentin and I had a quarrel, Tony. I came to apologize."

The matter-of-fact statement did much to cool Anthony's anger. This he could understand, though not the reasons for it. What, he wanted to know, could have been serious enough to cause a breach between the two lifelong friends?

Crispin began a halting effort to explain the quarrel without involving Claris. While the others' attention was taken, Henry left the terrace and ran swiftly across the lawn, ostensibly to save a flower bed from Hermia's depredations. Philippa ran after him, grateful that he had given her a moment to explain. "It's St. George," she whispered as he handed her the dog, "we think he took the bracelet. We came down so Lord Christopher could find—"

Her words were interrupted by a scream. Maria Doddington had come out on the terrace, without the shawl she had gone to fetch and with a look of utter distress upon her lovely face. Her voice carried clearly across the lawn. "My necklace, Quentin! The pendant! It's been stolen!"

Chapter 23

With admirable self-restraint, Philippa avoided casting as much as a glance in Crispin's direction as she ran back to the terrace. Henry, rapidly piecing together the little information he had, did likewise. Hermia scampered after them, barking sharply.

Had Henry and Philippa been less circumspect they would have observed that Crispin was giving an excellent portrayal of the disinterested onlooker. Claris and Anthony wore expressions of hopeless confusion. Anthony's was genuine.

St. George had taken his distraught mistress by the shoulders. "Control yourself, Maria. Are you certain the thing is lost? You haven't mislaid it?"

"Of course I'm certain." Maria shook herself free of his grasp and stared up at him defiantly. "You know what care I take of my jewels, and you warned me to be particularly careful with this piece."

"Yes, yes, but couldn't you have put it in a different place perhaps and forgot—"

"I would *not* forget," Maria insisted. "You *know* I would not!"

"Maria—Miss Davenport, do you think you could possibly keep that dog quiet?"

Philippa bent over Hermia but made no attempt to silence her. The more distractions the better.

"Maria—" the viscount began again.

"It has been stolen, I tell you," Maria exclaimed impatiently.

"It must have been stolen this afternoon, for I was wearing it when we went upstairs after luncheon, as you know perfectly well—"

"Quentin." Anthony had been staring at Maria, first in puzzlement and then, as he realized who she must be, in mounting outrage. "This is disgraceful!"

"Exactly." Maria turned her flower-like blue gaze on the marquis. "That such robbery could be committed in the home of a gentleman! Thank goodness you at least understand, sir."

"You mistake my meaning, madam." Anthony was still looking at St. George. "Dash it, Quentin, you know what I'm talking about."

"No, Tony, I'm afraid I don't," the viscount said pleasantly. "What are you talking about?"

It was one more frustration in a day full of them. The marquis made an effort to control himself and turned to Philippa and Claris. "If your business here is done, ladies, perhaps you will allow me to escort you back to Raynley."

"Quentin!" Maria exclaimed, before either of the other women could respond. "You won't let anyone leave until my pendant is recovered, will you?"

"Now see here, Miss—ma'am—" Anthony began.

"Oh, you aren't acquainted, are you?" St. George showed all the horror of one who has just discovered a sad social lapse. "Maria, allow me to present my cousin, the Marquis of Carteret. Tony, this is Miss Maria Doddington, a very dear friend of—"

"There's no need to go into the details, Quentin," Anthony said sharply. "Miss Doddington, you can't seriously think any of us was responsible for the loss of your necklace."

"Well, someone took it," Maria said, not unreasonably. "I don't think it was Quentin, and I didn't bring my maid down with me, so unless you suspect one of the servants—"

"Or Hermia," Henry muttered.

Hermia had settled down, but she barked at the sound of her name. Anthony looked at Henry in revulsion and said repressively that it was high time Miss Davenport and Miss Ashton returned to Lady Francesca's entertainment.

Philippa did not like being managed so but hesitated to

object, for Carteret's suggestion might be the perfect way to get them all away from Cranford. Assuming that Crispin's mission had been successful. It seemed likely that it had, but Crispin himself had made no effort to leave. Could someone else have taken the pendant? Or could Lord Christopher have been forced to leave it in the house? Or—of course, his missing coat. He must have put the pendant in his coat pocket and then removed the garment when he was asked to help with the furniture. Should she fetch it, or would that only arouse the viscount's suspicions?

"No, no," St. George exclaimed, "you mustn't depart so quickly. Not when you have come all this way. Stay and drink a glass of champagne with me."

"Very good of you, Quentin," Carteret said coldly, "but—"

"Tony, I insist."

He knows we have the pendant, Philippa thought, watching the viscount. It would indeed be folly to go after Lord Christopher's coat.

St. George shouted for Luscombe and smiled at his younger cousin. "After all, we must drink to the healing of the family breach. I'm sure Cris will agree with me."

"I'm in no hurry, Quen," Crispin said easily. "To tell the truth, I don't much fancy driving all the way back to Raynley with a parched throat. By all means let us have a toast."

Lord Christopher, Philippa thought, was behaving with admirable sense. They needed to calm St. George's suspicions. If the pendant was in the coat, they were safe enough, for while there was no way they could get their hands on it while they remained on the terrace, there was equally no way St. George could recover it. Philippa sat down beside Claris, demonstrating with alacrity that she was in no hurry to return to the crowds at Raynley. Henry said cheerfully that he was all for fostering family unity. Anthony, seeing no tactful way to remove Miss Davenport and Miss Ashton from Maria's presence, strode impatiently to the balustrade at the edge of the terrace.

Luscombe came out of the house, muttering that to his way of thinking if a gentleman was going to rearrange his furniture he should rearrange his furniture and if he was going to entertain guests he should entertain guests, but to do both at

358

once was asking for trouble, though of course it wasn't his place to say so and was there something his lordship wanted?

"Champagne," St. George informed him. "And some cakes or sandwiches or some such thing. Whatever Mrs. Luscombe thinks appropriate. Oh, and Luscombe," the viscount added, as Luscombe turned to go, "bring Lord Christopher's coat outside. Apparently he took it off when he was helping you with the furniture. Where did you say you left it, Cris?"

"That's all right, Quen." Crispin was already on his feet. "I'll fetch it myself. No need to trouble Luscombe further."

"I hardly think a coat will strain Luscombe's back," St. George returned. "I consider it the least he can do as reparation for forcing you to hoist furniture. I fancy you'll find the garment by the stairs, Luscombe. Bring it here directly."

Luscombe went inside. Crispin hesitated. If he followed, he would likely find himself racing his cousin. Best to wait until Luscombe returned and grab the coat before Quentin could. Crispin sat down.

"See here, Cris," said Anthony, turning back from the balustrade, "I still don't know what caused this breach between you and Quentin in the first place."

"It was private, Tony," Crispin informed him.

Anthony stared at his brother, stupefied. "You said it was a family breach. Damn—you might remember, Crispin, that I am the head of the family. If you think—"

"Carteret." Henry gave a discreet cough and addressed the marquis in lowered tones. "I fancy that your brother and cousin do not care to discuss the source of their quarrel in the presence of ladies."

It was the perfect—perhaps the only—argument to silence Lord Carteret. Anthony gave it up and sat down. Philippa looked at Henry appreciatively.

"Quentin," said Maria plaintively, unaware of the eddy of undercurrents which surrounded her, "have you forgotten about the pendant? You told me how valuable it—"

"My dear girl, what would you have me do?" St. George cut smoothly into his mistress' speech. "Subject my guests to a search?"

359

Anthony, who had been staring at his boots, looked up at that. "What is this problem your women have with their jewelry, Quentin?" he demanded.

It was dangerously close to the truth, but Anthony, of course, did not know that and the others pretended not to. St. George, Philippa was forced to admit, was handling the situation admirably. Luscombe seemed to be taking longer than was necessary. Could he be searching the coat himself? No, there was no way the viscount could have ordered him to do so. If St. George took the coat from Luscombe before Lord Christopher could, should they try to overpower the viscount? Their forces were larger, but the viscount would have Miss Doddington on his side, and Luscombe might come to his aid, and there was no telling what Lord Carteret would do. Philippa was still considering alternatives when she heard Luscombe's returning footsteps.

Several pairs of hands poised to reach for the coat. The French windows opened and Luscombe stepped onto the terrace. His hands were empty.

"Where the devil is the coat?" St. George demanded, his polished veneer quite gone.

"No sign of it in the hall, my lord." Luscombe looked at Crispin, whose face bore an expression of genuine bewilderment. "Are you sure you had it with you?"

"Of course he had it with him," St. George snapped. "Even Crispin wouldn't come calling in his shirt-sleeves. All right, Cris, let's stop playing games. Where did you leave it?"

"On the stairs. I told you."

"I know what you told me. Now you can tell me the truth."

"That is the truth! I'll go inside and have a look around. I'm sure I can find it."

"Oh, no, you don't." St. George's arm shot out, blocking his cousin's way. Henry took a step forward.

"Quentin," said an authoritative voice which caused Hermia to retreat under the nearest chair and most of the other occupants of the terrace to wish they could do likewise, "I should like to know what you mean by pushing half the drawing room furniture into the—good God," exclaimed the Countess Buckleigh, her sharp eyes sweeping the terrace, "what on earth is going on here?"

"Mother," said St. George, releasing his hold on Crispin, "this is an unexpected pleasure. Sir," the viscount added, as Lord Buckleigh strode onto the terrace after his wife.

"St. George," the earl said to his heir, "I should like to know—what the deuce is going on here?"

"Exactly," said his wife, "what I am attempting to discover. Anthony, Christopher, I was under the impression that you were spending the afternoon at a breakfast given by Francesca Scott. As Miss Davenport and Miss Ashton both reside with Lady Francesca, I assumed that they and Mr. Ashton would be in attendance as well. Am I to understand that the entertainment has been called off?"

No one answered this question, for even the story that Crispin had come to apologize to St. George would not serve. Lady Buckleigh would have a number of questions about the quarrel, and she would not be fobbed off as easily as Lord Carteret had been.

Philippa stepped into the breach. "No indeed, Lady Buckleigh," she said warmly. "The entertainment is most successful but shockingly crowded, of course, and as we were already so close we decided to pay a call on Lord St. George."

"Indeed." Lady Buckleigh appeared far from convinced. She had not yet sat down and so was keeping the gentlemen on their feet. "All of you?"

"Yes," said Philippa firmly—there was no need to explain about Maria—"it is so much cosier with a large party, don't you think? Of course it was inconsiderate of us to impose ourselves on Lord St. George, but he has been most hospitable." Philippa flashed the viscount a smile dripping with honey.

"Not at all." St. George's answering smile was equally as sugary. "Any man would be happy to be imposed on by such charming company."

"I see." Lady Buckleigh was by no means convinced by Miss Davenport's story. She and Lord Buckleigh had stopped at Cranford on their way back from Berkshire to discover why

361

their son and heir had chosen to rusticate in the middle of the Season. For all her formidable exterior, Lady Buckleigh nourished a soft spot for her elder son. She had received a letter from her sister reporting his defection and hinting at trouble, and if Quentin was in trouble, Lady Buckleigh meant to help him. And to discover the cause of the trouble. Finding Crispin and Miss Ashton present, she had immediately suspected an elopement was in progress, though in that case Mr. Ashton's presence puzzled her. She was determined to get to the bottom of the situation, but before she could speak her husband made an observation of his own.

"About to engage in some sort of sport, Christopher?" the earl inquired of his shirt-sleeved nephew.

"No, sir," Crispin said quickly. "I was just helping Luscombe move a piece of furniture upstairs and I seem to have—er—mislaid my coat. I was just going to look for it."

"No one," said Lady Buckleigh, "is going anywhere until I have some answers. That applies to you too, Quentin."

"Certainly, Mother. Luscombe, Lord Christopher's coat must be somewhere in the house. Find it and bring it—"

"I cannot imagine," said Lady Buckleigh, "how Crispin could have come to mislay his coat, but there's no need to waste Luscombe's time searching for it. Crispin can find it himself—when I am finished with him. Luscombe, you may bring a fresh pot of tea—good and strong, mind you—as quickly as possible."

"Yes, my lady. Er—does that mean your lordship won't be requiring the champagne?"

"It most certainly does," said Lady Buckleigh. "The stories I am being told are quite addled enough without the addition of wine. And now that Luscombe is out of earshot," the Countess continued after a moment, "I don't want any more prevarication. What is going on here, Quentin? Why are all these people assembled in your house? And what have you been doing with the furniture, which to my recollection has not been moved since before your father and I were married?"

Before St. George could answer, Crispin seized on Lady Buckleigh's last question, seeing the perfect opportunity to divert her attention. "Well, you see, Aunt Catherine, Quentin had to make room for the billiard table."

"Billiard table?"

"Yes, I believe it is to arrive tomorrow."

"Am I to understand, Quentin," Lady Buckleigh demanded, "that you intend to put a *billiard table* in the drawing room?"

"Have to admit it's the largest room in the house, Catherine," Lord Buckleigh observed. "Just where were you thinking of putting it, St. George? Wouldn't want it too near the fireplace."

"Horace," said Lady Buckleigh, "I wish you would stay out of this. It is a domestic matter and really no concern of yours."

"Which is to say it's dashed silly," Lord Buckleigh returned testily. "What I want to know is why St. George came down here in the first place."

"All in good time, Horace." Lady Buckleigh at last moved toward an empty chair and as she crossed the terrace her eye fell on Maria. "I don't believe I am acquainted with this young lady, Quentin," the countess said.

"My apologies, Mother. I'm afraid I have been rather distracted since your arrival."

"If everyone allowed such paltry considerations to interfere with the social amenities, Quentin, society would come to a complete standstill." Lady Buckleigh began to draw off her gloves. "Who is she?"

Lord Buckleigh, Philippa observed, had also noted Maria, though he seemed less interested in her name than in her personal charms.

"Mother," said the viscount, "pray allow me to present Miss Maria Doddington. Miss Doddington, my parents the Earl and Countess Buckleigh. Miss Doddington is a friend of Miss Davenport's and Miss Ashton's," he concluded smoothly.

Anthony, like the others, had seen the wisdom of closing ranks in the face of the Buckleighs' invasion, but this slander on innocent womanhood was more than he could stomach. "Quentin—" he began on a warning note.

"That's right," Claris said sweetly at the same time. "We met at a luncheon last week, did we not, Miss Doddington?"

Anthony looked at Claris in surprise, but fortunately no one noticed. Maria, who was growing bewildered and felt that the loss of her pendant had most unfairly been forgotten, murmured something inarticulate.

"Well, well." Lord Buckleigh moved toward the settee on which Maria was seated. "Tell me, my dear, are you any relation to the Doddingtons of Hammond Hall in Northumberland? Old Reggie Doddington and I were in the 41st together, back in the '90s."

Maria had never heard of Hammond Hall and had only the vaguest idea of the location of Northumberland, but she did know she had at last found a sympathetic ear.

"Oh, Lord Buckleigh," she exclaimed, "perhaps you will help me. My pendant has disappeared and no one will make the least effort to recover it and I do not know what I am to do!"

"Eh, what's this?" said the earl, lowering himself onto the settee. "Lost your jewelry? Poor child!" Lord Buckleigh seemed to have quite forgotten his lack of interest when his own daughter found herself in a similar predicament. "When did you last see it?"

St. George, who remembered only too well when and where he had last seen the pendant, said hastily, "There's no need to concern yourself, Father. I assure you every effort is being made— Ah, Luscombe. Your timing is impeccable."

Luscombe set down a tray bearing a fresh pot of tea and a plate of Mrs. Luscombe's excellent saffron cake, then beat a hasty retreat before anyone could ask him to do anything else. Lady Buckleigh, never one to abandon her social duties, poured tea for the company, though the performance of this office did nothing to impede her inquisition. "I insist on being told the truth of what is going on here," she said, lifting the teapot. "I mean the real truth, not any stories about dashing off to pay a social call in the middle of another engagement or—"

"Just a moment, my dear. It appears we have arrived in the midst of a crisis."

Lady Buckleigh turned to her husband with raised brows. They seldom interfered with each other, but then they were rarely in each other's company. In fact their seven-day sojourn at Buckleigh Place had rather tried the patience of both. "I am quite aware of that, Horace," the countess said. "I am endeavoring to discover the nature of the crisis."

"Well, if you'd listened a little more carefully you would have discovered it long since. Miss Doddington has lost her pendant. As I was saying, Miss Doddington, when did you last—"

"Horace—" said Lady Buckleigh firmly.

"Father—" said Lord St. George, a shade desperately.

But at this point the viscount received succour from an unexpected source. Satisfied that the new arrivals were not bent on mayhem, Hermia crawled out from beneath Henry's chair.

"What," Lady Buckleigh demanded, "is that?"

"It's a dog, Catherine." Lord Buckleigh's impatience was increasing. "Any fool could see that."

"I know it's a dog, Horace. I did not know Quentin had taken to keeping them here or that he allowed them on the terrace."

"You mustn't blame Lord St. George, Lady Buckleigh," Philippa said quickly, welcoming the diversion. "Hermia is mine."

"You brought your dog with you, Miss Davenport?"

"Oh, no," Claris hastened to Philippa's defence. "Henry and Lord Carteret brought her."

"Anthony," said Lady Buckleigh, eyeing her nephew, "I wish you would tell me—"

"It would be more accurate," said Henry, "to say that she stowed away."

"Stowed a—"

"Catherine," said Lord Buckleigh, "the dog is immaterial. Where did you last see the pendant, Miss Doddington?"

No more eager than St. George to reveal their relationship to his parents, Maria murmured that she thought it had been somewhere in the house.

"Well," said Lord Buckleigh heartily, "that's something to start with. A search must be organized. We'll have your necklace back in no time. Quentin, don't just sit there, there's work to be done. You have a look about the kitchens. We don't want to upset Mrs. Luscombe, but we can't be too careful. Mustn't let it be said a guest's belongings aren't safe under your roof. Christopher, you take charge of the drawing room.

Anthony, the dining room and study. You, sir—" his eyes fell on Henry. "I don't believe I know you."

"Mr. Ashton, Father," St. George supplied.

"Ashton? Oh, yes, the friend of that dashed Jacobin who stole Edwina's bracelet. You can help, too. Check the library first, then the hall. Never know where these things will turn up." Lord Buckleigh had been obliged to resign his military commission when his elder brother's death left him heir to the earldom. Buckleigh had had no particular fondness for his brother, but he rather regretted leaving the army. Somehow politics did not afford the same straightforward opportunities for command.

But though for a variety of reasons the gentlemen fell in with Lord Buckleigh's plan, Lady Buckleigh was less ready to acquiesce. "Quentin," the countess said, "sit down. Horace, you may carry on a very thorough search with the other three gentlemen. Quentin is going to remain here and provide me with a satisfactory explanation."

"Dash it, Catherine," the earl protested, "he can do that later."

"He has already delayed long enough. Quentin—"

"St. George—" the earl commanded at the same time.

"Crispin!" shrieked a voice from the drawing room. "Oh, my darling, thank heaven!" The Dowager Marchioness of Carteret rushed onto the terrace and fell upon her son. "Tell me that you aren't married!"

Chapter 24

"Who," said Lady Buckleigh in a voice that demanded to be heard, "said anything about getting married?"

"My aunt, Mama." Lady Edwina had followed Lady Carteret onto the terrace, looking composed and not at all as though she had spent the best part of an hour in a carriage driven faster than the roads would allow. She took a chair beside her mother and opened a ruffled silk parasol of a hyacinth violet that just matched the ribbons on her leghorn bonnet. "She persists in believing that Crispin has eloped. Could you give me some tea?"

This heartless response did not escape the notice of Lady Carteret, though she appeared quite distracted. She clutched her heart with one hand and clung to her son with the other. "You aren't married," she repeated, "tell me you aren't married!"

The Thane family, used to Lady Carteret's ways, remained singularly unimpressed by this outburst, though Lord Buckleigh was heard to mutter that it was just like his sister-in-law to get a bee in her head. The others hovered around, looking helpless or uncomfortable as the case might be, while Crispin earnestly assured his mother that no marriage was contemplated. "At least today," he added, which sent her off into fresh paroxysms.

It was Claris who finally calmed her down. She guided Lady Carteret to a chair and searched in her reticule for the bottle of vinaigrette that the marchioness was sure to carry. Kneeling before the woman she intended to make her mother-in-law, she unstopped the bottle and waved it gently beneath Lady Carteret's nose, all the time patting her hand and uttering soothing words. When Lady Carteret's hysteria had subsided, Claris took a seat beside her, poured her a cup of tea, ascertained her wishes as to cream and sugar, and handed her the cup and saucer with assurances that she would soon be feeling much better. She was, she said, very attached to her own mama who would never speak to her again if she so much as dreamed of an elopement.

Lady Carteret had managed to draw everyone's attention. The search was momentarily forgotten, and even Maria did not appear to recollect her loss. No one noticed that Elliot Marsden had appeared on the terrace until he crossed to Philippa and raised her hand to his lips. And no one then thought to remark it, save for Anthony who moved forward with a proprietary air.

Philippa removed her hand from Mr. Marsden's grasp and smiled brightly at the two men, wishing them both at the devil. "I'm afraid we have caused a great deal of trouble for everyone with this impulsive visit," she said. "It was ill-advised but quite harmless. We would have left by now had it not been for Lord and Lady Buckleigh's arrival."

And the still missing pendant. Why should Lord Christopher's coat have disappeared? Lord St. George obviously suspected that his cousin had taken the pendant, but he had not himself left the terrace and he had given his man no orders but that the coat be brought outside. He was clearly just as upset as Lord Christopher about its disappearance—unless that had been a pretence. Philippa wished she could talk to Henry, but he was nowhere in sight.

Philippa continued her conciliatory remarks to her suitors, neither of whom showed any disposition to leave her side, and kept a watchful eye on the Viscount St. George.

"I can't understand why you had to pay Quentin a visit." Lady Carteret addressed her son in plaintive tones.

"Nor can I," her sister added. "Sit down, Crispin, and stop

368

fidgeting. You, too, Quentin."

The young men complied, looking warily at each other.

"There's something between the two of you," Lady Buckleigh went on. "I don't demand a complete explanation, but you owe us something. And if you can't tell the truth, pray make it plausible."

"The truth, Mother, is rarely plausible. Which do you prefer, verity or sense?"

Lady Buckleigh regarded her son with disfavour. He was much too inclined to be clever.

"Proceed," she said coldly.

"We quarreled last week. Did we not, Crispin?"

His cousin nodded. "I said some things I later wished I had not. I drove over today to apologize."

"With Miss Ashton? And Miss Davenport?" Lady Buckleigh's tone indicated her disbelief.

"It would not have been proper for me to come without her," Claris explained.

Lady Carteret stared at the girl by her side. "But why should you come at all?"

"I'm rather afraid it was my fault," Claris said, taking it boldly on herself.

The two men looked at each other in a rare moment of accord. Was Claris foolish enough to blurt the story out?

"Crispin—Lord Christopher—was very unhappy on account of the quarrel," Claris went on, "and I told him he had to make it up. I have sisters, you see, and we were forever at each other's throats, but Mama never let us carry a grudge for long. Then, when I learned that Lord St. George was only a few miles away, I insisted Lord Christopher go at once. One is always rather shamefaced about apologizing, and it's best to get it over as quickly as possible."

Lady Edwina looked at Claris with admiration. She did not believe a word of it.

Lady Buckleigh suspended judgement, but her sister thought that Miss Ashton had shown surprising sense. Crispin and St. George visibly relaxed.

"But why should you quarrel in the first place?" Lady Carteret wanted to know.

"Oh, I imagine that was just something between men," Claris said hastily. "They have a way of looking at things that we women do not really understand. I think it best if we do not press them for explanations."

"Well done," Edwina said to herself.

"Hear, hear," St. George muttered.

"I say," said Lord Buckleigh who had been in conference with Maria Doddington, "time to get on with the search."

"Of course." St. George jumped up with alacrity. "Miss Doddington, how could we forget you?"

"Sit down, Quentin." Lady Buckleigh's voice was peremptory. "I haven't finished with you."

Out of long habit, St. George hesitated, but only for a moment. "Later, Mother, I promise you. Father needs me."

"If I were you, Quen, I'd stay with Mama." His sister was relishing his unease. "I'm sure Mr. Marsden will be glad to help with the search."

Her voice carried to Mr. Marsden who was still in conversation with Philippa and Anthony. He looked puzzled, but indicated he was willing to perform any service that might be required.

"Miss Doddington has mislaid a valuable pendant," Lord Buckleigh explained. "A red stone set in gold filigree, on a gold chain. St. George, come along. Tony, Cris, you too, Marsden. We need all the help we can get." He looked around, counting his troops. "Where the devil is that fellow Ashton?"

"Here, sir." Henry came out onto the terrace, a brown coat over his arm. "I think this is yours, Paget."

Crispin moved forward eagerly, but St. George was quicker. He plucked the coat from Henry's arm and searched rapidly through the pockets. Philippa had to admit it was skillfully done. To someone not attending, he appeared to be merely shaking it out.

"I say, Quentin, that's *my* coat," Crispin said in an aggrieved tone.

He reached out to take it from his cousin's hands. St. George seemed to be in a fit of abstraction—disappointed, Philippa would have said—but at his cousin's words he recollected himself. "Allow me." He held the coat so Crispin could put it on.

Crispin shrugged his shoulders into the garment and patted his hips as though he would make sure it sat him properly. He seemed disconcerted. His cousin observed this reaction and smiled.

"I'm glad to have found it," Henry observed. "Mrs. Luscombe—is that her name?—saw it on the stair-rail and took it up to Lord St. George's room, thinking it one of his. I fetched it from the wardrobe. I must say I envy you your tailor, St. George. There's a handsome waistcoat I wouldn't mind wearing myself."

St. George glared at Henry. His mother drummed her fingers on the table, a sign that she was agitated. "I fail to comprehend this concern for a simple coat," she said to the group at large. "And I fail, Mr. Ashton, to see why it was necessary for you to investigate my son's wardrobe." She did not need to add that she considered it insolent presumption.

"My apologies, Lady Buckleigh. It was to save Mrs. Luscombe the steps. She complains of the rheumatics."

Philippa silently applauded Henry's enterprise. But where was the pendant? It was clear that St. George had not found it in Lord Christopher's coat pockets, and equally clear that Lord Christopher must have put it there. Must they begin all over again? And how were they to proceed when the Thanes and the Pagets made it impossible to confront the viscount?

Lord Buckleigh's patience was wearing thin. "The devil with the coat, and the devil with Mrs. Luscombe's rheumatics. Let's get on with the search."

"For this?" Henry pulled a gold chain from his pocket and held it up for all to see. A glowing red jewel set in a fine frame of filagree depended from it.

Maria gave a joyful cry and ran forward, but Henry held the necklace out of reach. "The chain is undoubtedly yours, Miss Doddington, but not, I think, the stone. Lady Edwina?" He laid it on the table in front of her. "Do you recognize it?"

"Don't be ridiculous, Ashton, the necklace is Miss Doddington's." St. George moved toward the table with decision.

Edwina was Lady Buckleigh's daughter. She clapped her

hand over the stone and dared her brother to come closer. "Not so fast, Quentin." She rose gracefully and held the chain aloft, studying the play of light on the jewel. "It's mine," she said in wonder. "It's mine, I'm sure of it. See, there's a small chip on one side."

The terrace was suddenly quiet. Then Edwina realized the implications of her discovery. She stared at her brother in momentary disbelief. "Quentin, how dare you?"

Maria gave a cry of outrage. "It's mine! It's mine, he gave it to me!"

Lady Buckleigh looked at her in surprise. Miss Doddington had seemed like a well-bred young woman, but she evidently had some intimate relationship with her son. Strange that the other women had claimed her as an acquaintance. Wasn't there something about a luncheon? She put the problem of Miss Doddington away for future scrutiny and turned to her daughter. "Edwina, are you saying that Quentin has appropriated one of your jewels?"

"Yes, Mama. No, it's *the* jewel, the missing one. It's from my bracelet."

Lady Buckleigh's composure was shaken. "Your bracelet?" she whispered.

Edwina was triumphant. "Yes, Mama. Quentin stole my bracelet."

There are moments, Philippa thought, when everything comes to a head, when passions and thoughts, carried on a whirlwind, settle at last in a new arrangement, like the pieces of glass in a kaleidoscope. In a novel, it would be time for a new chapter, or a new section within a chapter, to give the reader a chance to adjust to the different pattern. If there was such a time here, it lasted no more than a fraction of a second, but Philippa knew that everything had changed.

"You're a fool, Edwina." St. George's voice was contemptuous. "Any stone can be chipped."

"The cut is unique," she insisted.

"And can be copied."

"I'm sure it's mine."

St. George shrugged. "I had it from a jeweler in the Burlington Arcade. I don't know where he got it. That scoundrel Murray probably needed ready money."

"Let me see the stone, Edwina." Lady Buckleigh held out her hand. "I've handled that bracelet since I was a girl." She spent a long minute examining the stone, then set it down with a sigh. "It's very like."

"May I have it back now?" Maria addressed Lord Buckleigh, the only one present to have shown her any sympathy, but he shook his head. He turned to Henry and his voice was hard. "Are you accusing my son of being a thief?"

Henry's voice was equally hard. "I accuse him of having a jewel in his possession which came from your daughter's bracelet."

"It was *my* pendant," Maria said. Tears ran unheeded down her face.

"Which my cousin stole from Miss Doddington." St. George's eyes were on Crispin.

"Which I returned to my cousin," Crispin said, his eyes on Edwina. "Or tried to," he amended. "Thanks for your help, Ashton."

Lord Buckleigh's voice cut across this exchange. "Where did you get the pendant, St. George?"

"I told you. A jeweler in the Burlington Arcade."

"His name?"

"I don't recall."

"Look at me!"

St. George turned on his father in fury. "Am I to be subjected to an inquisition on the word of this man Ashton? Do you know who he is? He's a scribbler, a friend of that scoundrel Murray, and he has no liking for his betters."

"Quentin!" Lady Buckleigh could not allow this to pass. One might think such things, but one did not say them.

Lord Buckleigh was troubled. He was a man of fixed opinions, unyielding in his opposition to change, hostile toward those who would bring it about. He was allied with the most conservative members of the government, among whom his harsh tongue and readiness to take unpopular measures had earned him considerable respect. He did not hesitate to use the law to his advantage, nor to go around the law in order to gain his ends. But he had a rough morality and his son had violated his notion of what was right. "I have no liking for Gordon Murray," he said, "but he lies in prison on a charge of theft. What happened, Ashton?"

"I don't know," Henry said, "but I can guess. Lady Edwina's bracelet dropped unnoticed and was picked up by her brother. He did not immediately return it. Perhaps he forgot about it, or perhaps he intended to torment her, or perhaps even then he had another scheme in mind. The next morning he visited Murray's office and left the bracelet as a souvenir. I suspect he intended to send an anonymous message to the magistrates, but, fortunately for him, Lord Sidmouth ordered a search of Murray's rooms first."

"And the pendant?"

"There are two possibilities. The stone came loose and he discovered it in his pocket, or he pried it loose deliberately. In either case, he took it to a jeweler—I'm sure the man can be traced—and had it set in a pendant which he then presented to his—to Miss Doddington, telling her to take great care of it as the necklace was valuable. As indeed it is. I cannot swear to this, Lord Buckleigh, but I'd wager something very like it took place."

"A cock-and-bull story!" St. George spat his contempt.

"The man who visited Murray's office was seen. We have a reliable witness."

St. George was shaken. "Impossible! There was no one there!"

There was a moment of absolute quiet. Hermia, made anxious by the shouting voices, moved close to Philippa and whimpered. Philippa stooped and picked her up.

"Horace," Lady Buckleigh said in a parody of her former manner, "it can be handled."

"Handled, Lady Buckleigh?" Henry's voice was gentle. "What is it you propose to handle?"

Anthony came forward. "Murray will be freed, that's the main thing. You'll withdraw the charges, Edwina."

"It's too late for that, Carteret," Henry said.

"It will be explained. A jest gone wrong." Lady Buckleigh turned to her son, her voice bitter. "You were clever enough to have done it, you can think of a reason why. Better to be thought a fool than—"

"No!" Henry's voice cut like a whip.

"It will be your word against ours, Mr. Ashton. How will you stop us?"

"With my pen, madam."

They took each other's measure. Ashton, Lady Buckleigh saw, had a strength she had not suspected. Could he be bought? He would have to be, for Quentin's reputation must be saved, though he ill-deserved it. She looked into Ashton's eyes and knew it could not be done. They were implacable, exultant, and—the final humiliation—pitying.

Philippa watched the play of feeling across Lady Buckleigh's face, knowing she was more formidable than her husband, knowing the moment she admitted defeat. She saw the pity in Henry's eyes and wondered again, as she had the day in Mr. Murray's office, how he could keep his humanity without compromising his anger.

Then she looked around. St. George was perfectly still and the others seemed to have withdrawn from him, though no one had actually moved. Lady Edwina, Philippa thought, had satisfied a private grudge. Lord Carteret's face mirrored his inner conflict: he detested his cousin and what he had done, but the family must hold together. Lady Carteret appeared bewildered, and Lord Christopher, now that the thing was finally over, looked as though he had lost something he had never known he valued.

"It won't do, Catherine." Lord Buckleigh turned to his son. "You will come with me to London, and you will make a full confession. You will make it in writing so that there can be no doubt of Gordon Murray's innocence."

St. George raised a brow in mocking inquiry. He had himself in hand once more. "Dear me, Father, surely this is carrying notions of fair play too far. I never thought to hear you defending a Jacobin."

"What you did is dishonourable, Quentin," Lord Buckleigh said grimly.

"I see, Father. But paying men to incite a mob to riot, as you and your colleagues have done on more than one occasion, that, I take it, is highly honourable?"

Lord Buckleigh frowned. "This was different. You were in a gentleman's house, and he was a gentleman's guest."

St. George stared at his father in disbelief and gave a harsh burst of laughter. "If that's the way *you* choose to play the game, Father, you're going to lose."

"Perhaps the game's not worth winning," Henry said quietly.

"You can hardly expect me to take your advice seriously, Ashton," St. George said dryly. "It was purely a matter of personal safety. I view Murray as a danger. Are you saying I am wrong?"

"No, thank God," said Henry. Philippa had never agreed with him more.

"Horace," Lady Buckleigh whispered, "what will happen to him?"

"Not half of what he deserves. Ashton, will your friend bring suit?"

"My guess is that he'll settle for public vindication. But you can't silence him."

"I accept that." It was an enormous admission from a man of Buckleigh's persuasion. "If I can compensate him in any other way for the ordeal he's undergone on my son's account—"

"He won't take your money."

Lord Buckleigh nodded. "Very well." He roused himself. "St. George, tell Luscombe to pack your things, we'll be leaving in half an hour. And have him order the carriage. All the carriages. I doubt any of us will be staying."

It was time, Philippa thought, for a new chapter. People moved from the positions into which they had been frozen, and there was a murmur of voices. St. George went into the house, followed shortly by Maria Doddington. He had not once looked at her, and this casual cruelty was written on her face. Philippa was sorry for the girl.

Lady Buckleigh stared mutely at her husband. He answered her unspoken question. "I daresay he'd best go abroad for a time."

She nodded. She was recovering from the shock and making plans. "I'll put it down to his zeal, and the idiocy of the young. In three months, no one will remember."

"I will," her husband said, and he descended the terrace steps and disappeared around the corner of the house.

Philippa turned to Lord Carteret. "I'm sorry," she said. Not that his cousin was exposed, but that it might give him pain.

Hermia barked to be let down, and Philippa gave her pet her freedom. When she rose she found that Henry had joined them. "Carteret," he was saying, "I'm following Lord Buckleigh to London, I mean to see Murray. Do you want to drive with me?" It was a handsome concession. Henry wanted none of the marquis at this moment, but neither did he want him left with Philippa.

"I have my curricle, Ashton, I'll see that Miss Davenport and Miss Ashton are returned safely to Raynley. Crispin can take care of himself." He moved off to speak to his brother.

"Will he be all right?" Philippa asked Henry. She was not talking about Lord Christopher.

"I'll see that he is. I mean to have him out of prison this evening."

"Come to Green Street later. I'm sure we'll all return to town tonight." Then she laughed. "Better yet, bring Mr. Murray so we can see for ourselves."

Henry smiled and went off in search of Lord Buckleigh.

Elliot Marsden, who had been standing near Philippa all this while, took advantage of the lull to draw her down the terrace steps. "I'm happy for you," he said, "and for your friend. And may I say, for myself? Will you walk with me a little?"

Only then did Philippa remember that the conclusion of Mr. Murray's problems meant the commencement of her own. Surely he would not expect an answer today, not so soon, she had had no time to think. She tried to mask her consternation, wondering what she would say to him, how she could put him off.

"I shall be leaving in a few minutes," she said. "We've been gone much too long from Raynley."

"Then give me those few minutes."

She did not know how to refuse and was about to take his

arm when they were interrupted by Anthony who had followed them onto the lawn. "Miss Davenport was speaking with me, Marsden."

Elliot stared boldly at his rival. "I have asked Miss Davenport to walk with me, Carteret. I have a right to make the request."

"And I have a right to refuse it!"

"Wait, wait!" Philippa put up her hands to separate them lest they come to blows. "No one has any right to my person. Not, that is—" She faltered. They had every right to demand an answer of her, she had given it to them this very day. She would have to plead for time. She glanced at Claris, still seated by Lady Carteret, and wondered wildly if she should beg a seat in the marchioness' carriage. Anything to avoid a drive in Lord Carteret's company. "This is not the time for private interviews," she said, "nor the place. I will be at home tomorrow, I will be glad to receive either of you then." And she fled toward the safety of the terrace where the rest of the women were gathered.

The men looked after her, then turned to face each other. "You should know, Marsden," Anthony said, "that I have offered for Miss Davenport some days since. The morning after the Warwicks' affair, at half past twelve to be precise."

Elliot seemed amused. "You should know, Carteret, that I have done the same. At a quarter past eleven."

At this, all of Anthony's control snapped. The sight of Philippa slipping into the secrecy of the oak trees at Raynley, the inconclusive contest with bow and arrow, the sense that he had been made a fool of by Crispin, by St. George, and even by the Ashton chit and her brother, combined with the fresh humiliation of being second to this damn' barrister who seemed to live in his stepmother's pocket— He grabbed the lapels of his rival's coat. "I want this settled, Marsden. Now."

Marsden stepped back. There was no trace of amusement on his face. "Agreed." Of one accord they walked to the far end of the lawn and stripped off their coats.

The five women on the terrace were not aware of their departure. Nor was Crispin, who had been unwilling to leave Claris' side. Lady Buckleigh was locked in her own misery. Her sister, too, was quiet, but with her son's reassuring presence at her side she could not but feel complacent. The young people kept up an inconsequential chatter in an effort to relieve the tension of the scene they had recently witnessed. And in Philippa's case, of the one she had just avoided.

Then Hermia, who had followed Philippa back to the terrace, suddenly ran off again. Philippa looked up and saw her dog bounding across the lawn in the direction of two men who seemed to be removing their coats. She might have known. What a coward she was! She raced after Hermia and caught her just as she reached Lord Carteret and Mr. Marsden. "No!" she said breathlessly, "you must not! Not on my account."

"Leave us," Anthony said. His face was unyielding and he did not look at her.

"Of all the ridiculous—" Philippa began.

"No!" came a scream from the direction of the tea table. "No!" The three turned around in time to see Lady Carteret clinging to the balustrade at the edge of the terrace. Her soft, plaintive voice was sharp with distress, and her words carried clearly across the lawn. "Stop it!" she cried. "Stop! He's your brother!"

Chapter 25

Philippa stood motionless but her grip on Hermia must have slackened, for Hermia wriggled free and ran to bark at Carteret's and Marsden's feet. Lady Carteret remained at the edge of the terrace, her hands gripping the balustrade, her eyes on the two shirt-sleeved men. Lady Buckleigh stared at her sister in astonishment. Claris looked at Crispin. Crispin looked at Edwina, then of one accord the two cousins started down the terrace steps.

For a moment Anthony stood frozen. Then he looked from his stepmother to Marsden. Marsden shrugged. He did not seem in the least surprised, which perhaps galled Anthony as much as anything.

"No," the marquis said, striding toward the terrace. "It's not possible."

"Don't be an idiot, Tony," Crispin advised as they met in the middle of the lawn. "Knowing Father, anything's possible. I suppose this means you're my brother, too," he continued, holding out his hand to Marsden who had followed Anthony. "Sorry I didn't know it earlier."

Marsden accepted his hand. He seemed almost amused. Edwina offered her hand as well. "Welcome to the family, Mr. Marsden. Or may I call you Cousin Elliot?"

"I should be honored, Lady Edwina, but I fear I cannot claim the title. My connection is entirely with the other side of the family."

"We don't bother with such trifling distinctions," Edwina

assured him. "Tony has always treated me just like a cousin, haven't you, Tony?"

"I—" the marquis realized the idiocy of trying to answer Edwina's question. "Stay out of this, Eddy," he commanded. "I tell you the thing's impossible. Marsden already has a father."

"Everyone has a father, Tony," Edwina murmured sweetly.

"A different father. You know what I mean."

"My dear Carteret," Marsden said mildly, "you of all people ought to realize that when a woman gives birth to a child there is no guarantee her husband is the father. Even in the best of circles."

"Especially in the best of circles," Edwina said.

"When?" Anthony demanded, his eyes on Marsden.

"1789, the 25th of January," Marsden said, his voice composed.

Anthony had been born in April of the same year. Marsden was some three months his elder. His elder brother. His father's eldest son. Or at least, Anthony amended bitterly, the eldest that he knew of. How many other bastards had his father kept secret? Or not so secret. The late Lord Carteret had evidently taken his fool of a wife into his confidence. It was only his son and heir who had been kept in the dark. And it was not only his father who had kept the secret from him. Father might have had some right to do so; Aurelia had none.

He stalked to the edge of the terrace, intending to voice his outrage to his stepmother, but was forestalled by Lady Buckleigh who had been thinking along the same lines. The countess was not herself and it had taken her some moments to assimilate the situation, but despite her concern about her own son, she was by no means past taking an interest in other members of the family.

"Aurelia," Lady Buckleigh said, "you never mentioned any of this to me!"

Lady Carteret, who was still standing, turned to her sister, who was still sitting. "No, Catherine," the marchioness said— Claris thought her expression couldn't have been more smug—"I did not. Contrary to what you have always believed, I am capable of keeping a secret."

"I should think," said Anthony before Lady Buckleigh could respond, "that I might have been informed."

Lady Carteret—still, Claris judged, looking smug—turned her eyes on her stepson. "Your father did not want it that way, Anthony."

"And after his death?"

"I have always," the marchioness informed him in her most long-suffering accents, "done my best to respect your father's wishes."

"Aurelia—"

"What's the trouble, Anthony?" Lord Buckleigh had come around the corner of the house.

"Aurelia says Elliot Marsden is my father's son!"

"Oh, she's finally told you, has she?" Buckleigh was still preoccupied with St. George's disgrace. "Well, I suppose you were bound to find out sooner or later."

Anthony stared at his uncle. "You knew, too!"

"Your father took me into his confidence, yes."

"And I suppose he's known all along," Anthony continued, gesturing toward Marsden.

"Oh, no," Marsden assured him. "I didn't learn the truth until after our father's death. Trenchard told me."

"Trenchard? Do you mean to say," Anthony demanded slowly, looking from Buckleigh to Lady Carteret, "that our *solicitor* knew all the details, and no one bothered to inform *me?*"

"Calm down, Tony," Crispin advised. "If it weren't for solicitors, no one would know family secrets."

"I think," said Anthony, ignoring Crispin and mounting the steps, "that you owe me an explanation, Aurelia."

"By all means, Anthony," Lady Carteret said sweetly. "I am quite prepared to give you one, as soon as you are prepared to listen."

Having retrieved Hermia again, Philippa had remained quietly in the background, holding tightly to her pet. She felt oddly detached. She looked involuntarily to Henry who had followed Lord Buckleigh and knew that he shared her feeling.

382

One could not quite laugh, but one could not deny that it was a situation ripe with irony, both comic and dramatic.

And yet, Philippa thought, it was odd that she should feel so, for, unlike Henry, she was not a disinterested observer. As Marsden's or Carteret's future wife she was very nearly as interested in the events now taking place as they were themselves.

It was then, when for once neither of her suitors was paying her any heed, that Philippa realized she had no intention of marrying either of them. She was quite sure of her resolve. How strange. And yet it seemed less that she had come to a decision than that she had acknowledged something she had known for a long time. It was an odd moment to make the discovery. Or perhaps it wasn't.

Philippa surveyed the two men with rueful affection. There was Carteret, angry and frustrated thanks to the family pride she could perhaps understand but would never be able to share. And there was Marsden, amused, aloof, apparently unconcerned with the feelings of those about him. She could like and sympathize with both. She could spend the rest of her life with neither.

"By all means, Anthony," Lady Carteret was saying. "I am quite prepared to give you one, as soon as you are prepared to listen."

The marchioness' statement ended Philippa's reflections. Carteret was already on the terrace. Crispin started after him. Marsden gave Edwina his arm and they followed. Philippa reached the terrace at the same time as Henry and Lord Buckleigh. She wondered if she and Henry and Claris should withdraw, leaving the Paget and Thane families to sort the matter out, and she cast a glance at Henry. But Buckleigh, interpreting the glance, said gruffly, "You'd best stay. Better you know the truth than the sorts of things you must be imagining."

Rather to Philippa's surprise, Lady Carteret did not contradict the earl. Lady Buckleigh, however, maintained enough presence of mind to realize that her late brother-in-law's excesses were not appropriate material for her own daughter's ears.

"Edwina," said the countess, "you will oblige me by waiting in the house."

"Thank you, Mama," Edwina said with due deference, "but I see nothing in the atmosphere outside to force me indoors." She seated herself beside Marsden, well away from her mother. Lady Buckleigh did not press the issue.

The others found seats—Crispin went inside briefly and emerged with two extra chairs—and Lord Buckleigh turned to Lady Carteret. "Would you prefer that I do the talking, Aurelia?"

Lady Carteret hesitated, her distaste for the unpleasant and indelicate facts of the story warring with her reluctance to relinquish centre stage. "No, Horace," she said firmly. "I will do the talking." She paused a moment to be sure of her audience's attention, then continued. "The story begins many years ago, when I was still in the schoolroom." She enunciated the last with obvious enjoyment. It was the fact of her youth, Philippa suspected, that allowed Lady Carteret to speak of the events with such composure. The late Lord Carteret had committed this particular indiscretion long before he married Aurelia Montagu.

"Before your birth, Anthony," the marchioness went on, "your late father formed a—an attachment—for the Baroness Scargill. I never met her but she was said to be very pretty and to be somewhat—ah—unfortunate in her marriage."

"My father," said Marsden, "my putative father, that is, the Baron Scargill, was a sour-tempered drunkard."

"At all events," Lady Carteret continued hastily, "Lady Scargill returned Lord Carteret's affection and eventually there was a child. Elliot. Lord Scargill was aware that the baby was not his, but he had no wish to go through the scandal of a divorce—that is hardly to be wondered at, I'm sure no sane person would, and whatever else was said about him, I don't believe anyone ever questioned his sanity—and he already had an heir, and from all reports he never interested himself much in anything relating to his wife or children."

"Very true, ma'am," Marsden agreed dryly.

"Yes. Well," said Lady Carteret, "Lord Scargill acknowledged the child as his own, but the Scargill estate was sadly encumbered and Lord Carteret was very properly concerned for the boy's future—especially as poor Lady Scargill died not long after Elliot's birth—so he made certain provisions. I don't know the particulars. That, Anthony, is where Trenchard comes in, and you must see that he had to, for Horace is much too busy to have time for such details, and you are always saying that I have no head for business, and you claim to find it deadly dull yourself, which it is, but someone had to see to it. It was Trenchard and Horace, at your father's request, who helped see Elliot established in the law. Not that Elliot could not have managed on his own, of course, but a word in the right place does help, you know."

"Yes, yes," Anthony said impatiently. "And you, sir," he turned on Marsden, "you knew none of this until after my father's death?"

"I was told none of it until then," Marsden returned calmly. "Lord Carteret had instructed Trenchard to inform me of the facts on his demise. But I admit I suspected something before then. I thought perhaps Lord Carteret had helped with my education. He visited me once or twice when I was at Winchester."

"He—" Anthony stared at his half-brother in outrage. "He never visited me at Harrow."

"Anthony! Elliot!" Lady Carteret said reprovingly. "I am sure your father would not wish you to quarrel. Say what you will about him, he was concerned with his sons' welfare."

"And did you, ma'am," Anthony inquired of his stepmother, "accompany my father on these visits to Winchester?"

"Oh, no. Lord Carteret told me about Elliot soon after our marriage, but I did not actually meet him until much later. After your father's death. Elliot most kindly called and offered me his condolences, and I must say he was a great deal more solicitous of my feelings than you were, Anthony—or even you, Crispin, though of course I make allowances for you, dear, for you were still at Harrow at the time."

Philippa looked at Marsden with wry appreciation. He had clearly won Lady Carteret over with that first call. And she had no doubt that that had been his intention. Trenchard and Buckleigh had been able to further his career, but Lady Carteret, with more influence than Trenchard and more leisure than Buckleigh, had been able to do a good deal more.

Carteret was angry because the secret had been kept from him and, perhaps more importantly, because this man of whom he had grown so jealous proved to be his elder brother. But what, Philippa wondered, must Marsden's feelings be? For some four years he had known, and even earlier had guessed, that he was the eldest son of the Marquis of Carteret. Had he been born on the right side of the blanket, all Anthony's wealth, position, and power would be his. Suddenly, Marsden's ruthless ambition was very understandable. And perhaps the reason he had been so determined to win her from Carteret. Now it almost seemed she had been forgotten in the face of this new source of conflict between the two men.

But in this Philippa was mistaken. "Miss Davenport," said Carteret into the silence which had fallen over the company, "I hope you understand that under the circumstances neither of us can wait until tomorrow." He turned to the others. "Please excuse us. Mars—my brother and I have something of great moment to discuss with Miss Davenport."

Carteret had risen and was holding open one of the French windows. There was no sense in delaying the unpleasant. Best to have it over and done with. Hermia, scenting fresh adventure, made to follow her mistress. Philippa would have been grateful for the dog's support, but decided it would not be fair to her suitors. She looked at Henry. His face was strangely bleak, but as he met her eyes he smiled and lifted Hermia onto his lap. Philippa smiled her thanks, squared her shoulders, and walked into the house.

Carteret led the way through the denuded drawing room and the crowded hall to the library, which had the advantage of not overlooking the terrace. Once they were all inside, he closed the door firmly and said, "Miss Davenport, I don't mean to be importunate, but—"

"You want your answer. And Mr. Marsden wants his. I am glad you are both here, because what I have to say concerns both of you." How idiotish, of course it concerned both of them. She was more nervous than she had realized. She must come to the point as quickly as possible. She forced herself not to avoid their eyes. "I fear I have ill-used both of you. I have hesitated and, well, there's no sense in dithering any further. I want each of you to know that my decision has nothing to do with the other. But I find—I am afraid that I cannot marry either of you."

For a moment the room was quiet. Then Marsden began to laugh softly. Anthony, who had been staring incredulously at Philippa, turned on his brother. "She isn't joking," he said sharply.

"I am well aware that she is not. But I think she cannot fail to see the ironies of the situation."

Philippa had positioned herself behind a strategically placed table. Anthony moved forward and placed his hands on its polished surface. "Philippa, if this has anything to do with what my stepmother has just been saying—if you fear to make a rift between—between brothers—"

"No, Lord Carteret," Philippa interjected, "it has nothing whatsoever to do with that."

"But—why?" the marquis demanded. Why, though he could not quite say it, would she possibly refuse him, especially as her affections were not engaged elsewhere?

"We aren't suited," Philippa said quietly. "I think even you must realize that."

The thought had once or twice crossed his mind, but he refused to acknowledge it. "Damn it, Philippa, I love you," he insisted.

Philippa looked into the attractive face which suddenly seemed younger than Crispin's. "Dear Anthony," she said, addressing him thus for the first—and perhaps the last—time. "I won't say you don't. But you would tire of it, you know. Oh, perhaps not of me," she went on, forestalling his protest, "but of having a wife who read you reform lectures over the breakfast cups and invited Mrs. Robinson to take tea in the nursery."

Anthony was almost disposed to smile at this last. "But you wouldn't—" he began reasonably.

"That's just it," Philippa returned gravely, "I would."

Carteret fell silent at that. Philippa turned to Marsden. "*And what to me, my love? and what to me?*" he quoted softly.

Philippa smiled. "A year's penance wouldn't change either of us. You once told me you could make your way in the world without me. I believe you."

"I believe I also said I cared for you. Do you doubt it?"

"No," Philippa said after a moment, "but you care for other things as well."

"Is that so bad?"

"Oh, no. I don't think I could be happy with a man who didn't. But they're not the things I care about." She moved toward the door. "If you'll excuse me, I think I should return to the others."

"Wait!" Anthony's voice held a note of desperation.

"There's nothing more to say, Lord Carteret."

Carteret stared after her, then turned back to Marsden who had not moved. "Damn it, man, are you just going to let her walk away?"

"What else can we do?" his brother said. "She's made her choice."

How odd, Henry thought, that all his future happiness should be determined while he sat on the terrace at the home of a man he despised, holding a squirming dog, surrounded by a set of people whom he scarcely knew but whose family secrets had just been poured into his ears. Hermia, perhaps sensing Henry's mood, stopped squirming and licked his face. Henry pulled absently at her ears.

He was not the only person who was acutely conscious of the scene taking place within the house. No one who was aware of Marsden's and Carteret's pursuit of Philippa Davenport, and that included all the company, with the possible exception of Lord Buckleigh, could fail to guess at the business the two gentlemen had with her. Lady Carteret, who had grown quite calm when there was a task at hand, felt a return of anxiety. She had left the Warwick House ball fearing the worst about her stepson and Miss Davenport, but when the succeeding days brought no announcement of a betrothal she had taken heart. Now it appeared that her hopes had been in vain.

"Catherine," the marchioness exclaimed, "do you realize what is going on in there?"

Lady Buckleigh eyed her sister wearily. "I can guess at it, Aurelia. I must confess it does not concern me much at present. Horace, I wish to say a few words to you before you leave for town." The countess rose, took her husband's arm, and proceeded across the lawn, out of earshot of the group on the terrace.

Lady Carteret was affronted. It was too late to do anything for Quentin, but Anthony could still be saved. "Edwina—" the marchioness turned to her niece.

"I wouldn't waste time worrying about it, Aunt Aurelia," Edwina advised with what Lady Carteret considered to be a shocking lack of feeling. "Tony will do just as he pleases. He always has." Edwina did not care in the least whether or not Tony married Philippa Davenport. Except, she realized with faint surprise, that she rather hoped Miss Davenport would not accept Elliot Marsden's suit.

Thus spurned by the female members of her family, Lady Carteret appealed to her son. A resigned Crispin turned to his mother but received such a ferocious scowl from Claris that he held his tongue.

Henry, not unaware of this byplay, could not forgo a smile. Claris was handling Lady Carteret far better than even he would have expected.

"Dear Lady Carteret," Claris said soothingly, adding some more tea to her ladyship's cup, "you mustn't fret so, you'll make yourself ill. Philippa may refuse him, you know."

"Refuse him?" Somehow, despite Miss Davenport's surprising hesitation and Elliot Marsden's surprising success with the lady, it had not occurred to Lady Carteret that Philippa Davenport would actually refuse her stepson. She was not even sure she found the possibility reassuring. "Nonsense," the marchioness said, "he is a Paget."

"So is Marsden," Crispin muttered, drawing another smile from Henry, a laugh from Edwina, and a sharp look from his mother.

"At all events," Claris continued hastily, "you have done everything in your power to assure his happiness. Whatever steps he may now take, whatever the result, you are absolved of all responsibility, dear ma'am."

Lady Carteret was much struck by this line of reasoning. *She* had done her duty by Anthony. If he chose to ruin himself it was quite his own affair. The marchioness took a sip of the tepid tea and patted Claris' hand. "I am glad that you at least sympathize with me."

"Well, ma'am, I daresay it is because you remind me so excessively of my own mother." Claris spared her brother a brief glance, daring him to give her the lie. "Of course she is not as pretty, but she has just the same sweetness of manner."

Doing it much too brown, my girl, Henry thought, willing his thoughts away from Philippa Davenport. Lady Carteret, who mercifully was unacquainted with the vigorous, strong-minded Judith Ashton, did not find the words excessive and was far from impervious to their flattery.

Claris decided to press her advantage. "Lady Carteret, I beg you to accept my assurances that however strong my feelings for Lord Christopher, I will never marry him without your blessing."

"Claris!" Crispin exclaimed involuntarily, for his beloved seemed to be dooming them to a lifetime apart.

"No, Crispin," Claris said firmly. "Much as I love you, I know I could not be happy as your wife if your family did not countenance our union."

Lady Carteret regarded Claris with genuine affection. Such a dear, sweet child and so prettily behaved. She showed none of Edwina's unfortunate flashes of temper, not to mention the disgraceful lack of deference toward her elders which Edwina had displayed this afternoon. The day's events had left Lady Carteret feeling, among other things, sadly disillusioned with her niece, and the disillusionment only made Claris seem more appealing. She was, in fact, not unlike the daughter for whom Lady Carteret had always secretly longed. Having been the sole female—except for the servants, who of course did not count—in Carteret House for over twenty years, Lady Carteret had frequently considered how pleasant it would be to have an affectionate, sympathetic young girl about to keep her company. Of course, a daughter-in-law would do almost as well as a daughter. . . .

"Well, my dear," Lady Carteret temporized, "I'm sure it is very proper of you to say so." Crispin was young, of course. But the afternoon's revelations about her nephew had caused Lady Carteret to think that young men might be safer married. And marriage could be the very thing to save Crispin from the excesses in which his father and brother indulged. Lady Carteret had frequently thought that her own Bertram might have been much improved had she married him ten years earlier—that is, had he been ten years younger, for of course she could not have married him at the age of eight. . . . "You know, my dear," Lady Carteret confided delicately, bending her head close to Claris', "there is not merely the matter of my own opposition. Your brother quite forbids the match."

But Henry was already on his feet. He set Hermia down, flashed a quick grin at Crispin, and crossed to the marchioness' chair. "Lady Carteret," he said, with one of his sweetest smiles, "I will not deny our differences. But my temper, as my sister will tell you, is frequently short, and I believe it has led me to say some unfortunate things. I hope you will accept my apologies. More important, I hope you will not let whatever differences we may have stand in the way of two young people who have proven themselves sincerely attached."

"Oh, dear!" Lady Carteret exclaimed. "I do not know—that is I really think—"

Three minutes later Philippa returned to the terrace to find Crispin embracing his mother, Claris flinging her arms around Henry's neck, and Lady Edwina offering congratulations in her beautifully modulated voice.

"Oh, Philippa!" Claris released Henry and ran to her friend's side. "Henry and Lady Carteret have given their consent and Crispin and I are properly betrothed at last, isn't that splendid?"

"Splendid," Philippa agreed, pleased but surprised at this turn of events. She hugged Claris and met Henry's eyes over his sister's shoulder. She was seeking some clue to his sudden about-face in the matter of Claris' marriage but saw a very different question in his eyes. Of course. He would have realized why she had gone apart with Marsden and Carteret. Most of the company, even those who did not actually know the two men had proposed, must have guessed at the truth of it. Philippa gave a slight shake of her head.

Henry felt as if the weight of the universe had suddenly been lifted from his shoulders.

Claris released Philippa, looked into her face for a moment, then returned to Lady Carteret. "It isn't Lord Carteret," she whispered into her future mother-in-law's ear.

Lady Carteret stared at Claris in disbelief. "Not Anthony?"

"No."

"Then it's Elliot?"

"No," Claris said, "not Mr. Marsden either."

"So," Henry murmured to Philippa, "you made up your mind at last."

"I made it up a long time ago," Philippa returned. "I just didn't realize it until today. But," she continued, looking at the smiling Crispin and Claris, "I understand you've recently changed yours."

"Paget's a good lad. Both Murray and I have cause to be grateful to him."

"So you're giving him Claris in recompense?"

"Hardly. Even if I wanted to, I don't think Claris would let herself be given. Haven't I already admitted I misjudged Paget in the past?"

"You also," Philippa reminded him, "claimed their attachment could not survive in the face of his family's opposition."

"It seems I misjudged Claris as well. She has just demonstrated that she can turn the opposition around."

Before Philippa could respond, St. George returned to the terrace. The viscount leaned negligently against the wall of the house and surveyed the company, and the company fell into an awkward silence. A few moments later Lord Buckleigh came striding back across the lawn and curtly informed his son that it was time they were off. "We'll take whatever carriage you keep here," Buckleigh went on, mounting the terrace steps. "Your mother, of course, is taking our coach directly back to Bruton Street." He turned to his wife, who had followed him more slowly.

"I will accompany you, Catherine." Lady Carteret, all self-assurance, rose and moved toward her sister who for once did not appear in the least self-assured. "You should not be alone at a time like this."

Philippa could not determine whether the look Lady Buckleigh gave the marchioness was one of thanks or loathing. Very likely, she thought, Lady Buckleigh herself could not have said. Having three sisters of her own, Philippa was familiar with the feeling.

Lady Buckleigh glanced at her son who met her eyes, his own defiantly impassive. Lady Carteret cast a brilliant smile at her son and future daughter-in-law. Lady Edwina made no move to accompany her mother and aunt, and Lady Buckleigh did not seem to notice. Perhaps her mind was still too preoccupied with St. George to leave any thought to spare for Edwina.

"I'd best be off myself," Henry said to Philippa. "Make my apologies to Francesca."

"Of course. And you will bring Mr. Murray to Green Street tonight?"

"Without fail." He looked at her a moment longer, but Philippa's eyes had gone to the French windows through which Maria had just reappeared. She showed no trace of tears and was looking very pretty. She had put on a delicate pelisse of sapphire silk and a matching hat ornamented with a gracefully curling feather, and she carried a painted velvet reticule. Luscombe, she said in subdued tones, had placed her trunk in the hall, but she feared she would have to beg a ride to town.

"Of course, my dear, of course." Buckleigh's haste to depart had dimmed considerably with Maria's appearance.

"Of course," St. George echoed. "I'm sure the three of us will have a most cosy journey together. Shall I make you a present of Maria, Father?"

Buckleigh glared at his son, started to speak, restrained himself and turned to Henry. "Ashton, do you think you could—"

"Certainly. I should be pleased to escort you to town, Miss Doddington. What is your direction?"

"I have rooms in Marylebone Lane. I do not know how much longer I will be able to reside there, but I can at least return for tonight."

Lord Buckleigh took the hint with no difficulty. "Nonsense, my dear," he declared. "Shouldn't like to see you suffer for my son's folly. You let Ashton take you home and don't worry about keeping your lodgings. Come along, St. George, it's time we were leaving."

The viscount bestowed a final mocking smile on the company and preceded his father into the house. Henry gave Philippa a far warmer smile, said good-bye to his sister, Crispin, and Lady Edwina—whom her father seemed to have

393

forgotten—then gave Maria his arm and followed.

Seeing the sorrow in her betrothed's eyes as he looked after St. George, Claris gave his hand a comforting squeeze. "Well," Crispin said briskly, "no sense in staying here any longer. Where are Tony and Marsden—er—Elliot?"

"Still in the house," Philippa told him. "I don't think we should disturb them."

"No," Crispin agreed. "But I suppose I'd best leave Tony's curricle—"

"I think you should take it," Edwina said. "I'll make it right with Tony."

"Aren't you coming with us?" Crispin asked, surprised.

"No," his cousin said simply. "You'll make my excuses to your cousin, Miss Davenport?"

"Certainly."

Crispin looked at the three women in puzzlement. Neither Claris nor Miss Davenport seemed to find Edwina's behavior in the least surprising. Oh well, he had more important things to think about than Eddy's whims. He tucked Claris' hand beneath his arm. Much more important.

Lady Edwina was sitting alone, her parasol tilted over one shoulder, when Anthony and Marsden returned to the terrace some fifteen minutes later. Edwina, a sharp-eyed observer, judged that if the two men had not become fast friends, they had achieved a certain level of understanding. There was nothing like shared adversity to banish differences.

Edwina rose gracefully. "The others have all left."

"Why are you still here, Eddy?" Anthony demanded, not very graciously.

"I imagine because she needs an escort back to town, Carteret," Marsden told him. "Am I correct, Lady Edwina?"

"Perfectly correct, Cousin Elliot." She closed her parasol. Marsden held out his arm. Edwina laid her hand on it. Anthony looked at them for a moment, then laughed and took his cousin's other arm, and the three of them descended the terrace steps.

Chapter 26

"Any sign of them?" Nicholas Warwick asked.

Francesca shook her head. She and Nicholas were standing in relative privacy on the lawn. The terrace above them was crowded with dancing couples, with more dancers overflowing into the drawing room. The guests had long since finished eating, and the servants were already clearing away the remains of the meal. It was still light, but it must be several hours since Gwendolen had brought her Henry's brief message.

"It's just past seven," Nicholas said, glancing at his watch. "Don't worry. They can look after themselves. And if they aren't back within the hour, Gerry and I will go after them."

Francesca smiled. "If they aren't back within the hour, I'll be tempted to go after them myself. Do you suppose—"

"What a wonderful party, Francesca. We've been enjoying ourselves tremendously. How odd that we haven't seen you since four o'clock."

Philippa had come round the side of the house from the direction of the stables. Claris and Lord Christopher were following close behind, their hands clasped together. Francesca surveyed the trio with relief. Philippa's hair was in a predictable state of disarray, but otherwise they looked quite presentable and remarkably cheerful.

"Not at all odd," Francesca said, "considering the crowd. I told anyone who asked after you that I was sure you must be somewhere about."

"Very sensible," Philippa returned. "I knew we could depend on you. I'm afraid it's all excessively complicated. Would you mind terribly if we returned to London tonight?"

It was nearly midnight when they at last returned to Green Street. The party was a large one, for Francesca had asked the Warwicks to stop by. Claris had told her of the betrothal and she had asked Crispin as well. They were now all acquainted with the events at Cranford that afternoon and were eager to see Gordon Murray.

Tuttle, apparently not surprised by their unexpected return, informed Lady Francesca that Mr. Ashton and Mr. Murray were upstairs in the drawing room. Philippa noted that Tuttle seemed in a singularly cheerful humour. Mr. Murray's release no doubt accounted for some of it—concern about his plight had spread below stairs—but she could have sworn there was more.

There was. When the party entered the drawing room they found Henry and Murray were not its only occupants. Murray was seated by the fireplace, in heated discussion with a tall, thin, elegantly dressed gentleman, and Henry was near one of the windows, conversing with a vivacious lady whose gown of amber sarcenet looked as if it had come straight from Paris—

Hermia gave an ecstatic bark. Philippa stopped, transfixed, in the drawing room doorway.

"Mama!"

The former Rowena Davenport and her new husband, Kenrick, Lord Braithwood, were an impressive couple. In addition to an exquisite face and figure, Rowena possessed a warmth and charm which had instantly reminded Henry of Philippa. Kenrick was not as classically handsome as the Marquis of Carteret (though some observers might have said he had the more interesting face) and did not possess as large a fortune, but he was sufficiently well-endowed with both commodities to have attracted his share of interest among matchmaking mothers and their romantic daughters before he caused a minor scandal by marrying a woman ten years his senior. Neither he nor his wife seemed to find this notoriety in the least disturbing.

Rowena came forward quickly and embraced Philippa, then held her at arm's length. "Darling! You look splendid. Yes, Hermia, I'm delighted to see you, too. Francesca, I apologize for descending on you so precipitately, I know you hadn't looked for us for at least another fortnight."

"Nonsense, Aunt Rowena." Francesca handed Linnet to Gerry and reached out to embrace her aunt. Philippa kissed her stepfather, and somehow in the flurry of greetings and introductions nothing further was said about the Braithwoods' unexpected return from their wedding journey. Philippa was too happy to have her mother back to question the reason for her early return.

While the others were congratulating Claris and Crispin, Murray made his way to Philippa's side. He looked well, if a little tired, and was evidently enjoying himself.

"Seems I'm in your debt, m'dear," he said in a low voice. "Henry's been telling me what you did."

Philippa protested that very little credit was due to her. "It was Claris who first thought to suspect Lord St. George, and Lord Christopher who stole the pendant, and Henry who tricked St. George into confessing."

"But none of it would have come off if you hadn't kept your head. By the way, I've been having a most interesting talk with your stepfather. Didn't know he was *your* stepfather or I'd have said something earlier. Always thought Braithwood was a sound man, even if he is a baron."

Philippa looked at him in surprise. "You know Kenrick?"

"Met him years ago. Come to think of it, I believe it was Warwick who introduced us."

It really shouldn't surprise her. Kenrick sat in the upper house, but his politics were similar to Nicholas Warwick's. She was tempted to bring the matter to Henry's attention. Her world and his weren't so very far apart after all.

It was a convivial party. Linnet, who had slept on the drive to London, was wide awake and in an angelic temper, delighted to let the adults fuss over her without fussing in return. Tuttle came in with champagne and sandwiches and they toasted Crispin and Claris' future. Philippa could not have said when, in the midst of all this good will and family feeling, her elation began to fade, but she had a sudden sense that, despite Mr. Murray's freedom, despite Claris' betrothal, despite her mother's return, life was not at all what it should be.

She glanced around the drawing room and saw her mother's eyes meet Kenrick's in unspoken communication. Crispin and Claris were seated side-by-side on the sofa, not saying a great deal and not looking at anything but each other. Francesca had settled herself in a satinwood armchair with Linnet on her lap, and Gerry was leaning over the chair back with his hands resting on her shoulders. Nicholas had his arm around Livia, who was sitting beside him on a small settee.

Philippa's gaze fell on Gwendolen Warwick, perched on a stool beside her parents, and she felt sudden kinship with the younger girl. Except that love and romance were still in Gwendolen's future. Philippa was quite certain that today she had put them irrevocably in her own past.

Philippa looked at Henry, wanting the reassurance of one of his smiles, but he was talking to Livia and Nicholas. He had scarcely said a word to her since her arrival in Green Street.

She laughed and smiled at the appropriate times, but her depressed feeling continued. At length the Warwicks rose to leave, taking Henry and Mr. Murray with them, and a reluctant Crispin also said good-night. Francesca took Linnet up to the nursery. As the others began to drift upstairs, Rowena put an arm around Philippa. "Come into my dressing room and talk for a bit, darling. If you aren't too tired."

Philippa had been wanting to talk to her mother for weeks, but now that she had the opportunity she was not sure where to begin. Though she had talked about Carteret and Marsden in her letters, she had not said how serious her involvement with them had become, let alone mentioned their proposals. So when Rowena dropped down on the green satin sofa in her dressing room and patted the seat beside her and said, "Now tell me what you've been doing with yourself?" Philippa answered with a question of her own.

"Tell me why you and Kenrick came home so suddenly,"

she countered, sitting beside her mother.

Rowena had bent down to unlace her half-boots, but at that she looked up, laughing. "The truth is, love, Francesca's letter had me rather worried."

"Francesca's letter?"

"Yes, the last time she wrote she said you seemed to be in a bit of a quandary about a pair of gentlemen. Being as anxious as most mothers, I told Kenrick I thought it was high time we returned home."

Philippa stared at her mother. "You hurried home from Paris because of what Francesca said about Lord Carteret and Mr. Marsden?"

Rowena finished with the half-boots and tucked her legs beneath her. "Well, darling, you know I've always tried to leave such decisions up to you girls—though I must say I never could like that captain with whom Violet was so taken—and of course I'll accept whatever choice you make, but I really have difficulty seeing you married to the Marquis of Carteret."

"But you don't even know him," Philippa said. "Do you?"

"I haven't met him," Rowena replied, "but I know the type. Quite charming and very agreeable for a flirtation—or even a liaison—but not the sort of man you'd want to face across the breakfast cups for the rest of your life."

It was such an accurate description that Philippa almost laughed. "And Mr. Marsden?" she asked. "What do you know about him?"

"Only what Francesca told me."

"She said he was after my money?"

"She had some concerns about him."

"She was right. Though I like to think he was also interested in me. They both proposed. I don't suppose Francesca can have written you about that. I only told her myself a few days ago."

"No, she merely said she thought it likely they would do so." Rowena looked at her daughter expectantly. "Dearest, if I've insulted the man you mean to marry, I do apologize."

Philippa shook her head. "I refused them both. And you were right to be concerned, I wouldn't have been happy with either of them. But it is rather vexatious. I'd decided I'd quite like to be married."

"Isn't it a bit drastic to swear off marriage altogether?"

"I'm trying to be a realist. I used to think the problem was that no interesting men were interested in me. But now I've had two interesting—and attractive—men actually offer for me, and it turns out they aren't right either. Even if I do arouse another man's interest, and I'm not at all sure that I will, I expect I'd have the same doubts about being happy with him. And I expect I'd be right. I tried writing about it, you know, what it would be like to be married to Lord Carteret and what it would be like to be married to Mr. Marsden. It was quite horrid. I'm beginning to wonder if perhaps marriage isn't for me at all."

Rowena brushed a strand of fly-away hair out of her daughter's eyes. "Don't despair, darling. You're still absurdly young. For years after your father died, I swore I'd never marry again. It's difficult to find one person to spend the rest of one's life with. Not that you necessarily have to settle for one. Look at Emily Cowper."

Philippa laughed. "Very true. But I don't think that would do for me."

"No," Rowena agreed, "I don't think it would." She looked as if she might have said more but instead asked for Philippa's latest news from her sisters. When Philippa at length kissed her mother good-night her mood was considerably lightened. But as she rose to leave, her eye fell on the door to the adjoining bedroom. Kenrick would be waiting for Mama. Philippa sighed. She had made the right decision, she was sure of it. But there was such a lot of life that she was missing.

It was past ten when Philippa woke the next morning. She lay in bed, savouring the pleasure of Mr. Murray's release. It was as good as a novel, and not unlike one. In the real world, iniquity was not always punished.

Well, the adventure was over. All her adventures. She was not likely to find a new suitor with Carteret's charm or Marsden's compelling force. How strange that they should be brothers. She might have guessed, for those grey eyes were much the same. She understood Elliot Marsden better now,

400

and she rather hoped the two would mend their differences. Lord Carteret could use a friend.

Philippa was not sorry for her experience. She had tested herself in these last few weeks. She was no longer content to be an observer, and she was not afraid of being something more. As for her regrets of the night before, she would put them out of her mind. She was a writer, and her life was quite full enough.

She sat up and saw Hermia still asleep at the foot of her bed. "Poor Hermia, you had an eventful day, didn't you? Didn't we all? But it's time to go back to work."

She rang for her maid, bounded out of bed and threw open the drapes. It was a glorious day. Hermia jumped down and sat beside her, tail thumping on the carpet. "No run today," Philippa said, "I'll send you out with Nancy. I want to breakfast with Mama."

But Lady Braithwood, Nancy informed her, was not yet up, nor were the other ladies, and was it really true that Miss Ashton was going to be married to that handsome Lord Christopher? So the news was out. Well, of course it was, secrets did not thrive in this house. Philippa assured her that it was true and, because Nancy was longing to be the bearer of fresh news, added some details about Lady Carteret's and Henry's capitulation.

"I'm that happy for her, miss, but I rather thought it might be you."

"That's not likely," Philippa said, glad that Nancy was behind her, fastening her dark green dress, and could not see her face. "Don't fuss now, I'm quite presentable. See that Hermia gets a walk and tell me when my mother comes downstairs. I'll be in my study."

She was determined to work, but she did not immediately go to her desk. Instead she stood at the window, watching Linnet take uncertain steps down one of the garden paths while Adèle followed vigilantly behind. Philippa sighed. This would not do. She turned back to the desk. It seemed an age since she had last sat there.

But not so long that she did not recall how the desk had been left. There was a sheaf of papers piled neatly just in front of her chair, and the hand was not her own. Were these Kenrick's? Or had someone left her a letter? Philippa settled in the chair and picked up the first page.

It had been a happy idea to have the wedding at Raynley. Francesca had suggested it, and Philippa had eagerly accepted. The drawing room was large and designed for comfort, they could breakfast on the terrace, and there would be none of the stiff formality of a proper church and a droning bishop.

A droning bishop?

The party included only the families and a few close friends, but it was larger than Philippa expected. She had not quite realized just how many sisters Henry had.

Henry? She scanned the page again. She had not often seen his hand, but this looked something like she remembered. How like him to write her a story. Then she realized that the story was a parody of her own. He had read her stories. He had come into her study and read something she had written for herself alone. How dare he trespass on her privacy?

She put down the pages, then picked them up again. At least he had made a fair imitation of her style. Was he chaffing her on her failed courtship? Or telling her that there was still room for hope? Or both? And who on earth would he select as her groom? Hastily she resumed her reading.

Everyone said that Philippa had a special radiance that day— isn't that always said of brides?—but those who knew her best knew that the radiance was always there, and part of her special charm.

Philippa smiled involuntarily. His description was generous but quite stretched the bounds of belief.

Henry, however, was inclined to be agitated. He could not believe his good fortune, and he was afraid that Philippa would change her mind. He managed to drop the ring.

Philippa grinned. Henry had the gift of not taking himself too seriously. But why should he make himself the hero of her story? She had thought him one of the guests.

When the couple had been united, the party moved outdoors where Francesca had arranged a splendid wedding breakfast. There was a great deal of kissing—how fortunate, Henry thought, that Philippa has all these sisters—

Philippa laughed. She wondered what he would make of

Ianthe's bustling maternity and Violet's caprice and Juliana's single-minded devotion to her animals.

—and laughter and general hilarity. But while the festivity was at its height, Henry drew his bride away from the table. He was taking her to Paris, and they would lie that night at Dover. "Or someplace closer," he whispered, "for I do not think I can wait."

Philippa let the paper fall. She had thought the story a jest, but this—

He could not be serious. Henry had been an adversary, and he had become a friend—at least, she hoped he was her friend, though he had shown her no special favour—but he would not look upon her in this way, not as a man looks upon a woman.

Or would he? He was not given to dalliance, but surely he had a man's desires. What kind of woman would stir them?

Philippa had a sudden recollection of the first time she had seen him, surrounded by a bevy of eager young women all vying for his attention. She had thought him singularly attractive then, though their subsequent encounter had driven this image from her mind. What would it be like to be kissed by Henry Ashton? She imagined his arms around her and felt her breathing quicken. Yes, she would like it very much. Of course, she had quite enjoyed kissing Anthony Paget and Elliot Marsden, but kissing Henry seemed so much more—so right.

How curious. Why should she find it so? Henry was an attractive man, but no more attractive than her former suitors. He did not have Carteret's dash or Marsden's bold arrogance, though she suspected he passed them both in understanding. And he was easy to talk to, and they laughed at the same things, and she could quarrel with him without a trace of guilt. She would miss him dreadfully if he no longer called in Green Street.

She had never had a friend quite like Henry Ashton. She thought of the way he challenged her mind as no one else had ever done, and the way their eyes sometimes met in sudden understanding. He was more than her friend, he was her companion, her partner, her lover—

Lover? Well, why not, she was desolate at the thought of losing him. Was that what it meant to be in love? Could she be in love with Henry?

She picked up the discarded page and read the last few lines again.

. . . they would lie that night at Dover. "Or someplace closer," he whispered, "for I do not think I can wait."

Philippa felt her face grow warm. Would he go on to describe—? Impatiently she turned to the next page.

Philippa Davenport Ashton entered the breakfast parlour of the Ashton house on a brisk morning in the spring of 1825 to find her husband already at the table, engrossed in the Morning Chronicle.

He rose as she came in and his smile told her of his delight in seeing her. They did not kiss, for they had exchanged such pledges, and more, the night before, and Philippa had fallen asleep in his arms. He was not there when she awoke, for he was an habitually early riser.

Wretch, she thought, I rise early myself.

"I finished the article for Gordon," he said. "Gordon's very grateful to you, you know. Now that we're married, he doesn't have to feel guilty about not paying me." Henry had learned to laugh at the disparity in their fortunes.

Philippa laid down the page abruptly. She read the last paragraph again. It had never occurred to her that her fortune would be a barrier to seeking her hand. How different it is for men, she thought, and how unjust that it should be so.

They had spent the previous evening at the Warwicks' where much of the talk had turned on The Prime Minister's Indiscretion. *Gordon Murray, who made one of the group, said that it was the funniest thing he had read in years, and Mrs. Ashton was likely to do more good with her wit than he had ever done with his exhortations. Henry regretted his execrable behaviour as Chiron—no, he did not regret it. It had made her angry, but it had made her think. And she had found her own voice.*

And that, Philippa thought, is as near an apology as Henry Ashton will ever give me.

"Nicholas and Livia want us to come to Waverley before we go to your mother's," he said. "Gerry and Francesca will be there, too. Would you like to go?"

"I'd love to go to Waverley," she said, thinking of the

Warwicks' Sussex estate with pleasure. "Justin and Linnet are so good with Belinda and Robert."

Robert? Well, why not? If their daughter took her name from Philippa's first novel, their son should take his from Henry's.

He smiled. "I confess I'd like to go, but I don't want to take time from your writing. You have little enough as it is."

"As much as you," she said tartly, for they had produced four books each since their marriage.

"Waverley, then." He left his chair and stood over her. "I'm going up to the children. I promised them a story. Then I must be off. I'll be back by four. I understand you've asked Mrs. Robinson to call, and I wouldn't miss it for the world." He bent down and kissed her quickly, then kissed her again because he so enjoyed it. And at last, his cravat somewhat askew, he left the room.

The manuscript stopped there. Philippa put the pages down reluctantly, musing on the scene she had just read. Henry's story showed the best of her hopes, as her own had told the worst of her fears.

She looked up from the manuscript, wondering how she could possibly face Henry Ashton again, and found herself staring into a pair of intense green eyes.

Philippa rose hastily, her feelings a mixture of embarrassment, anger, and joy. It was her anger that surfaced first. "Henry, how dare you read my private papers!"

"Ah, I was afraid of that." He closed the door behind him and came into the room. "I'm sorry, it was not the act of a gentleman."

She glared at him, trying to control the beating of her heart. "It was not. Do you make a practice of rifling other people's desks?"

"No," he said simply, "only when I am trying to ascertain the feelings of the woman I love."

Her breath caught in her throat. "You might have asked me," she said, her anger somewhat abated.

"Would you have told me?"

She was silent.

"I thought not. As a matter of fact, I asked Gerry. He said he really didn't know, but you'd written some stories about

Carteret and Marsden, and why didn't I have a look at them. No," he continued, holding up a warning hand, "I take full responsibility. It was the night before we went down to Raynley. I'd joined him here for dinner."

Philippa did not reply. He'd had no right. And yet . . . And yet . . .

"I didn't know how you felt about them, you see, and if you cared for them, or even one of them, I didn't want to interfere."

She challenged him. "But you did."

"Oh, no, not then. I could tell you weren't yet clear in your mind, and until you'd made your decision there was nothing I could do. But after you gave them their *congé*, I knew I might have a chance."

"But when?" she asked, remembering the events of the past twenty-four hours.

"Last night, after I took Gordon home. I brought it by this morning." He moved closer to the desk which still stood between them. "I thought I did it rather well. The story, I mean. Did you like it?"

She nodded, unable to trust her voice.

"I rather hoped you would. You see, that's the way I see the future, or would like to see it. Does it—? Is it—?" He faltered.

Philippa realized that she had just received her third proposal. "Oh, Henry," she burst out, "I don't know! I'm not sure I'm fit for marriage. I expect too much!"

Henry had a moment of doubt. Had he misread her? Then he staked it all on a final, desperate question. "Philippa," he said, holding his anxiety in check, "can you imagine spending the rest of your life without me?"

She came to him then. She left the safety of her desk and walked up to him and put her arms around his neck and pressed her lips against his own. It was her surrender, given joyfully and willingly and in perfect confidence that he would surrender himself to her as she did to him.

The embrace shook them both. Philippa looked at him in wonder. It was quite as exhilarating to kiss as to be kissed. It was even better when both things happened at once. She decided to put this discovery to the test once more.

After a long moment, she drew back. "Henry, do you really think we can produce eight books and two children in six years?"

"I don't know," he said, bending his head to hers once more, "but I'm willing to try."

They were interrupted by a scratching at the door. They separated and Philippa hastily jabbed the loosened pins into her hair. "Yes?" she called, and the door opened and Hermia ran into the room, delighted that she had found not only her mistress but Henry Ashton.

"If you please, miss," Nancy said from the doorway, "your mother has come down and would be pleased to have you join her in the breakfast parlour."

Claris looked up as her brother followed Philippa into the room. "Oh, Henry, I'm so glad you've come, we've been talking about an August wedding. Lady Braithwood says we may have it here and Francesca says we may have it at Raynley and I think I would prefer that because Mama is more comfortable in the country, but what do you think?"

Yesterday, Henry would have advised a long betrothal. This morning he did not even think to question the imminence of the ceremony. "Whatever you like, bunny."

He had not called her that for years. Claris looked at her brother sharply. Was he sickening for something? He had the strangest expression on his face.

Rowena's attention was focused on her daughter. She seemed unusually pale. Francesca observed the couple and sent a meaningful look to her husband who was deep in conversation with Kenrick. Gerry failed to notice it.

Philippa took a chair beside her mother, and Hermia, who had followed them in, lay down near her feet. Henry remained standing. Rowena looked at him curiously. "Please sit down, Mr. Ashton. Have you breakfasted?"

"Hmm?" Henry came out of his abstraction. "Yes. That is, no. At least I don't think so. I've been up all night."

He sat down beside Gerry who at last noticed that something was amiss. "How's Murray faring?"

"Oh, Murray's fine. Quite beside himself, in fact." Henry accepted a cup of coffee from Rowena but left it untasted. He glanced at Philippa, then turned back to her mother. "Lady Braithwood, there is something I would like to tell you. To ask you. Purely as a matter of form, because it matters not one whit whether you like it or not. I intend to marry your daughter."

Rowena looked at the young man seated on the other side of the table. His clothes were rumpled, his hair fell carelessly across his forehead, and his face showed an implacable determination. She suppressed a smile. "And does my daughter intend to marry you?"

Philippa reached across the table and clasped Henry's hand. "As soon as I may," she said. Their eyes met and for a moment they shut out the whole world.

"What a good idea," Rowena said. "I thought when I met him last night that he'd be just the man for you. Don't you agree, Francesca?"

"I've thought so for a good two years."

Philippa gave her cousin a speaking look.

Gerry and Kenrick smiled warmly. Claris looked round the room, a stunned expression on her face. She had not quite given up hope for Lord Carteret. "And I never thought of it," she said with dismay. "I never thought of it at all." Then her face brightened. "But it's an absolutely splendid idea. How did it happen?"

"Henry wrote me a story," Philippa said. "It was a very clever story. I may even use it in one of my books."

Hermia barked and Philippa reached down to scratch her ears. "That is," she said, with a provocative glance at her future husband, "if you promise not to sue me for libel."